# Perilous Journey

# Perilous Journey

## The Founding of
## Nashville, Tennessee
## 1780-81

*A Novel by*
# PEYTON COCKRILL LEWIS

Published by:

Channing Press
3900 Georgetown Ct, NW
Washington, DC 20007

1st printing 2005

Printed in the United States

Library of Congress Cataloging-in-publication Data
Lewis, Peyton Cockrill.
Perilous journey : the founding of Nashville, Tennessee, 1780-1781 / Peyton Cockrill Lewis.
p. cm.
Includes bibliographical references.

ISBN 0-9761190-0-5

1. Young women—Fiction.  2. Widows—Fiction.
3. Nashville (Tenn.)—Fiction.  4. Historical fiction. I. Title.

PS3612.E973P47 2005
813'.6      QBI04-700434

Library of Congress Control Number: 2004097322

Cover photograph by Peyton Lewis
Author photograph by Ruth Kincaid

Book and cover design by Jill Dible Design

*To my family:*
*the ones who went before me*
*and*
*Bill, Ashley and Rebecca*

# ACKNOWLEDGMENTS

To write this book, I traveled my own journey, but happily it was not a perilous one. In fact, it was one filled with enriching experiences that began with my trip to Kingsport, Tennessee to explore the place where this novel begins. I thank Muriel Spoden for her guidance in showing me the historical sights of the area, as well as for the valuable information in her book, *Kingsport Heritage.*

I visited the "October Homecoming" at the Museum of Appalachia and saw for myself many examples of the way people lived in the 18th century wilderness. I touched a flintlock rifle, felt the heat of the blacksmith's forge, and watched a deerskin being tanned in the old fashioned way. I also enjoyed the music which lightened the lives of the early pioneers.

I moved on to the mountains surrounding Chattanooga where Indians performed one of their most effective attacks on the Donelson party at "The Suck," a whirlpool in the Tennessee River which no longer exists. And I wound up in Nashville, the place of my birth, where I was aided greatly by the able staff at the Tennessee State Library and Archives.

A special tribute goes to Linda Aaker and Rangeley Wallace who were present at the birth of this novel and who gave many critical suggestions along the way. Early readers who also gave sage advice were Judy Greene, Nancy Fisher, Diane Rehm, Kate Lehrer, Roger and E.J. Mudd, Ellen Atwell, Mary Beth Busby, and Sue Tolchin. And a particular thanks goes to my family; husband Bill, and daughters Ashley and Rebecca, who were always encouraging and supportive.

I also give thanks to the Robertson family, the East Tennessee Historical Society, Honey Alexander, Molly Pratt, Suzanne Toyne, Cuddy and Marie Viall, Annie and Charlie Trost, Eleanor Dore, Jamie Burnett, Kay and Rod Heller, Elizabeth Queener, Ron Dreben, Lynne Glassman, Jill Dible, Walton Beacham, and Dave Avesian. It takes a village to raise a book, even as it does to raise a child.

# INTRODUCTION

In December of 1779, a small group of men, women and children left the Watauga Settlement in East Tennessee on a harrowing river journey to a wild, new land on the banks of the Cumberland River. Little did they know that their trip would take place during one of the coldest winters in recorded history, and little did they know how many of them would perish.

On the first of November, a party of men and animals had preceded them, traveling overland on a proven trail to the new territory known as the French or Great Salt Lick. That group, led by James Robertson, had not included the families because the river route was considered a safer venue. The organizers chose Colonel John Donelson to transport the families on flatboats down the Clinch River to the Tennessee and on to the Cumberland country. Their supposition of safety would prove to be devastatingly inaccurate, however, due in large part to a map that greatly underestimated the distance to be traveled. The Robertson party had no conflicts and took two months to complete. The Donelson journey stretched over four months, and the voyagers were repeatedly assaulted by Indians.

Why would anyone undertake such a perilous journey while the Revolutionary War still raged and the British had financed the Indians to attack such expeditions? Some of them undoubtedly traveled for the promise of owning rich land in their own names, since their current land in East Tennessee was leased from the Cherokees. Some may have gone simply for the adventure of it. And some undoubtedly thought it was God's will to civilize the new land and populate it with Christian souls. All of them were later called the "Advance Guard of Civilization."

I have a particular reason for telling this story. Both my paternal and maternal great-great-great-great grandmothers were on the river journey to Nashville: Ann Robertson Johnson Cockrill and Elizabeth Jennings Peyton. I have chosen Ann as my narrator because her courage has been an inspiration to me since I was a young girl growing up in Nashville. She was the sister of James Robertson and a twenty-three-year old widow with three children when she embarked on this journey. Each chapter of this novel begins with an entry of her fictional journal, and I have tried to base the book's events as closely as possible on actual historical fact. In some cases, I found conflicting reports of the same event, and I chose the version that seemed most plausible. In other cases, I chose details that helped bring situations to life and made them dramatically plausible. For instance, I have no information that Ann and her family actually traveled on Colonel Donelson's boat, *The Adventure,* but placing her there helped to bring the story to life.

We are all in debt to Colonel John Donelson for keeping his own record of this trip, which he introduces with these words: "Journal of a voyage, intended by God's permission, in the good boat Adventure, from Fort Patrick Henry, on Holston river, to the French Salt Springs on Cumberland river, kept by John Donelson." His journal is published in A.W. Putnam's book, *History of Middle Tennessee or Life and Times of Gen. James Robertson.* I also used Putnam's book as a reference for numerous stories of the early days at Fort Nashboro. And anyone who writes of this time period is grateful for the collection of Lyman Copeland Draper, whose letters and interviews of pioneers are invaluable in understanding this turbulent time. Also of note are books by Harriette Simpson Arnow which provide a wealth of information on 18th Century life in the Cumberland country.

# Perilous Journey

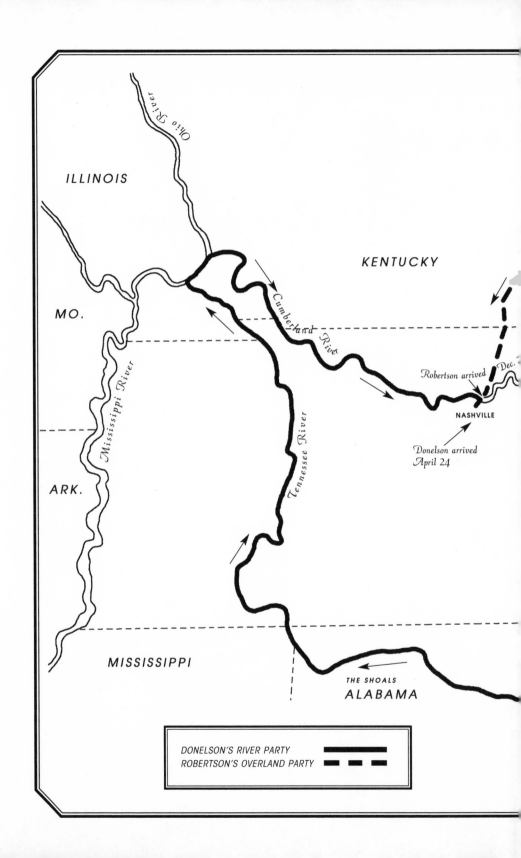

ILLINOIS

KENTUCKY

MO.

*Cumberland River*

*Ohio River*

*Mississippi River*

*Tennessee River*

*Robertson arrived* Dec.

NASHVILLE

*Donelson arrived April 24*

ARK.

MISSISSIPPI

THE SHOALS
ALABAMA

DONELSON'S RIVER PARTY
ROBERTSON'S OVERLAND PARTY

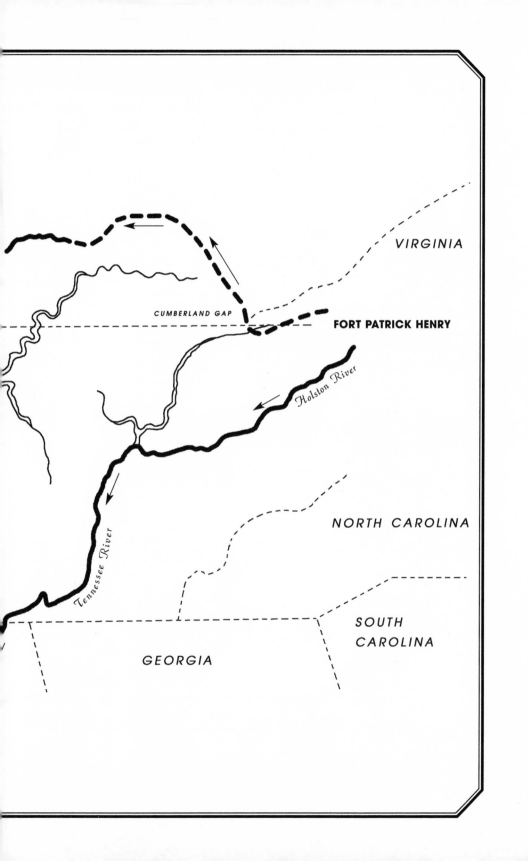

# *One*

FEBRUARY 10, 1780 — *First light. I take my quill in hand on this, my twenty-third birthday, to start a record of the great journey I will soon begin. My fingers stiffen and ache from the cold, and I find it difficult to write while I am huddled beneath a buffalo robe. Surrounding me on the river bank are thirty boats, dugouts and canoes that should have left almost seven weeks ago. On December 22, Colonel John Donelson led sixty families cheering and singing down the South Fork of the Holston River, bound for our new life at the French Lick, yet almost immediately we foundered on shoals. As we tended our boats, a further calamity occurred when the ice set in, trapping us with only three miles traveled. Since then we have been forced to wait, and the good Lord knows I was not made for waiting.*

*I despair in seeing our canoes as useless as jewels, their gunwales strung with icicle fringes. Our flatboats lie paralyzed in drifts of snow, like so many wounded animals. I will not look at them. I also avoid looking in the distance at Fort Patrick Henry, where neighbors have expected our departure for so long. How can they keep from mocking us? Instead I turn my gaze to the sky where the moon droops a thin smile, and to the horizon where mountains wear a crown of blue haze.*

*When my brother, Jamie, returned from the Cumberland Country last year, he said the new land we seek has mountains too, but will they look like these old friends I have come to love? When I climb those new mountains, will my heart tremble as it does here surveying the gray-green hills? This waiting gives me too much time to think of what I leave behind.*

*Maybe if I knew exactly where the river will take us, I would have less apprehension, but our party has only a crude map to show how the rivers feed, one into another. The sketch Jamie drew with the help of a friendly Cherokee is a rough drawing and no one can swear to its accuracy. Perhaps this map is a symbol for our whole expedition, an endeavor we must accept with hope and faith.*

*Some might think my age of twenty-three is young, but I have been a widow for two years and am the sole provider for three daughters. I was a bride the year I turned thirteen, as if I suspected my married life would be cut short, and I needed to make an early start. Even though David and I were wed for eight years, it was too little time. Maybe I could have borne his loss more easily if he had experienced a hero's death, losing his life while fighting the dreaded Indian Chief, Dragging Canoe. Then I might have seen a reason for his loss. Instead, he was killed in a senseless fashion, crushed beneath a falling oak. I still struggle to see God's Will in such a tragedy.*

*In these odd hours when I look back on my marriage, I believe I knew my husband only when the dark shadows of night settled upon us. Chores of survival consumed our days, with evening bringing our sole intimacies. I have no idea if our marital dance was like that of others, but David and I made a good life. Pretty words never passed between us, but we forged our bonds all the same. After his death I felt as empty as a hollow gourd and neither prayer nor fevered activity could dispel the sensation.*

*I found a way to carry him with me, at least a part of him: the masculine smell of tobacco, leather and sweat. Underneath my mole-gray woolen cloak, I wear his hunting shirt and leggings like a second skin.*

*My sister-in-law, Charlotte, thinks I have lost my senses, but these garments keep him near. I labored long in tanning the deer skin for his shirt until its touch became as soft as the skin of our children, and I imagine his britches still hold the shape of his strong legs. These clothes suit me well since I must be both father and mother to our daughters who curl against me now like puppies seeking warmth. I have already killed to save their lives, and by Heaven, I'll do it again if I must.*

*Jamie gave me this journal before he and my brothers, Mark and John, left in October for the French Lick with the other men. It was his suggestion that I record the wondrous things we will see and do as we travel to the Cumberland. I believe it is equally useful to record my thoughts, for the mind has its own journeys.*

We had an eventful day at last. This morning, just after I tucked my journal into its scarred leather knapsack, I observed Charlotte talking with Colonel Donelson near our boat, *The Adventure.* I must admit I indulged in critical thoughts about the Colonel's incompetence and enjoyed the process quite a bit. Charlotte always defends him, saying he can't be held responsible for the terrible weather that slowed boat construction or the thick ice that trapped our vessels. But I believe that at sixty-one, he is more suited to being a gentleman land speculator than the leader of this assorted fleet. How foolish he was to wait until December to begin the journey in the first place. He should have instructed the shipbuilders to work double time. If I force myself to be reasonable, however, I acknowledge this winter has been unusually harsh, with fog freezing in large white knots on the bushes. The first time I have ever seen such a thing.

Charlotte motioned for me to join her at the river. I was reluctant to leave my warm spot even though my straw mattress can be maddeningly prickly at times. But rise I did. On seeing me, my hound, Bruno, slung his large head upwards in alarm. Now that David is gone, he feels a responsibility to protect us, but I raised my hand to ensure his silence. I wanted the girls to sleep as long as possible, the oblivion of slumber being one of their few blessings.

As I threaded my way through the campsites where families still bunched beside low fires, I considered the differences between Charlotte and me, beginning with the most obvious one: our appearances. Charlotte is a dark brunette who always wears a white cap with feathery ruffles framing her face. It is my belief she favors such frills to soften a face stronger than the countenance of many men. I don't mean that she lacks a womanly aspect. Not at all. Her lips are as fine and delicate as any I have seen, a dainty curve across her pale white skin. But her nose is straight and strong and her glittering black eyes have the power to reach into one's soul and pluck out the truth, no matter how painful.

I, on the other hand, possess a far more intemperate demeanor. My coppery hair burns like a robust fire even on the coldest day. And to my everlasting dismay, it curls and springs from my head like thick coils of hemp. Although I try to subdue it under a knitted cap, it still escapes and fans over my shoulders like a flaming cape. My eyes, too, have an unusual appearance, hazel with prominent flecks of yellow. My mother used to say they were the eyes of a cat, and that only my long tapering fingers showed the mark of a lady. I hope she does not look down from heaven and despair at my wearing trousers. I can sum up the disparities between Charlotte and me by saying that she is a woman of reflection, and I am one of action. She is the warm hearth, and I am the blazing coal upon it.

When we reached the river's edge, I in my gray cloak and she in her green one, I witnessed the cause of her excitement, for etched on the river's frozen surface was a fissure, a dark jagged promise. Charlotte had heard the ice crack during the night, the first sign a thaw is coming. I wanted to spread the good news to my friend Elizabeth at once, but Charlotte knelt beside the silver-white river and insisted I join her in prayer. I have learned that when Charlotte draws down her eyebrows, one might as well relent, so I also knelt on the buckled earth and felt its iciness creep into my knees. Before she began the prayer, however, she proposed the most extraordinary thing . . . that I become a teacher for the children on *The Adventure*. Everyone knows Charlotte is the most learned person in our community, the one who taught both Jamie and me to read, and if anyone should be the teacher, it is she.

Before I could refuse, however, she provided the reason for her suggestion. She did not humor me by saying that I was the obvious choice because of my education. Charlotte is far too honest for that maneuver. No, she explained how she had observed my entertaining the children with stories during the months of our confinement, and she thought I could enlarge my efforts with lessons in reading and writing as well. She did not add that my loud voice carries well over the sound of wind and rushing water, but it is true.

I protested that I wouldn't know where to begin since we have no primers, no slates, no writing papers. In response Charlotte suggested I ask Major John Cockrill for assistance, as he is both an able blacksmith and a carpenter who might devise tools to fit my needs. I am reluctant to speak with the man, however, since I barely know him. He has only lately come from Virginia and keeps to himself, working quietly at whatever job the Colonel assigns.

I told Charlotte I would give her suggestion my serious consideration, but first I wanted to inform my friend, Elizabeth Peyton, about the ice's changing condition. Elizabeth is heavy with child and most eager for the journey to begin. She hopes we will reach the French Lick before she gives birth so that her husband, Ephraim, will be by her side, but given her advanced pregnancy, I believe it impossible. She travels with her parents, Mary and Jonathan Jennings, on a flatboat not nearly so large as *The Adventure*, which can carry twenty of us. But their craft is adequate to accommodate Elizabeth, her parents, two slaves and two devilish boys, Elizabeth's younger brother Johnny and his friend Robert Wood. The boys weren't old enough to travel overland with Jamie and the other men, but are quite old enough to be a continuous source of mischief.

Elizabeth is a beautiful girl, angelic in quality, with long honey-colored hair that gleams even in dim morning light. Her face is an almost perfect heart shape, with broad brow and pointed chin. As I approached, she lifted her slate-gray eyes which took on an added light at seeing me. She was sitting on a wooden bench dressed in a voluminous red cloak and binding a wheat-colored baby blanket. Her good-for-nothing brother sprawled on the ground nearby, poking roughly with a crooked stick at the family hound.

I cannot abide cruelty to animals, so my first act was to seize the branch from Johnny, crack it across my knee, and throw it into the fire. I admonished him for his low-minded actions, and suggested that if he wanted to play with sticks, he and his friend Robert could collect wood for the morning's fire. This advice was met with a sulky expression and a complaint that such work was fit only for slaves. But I stamped the ground with such a force that those two shiftless boys sidled off rather than deal with me further.

I didn't come to upbraid Johnny Jennings, however, so I proceeded right away to deliver my news, that the ice was breaking and we would soon be underway. On hearing my words, Mrs. Jennings skirted the fire to join us, wearing a gray cloak similar to mine. She is solemn like her daughter, but built tall and strong with a craggy face, her forehead defined by thick dark eyebrows that curl over smoky eyes. Because of Elizabeth's fatigue, she was reluctant at first to view the new development at the river, but her mother convinced her that walking makes a happy child.

Elizabeth was sure of his happiness already, she said, since just the previous evening she had felt his little hand stroke the full length of her stomach, waving a glad hello. She drew her mother's hand slowly across her swollen belly, and Mrs. Jennings smiled broadly. "I wager he was, Honey," she said. "All the more reason to show him the river."

While Mrs. Jennings and I supported Elizabeth between us, steering her like a fragile craft across the icy patches, I took the opportunity to inquire as to the whereabouts of Mr. Jennings. His wife explained that he had gone hunting for fresh meat so they could save their dried provisions for the trip. This worry about their food supply stirred up Mrs. Jennings' memories of her former life in Virginia. She described in great detail the sweet taste of gingerbread that used to sting her tongue and the butter that would stream down her chin. Of turkeys practically as big as small hogs laid out on giant platters. And juicy pork, cracklen bread, and sausage seasoned with sage and the bite of strong red pepper. By the time we reached the water, I was fairly weak with hunger from hearing talk of such grand food.

I was pleased to interrupt her litany by pointing to the ice fissure that had grown even larger than before. Soon it would spread further, racing the length of the river, pointing the way toward the land of good springs and rich soil, and a life that one day would rival any in Virginia.

# *Two*

FEBRUARY 11, 1780 — *To our dismay, shortly after noon yesterday more cold air rushed into the valley and dark clouds tumbled in the sky as if God had set a pot to boiling. The wind whipped us without mercy, punishing us for some unpardonable deed. My own misery lessened when the children brought me a present they had made for my birthday, a doll fashioned of corn husks, its features drawn with charcoal from the fire.*

*What a delight these daughters are, as different from each other as the three leaves of the sassafras tree. Charity, just shy of her third birthday, surprises me upon occasion with large questions about life and death. I cherish her dark, straight hair, so like David's. My five-year-old Betsy, whose personality is closest to mine, has a head covered with blond ringlets that keep anyone from guessing she is my child. Only Polly's red hair identifies her immediately as mine, but her solemn brown eyes come from my mother. When Polly presented the doll to me, I had the oddest sensation that my mother was reaching directly from the grave to touch me again.*

*When I cried from the pain of missing my mother, the girls feared I didn't like their present, but I pulled them close and assured them that no gift could have pleased me more. As I nuzzled my cheek against their dear faces, I thanked God for giving me these wonderful children. A special attachment exists between mothers and daughters. When I see the promise of my best self in their unformed spirits, I pray I will have the wisdom to teach them how to have full and useful lives. More than sewing a fine seam or molding a flawless candle, I want them to develop fearless hearts. Because my father died when I was only four, I don't remember much of his teachings, but I do remember how my mother instilled in me the importance of courage. As her only daughter, and all the more special because of that, she taught me to face life bravely, just as she taught my brothers. Although she died shortly before my marriage, I have not forgotten her lessons these ten years hence.*

*This morning it is so cold that if I could lick the air, my tongue would freeze. Across the frozen ground, other families slumber near their fires, some under tents, but most unsheltered from the winter air. It is as if we form one body, breathing together, determined to survive. May God answer our prayers and deliver us safely to the Cumberland Country.*

All morning the wind blew steadily, sending the ice-sheathed trees into a frenzy of clattering. As an exercise to warm myself, I imagined the trees ripening into spring: lavender petals exploding on the black branches of the red bud trees, patches of white dogwood, delicate as lace, dotting the thicket. I pictured the fruits of summer: ripe purple plums splitting their skins, soft peaches hiding scarlet hearts. The thought of their taste pooled saliva beneath my tongue, and forced me to swallow hard. Better to think only of meat, potatoes and corn pone. Then I will not be disappointed.

Betsy interrupted my thoughts, tugging at my shirt with her thick brown mitten. Her cheeks were burnished crimson from the harsh wind, but she was warm beneath the robe, her knitted cap pulled tightly over her ears.

"Mama," she said in a loud whisper, drawing the word out slowly from her cupid bow mouth.

"Yes, honey," I replied, centering my finger on her lips, a gesture to speak softly.

"I know God wants us to share," she began, her blue eyes opening with such righteousness I could tell she hatched a plot. "So if you're not playing with your birthday doll, may I?"

I shuddered at the idea of encountering the brutal wind on our way to the boat, just to retrieve a doll and cautioned her to go back to sleep. But she continued, sensing why I was reluctant. "If you give me the key, I can get it all by myself."

I sighed deeply at the image of Betsy scrambling through the trunks and boxes, creating a veritable avalanche of baggage. It was obvious she could not go alone, and when I considered how small was her request, I relented.

"Well, you'll have to be very careful with her," I said, summoning what I hoped was the proper parental tone. "And be very quiet when you get . . ."

But she was already out of the covers, moving lithely as a snake, and it was all I could do to catch up with her. The cutting wind made us hunch and duck our heads, so when we reached *The Adventure*, we headed straight for shelter in the cabin where our goods were stored. Although *The Adventure* is the largest boat in the flotilla, a good thirty by forty feet, it is barely adequate to accommodate all our luggage, tools and foodstuffs. The cabin was stuffed with a jumble of things: animal traps and fish baskets; kettles and skillets; and an assortment of broad axes, hoes, augers and adzes. Oaken barrels stacked against the wall were filled with meal, corn, salt, flour, bacon and ham. Barrels of cabbages and potatoes nestled beside containers of whiskey. And bags of seed gave promise of crops to come: corn, oats, beans and pumpkins. The sight of such abundance comforted me, that we would not go hungry on our journey to the new land.

I found my walnut trunk with little difficulty for it is as familiar to me as my own hand. David fashioned both the trunk and its iron key which hangs on a thin leather strap around my neck. I opened its solid lid to reveal all the objects of my past. On the very bottom were thick blankets, followed by the quilt my Gower relatives gave me on my wedding day. Next was the red coverlet David and I slept beneath every night of our married lives. On top were my Bible, the pewter plates and cutlery that once belonged to my mother, David's hunting knife, and a brown straw sewing box with a broken lid. Tucked among these items were dun-colored pouches containing gourd seeds, the maple sugar I saved for the darkest days of the trip, and perhaps the packet I value most: the one with flax seeds that will become material for shirts, sheets, towels and even fine linen. The last item was the little doll whose rough dot eyes gave it a bewildered expression. I handed the doll to Betsy who took it quickly between her mittens.

"You'll share with the others now," I reminded her.

She nodded gravely and found a corner of the cabin where she could play with the little doll. Near her was Hagar, the Robertsons' slave, who had also sought shelter from the wind to protect the sleeping toddler, Charlotte. Hagar's head was wrapped warmly with a dark red scarf, its fabric decorated with small blue squares. A thick wool cape the color of her skin draped from shoulder to foot. I knew Hagar was as ready as the rest of us to begin our journey, since her husband, Henry, had gone ahead with Jamie and the other men. She slowly rocked the child from side to side, comforting little Charlotte who was often sick during the night.

After I said good morning, Hagar surprised me with an announcement that we would leave this place in two days. I asked her if she had heard the news from Colonel Donelson, but she rested her hand on Charlotte's forehead, testing for a fever, and replied it had come to her in a dream. The Lord told her He would lead us out of here just as He led the Israelites. Hagar is known to see visions and hear voices inaudible to the rest of us, and I would dismiss her superstitions if they did not so often prove true. So I simply responded that I hoped we wouldn't have to wander forty years.

"If we behave ourselves," she said, "it won't take us nearly so long. But if we don't . . . well, I guess Captain Robertson will come back to straighten us out."

"We need more than one Captain Robertson, don't we Hagar?" I answered, glad to focus on the tangible. "If Jamie were one of a pair of twins like Ephraim and John Peyton, then he could be with us and with the men at the Cumberland too."

"Just because folks are twins doesn't mean they're alike," she said. " I see a big difference in those Peyton men. Miss Elizabeth picked the wrong one." Hagar nodded for emphasis.

Admittedly, it took no conjuring to see a difference between John and Ephraim Peyton. It was true that physically they were as alike as two people could be, both fiery-haired, of medium height with slender, wiry bodies. Whereas I have only a few freckles to accompany my red hair, they look as if God fired a shotgun of brown spots to cover their faces as thoroughly as a bad case of hives. Their disparity, however, lies in the expression of their brown eyes. John's appear clear, as if no secrets reside in his soul, while Ephraim's eyes have a guarded aspect, an opacity that blocks any revelation of his inner life. I worried that Hagar had some further clue as to Ephraim's nature, something revealed by her second sight, so asked for any information she might have. But she began chanting to the baby in some unintelligible language, indicating she had revealed all she planned to say. It was with an unsettled heart that I took my leave, gathering Betsy and returning to our campfire where my other two children still slept.

The wind had lifted the blue haze from the mountains, exposing their dark outline etched against the milky sky. I kissed each of my sleeping girls on the forehead, and Betsy joined the wake-up ceremony by crying, "Look what I've got," sweeping the doll tauntingly over their heads. After they were thoroughly awake, I noticed Major Cockrill already working at the fire he shared with Hugh Rogan, so I hurried my daughters to play with Charlotte's children, and went to join him, thinking it might be a good time to talk about teaching supplies.

Major Cockrill is not what I'd call a handsome man. His features are too irregular for such a description. His nose is a bit prominent on an angular face and thick eyelids shelve his deep brown eyes. But the corners of his mouth turn up in a pleasant way, and years of being a blacksmith have left him with broad shoulders and a deep, thick chest. Under his sweeping cape he wore leggings of beige linsey-woolsey and a loose hunting shirt tied in back with a sash. On his head sat a floppy rust-colored hat. He was pouring melted lead from a heavy iron saucepan into bullet molds when I arrived, and I took a moment to appreciate the extent of his equipment: a small bellows, anvil, tongs, screw plates and files for fixing guns.

"Morning Mrs. Johnson," he said, attempting to wipe the black iron scale from his hands.

"Morning Major Cockrill." I answered stiffly. I'm afraid I have little facility for trivial talk, and went right to the subject, saying I needed to ask a favor. He thought I needed my rifle repaired, but I explained that Charlotte wanted me to set up a school, and I came to see if he might construct a slate of some kind. He gazed at the fire in contemplation but said nothing.

"I know you're busy," I added, wondering if he thought the request a frivolous one. After all, he had no children of his own, but he surprised me by changing the subject entirely. He said he had seen me once before, three years earlier. At that time, he had come with Colonel Christian to save Fort Caswell from an Indian attack, but when they arrived he heard the story of how I had already saved the fort.

Well, I confess that this turn in the conversation made me uncomfortable. I didn't think of myself as a heroine. I had only done what was necessary with much help from others, so I returned to the subject of teaching tools. But he added not another word, only continued to stare into the fire.

"I'm sorry to have bothered you, Major," I finally concluded, exasperated at his lack of response. "I'll be on my way."

"I'll think on the problem, Mrs. Johnson," he said, kneeling to resume his bullet making.

So much for Charlotte's suggestion that he would be useful. It appeared he had no understanding that the children's education was important. I returned to *The Adventure*, already in a disgruntled mood, only to find Charlotte deep in conversation with Colonel Donelson. I listened with annoyance to the Colonel's lofty tone of voice and wondered if he thought himself better than the rest of us since he had once served in the House of Burgesses. I tried to imagine him in dignified surroundings with Governor Jefferson, but there was nothing particularly elegant in his fleshy demeanor. He was a man of medium height, with square shoulders and a slightly curving spine. His gray hair was rather sparse and the skin gathered around his eyes like crushed fabric. Those dark eyes might have seen grandeur in the past, but it was well known that he had fallen on hard times of late and was staking his family's future on land speculation in Kentucky. He was accompanied by his wife, son Severn and daughter Rachel, as well as two married children, John Junior and Mary Caffrey . . . enough to make a settlement of his own.

"Ah, Mrs. Johnson," the Colonel said. "I was just telling Mrs. Robertson that I've had good news from Hugh Rogan. He and my man, Somerset, have been scouting the river, and Rogan says the ice is breaking up along the banks for several miles. We'll be able to set sail in a day or so."

"Good news indeed!" I put my arm around Charlotte. "I was afraid I'd have to raise my children right here on Reedy Creek."

Charlotte arched her brows, giving me a look of reproof.

"I hope I can count on you to rally the troops, Mrs. Johnson," added Donelson, determined to maintain a cheerful manner. "Everyone looks up to you, and there's much you can accomplish to keep up their spirits."

"What a nice compliment," said Charlotte, looking at me as if to say "I told you so."

But I didn't believe it was a compliment, only a move worthy of the politician he was, shifting focus of the conversation from his own failure.

"We're hoping Ann will be our school teacher," added Charlotte, eager to maintain a pleasant conversation. "Have you spoken with Major Cockrill about the supplies?"

"Charlotte thinks the Major can print readers overnight," I said. "But all he did when I asked for help was say he'd think about it."

"Major Cockrill has been quite helpful in repairing our boats, and no doubt he can help us in this matter as well," said Charlotte. "Wouldn't you agree, Colonel?"

"I believe, Mrs. Robertson," said Colonel Donelson, "you are as correct as ever. And if you will excuse me." At this point the Colonel took his leave, happy to withdraw.

I was sorry to see him depart so abruptly, only because I wanted to add a few more complaints, but I knew my energies would best be spent on analyzing how to teach the children. First I should canvas the group to see what books were available. Almost everyone had a copy of the Bible, but surely other books existed too. Hymn books. Nothing helped to lift the spirits and invigorate the body so much as the healthy singing of a hymn. I began to warm to the idea; Charlotte was right, as usual. Being the school teacher was the perfect activity for me, and I vowed to start that very afternoon.

———

It was almost three o'clock when the children sat in a half circle around a fire that burned near *The Adventure*. The black smoke from the flickering flames drifted occasionally into one face and then another. My own children, Polly, Betsy, and Charity, sat beside Charlotte's little ones: Randolph, Delilah, Peyton and little Charlotte cradled in her mother's lap. I marched back and forth in front of the children to capture their attention, counting my footsteps loudly, trying to compete with the distant pounding of Major Cockrill's hammer and the distracting aroma of baking corn bread. A few dogs barked in the distance, but Bruno lay stretched beside the children, as if he too had come to study.

I was ready to start their lesson, when the children began with questions about the day I saved the fort, begging for the story. Although I knew they had heard the tale many times, I thought it might be fitting to repeat it once again before we began a journey that might well bring perils of its own . . . to reinforce the importance of vigilance where Indians are concerned. And so I began.

To provide a background for that day's events, I started with the tale of what happened five years ago in March of 1775 at Sycamore Shoals just outside Fort Caswell, when Colonel Richard Henderson bought the very lands we plan to inhabit. At the time, it seemed that nothing could interfere with the treaty's success because no Indians of any tribe actually lived in that territory, and the Cherokees had indicated they were willing to trade. A rumor spread that the land was not the Cherokees to sell, but no one took it seriously. We eagerly waited for the great party of Cherokee Indians, led by Chief Attakullakulla, to come and exchange their land for the fine goods that Henderson had brought in six enormous wagons across the mountains. And what riches they heaved from those wagons and stored in huts built just for the purpose of displaying them. I thought we needed the guns and ammunition for ourselves, but I forced myself to remember that the knives, axes, hoes and rum were buying us land for the future. Actually buying it outright so we would never again have to worry about giving it back to the Indians. The land would belong to us and our children forever.

The Indians were excited about the treasure too. They started gathering at Fort Caswell two months before the treaty was to be signed, bringing their wives with them. It was the first time I had seen so many Cherokee women, and I watched carefully as they bent their slim and graceful bodies to study the bolts of bright cloth spread upon the ground. Many of them dressed in leather skirts with leather capes about their shoulders, but some dressed just the way we women at Fort Caswell did, except I must admit they were taller and more beautiful than we. As I observed a Cherokee woman string bracelets on her long, slender arm, I'd never seen anyone more elegant, not even on the other side of the mountains.

When it was time to begin the negotiations, our men turned out in their best clothes to impress the Indians during the talks. Jamie wore a dark blue waistcoat that Charlotte had made, and knee breeches with silver buckles. Colonel Henderson, being a judge, wore a tall powdered wig and black leather military boots. But they couldn't compare to the clothes Lieutenant John Sevier wore, a scarlet jacket and silk stockings, with elaborately chased silver buckles glistening on his shoes.

The Indians were dressed in their finery as well. For the first time I saw old Chief Attakullakulla himself, sitting still as death on a huge pile of thick furs: fox and beaver spread around him. From his ears hung a pyramid of silver spangles dropping almost to his shoulders and feathers crowned his gray head. He carried the signs of his fierce culture in the deep slashes that decorated his cheeks. Jamie had told me the reason the Chief was willing to make a treaty with us was to encourage our move to the West so we would leave his Cherokee Overhill settlement alone. He understood our land hunger and was trying to do the best for his people. So the talks began, with both sides sitting in one circle.

The work of coming to an agreement went on for days, and Chief Attakullakulla was almost ready to sign the treaty when his son, Dragging Canoe, rose to address the entire group. He is tall for an Indian, almost six feet, and his face is fearfully pitted with smallpox scars that must remind him of the pain our diseases have brought to his people. He told everyone at the meeting how the Indian nations "have melted away like balls of snow before the sun," and he warned that the white man would never be satisfied until we had taken everything. In front of the whole company he pointed to the very land we'll cross when our boats start again, saying, "A dark cloud hangs over the land known as 'The Bloody Ground.'" And with that message, Dragging Canoe split with his father forever and is no longer a Cherokee, but has formed his own renegade tribe, the deadly Chickamaugas. He does not accept the terms of our treaty, and the fear of him lies at the center of all our hearts. He left the treaty talks to meet with the British in faraway Florida and brought back sixty horses loaded with guns and ammunition he later used to fight us.

Over a year later when the word came down to Fort Caswell that an attack was imminent, people from nearby Fort Lee joined us, since their fort wasn't strong enough to stand against the Indians. Two hundred of us jammed together, many of the new arrivals with no beds or any possessions other than what they could bring on the run.

We had to put our cows outside the walls because we were so crowded, but we depended on them for milk. At daybreak on the morning of July 21, several of us women took our milking stools and left the fort early. Jamie and Lieutenant Sevier watched over us that morning as we took a few dogs who were trained to bark at the sight or sound of Indians. The grass was wet and my cow, Miss Priss, kept nuzzling after the fresh blades as I tried to milk her. Even though the air was cool, sweat strung across my upper lip, and when I lifted my sleeve to wipe it off, the first dogs barked. I couldn't breathe. It wasn't five seconds later that we heard shrill screams as the savages rose up from the forest like bats flying up at twilight. They rushed across the clearing, some shooting arrows and guns, others running wildly with their tomahawks raised, all painted black in the most grotesque fashion. We leapt from our milking stools and ran toward the fort.

Once inside, we slammed and barred the gate, only to hear more cries coming from the distance. Much to our horror, Kate Sherrill was still outside. Lieutenant Sevier and I climbed the ramparts to see Kate coming, just in front of an Indian who held his tomahawk high. With one hand the Lieutenant shot at the Indian and with the other he reached toward her with a shout, 'Jump Kate!' The bullets and arrows poured like hail and she knew she had to jump or die, so jump she did, and Sevier pulled her safely over the stockade walls. Her clothes were ripped and her body scraped by the sharp points of the stakes, but she was alive.

All of us were spared for the present, huddled together inside the fort, but the Indians wouldn't go away. On some days they fired at us repeatedly and on other days there was no shooting, and we thought perhaps they had left. On one of those quiet days when we thought it safe to carry on our chores, the real battle began.

Most of the men, including my husband David, had gone to get more ammunition and supplies, leaving only a few to stand guard. Since it was my turn to be in charge of wash duty, I organized the fire builders, and soon we had our kettles boiling for the piles of laundry we'd assembled. Perhaps because I was so busy with my own fire, I didn't notice what was going on outside the fort walls. Not until I heard someone scream, "Fire! Oh, Lord help us! They're burning the fort!"

I rushed to the ramparts with one of the men. "Do something!" I cried, but the Indians were so close to the fort it was impossible for him to aim his rifle downward and catch them in its sight. The overhang of the palisades interfered. The Indians who set fire to the walls were joined by others who shot from a distance. All I could think was that I must save my daughters. I cried to the women at the wash pots, "Make a line! We're going to put out this fire."

They brought me the first pot, a huge iron vessel I could barely lift by gripping each of the handles with my doubled-over apron. Just as I spilled the first pot over the stockade and heard the fire's hiss, I felt an arrow enter my arm, a little below the shoulder. I called for another pot and emptied the scalding rain upon the Indians' backs. Once again I felt the sting of a wound, this time a shot. But I kept to my post until the fire was out, and the Indians retreated. I later counted many wounds on my body, and regretted not a one. It was an honor to defend my family and my country.

When I had finished the story, even though it was not new to the children, they stared at me in awe, their eyes open wide and spiked with fear.

"You weren't afraid?" Polly finally asked, breaking the gripping silence.

"Of course I was," I answered. "An Indian attack is something to fear, but I wanted to do my best, and I'm proud as any soldier that I did." I added an even more important message. "But remember, I couldn't have done it myself. Every last woman in the fort helped me lift those pots."

I studied their young faces and prayed that none would ever witness such terrible events. But if they did, I hoped the impulse to fight together would be as instinctual as breath itself.

# *Three*

FEBRUARY 13, 1780 — *When I told the children my story, I recounted only the parts I thought they needed to hear. I saw no reason to describe how one arrow was later removed from my arm, how Jamie held whiskey to my lips and had me drink until I could barely focus on his face. How he broke off the arrow's point and wrenched the shaft from my arm. I didn't relate how the blood covered his hands as if he wore shiny, scarlet gloves, and I fainted from the pain. How I woke again, aching in every part of my body, scalp wounds streaming blood onto my eyelashes where it later matted and dried. Other arrows had hit my upper body leaving five puncture wounds, one just below my left breast. After more than three years, I still tremble at the thought of revealing my naked skin to another human being. I should consider these scars as signs of courage, but I feel a deep and abiding shame at how they have disfigured my body. I do not dwell on it, however. I survived.*

*The cold weather continues, and with it come new maladies. Yesterday Mr. Jennings, returned from his hunting trip with a strange tale. Usually he sets his hounds to follow turkeys until the birds take roost in the trees. Then the turkeys are so distracted by the dogs' howl-*

*ing that they are unaware of humans approaching, and can easily be shot. Yesterday, however, as he and the dogs stalked the woods, he came to a sight he had never before witnessed. A number of the birds had frozen in the trees from the excessive cold and tumbled dead to the ground. He slung one of the poor, scraggly creatures across his shoulder to bring back for our inspection only, since it was not fit for eating.*

*The sight of the diminished bird struck at my heart. I have seen turkeys that weighed as much as fifty pounds, turkeys so fat they burst when shot from the trees. But this bird, our neighbor, so to speak, was as thin as ever I have seen, its once proud breast shrunken. Even his red neck had turned an ashy gray. Oh, Heaven protect us. This cold is our proven enemy. I pray we encounter no others.*

*If it please God, today is the day we shall take leave of this place. Colonel Donelson has spread the word to assemble this morning for a departing prayer. At last.*

As the sun struggled to penetrate the clouds, the sharp sound of a horn drew us to the river bank. Chunks of ice bobbed on the water's surface, a reminder of the booming noise we heard when the ice finally broke up, as if the very earth was ripped apart and roared with pain. At that time, the river sped ferociously, desperate for release after its long confinement, but now the flow has returned to normal. Colonel Donelson raised his hands for silence.

"It seems God thought we needed some extra seasoning," Donelson began, "before we got our real start. But Hugh Rogan tells me the river is ready now. At least I think that's what he said. You know his thick Irish brogue takes a bit of translation."

The crowd laughed, glad to make a boisterous noise in defiance against our old foe, the weather. I spotted Hugh drop his head in embarrassment, a short, chunky man built like a boulder.

"Today, with God's permission, we begin our journey to the French Lick," Donelson continued. "We will travel through territory that has never been mapped with precision. We have chosen to pursue a land we have never seen," he went on gravely, turning his gaze on first one and then another of us. "But we are armed with something far more powerful than the four- pound cannon I carry on my boat. We are armed with faith: faith in our God who has sustained us thus far.

"Before we launch our boats, I'd like each of you to join me in singing the Doxology, our hymn of Praise and Thanksgiving."

A sudden burst of emotion tightened my throat and dried the juices in my mouth, but I struggled to sing with the others.

*"Praise God, from whom all blessings flow;*
*Praise Him, all creatures here below;*
*Praise Him above, ye heav'nly host;*
*Praise Father, Son and Holy Ghost.*
*AMEN."*

As the last strains of "Amen" lifted above us, I was amazed to see how the familiar faces of my neighbors shed their wrinkles and scowls. All fears were drained away in this one moment of startled grace. The future was ready to unfold at last; there would be no more wondering.

"And now a moment of silent prayer," added Donelson, closing his eyes, "each in his own way."

I squatted low to the ground on my haunches to get as close to my girls as possible; then bowed my stubborn head and squinted my eyes until my brow cramped in the process. I put my arms around my children, breathing deep of their warm scent of spice and wood smoke and began a prayer for their well being, for their survival even if I perished. Their deliverance was all I prayed for — the hope of food to sustain them, fair weather to hasten their journey and a trip without the horror of Indian attack. I remembered that we would travel through the country where Dragging Canoe had established new towns, and his dreadful curse echoed in my mind. "A dark cloud hangs over the land known as 'The Bloody Ground.'" I shivered and pulled the children even tighter. My eyes were still closed when I felt a tap on my shoulder.

"Ann," said Charlotte. "It's time."

When I opened my eyes, I discovered that the magic of The Doxology had lifted, and our expressions were once again hardened into the determination necessary for the enormous task at hand. But surely God remained in our hearts.

———

What a thrill it was to see our boats being launched once more! Because it was the largest, *The Adventure* went first; a group of ten men straining to push its timbers over log rollers, bumping it toward the water's edge. It was a fine vessel, the deck constructed of dense poplar timbers joined with more than a thousand maple pegs and caulked with tar and oatum. The cabin took up half of its forty-foot length, the roof covered with white oak shingles. Once we were underway, one man would stand on the cabin roof to steer, using the long sweep of the tiller. Two more would use broadhorn oars to keep the craft moving in shallow water or when going upstream. No one could say it was a graceful way to travel, but its size provided us a maximum amount of space. Still, for a long time we would be packed as close together as the kernels on an ear of corn.

We cheered when *The Adventure* hit the water with a loud splash. Donelson's canoe followed quickly behind. Other vessels came after, crashing into the swiftly moving water while the children screamed and jumped on the riverbank, clapping their hands.

"Can we get on now, Mama? Please," begged Polly, her red hair switching on her shoulders.

"Please?" added Betsy, pulling on my leggings.

"Good heavens, girls. They've got to load the boat first."

"When will they put on our mattress?" asked Charity, wanting to be treated like a baby for the occasion. "I want to go back to bed."

"No sleeping now, Honey," I said, "This is a day you will remember all your life ."

I hastened them toward Hagar for their breakfast and watched the flurry of activity around me as people finished their packing. While the men launched boats, the women stored their last cooking implements, checked their trunks, and gave slaves instructions for moving the goods. I was happy to see that Mr. Jennings had succeeded in getting Johnny and Robert Wood to help push their boat toward the river. Elizabeth and her mother followed, walking straight toward me with baskets of linen slung across their arms.

"Isn't it wonderful?" shouted Elizabeth as she waddled toward me, her feet turned out like a duck to accommodate her pregnant belly. "Maybe I'll be with Ephraim when our baby is born after all. And even more good news!" Elizabeth gestured for Nancy Gower to join us. "Your cousin has agreed to come on our boat to keep me company."

Nancy, a sunny girl of seventeen, had raven hair that curled thickly around her face. I imagined she would be a good traveling companion indeed, and maybe Johnny and Robert would be too embarrassed to pull lazy tricks in front of her.

"Oh, we're going to have such adventures!" said Nancy, twirling her skirt like one of my children. "Imagine what we'll see!"

"A good deal more than we'd like, probably," I said.

"Oh, Ann," said Elizabeth, pushing my arm gently. "You know you're excited too."

"Of course I am." I returned Elizabeth's gaze. "If I had to stay here even one more day, I might jump in the river and start swimming on my own. I'm just more wary than you."

"Ah," said Elizabeth. "Probably because you're a mother. I imagine I'll be more cautious very soon. By the way, did Major Cockrill find you this morning? He said he had something for you."

"Now what sort of present would the Major have for you?" teased Nancy, a sparkle in her coffee colored eyes.

"I asked him for some teaching equipment," I said. "Perhaps it's ready."

"They say his father was in the House of Burgesses, just like Colonel Donelson," Nancy continued.

"I imagine being a blacksmith will serve him much better out here," I responded, giving a final hug to Elizabeth. "Now I must gather up my girls. I'll see you this evening."

I hastened through the crowd, greeting my fellow travelers: old Mr. Harrison, his snowy hair tasseling in clumps beneath his brown felt hat, his woolen stockings bunching at the ankles. And Mrs. Harrison and Susanna Henry, plump and round under their greatcoats, looking like two hens in eager conversation. I saw John Cockrill making last minute repairs to his equipment, absorbed with the work.

Excitement swept my body, inching up from my feet as I walked faster and faster. My stomach tightened with anticipation and my breath quickened. I released a cloud of steam as I yelled, "This is the day which the Lord hath made. Rejoice and be glad in it."

I had reached the river's edge when I heard the cry of "Mama, Mama," and turned to see my three daughters running toward me, hand in hand like daisies on a chain, their caps bright in the morning sun. And I was filled with joy.

# *Four*

FEBRUARY 21, 1780 — *Such happiness we had for a week, our boats moving at a good pace each day. But the weather has arrested us again, this time at the mouth of Cloud Creek. The air is so thick with fog I can barely distinguish the individual boards beneath my feet. I stand inside a boll of cotton, surrounded by endless puffs of white.*

*The Colonel just gave the order for all boats to find shelter, but how can we find a place to dock in this land of mist?*

FEBRUARY 27, 1780 — *After remaining cold and distressed for a week at Cloud Creek, we cast our fortunes to the river, only to be stuck again at this wretched place called Poor Valley Shoal. It is aptly named. Our boat is trapped on the shoals and beaten hither and thither by the rapid current. I write as the light of day fades, wondering if our boat will be shattered and tomorrow may never come. This whole endeavor seems more a folly every day. Is there no one amongst us who can steer a boat with success? We are supposed to meet a Captain Blackmore and his party at the mouth of the Clinch River and maybe he will prove a better navigator. With our slow progress, I fear he will proceed without us. Alas.*

**FEBRUARY 28, 1780** — *I write in haste. Colonel Donelson has ordered some of us to disembark to lighten the load. Only his family and slaves remain on board. God help us all!*

The surrounding mountains had protected the area from a heavy snow accumulation, and the straight dark cedars wore only thin white swags along their boughs. I instructed the children to link hands firmly, and we splashed into the shallow water with Bruno close behind us. Each step I took landed on slippery rocks streaming with long threads of green moss, making my progress most perilous. At one point I twisted my ankle, jerking the girls and creating a wobble along our line. For some seconds I feared the four of us would tumble into the icy current, but with God's help, we continued to move slowly until we reached the river banks.

Once out of the water, we stamped vigorously to dislodge the water from our soggy boots. But just as we became a little drier, Bruno shook himself furiously, adding an icy shower to our misery. Although I felt as forlorn as an abandoned duckling, I remained cheerful for my children, sending them on a game to search for wood, knowing the vigorous movement would bring warmth even before we lit fires. In a matter of minutes, Charlotte arrived with the baby, followed by Hagar and the rest of the Robertson children who joined mine to bring back timber. Charlotte collapsed on the snowy earth beside me and took up rubbing the toddler's back.

"We'll get the fire started soon," I encouraged, gently stroking little Charlotte's cheek. "Then she'll be warm."

"Just look at this place," said Charlotte, surveying the bleak landscape. "We might as well be back where we started."

"That doesn't sound like you, Charlotte," I said, although the words mirrored my thoughts.

"No," Charlotte admitted, resting her chin on her daughter's head. "But when you have a sick child, it's hard to see things straight."

Hagar knelt near us, scraping snow from some stones at the river's edge.

"What are you doing?" I asked.

"Looking for a sign," Hagar responded, sifting the stones through her hands.

"Of what?"

Hagar chose a perfectly round, flat stone from the rest and held it between her thumb and index finger.

"This place is a safe one," she affirmed.

"I could have told you that," I said. "Not a sign of Indians."

"A lucky charm tells more than a body can see." Hagar rolled the stone between her fingers, as if its good luck could rub off. "It's round like the sun. Round like the moon." She slipped the stone into a small pouch worn at her waist.

"Luck can travel with you," Hagar added, looking straight at me with her wide-set eyes. "And we need all the help we can get."

I studied her pouch with curiosity, a tan, unobtrusive bag.

"What else do you carry in that bag?" I reached toward it.

"Nothing you'd want, Miss Ann," said Hagar, swiftly tucking it into the folds of her cape. "Just a slave's cautions. Some roots, beads, shells. If we need them, you'll see them."

"But what do you . . ." I continued.

"Don't you pay any mind," said Hagar, joining Charlotte in rubbing the child's arms.

Hagar harbored beliefs I would never understand, but I prayed she was right about the good luck part.

The children returned with a combination of fallen logs, branches and vines that were dry enough to make a fire that leapt quickly skyward. Other stymied boats followed Colonel Donelson's lead, seeking to improve their chances by putting passengers ashore, and soon a number of fires burned brightly on the shore. I settled the children, turning them first to the fire to warm their faces and then insisting they warm their backs as well.

As heat spread across my own back, I studied the unfamiliar, shadowy wilderness and wished that we carried an accurate map for our journey, or were accompanied by someone who had traveled this route before. I had heard tales of men becoming lost and disoriented in the woods and going mad. The tangled branches, the sameness of the underbrush, became hell to a traveler in a strange land. Even Jamie, on his first trip over the mountains from North Carolina, had fallen victim to the dense forest.

He struck out alone for the new land ten years ago, taking his rifle and his favorite horse to follow the Indian Warrior Path to the Watauga River. He had no trouble picking his way across creeks, deep into the new country. At the Holston River he turned south until he came to the fine land he was looking for along the river, but his return trip was not so lucky. He took a more southern route, through Georgia, and found he had made a critical error. He carried no compass, and heavy rains soaked his gun powder while fog obscured his vision and rattled his senses. At one point he came across rhododendron and laurel too thick for his horse to penetrate, so he sent the animal back the way he had come. For two weeks he wandered, unable to hunt for food without usable gun powder and dependent on roots and berries for survival. He would have died except for a miraculous encounter with two hunters who fed him and gave him a horse, allowing his return home.

If not for the success of Jamie's first pilgrimage, maybe I would be sitting inside a house of dark red bricks, stitching a Bible verse on a sampler and contemplating a long life. Maybe I would be in Virginia, eating from china plates, with a gold locket dangling from my neck instead of the weight of a heavy iron key. But would I be bored with such a life? Or would boredom be preferable to sitting in snow and praying for deliverance?

Recalling Jamie's struggle in the wilderness reminded me that anyone could falter given the great mission we were trying to accomplish: to establish a new frontier. And I must, must develop my patience. I examined my boots of elk and deerskin and knew that I would not trade them for fine slippers with a neatly turned heel. They were darkly wet now, but they would dry easily and carry me many a mile. And my children were safe beside me. Nothing else mattered. My thoughts were interrupted by a man's voice, and I looked up to see John Cockrill looming above me in his caped greatcoat, his brimmed hat casting a shadow across his forehead.

"I'm sorry to disturb. You looked as if you saw the French Lick right before you."

"Good evening, Major." I stood, tipping my head so I could look him eye to eye. There was something rather haunting about his deep-set eyes.

"I've made you a slate," he said simply.

"A slate? Wherever did you find the material?" I asked, surprised.

"Not a slate exactly, but it'll do," he said mysteriously. "As soon as we have a proper landing, I'll bring it to you."

He addressed my daughters who stared at him silently, their faces glowing in the light.

"And who might these be?" he asked, letting his hands rest on his thighs. "Animals you found in the woods?"

"No sir," giggled Betsy. "We're girls."

"He knows we're not animals," said my solemn-eyed Polly, nudging her sister.

"Sometimes my Mama says I'm a honey bear," said little Charity, pleased to add something to the conversation.

"And that's just what I was about to guess," the Major said seriously. "And you Miss," he addressed Polly, "Are clearly a fox. I can tell by your red hair."

Polly eyed him warily and tightly pressed her lips together.

"And you," he said moving on to Betsy, "Are a puppy. And I bet you'd like to have your stomach tickled."

He leaned toward her as if to tickle, his large hand casting a shadow, and Betsy doubled over with squeals. I was surprised he could make them laugh. At least two of them.

He left without further conversation to return to the fire he shared with Hugh Rogan, the folds of his dark blue cape fluttering behind him, his heavy black boots making a crunching sound in the snow. What an odd pair he and Hugh made: Hugh short, stout, talking continuously in his heavy Irish accent, the Major much taller but given to brief conversations.

"I've seen him before," said Polly. "He's the one who fixes the guns."

"Then he's important," said Betsy.

"We're all important in our own way," I added. "Look who built this fire."

At that moment Charlotte joined us smiling, the fire's warmth having restored her humor.

"Wasn't that Major Cockrill?" she asked.

"You know very well it was. He says he has a slate for me."

"And what good timing," said Charlotte, seating herself. "When *The Adventure* gets underway again, your teaching can help the children forget this terrible cold."

"If *The Adventure* gets underway again," I said sourly. "Actually, I'm looking forward to teaching. I'm even dreaming of starting a school for all the children when we get to the French Lick," I added, stroking Bruno's furrowed head, his fur warm velvet beneath my fingers. "What do you dream of, Charlotte, when we finally settle down?"

"When I have time to dream, it's of a brick house, with columns and great glass windows.

"Oh my. Such big ideas."

"And then, in the garden," Charlotte continued, "I'll plant

hedges of lilacs like we had back home . . . and sweet violets . . . long stretches of them . . . like puddles of purple rain." She paused and threw a small stick into the fire. "But most of all I dream of having James with us. I've grown so weary of our long separations."

"It's a wonder you've had time to bring five children into the world," I said mischievously.

"Ann!" Charlotte answered sharply.

"Well it is," I continued. "He's always off scouting or making treaties with the Indians."

"I'm proud of what he does," said Charlotte adjusting the folds of her skirt. "And not many white men have learned to speak the Cherokee language as well as James, but it's time for him to be with his family."

I couldn't imagine Jamie staying home as long as there were settlements to provide for, or men to organize for Indian skirmishes. But I said nothing. Fortunately Charlotte could manage very well on her own, and with five children to care for, she had little time for fretting.

"This war will be over one day," continued Charlotte, "And the Indians will cease their attacks. You'll see."

She turned her black eyes on me, and all the longing she felt for James lay naked there.

"Of course," I said hastily. "Of course," I added with emphasis as I drew Charlotte close to me. I wondered why I felt so much like crying when we spoke of happy times. For all my bluster, I found it difficult to imagine a world in the wilderness where glass windows did not invite the Indian's rifle fire. Or where anyone had the leisure to tend flowers.

At that moment, we were startled by a loud crashing from *The Adventure* which had broken loose from the shoals and slammed into an island. Charlotte and I rushed to the river's edge to see Somerset lean over the boat's narrow gunwale, trying to rescue a box from the water.

"Look," I said. "The four-pounder." The cannon lay on its side, sliding back and forth on the boat's deck.

As I screamed a warning into the wind, John Cockrill threw off his greatcoat and strode into the shallow water, pulling his canoe beside him. In a matter of seconds, he had swung into the boat and was paddling furiously. The water swept his canoe off course, but he battled on until he reached *The Adventure* where Somerset pulled him aboard. I took a deep breath for the first time in minutes, but watched anxiously as Cockrill approached the cannon which still flailed about. After he secured it, he provided poles for two of the slaves and instructed them to push *The Adventure* from the island while he took the tiller from the Colonel to steer the boat. Little by little the vessel shifted and gradually lurched toward us. Men stood anxiously on the shore, waiting to help with a rough landing, but amazingly *The Adventure* slipped to shore with surprising ease and lodged in a safe berth. Praise God.

———

It was already dark by the time we reassembled for dinner. All the boats had landed and our full party of two hundred spread along the snowy savanna. The earth surrounding our camps was a filthy mixture of mud, sedge grass and dirty snow, but we did what we could to prepare a decent dinner after the ordeal. As a gesture of thanks, Colonel Donelson asked Major Cockrill to join us, and he sat near our fire, warming his chilled bones. His wet clothes hung on hastily-assembled sticks before the fire, and he sat wrapped in an enormous buffalo robe.

Patsy was preparing a stew of dried venison, while Hagar and I chopped a few of our precious onions to add as seasoning. I observed the Major sitting in firelight, the evening dark behind his head, and it occurred to me that he must be lonely, a man new to the community with no family to sustain him. He slouched forward, his head resting on his bent knees. When I finished my task, I wiped my hands and strolled to join him by the fire.

"It'll be awhile before you're warm, I expect," I said.

"Colonel Donelson gave me a swallow of whiskey," he answered. "It helped mightily,"

"That's the least he could offer after you saved our boat."

"Have you ever piloted a flatboat, Mrs. Johnson?" he asked in a steady voice.

"No, but I've got common sense," I said. "I think I'd know to push off an island if I was stuck on one."

"It's not like paddling a canoe, Mrs. Johnson. More like trying to steer a house."

"But surely you wouldn't have landed on that island if you'd been in charge."

"That depends. If the boat wanted to land there," he said, rubbing his forehead with his wide hand, "my vote wouldn't have made a difference."

"Well, it was a brave thing you did to retrieve it."

"I couldn't have done it without the men paddling." Gesturing to the ground in front of him, he said, "Won't you sit down, Mrs. Johnson? No chair to offer, but there's plenty of dirt for the two of us."

I sat a bit reluctantly, not knowing what more I had to say.

"Was there much damage to *The Adventure*?" I asked, thinking he should untie his brown hair so that it could dry more easily. It was caught in a tail that disappeared down his back into the buffalo robe.

"Nothing I can't fix before we start tomorrow," he answered. "We lost some blankets, though, and a box with Mrs. Donelson's pewter plates."

"Ann!" called Charlotte from the other side of the fire. "I need your help."

I rose, agitated that Charlotte had not granted me time to make myself comfortable.

"The things I made for you are still safe on Hugh's boat," the Major added. "Maybe I can set them up tomorrow."

"I'd be obliged," I answered.

"Ann," called Charlotte again, with some urgency.

"I'm coming." I approached where she stood with hands placed firmly on her hips.

"What has gotten into you?" asked Charlotte, her brow as wrinkled as a withered apple.

"I was thanking Major Cockrill," I said defensively. "What's wrong with that?"

"Thanking him is one thing, but sitting down beside a man when you know he's naked is quite another," said Charlotte.

"Oh, Charlotte," I laughed out loud. "Is that all you're worried about?"

"This is not amusing, Ann. Think of your daughters."

"The man was covered with a buffalo hide," I said. "I couldn't see a thing . . . even if I'd wanted to," I added devilishly.

"I can see you're in a mood to torment me, but this is not funny," Charlotte continued angrily. "That robe could have fallen off, and then where would you have been?"

"Knowing the Major a great deal better, I suppose," I said.

"Look me straight in the eyes, Ann," said Charlotte. "Right now." I looked at her reluctantly, resenting her way of addressing me as if I were a child. "We are trying to create civilization in God's wilderness, and every day takes us to the edge of barbarity," Charlotte continued. "Our only chance for success is to be civilized in every way we can. It's bad enough that you wear leggings!"

Charlotte's dark eyes turned down at the corners, her thin lips a slash across her face. I bowed my head in the face of her indignation. I had never thought of civility as a weapon against the frontier's harshness. Civility to me was mostly a nuisance.

"Just try to see things the way others do," said Charlotte firmly. "That's all I'm asking."

I sighed. "I will try, Charlotte. I promise." But much as I loved my sister-in-law, I couldn't imagine being able to see life from her perspective.

The next morning, strings of ominous dark clouds threaded the gray sky. I lay near the dying fire, and from my makeshift bed, I could see Mrs. Donelson bustling near *The Adventure*, counting spoons and bowls in preparation for breakfast and trying to cheer her daughter-in-law. I rose to join them.

"Now Mary," Mrs. Donelson was saying, "We may miss the pewter plates, but we still have our husbands. Just think on that. I guess God thought wooden chargers were good enough for us wanderers."

Mary Purnell Donelson shook her head miserably. She was pregnant, but not nearly so far along as Elizabeth. Mary's wide nose kept her from being a pretty girl, but I could see how the young John had been drawn to her. There was strength in her broad face and square shoulders, a competent air about her that was reminiscent of his mother.

I settled beside Mary and watched Mrs. Donelson deftly stack the dishes on top of a bench which served as a table.

"No one was hurt on the boat yesterday?" I asked.

"We've got our bumps and bruises. Rachel had her wits scared out of her. But we're fine. Don't know what we would have done without Major Cockrill." She grabbed a stack of bowls. "Now Severn, you take these to Patsy," she said, thrusting them into the boy's hands.

"And you're feeling all right, Mary?" I asked, patting her on the knee.

"I was afraid all that bumping would bounce my baby right out," said Mary.

"I wish they came out that easily," I said. "It takes a far sight more than a bump."

"When you've had eleven of them like I have, you take it all in stride," said Mrs. Donelson, joining us on the ground which she swept first with the flick of her hand. "Just a temporary inconvenience. Like that scuffle on the river yesterday. I always knew Mr. Donelson would see us through. I cast my lot with the man years ago and I've never regretted it. You know, Mr. Jefferson once said that Mr. Donelson could survey a line straighter than a knife could cut a sausage. Or something like that. Mr. Jefferson says so many fine things it's hard to remember them all."

Mrs. Donelson stopped for a breath. She glanced at Mary whose eyes rolled in her head as if she had heard "Mr. Jefferson" stories a thousand times.

"Listen to me chatter. You run along, Ann. You have more to do than listen to an old woman clucking like a hen."

But before I could move, John Cockrill appeared with a shallow wooden box, roughly a yard wide and a yard long.

"Here it is," he said as he deposited it on the earth at my feet with a loud thump.

"Here is what?" I asked, regarding the empty box with confusion.

"Your slate," he replied.

I couldn't fathom how a box was a slate.

"It's a slate that needs no erasing and no chalk, just these." He pulled from his pocket a handful of sticks whittled into fine points and handed them to me.

"If that's a slate, then I'm a mongoose," Mrs. Donelson said. "Your battle with the river washed the sense out of your brain."

"Look," he replied, hunkering down and using one of the sticks to demonstrate. You fill the box with river sand, and the children can write their letters and numbers in the sand."

"Now why didn't I think of that?" asked Mrs. Donelson. "Simply brilliant. Worthy of Mr. Jefferson himself."

"Hardly that," said Cockrill.

"I don't know how to thank you," I said, feeling awkward. "I wish you had children of your own, so that I could teach them to repay the favor."

"Some day I'll have a houseful, and you can repay me then," he answered, nodding his head and touching his hat.

"It's a promise," I said, standing. I extended my hand for a serious handshake which he returned with a steady grip.

"Let me know if I can be of further service," the Major added, and he walked away without either of us saying another word.

# *Five*

MARCH 2, 1780 — *Oh mercy, such a time we have had the last few days. I had planned to begin teaching in earnest today. We had secured my new box and filled it with sand, but then came an unending icy rain, the gray heavens sifting God's tears. At midday, when the rain finally subsided, the river itself wrought a great calamity.*

*Our boats had just passed the mouth of the French Broad River and were moving along nicely, lulling us into a sense of tranquillity, when suddenly the Henry's boat hit a rough current and lurched out of control, heading straight toward a rocky island. I watched in horror as their boat slammed into the rocks, spilling all three Henrys and their goods into the water. At first we could see no survivors, but thanks to the good Lord, the Henrys were spared. Colonel Donelson called for the whole fleet to go ashore, and we spent the rest of the day capturing the Henry's belongings. These efforts took such a long time that we set up a temporary camp for the night, building fires and arranging what comforts we could.*

*As we were doing so, Reuben Harrison, a young man I have always considered intemperate, took it into his head to go hunting in these strange woods and nothing could dissuade him. Reuben is like many young men I have known, inclined to pursue his own will, no matter what the consequences. So off he went, and tonight he has not returned.*

*A few hours ago, the Colonel ordered several men to fire rifles, hoping the noise would help Reuben to return. It was a generous use of our limited gun powder, but unfortunately has provided no results as yet. With sadness I observed the Harrisons by their fire, Mr. Harrison snatching at his disheveled hair while his wife sat glassy-eyed, rolling and unrolling the apron in her lap, her thick fingers as gnarled as twisted carrots.*

*The day brought additional anguish for Elizabeth. At our fireside this evening, she told me how Johnny had carelessly dropped their father's powder horn in the river while he and Robert were playing soldier: a heedless action that may bring grave consequences. I tried to reassure her by saying it was Johnny's age that made him act so foolish, but I didn't really believe it. A mean spark glimmers in his eyes, a devilment he was born with. Being a mother teaches you that children come wrapped like surprise packages, and you spend a lifetime watching them reveal their true selves.*

*And if that distress wasn't enough, next Elizabeth developed pains we thought were the beginning of labor. These contractions proved a false start, but the mournful sound of her voice calling her husband's name will haunt me for some time to come.*

**MARCH 3, 1780** — *All day we have awaited Reuben. The Colonel went to the extreme measure of firing the four-pounder, to no avail. This situation of one person causing misery for so many reminds me of the Prodigal Son parable whose message I have always judged unfair. I dislike the fact that the one good son who stayed home was taken for granted, while the wicked one who ran off was welcomed home warmly and rewarded with a fatted calf. Just as surely as my name is Ann Robertson Johnson, when Reuben Harrison wanders back from the forest, everyone will be thrilled to see him, even if his misadventure has caused us no end of worry. I know my anger is not a compas-*

*sionate response, so I have tried to imagine Reuben staggering back to camp with a tomahawk stuck in his skull. I did feel ashamed . . . for a minute. But another part of me still believed he brought it on himself.*

*I must end this day with a prayer for Reuben . . . and forgiveness for my impatient heart.*

**March 4, 1780** — *This morning the Colonel abandoned hope of finding Reuben and determined to restart our journey, leaving behind Major Cockrill and two vessels to help Mr. Harrison in a further search. We cast off with some reluctance, but a few hours later we found Reuben lounging on a rock that overhung the river like a pale ugly lip; he was calm as a bullfrog without a scratch on him. Mrs. Harrison, who had joined our boat, let out a sound like the call of a screech owl, and I again repented my hardened heart when I saw her pure joy. She whispered, as if talking to no one but herself and the Lord, "God be praised. God be praised." How could I have forgotten what it means to lose a child, no matter how ornery?*

**MARCH 5, 1780** — *Today when we passed the mouth of the Clinch River, I heard an alarmed murmur rise from the boats, even above the splash of the current. The original plan was to join Captain Blackmore and the Clinch River Company here, but we saw no signs of anyone. As we drifted on, each new bend in the river brought hope, but every turn revealed only disappointment, more empty river banks. About three o'clock, however, we rounded a particularly wide loop and came upon tall walls of sandstone providing a pale backdrop for dark hemlocks, pines and cedars: more vegetation than we had seen in some time. The air emitted a pungent smell, and before our eyes, tied up on the banks, was a group of flatboats and travelers, twins to our own party. They answered our cheers with shouts of their own, all of us celebrating the fact that something favorable had finally happened as scheduled.*

*Our night was filled with rejoicing. Old Mr. Harrison danced a little jig to fiddle music, and Captain Blackmore joined our fireside for a drink of Colonel Donelson's well-rationed whiskey. Mrs. Donelson had fished out her remaining pewter mugs, and we gathered for conversation while the children played chase, running from fire to fire. Bruno crouched near me and grumbled at the children's shrieks; other guard dogs prowled the perimeter of our camp in search of Indians.*

*Captain Blackmore is younger than Colonel Donelson by twenty-five years, and wears an air of authority, even a hint of ferocity. Both his long, unruly hair and his skin are extremely dark and a deep line cuts vertically between his eyebrows. To my knowledge, I have never seen a pirate, but he must look like one. When he disclosed the details of their journey, he explained that while they had avoided Indians thus far, cold had penetrated them most thoroughly, particularly affecting one of the slaves.*

*And he added a dreadful piece of news . . . a plague has befallen the Stuart party, a group of twenty-eight traveling with him. Five of their number are afflicted with the small pox! I shuddered violently when I heard those words, for I once saw the body of a woman who died of the pox, her face still red and swollen and dotted with milky blisters the size of coins. Before she died, she lost her wits, thrusting her hand into the fire to be rid of it. What a horrible disease that takes one's mind as well as one's life. Captain Blackmore added that the Stuarts travel apart from his group, and at night he blows his horn to signal when he's making camp so they can do the same . . . but at some distance away.*

*The pox! The word resounded in my head, its implications reminding me of a hundred ways that our lives can get worse. I could listen no more and left to find my children, to lay my hands on them at once, as if I could protect their small bodies through my touch. I can swim to save them in the river. I can shoot Indians to protect them in case of an attack. But the pox? How could I deliver them from such an appalling disease?*

**MARCH 7, 1780** — *It's been two days since I thought to write in this journal. The time has sped much faster since we joined the Blackmore* *party, a merger that brings both pleasure and pain. The pleasure comes from stories of their travels and their fiddle music at evening time. Captain Blackmore is a feverish dancer and has singled out Nancy Gower as his partner on more than one occasion. She declared that he twirled her so fast it sent the earth spinning. I warned she'd do well to keep both feet on the ground where he was concerned. When she laughed at me, saying his dancing kept her warm, I reminded her that might well be the problem. I confess I sounded exactly like Charlotte. I have danced only with my girls, and they prove music is a tonic for us all.*

*The pain brought by the Blackmore party lies in two areas. Last night, one of their number became our first casualty. Bill, a slave of Thomas Hutchings, fell victim to the cold, his feet and legs frosting over. The tragedy could have been avoided if Captain Hutchings had treated the man properly. Before Bill was buried this morning, we saw how his shoes were ragged and made of porous cloth instead of leather. He wore only a short homespun coat rather than the heavy woolen capes we supply our slaves, and nothing covered his poor head. Such treatment is more tortuous than a bloody beating, for it is steady with no end except in death. As surely as there is a God in heaven, we shall be judged by how we treat our slaves.*

*On a happier note, this morning we witnessed the sun rise at last, the gray clouds giving way to the glow of pink and violet in the east. A deep orange ball of sun followed, peaking over the mountains like a bald man with his head on fire. The rebirth of the sun and the death of Bill reminded me how good things and bad have the habit of tumbling one upon another. I guess God had in mind a balancing act when He created this old world, but I hope He's decided we're due for a string of good events.*

Since the river was calm and the day sunny, I decided to test my new teaching box and rounded up the children. I deposited

Charity next to Betsy on the boat's deck, not because I expected my three-year-old to learn much, but to keep her out of harm's way. Even in the sunshine, the girls still shivered beside the sand box, bunched over like little squirrels to keep warm. The rest of the children joined them, and as I handed out the sticks Major Cockrill had sharpened, Peyton and Randolph dueled with each other until Charlotte spoke to them sternly.

I began by marking a large A in the sand and said, "**A** is our very first letter, boys and girls. Think of it as a hay stack with a little room at the top where you can hide." I added a **B** and continued the lesson until I had gone over every last letter of the alphabet. After an hour of study, the sky filled with black clouds and a fierce wind kicked up suddenly, producing tall waves that slapped the side of *The Adventure* and splashed onto the deck. The boat lurched and swayed, making us abandon all thoughts of learning. I corralled my girls and hurried to the cabin for safety. Our boat spun on the waves, sometimes moving with its bow forward, but just as likely to proceed with its port or starboard side. Rough waves churned and twisted in white peaks, so I was terribly relieved when Colonel Donelson signaled for all crafts to land. Wherever we could tie up, would be preferable to riding this shifting monster.

From the cabin's door, I could see the remains of an abandoned Indian village where all but a few buildings were charred with fire. The damaged foundations suggested that many cabins had stood once in the clearing.

"This must be one of the villages that Colonel Shelby burned last year," Colonel Donelson shouted into the wind. "One of Dragging Canoe's settlements."

Dragging Canoe! His curse came alive in my mind at once. Here was evidence of our raids on his Chickamauga villages, and I could well imagine his anger. It had been almost a year since Governor Patrick Henry instructed Colonel Evan Shelby and nine hundred volunteers to destroy the Chickamauga settlements on the Tennessee River as a punishment for their continuous raids on us. The mission was successful and in two weeks of fighting, they demolished eleven Chickamauga towns. Now we were at the site of one of those very raids.

No sooner had *The Adventure* struck the shore than Nancy Gower leapt upon our slippery deck, her black hair snaking wildly about her head. Her dark blue cloak hung raggedly around her shoulders, and her brown eyes were watery and wild. Her aspect appeared so terrifying that I was sure she had spied Indians in the village, but as she seized my wrist, her fingers digging at the skin, her only words were, "It's Elizabeth's time." I hastily left my children in Charlotte's protection, and followed her to their boat which Mr. Jennings was securing to an oak tree that sagged over the water like a weary old man.

We jumped on deck, pushing past Johnny and Robert who stood gawking and wall-eyed outside the canvas tent where Elizabeth lay. Mrs. Jennings was already on land searching for shelter, leaving Elizabeth with their slave, Hannah. As we entered, the wind was tearing viciously at the tent, an invisible whip flaying its canvas sides. I was alarmed to see a purplish flush to Elizabeth's face as she struggled on a straw mattress, writhing in mid-contraction. Her waters had already broken, and an acrid smell filled the tent. Poor Hannah seemed undone and could only repeat, "Easy, Miss Elizabeth," while gripping Elizabeth's hand.

"Don't you worry," I said to Elizabeth, lowering myself beside her. "We're going to move you to a better place." When her contraction subsided, I slid my arm around her shoulder helping her to rise slowly. Her legs were wobbly and tentative as a newborn filly. Outside the wind blasted cold and hard at our faces, but I could see Mrs. Jennings in the distance, standing beside the door of a log cabin whose walls were plastered with a mixture of grass and clay, the roof covered with broad wooden shingles. She was motioning for us to advance, so I ordered Johnny to gather buffalo robes and follow. Elizabeth's gait was unsteady, but she proceeded, leaning heavily against us in a slow staggering progress.

When we reached the cabin, Mrs. Jennings held aside the woven mat, and we plunged into a dark room still scented with the hint of smoke from Indian fires. The dwelling had no windows, the only light slanting across the dirt floor from the door's opening and sifting through holes in the walls where chinks of clay had fallen away. Shards of broken pots littered the earthen floor like giant spiked teeth. The thought of Elizabeth giving birth in our enemy's home was a dreadful prospect, and yet I knew this refuge was a blessing.

Johnny spread one of the soft buffalo pelts on the ground, and at his mother's request, returned to the river for fresh water. Mrs. Jennings folded another of the robes to use as a pillow, and we settled Elizabeth gingerly on the earth, soothing her as best we could.

"I'm glad Ephraim isn't here after all," she managed to say, her face pale and silvered with sweat. "He likes to see me pretty."

I was stunned and deeply troubled at her words. Surely it was the pain speaking and not her true thoughts. I assured her that any man would want to be near when his wife was giving birth to his own baby. That there was no sight more beautiful than the fierce intensity of birth: the struggle of mother and baby working together in magnificent single-mindedness. Mrs. Jennings motioned for Nancy and me to move aside, and she put her mouth close to her daughter's ear.

"You listen to me," she said in a low growl. "What's going on here is way beyond pretty or plain. You are making a miracle." She kissed Elizabeth's shining forehead. "And I'll tell you something else. There's lots of pain in this here world, daughter, and very little of it rewarding. But you're getting a baby for your troubles. Don't you forget that."

Johnny returned with two buckets of icy water, placed them beside his mother, and exited quickly. Nancy tore a strip of cloth from her petticoat, dipped it in the water, and laid the cold, damp cloth on Elizabeth's forehead. At first Elizabeth jerked at the cold sensation, but soon called for Nancy to repeat it, and even asked Nancy to drip water on her hot, thick tongue.

Elizabeth continued her strangled screams, turning her head repeatedly from side to side, until strands of hair became small nests beneath her head. As I listened to her tortured moans, I remembered my own labors with Charlotte by my side, and the solace I felt when she sang hymns. Not so much that I found comfort from the words, but I was lulled by the regular cadence and tone of her sweet voice. I began to sing all the old hymns I could remember, crooning until my voice grew thin and reedy. When I could sing no more, Mrs. Jennings told stories of the days when Elizabeth and Edmund were small and recounted their mischievous ways.

Night seeped into the cabin, the light fading between the logs like a slow fire sinking to black. Dr. Henry arrived, bringing a lantern he salvaged from his overturned boat to provide light that drifted around us. I asked if he couldn't do something to help Elizabeth, but his only consolation was whiskey which might slow her labor. So we continued to watch Elizabeth struggle, Mrs. Jennings periodically pushing down on her daughter's belly to speed the baby's journey. Finally, at six o'clock in the morning, when the wind had finally subsided, the baby's head crowned and Ephraim Peyton Junior twisted and slithered his way into the world with all the promise of dawn. Dr. Henry cut the umbilical cord with the practiced turn of a knife and placed the wailing, blood-streaked baby into his mother's arms. I marveled once more at the miracle of birth. How suddenly someone completely fresh and untarnished existed where an hour before there had been no one.

At the sight of mother and child, of Mrs. Jennings' delight at her new redheaded grandson, I wished for the power to draw the scene, so that Ephraim might have a record of this joyful moment. Elizabeth was both laughing and crying, outlining the baby's small ear with her fingertip, letting his tiny fist close around her finger. At last she could see the hand that had waved to her for so long.

When I took my leave of mother and child some thirty minutes later, the cold air struck my hair which had grown damp around my face and neck, making me shiver deeply. I pulled my cape more tightly around my shoulders as I hurried toward *The Adventure* to tell Charlotte and my children the good news. I was remembering my own labors, and the inexpressible joy at the birth of my children when Major Cockrill interrupted my thoughts.

"Is everything all right?" he asked, his hooded eyes deep with concern. "Mrs. Robertson told me you were here."

I explained that the birth had gone well and added little more, hoping he would leave me since I was quite anxious to return to my own children. But he continued to speak, saying he wanted to show me a structure the Chickamaugas had built. I stared pointedly toward *The Adventure* to prove my lack of curiosity, explaining that I knew all I wanted to know about Dragging Canoe and his people. But he was persistent, adding that we could never learn too much about our enemies. I studied his countenance and found it more animated than I had ever seen, so when he assured me the tour would not take long, I allowed him to lead me to the Council House, a rectangular building that somehow had escaped Shelby's fire. The Cherokees always have seven sides to their Council Houses, representing their seven clans. Dragging Canoe had apparently established his own rules and designed his Council House with four sides.

We entered the building from the east through a winding corridor built to ensure privacy so no one could look directly into the hallowed ceremonial space. When we reached the dimly lit center, I was amazed at what I saw: a room large enough to seat a hundred people with tiers of benches surrounding the walls to form an amphitheater. I inspected a clay bowl which the Major explained was for the sacred fire they kept burning morning and night.

"They're spiritual people," he explained.

"Their persistent slaughter is not spiritual," I retorted.

"They don't kill us for sport, you know. They kill to defend what they believe is theirs."

"But they claim these lands they don't even live on, where they only hunt."

"And their people have been hunting here since the beginning of time," said the Major.

I chose to ignore his point and asked about the most startling detail in the room, a large throne-like structure painted an ominous scarlet. The Major explained that it probably belonged to Dragging Canoe and was painted red as a symbol of war. At the thought of the room filled with Indians in their war paint, praying for victory over us, I suddenly felt faint, as if all air had been sucked from the building.

"What's wrong?" he asked, moving toward me, but I darted for the corridor. My heart thudded in my chest as I pushed down the narrow hall, straining to reach the light, panting desperately. It was not until I was outside that I slowed my pace, the cold air clearing my head.

"Mrs. Johnson, wait," the Major called, finally grabbing my arm and turning my shoulders toward him.

"You shied like a horse who's seen a snake," he said, his brows tented above his eyes in confusion. "What's the matter?"

"Shouts," I answered. "I saw a hundred faces screaming, and heard that terrible whooping sound they make when they attack."

"I'm sorry," he said, his breath pouring into the freezing air in a smoky burst. " Most people never get to see a Council House.

I thought you'd be interested." He looked as if he wanted to say more, but he tucked his head and kicked at the dirt with the toe of his boot.

"Is there anything I can do?" he asked after a long hesitation.

I shook my head no, wanting only to be left alone.

"We're not likely to see any Indians here," he said, lifting his head to survey the demolished village. "Shelby saw to that."

"Why does it have to be like this?" I asked quietly, as if I were talking to myself. "I hate Dragging Canoe. And I know he hates us too."

"Wouldn't you?" he asked. "Wouldn't you hate us if you returned to this?"

I couldn't speak. Yes, the Chickamauga homes had been burned, but Dragging Canoe had brought the trouble on himself with his looting and killing. His Indians weren't like the Cherokees, the ones Dragging Canoe left behind. His people hated us with the depths of their souls.

"Please give my best to Mrs. Peyton," the Major finally said. He turned to march away with military precision until he disappeared into the crowd.

———

Soon after ten o'clock when the flotilla took to the water, my fear of Indians was realized. From my spot on *The Adventure's* deck, I saw them on the riverbank . . . Chickamaugas standing in a line, their voices carrying across the water, "*Brother . . . How do ye do-o-o-o?*"

The Indian women and children were dressed in deerskin clothes and behind them stood their men with heads shaved on the sides, leaving patches of black hair that formed stripes down the center of their skulls, extending to a tail in the back.

"*Come ashore,*" they repeated. "*Come ashore.*"

"They appear friendly," said Colonel Donelson, shading his eyes with his rough hand.

"What are you saying?" I fairly shrieked.

"Are you sure?" asked Charlotte warily, her eyes still fixed on the Indians.

"They speak English," continued the Colonel. "It's a chance to learn about the river ahead of us."

"Husband," Mrs. Donelson frowned. "I think we should keep away from those people."

"If we must speak to them," said Charlotte, always the peace maker, "let's tie up on the opposite shore, away from possible danger."

"Just keep moving," I pleaded.

To my consternation, however, the Colonel's son agreed that we should meet with the Indians. John Junior, a handsome, sturdy blond man, had been a quiet presence throughout the trip, and I wished he would remain so. Didn't anyone remember that Indians were killers? Couldn't John Junior take into consideration the welfare of his pregnant wife, Mary, and their unborn child? Or did he feel the need to demonstrate his so-called bravery to his father?

"I've got a plan for me and Johnny C.," he said.

Johnny C. was John Caffrey, husband of Mary Donelson Caffrey, John Junior's brother-in-law. The Caffreys had their own small boat and traveled separately from the rest of the Donelson party. I had wondered if their absence was due to Mary Caffrey's insistence that she do things her own way or Johnny C.'s reluctance to be under the strict guidance of his father-in-law, Colonel Donelson. They rarely joined the rest of us in the evenings.

John Junior announced his plan: the main party would land on the northern shore, opposite the Indians, while he and Johnny C. would take their canoe to investigate the Indian settlement. Although Mary Donelson tugged at her husband's shirt in protest, he carefully removed her hands and gave her a reassuring smile.

The fleet landed on the north shore safely, but remained perched precariously, ready to shove off if necessary. The two Johns untied the canoe from *The Adventure* and waded into the water to launch it: young boys striking off on a lark.

"Nothing good can come of this," I noted bitterly, watching them climb into the boat. The faint sounds of *"Brothers, Come Ashore"* did nothing whatever to reassure me.

"Doesn't he care a thing about me and the baby?" Mary paced *The Adventure's* deck as she studied her husband. "I can't be taking care of a fatherless child in this wilderness!"

"Don't talk like that Mary," said Mrs. Donelson. "John's not a man to take foolish chances."

"But to paddle right up to an Indian village!"

Colonel Donelson put his arm around Mary's shoulders. "He's a trained soldier. They didn't make him a Captain for nothing. He knows how to handle himself."

As the men dipped their paddles into the water and began their foray, I could see three Indians on the other side of the river launching a similar craft, a dugout canoe. Two of the men were dressed in traditional breeches and long fringed hunting shirts, but the third was outfitted like no one I had ever seen. In fact, he looked less like a man than an animal, for he wore an entire bearskin on his body. As the Indian canoe drew closer, I saw that his arms were fully covered with fur that had once covered the front legs of a bear, and the remaining part of the pelt was belted around his waist.

Abruptly the Indians motioned to young Donelson and Caffrey to return to *The Adventure*, the bear man waving his furry arms in large gestures.

"Oh thank God!" Mary moved forward to grip the ship's gunwales in her hands. "They'll surely turn back now."

"It could be a trick," I warned, unwilling to trust anything the Indians might do.

But the two men took the bear man's advice and reversed their direction to return to our shore. The first Indian boat followed them, and three more canoes filled with Indians started to cross the river as well.

"How I wish James were here," wailed Charlotte as she watched the four Indian canoes coming closer and closer. I put my arm around her waist and suggested we move the children into the ship's cabin to stay with Hagar.

Captain Blackmore had left his boat and approached the Colonel as the dugouts sliced through the water. He hopped easily over *The Adventure's* side.

"One wrong move," Blackmore scowled at the canoes, "and those Indians will be deader than door nails."

"I'm sure that won't be necessary," said Donelson firmly. "They appear friendly, and I've brought gifts for just such a time."

With that, Donelson instructed Somerset and Patsy to shake out a blanket and spread it across the uneven river bank. From a gray burlap bag he drew quids of tobacco leaves that were tied together in bundles, and lined them up in rows, like small brown soldiers fallen on a field of battle. Another bag produced blue, red and orange ribbons wound in circles and laid like a series of "O's" on the ground. Lastly, the Colonel assembled packets of the red dye, vermillion, sure to please the Indians because they used it for war paint. I shuddered at the thought of Chickamaugas wearing it to fight future settlers who might follow us.

John Junior and Caffrey stood beside the Colonel and Captain Blackmore, providing a thick human wall to wait for the dugout and its passengers. When the first three Indians landed, the bear-clad man stepped out first and came forward, extending his hand toward the Colonel.

"Arch Coody," he said in perfect English. "My father was Sam Coody. Maybe you've heard of him."

"No," said Blackmore abruptly, but the Colonel was more cordial and shook the extended paw.

A half breed. Probably the son of one of the many traders who had found comfort with an Indian woman.

"We come in peace," Coody said, revealing a mouthful of brown, broken teeth as disgusting as any I had ever seen.

The Colonel continued to shake his hand vigorously and explained his mission: to deliver the flotilla to the banks of the Cumberland River.

"You've a long way to go," said Coody. "But I believe I can help you."

"We'd welcome that," said the Colonel. "And we've brought gifts to show our good faith," he added, pointing to the blanket.

Twelve more Indians had beached their canoes and fallen in behind Coody and the two others. They were of medium height, with dark brown eyes, high cheekbones and the peculiar tail of hair hanging down their backs. Their faces were free of hair; their skin, the color of tea. Arch Coody looked quite different, however, with fierce green eyes that burned from his dark face, giving a hint of his mixed heritage. He wore a beard which further set him apart from the Indians, and the black hair on the backs of his hands was almost as thick as the fur he wore.

He gestured to the other Indians to approach the blanket, and they knelt beside the items, choosing carefully. One brave was particularly interested in the blue ribbons, letting the shiny cloth unroll and fall across his dark hand. He held one gingerly as if it were a strip of captured sky, and I wondered if he wanted to decorate a lover's black mane, or planned to tie back his own tangled fall of hair. Captain Blackmore kept a watchful eye on them all, his gun at the ready.

I was so absorbed in watching the brave with his ribbons that I was shocked to hear the crack of rifle fire. My first thought was that Captain Blackmore had shot one of the Indians, but the sound came from a different source. Turning, I saw the problem was Johnny Jennings who had aimed at a swan bobbing in the water but missed. The sound of the shot, however, had alarmed the Indian braves who remained across the river and a great cry rose from their camp. They thought the shot was intended as an attack, for within seconds their remaining canoes hit the water with warriors ready for battle.

A great scuffling occurred as Coody instructed his group to return and inform their companions that the shot was harmless. Then he spoke to Donelson.

"You've got to cast off," Coody insisted, his face filled with alarm.

"But you said you came in peace," the Colonel protested.

"Move!" Coody yelled loudly. "That fool boy set them off."

Donelson called for the horn to be blown and movement passed through the group like a shudder. I jumped to the shore to help Mrs. Donelson grab the remaining ribbons and tobacco, and noticed that all the packets of vermillion had been taken, a dreadful sign. While we scurried, John Junior tied our canoe to the boat and Somerset prepared to cast off.

"They'll have your scalps if you don't hurry," said Coody who had climbed aboard *The Adventure*.

Mrs. Donelson and I returned to the boat just as John Junior and John Caffrey pushed it from shore. It was soon in the river's grasp, fortunately well beyond the reach of gunfire, but the Indians were in rapid pursuit, their rifles cracking loudly above the sound of the river.

"Get down girls!" I cried. My daughters fell to the floor inside the cabin. "Cover your heads!"

The older children lay down as they were told, but baby Charlotte broke loose from her mother and toddled across the deck as a bullet hit the mast, just missing the little girl. Charlotte ran for her daughter and slipped her under the thick protection of her own skirts.

For an interminable thirty minutes the Indians pursued us, shooting and yelling, their muscular arms hurling their oars through the water. But little by little both *The Adventure* and the other boats pulled away, the screams of the Indians becoming more and more faint. The Chickamaugas finally ceased firing and turned their canoes toward home.

The fear they had brought remained.

# Six

MARCH 8, 1780 — *Colonel Donelson seemed much taken with the bear man, and Coody kept close to his side, laughing loudly at his own stories. The smell of bear still seemed strong upon him, and Bruno and the other dogs kept up a steady snarl in his presence. The Colonel questioned Coody about the possibility of Indians down river, and he assured Donelson that all the Indians had withdrawn to the mountains except for the ones we had already encountered. We'd meet no more of his half brothers with the red skins.*

*As The Adventure floated easily on the water, he proceeded to spin Cherokee tales which the Colonel enjoyed and the rest of us were condemned to hear. He told of the creation of the mountains that loomed on either side of us. The Cherokees believe that when the world was young, the Great Buzzard flew over the earth, and when he reached the Cherokee country, he had grown tired from his long journey. His wings became so heavy it was difficult to hold them aloft, and he drifted lower and lower. Finally, in a fierce effort to lift himself once more, he flapped his enormous wings striking the ground. Wherever his wings hit, the force created a green valley, and wherever his wings turned up again the land transformed into a mountain. The animals who lived in the country tried to call back The Buzzard to make more valleys, but he never returned, leaving the Cherokee country with many mountains.*

*It was a strange tale. Who would want to believe his land was conceived by a creature as awful as the buzzard? I have seen those birds do their dirty work, first circling in the air observing their prey, then attacking a dying animal, picking sharply at its eyes. It chills me to think of a buzzard so large it could cover the mountains with its wingspan. What a pity the Indians have not read our Bible and discovered the truth of how God created the world.*

*At least Coody's next story described something useful: the condition of the river in front of us. Here the river is almost a half mile in width, but soon it will narrow as it squeezes between two mountains. When the river narrows, the water begins to flow more swiftly and the convergence of currents produces two deadly obstacles, The Suck and The Boiling Pot. These two whirlpools cause the water to spin in a circle, drawing whatever they can into their deep centers. We will need the Lord's protection to pass safely by these terrible spots.*

*Late yesterday afternoon Coody asked Colonel Donelson to put him off the boat. He said his last farewells, once more promising we would suffer no more trouble from Indians. His expression appeared sincere, but I remembered his tale of the buzzard and thought he had the look of an old bird who could pick a skeleton clean. Bruno set up a rumble as if he wanted a piece of Coody's leg, and I felt like joining him in a growl myself.*

*When it was late afternoon, we made camp on a particularly rocky shore. The sky's sunset had colors pretty enough for a party dress; robin's egg blue, pale pink and peach. While I was trying to find a level place to put our mattresses, Major Cockrill ambled to my side, carrying a long rifle. Anyone could see it was a fine gun, and when I complimented the Major, he told me he had made it himself, back in Virginia. Then he said it was for me: a flintlock rifle finer than anything I had ever owned. When I was a girl hunting birds, I used a fowler which sent out a spray of shot and could sometimes bring down a bird or two, but had little accuracy. And when David died, he left me his musket, a tired old gun heavier to lift than a new fallen tree. But this gun. The Major might as well have laid a cloth of gold across my arms. I stared at the stock made of polished maple wood, embossed with an eight-point brass star.*

*I am ashamed to say I embarrassed both myself and the Major by almost crying right there. He had given me a gift of great beauty and also an instrument of security for my family. I tried to thank him, but found I could not look into his eyes for more than a few seconds. I was seized by the desire to hide behind a tree but none was available except a skinny cottonwood that wouldn't have hidden a snake on its tiptoes.*

*The Major helped me out of my misery by describing the gun, saying it would hit its mark for up to one hundred yards. It would give me good protection from the Indians, since their guns often shoot wide of the mark, even at fifty yards. I managed a muffled thank you. After what was the longest minute imaginable, he touched his hat and walked away.*

*Charlotte never misses a trick and lost no time coming to my side to question our interchange. She was shocked on two accounts; first, that he would make such a gift for me, a widow woman, and second, that I would accept it. But the truth is, I marvel that he thought I was worth such a gift. I wanted to name the gun "Betsy" to capture all the spirit of my own daughter, but I couldn't disappoint Polly and Charity. So I will call it "Hope." The name speaks for itself.*

*Just before the dark fell, I sat with my new rifle and watched the clouds settle in our valley, providing a soft silver cover. I felt more comforted than I had for a long time.*

The river was our friend this morning, snaking along lazily, its wide banks opening like a promise. We passed islands without incident, and the sun shone for a brief moment, providing a bit of relief from the cold. Somerset stood on the roof of *The Adventure*, steering with the thirty-foot oar that pivots in a forked stick. He did so without difficulty, but most days we have to be on the lookout for a variety of hazards: such as wooden islands, piles of dead trees matted together that can extend twenty or thirty yards across the river. Almost as troublesome are planters, logs whose roots are fixed in the river bottoms and stand like spears in the water; and sawyers, trees whose tops move in a saw-like motion with the river's flow. These trees are dangerous to boats when they break the water, but even more so when they are hidden beneath the surface and snag vessels unawares.

Life as usual was teeming aboard *The Adventure*. Charlotte and Mrs. Donelson washed petticoats with lye soap in a pot of hot water, while Severn, Peyton and Randolph played tag with the girls, and Hagar and I readied the sandbox for another lesson. The boat drifted lazily around a bend when John Junior shouted.

"Indian town. South Shore."

Everyone on the boat jumped to attention and crowded to get a look at the town which came closer and closer. A host of Indians shouted on the banks, and behind them I glimpsed the roofs of their cabins peeking above the corn fields. Coody had lied.

"Brothers, come ashore," they called, just as the previous group had beckoned.

I turned to Colonel Donelson, daring him to invite another encounter, and braced myself on the rough floorboards. My new rifle leaned against my shoulder; I was ready for an onslaught.

"The water is safer on this side of the river. Pass by here," the Indians called in voices wafting across the water.

"You're not listening to those savages again, are you?" I asked.

"I'm listening all right," he replied, "But I'm not heeding." He called for the boat to steer toward the north shore, the exact opposite of what the Indians advised.

I sighed with some relief but kept my eyes riveted ahead. The Blackmore boat was in front of us and swept along swiftly, skirting the northern shore as closely as the Captain dared. I was encouraged to see that the river was still wide enough at this point to ensure we could avoid the Indians' guns from the south. All the boats, canoes and flatboats alike, sped along the river, as far away as possible from the calling Indians. But suddenly, to our dismay, we saw a disturbance in the forest before us; something that made the trees tremble. It was as if the underbrush had become human and rushed to the shore. War shouts fractured the air, followed by the snapping pop of guns. Smoke rose in puffs from the pine trees: an ambush.

Donelson told Somerset to swing the boat toward the center of the river. Then he yelled at John Junior and Jeremy to paddle for their lives. I threw my daughters to the boat's deck and tried to cover them with my body. I heard bullets thud into the outside hull of the boat.

"Mama, Mama!" their cries thundered in my ears even louder than the gun fire. A bloody scream from the Blackmore boat filled my imagination with images of bullets crashing through bodies and blood streaking faces and clothes alike.

"Papa!" cried John Junior. "They're launching their canoes."

I wanted to see what was happening but resisted the dangerous urge to look.

"God in Heaven!" shouted Colonel Donelson, lurching to the rear to get a better look.

"What is it?" I cried, struggling to keep my head down when I wanted to see for myself.

"God in Heaven," he repeated. "They're taking the Stuarts."

I had forgotten how the Stuart boat lagged behind us with its cargo of twenty-eight, many of whom had now come down with the pox. Without the protection of the other boats, they were easy prey for the Indians. I could no longer restrain myself and slowly crawled to the boat's railing, lifting my head above the gunwale. The Indian canoes had blocked the Stuarts' passage. Some of the Braves had already boarded the craft, and I heard screams as the Indians plunged their tomahawks into flesh and bone. Even from a distance, I could hear the dull thud of their blows, as if they were felling trees. Over and over. Thump. Thump. When I witnessed a raised weapon sink into a woman's bonnet, I reached for my new rifle, loaded it in haste, and fired at the back of the closest Indian, but we were too far away for the bullet to hit him. There was nothing I could do to stop the melee. Twenty-eight people, doomed to be killed like pigs at slaughter time. Oh God, what a terrible end.

I turned my attention to the river ahead where more Indians stretched along the northern banks like a series of traps laid by a master hunter, and one warrior stood above the rest, perched on a rocky promontory. While the other Indians were dressed in buckskin shirts with mantles draped over their shoulders against the cold, this man alone stood bare chested, his skin slashed with red and black paint. He held his rifle at his side, as if he were saving his shot for none but Colonel Donelson. It had to be Dragging Canoe. Only he would have the arrogance to stand alone and wait to fire one perfect shot.

"Colonel," I called. "Over there."

Colonel Donelson saw the warrior lift his rifle and aim directly at *The Adventure.*

"Get down!" I yelled, but the old soldier stood his ground.

"He'll never reach me," said Colonel Donelson. "I will not bow my head to a savage."

As Dragging Canoe's shot rang out, I fired one of my own, but both balls fell far short of the mark.

"We'll be safe when we get to the gorge," the Colonel shouted. "Everyone hold on!"

In the distance was the place Coody had spoken of, where the river narrowed to half its normal width and thick vegetation cut off any path along the shore. Every moment dragged as our boats paddled and splashed toward the sloping mountains, leaving Dragging Canoe and the other Chickamaugas behind. Although the flatboats lumbered pitifully, still we advanced with increasing speed as the river current accelerated in preparation for pouring through the narrows. Larger and larger grew the mountains as we approached, and after we skirted a large island, our boats finally arrived at their protection. The Blackmore boat reached safety first, and then another, and another, until we too slid into the slender passage. Soon we could hear no more cries, either of war or of suffering, and a strange and unnatural peace fell upon the river.

Charlotte signaled for our entire party to assemble in a circle to pray for the Stuarts. The sounds of death screams were so fresh in my ears that I was almost deafened to her words. I squeezed Betsy to my side so hard I realized she could barely breathe in my grasp.

"God bless and protect our brothers and sisters in this hour of need," Charlotte began. "Commend their souls unto Thy care and bring them everlasting peace. We ask in Thy name. Amen."

I couldn't bring myself to echo Charlotte's "amen." It seemed to me that the Stuart party had been sacrificed as a peace offering so that the rest of us might go free. Wasn't it enough that they were struck down with the deadly pox and already isolated? Why did they have to be slaughtered as well? The Indians had shown no mercy to even the women and children, but killed them all in the most brutal and painful way possible: skulls crushed, left half-dead to suffer as their lives slipped away. What was God thinking? How could He let Dragging Canoe's men murder them? And was it only a matter of time before it happened to the rest of us? Although I hadn't known the Stuarts, I mourned their passing with a pain in the center of my chest as real as if a large stone had been flung there.

No sooner had we finished our prayers when a warning came from the Blackmore boat that The Suck was straight ahead. I heard a roar and saw a horrible churning in the water. Twigs and underbrush sped past on their unstoppable journey to the bottom of the stream. The narrow boundaries of the river made it impossible to swing wide of the whirlpool, so our boats struggled to keep clear of the vicious pull. The roar grew increasingly louder.

We drew perilously close to John Cotton's boat in front of us, as both vessels tried to maneuver The Suck. Somerset grappled with the tiller to avoid hitting the canoe Cotton towed behind him which danced and bucked upon the waters like a young horse being broken. Suddenly it jumped in a rearing motion, almost standing on its end, the cargo springing from it like a jumble of rocks sliding down a mountain. I could see Jemima Cotton's anguished expression as she watched her life's possessions disappear.

Behind us Major Cockrill's canoe spun in a circle, unaffected at first by the strength of his paddling, but finally pulling free. Other flatboats glided as helplessly as leaves on the water's surface, bouncing and swaying, but finally every one succeeded in passing the dangerous area. Colonel Donelson blew his horn to stop, and even though I wished we could put more distance between us and Dragging Canoe, I knew it was right to put ashore. We had rescued the Henrys' goods when their boat had overturned, and we should do the same for the Cottons.

After we tied up, Captain Blackmore was quick to approach the Colonel.

"You saw what happened to the Stuarts?" he asked.

Donelson shook his head, unable to find appropriate words to respond to the horror.

"God will deliver His vengeance," said Blackmore. "The pox will have its way with the savages."

"We'd better see to the Cottons' things," said the Colonel, not wanting to dwell on the tragedy.

"I lost a man myself back there," Blackmore added. "Mr. Payne. Shot clean through the head during the ambush." He turned from Donelson to scan the shore. "Reckon we'll have to bury him here."

"You'll need to be quick about it," said the Colonel. "We should retrieve Cotton's things in short order."

Blackmore nodded and started back to choose a digging crew. My heart ached for Mr. Payne, a man of about twenty whom I barely knew. No family to grieve over his body. Buried so far away from any patch of civilization. I tried to comfort myself with the thought that at least he had gone quickly, without the torture the Stuarts experienced. And I considered his spirit, gone to be with God. We will all be there sooner or later.

Stepping from *The Adventure* to the flat limestone shore, I saw Mrs. Jennings chasing a square package that bobbed in the frigid water like a duck looking for food, and I hurried to join her.

"Are Elizabeth and the baby all right?" I asked, watching the package float toward us.

"Little Ephraim was squalling loud as the Indians," said Mrs. Jennings, "But he's doing better now. The movement of the boat soothes him if there's not too much commotion."

As the box came closer, Mrs. Jennings walked rapidly into the river, the water surging on either side of her, tugging at her brown skirt. I marveled at her strength. She had spent the entire night bringing her grandson into the world, had suffered the indignity of having her son incite the Indians with his thoughtless shot, and still she found the fortitude to help her neighbor and the strength to fight the icy river's pull.

My gaze rose above Mrs. Jennings to the somber skies and the rugged face of the mountain where a craggy band of stone was exposed near the top, as if the mountain wore a stone necklace. Not even a touch of gentleness in the landscape.

My somber thoughts were followed by the crack of gunfire. I turned toward the sound and saw Indians standing high on the cliffs above us, like ominous spikes against the sky. Fortunately the distance was great enough that the bullets fell short, but Colonel Donelson shouted orders to halt the search at once. The burying party also stopped their efforts and hastily returned to the Blackmore boat with Mr. Payne's body slung heavily between them. Women screamed for children who strayed along the banks, and I desperately searched for my own Polly whom I found aboard the Jennings boat. I pulled urgently at her arm.

"We've got to go."

"But Mama," said Polly, still holding a shiny stone she had brought baby Ephraim.

"Come!" I said, dragging her across the deck, the bullets singing in the air around us. We ran in terror of being hit, Polly following me like a rock skipping across the water. A man staggered beside us, grabbing his shoulder where a bullet had struck him. We all returned with due speed to our boats which pushed off, this time with the added task of dodging both the swirling water and bullets. I held my girls as *The Adventure* struggled past the remains of the Suck's current, was thrown off course, but recovered well enough to forge ahead. It barely eased around a large series of rocks projecting from the water, but when I turned, I saw the Jennings boat hit the same formation and remained as if anchored.

"Colonel Donelson, look!" I cried.

Donelson was so involved in steering *The Adventure* he failed to respond.

"Colonel Donelson!" I repeated, scrambling to the cabin's roof and leaning close enough to feel heat radiating from his neck.

"The Jennings!" I exclaimed.

He threw a brief glance over his shoulder, replying, "We must go on."

Alarmed, I returned to the deck to speak to Mrs. Donelson and pointed to the struggling Jennings boat, but she only muttered that God would provide. I screamed above the roaring water, insisting we stop to help the Jennings. The slaves drew away from me, and even my daughters huddled together at the sight of my distress.

"Ann!" Charlotte clutched me by the shoulders and shook me harshly, her black eyes fierce.

"Think of your children," she said. "We can't turn back."

"But Charlotte, what if they're killed like the Stuarts!"

I was frantic imagining their terrible fate, rejecting the idea that nothing could be done. I ran to the side of *The Adventure* again, straining to see what was happening. But the Jennings boat grew smaller and smaller as we pulled away down the slow bend of the river. I saw a canoe bobbing near the Jennings boat. Then nothing, as the mountains slowly obstructed my view.

For the rest of the day I was wracked with worry over the fate of Elizabeth and her family. Did the same fate await my own children? Would my desire to follow Jamie and the others be the death of us? The river widened and grew placid, astonishing us all with its calm in contrast to the boiling soup we had just navigated. Waves splashed only occasionally, and the water turned from a dirty brown to a slate color reflecting the sky. Even though our perils seemed behind us, my thoughts never strayed from my friends. Night began to fall swiftly, and the banks were covered with mud that turned black in the fading light.

"Will you stick with the northern shore for landing?" I asked Colonel Donelson, the first words I had spoken to him all afternoon.

He pulled his coat higher around his shoulders as he squinted into the closing darkness. Only a pale pink cast in the western sky hinted at a sunset. He waited so long to answer that I wondered if he had heard my question. Finally he spoke.

"This won't please you, Mrs. Johnson, but we're not camping tonight," he said in a strong, measured tone.

"But we have to," I lashed back.

"No, we don't," he answered. "We have to save ourselves."

"But the Jennings boat will catch up with us if you give it a chance," I said. "And if they're separated from us, they're much more likely to be attacked . . . like the Stuarts."

"I must put as much distance as I can between us and those Indians," he answered. "If I don't, we may all be killed. I've more than the Jennings to think of."

"But Colonel . . ."

"Please don't be difficult about this, Mrs. Johnson. I know what I'm doing. They'll find us if they're able. Everyone on this river is heading in the same direction," he added sadly.

And there was nothing I could do but take to my mattress and float through the velvet night with the rest of the party. Sleep came for others, but rarely for me.

# Seven

MARCH 9, 1780 — *My attempt to sleep on a moving boat produced strange sensations, time and motion disordering my senses. All night I imagined Indians following our path, stalking silently along the riverbank, their black war paint rendering them almost invisible. I could hear their blood-stopping cries, a sound indescribable to one who has never heard it.*

*Jamie says that nothing fires the Cherokee like the desire for revenge. A brave will cross half a continent to sink his knife into an enemy and harvest the scalp of victory. So it is with Dragging Canoe and his band of Chickamaugas. Although we bought this land from the Indians, they still see us as intruders. But how can they pretend ownership of all these vast lands? Surely they cannot claim every mountain, or fields their people have never farmed, or herds of animals so numerous they could feed us all forever.*

*Nevertheless, Dragging Canoe seeks revenge on us, and his hate will grow stronger if the Stuarts' small pox festers among his men. I remember the deep pox scars on his face that showed he had conquered the disease and knew its ferocity well. I see an endless string of insults and retribution playing out between us. I don't know how we can break this chain of events, but break it we must.*

I lay on the cabin floor and watched the morning sky lighten, finding no comfort in its tint of violet clouds. Having a clear sky after so many days of gray seemed a further irony, given the fog that smothered my heart. I hoped the sun would bring solace to Elizabeth and the others wherever they were. The fire from the hearth still burned bright enough to throw shadows on my children as they bundled around me. Polly lay at my feet but slept no longer, her brown eyes staring vacantly at the sky just as mine had.

"Good morning, my big girl," I whispered, leaning over her. She did not respond. "It feels like we're floating on air, doesn't it?" I continued.

"Are they coming yet?" asked Polly.

I did not pretend to misunderstand the question. "Not yet, Honey," I answered, stroking her head.

"He was so little, baby Ephraim," she said. "Too little for anybody to kill."

"Don't you worry," I assured her. "That baby's safe. And his mama."

"Delilah says he wasn't baptized. That if he dies, he'll go straight to Hell."

"Whoever heard of such a thing! That baby's soul is as clean as newly fallen snow." I struggled to keep my voice low. "And besides, I'm sure he's fine."

"I'm scared of the Indians, Mama." She turned her deep brown eyes toward me.

"Oh, Honey," I said, taking her into my arms. "Don't you worry. We've got Colonel Donelson and all these other folks to help us. And look at that cannon outside. An Indian would think twice before running up against a cannon."

"And your rifle," said Polly, feeding me a line of consolation.

"And the rifle of course. That new rifle could hold off a whole tribe of Indians."

We huddled together, still as rabbits hiding in tall grass.

"Would the Indians like us if they got to know us?" asked Polly hopefully.

"Honey, they don't want to know us. We're at war with each other."

Polly pressed against me even closer. "War doesn't make a lick of sense."

———

All day I hovered at the boat's stern, searching the river behind us, but hour after hour I saw nothing in our wake but trailing curls of foam and the other boats. The rest of my fellow travelers talked on the open deck, even laughed occasionally. I didn't understand how they could think of anything but the Jennings' fate. At midday when Charlotte brought me a wooden plate with strips of venison on it, I refused to eat, as though this small sacrifice could somehow aid my friends.

"Your fretting helps no one, Ann," she said as she put the rejected plate beside me on the deck. "We must get on with our journey."

"How can we go on as if nothing has happened?" I flashed white hot. "Doesn't anyone care about the Jennings but me?"

"You forget yourself." Charlotte raised her palm as if to stop my words with the gesture.

"Well it's true, isn't it?" I pointed toward the cabin where the others ate their food with enthusiasm. "As long as we have survived, no one seems to worry about the others."

Charlotte's face stiffened, her cheekbones appearing even more prominent.

"I have not seen my husband in months," she said slowly. "I don't know if he's alive or dead. I have my worries, but I still think of others."

My self-righteousness evaporated at once. How could I dismiss her many sacrifices?

"Oh Charlotte, I'm sorry," I said immediately. "You know how I am. I can't stand it when I feel helpless." I moved toward her, but she offered no easy reconciliation this time. Instead she stepped away, lengthening the shadow between us, leaving me in an isolation that tore at my heart. I must change my frame of mind for sanity's sake.

I looked to my own children who kept their distance because of my wretched mood, stationing themselves at Hagar's skirts where she washed dishes in a large tub of river water. I wanted to give them hope but my own heart felt shriveled and hard. Tears sprang into my eyes unexpectedly, and I did the only useful thing I could think of at that moment. I sank to my knees on the hard timbers and prayed again for the Jennings party. I prayed for Polly, Betsy and Charity, and finally for myself that I might accept God's will. The rough boards pushed into my knees while the cold wind ripped across my back. I drew myself in close, pressing my elbows and palms together to ask God for guidance in this dark hour. The blood beat in my ears as I waited for an answer.

For at least ten minutes I knelt beside my sand box in prayer and contemplation. I remembered the power that surged through my body when I mobilized the women to save Fort Caswell from the Indians. I knew it must have been God who put the strength in my arms to hoist that heavy cauldron. And God, too, had given me courage at the palisade wall, even after arrows struck my body. God had been present in my greatest time of need, and I must have faith that He would always be with me. I was stirred from my prayers by a small mittened hand that touched my own clasped fingers.

"Mama," said Betsy, her eyes wide and guarded. "Are you all right?"

"Come here to me," I said, rocking back on my heels and grabbing my daughter close.

"Polly said you were crying," said Betsy, examining my face.

"I had some things to cry about, and pray about, but I'm finished now. And do you know what?"

"What?" asked Betsy, still eyeing me suspiciously.

"I'm in the mood to tell a story."

"What kind of story? Not Indians again," said Betsy warily.

"No. We've had enough about Indians. I want to tell you about another boat trip that happened long ago. Noah's trip on the ark."

"That's from the Bible," said Betsy.

"Right you are. You get all the children together beside our teaching box, and we'll have a lesson."

Betsy, pleased to have a task, ran from child to child with great enthusiasm, pulling at her sisters' skirts and tugging Delilah's braids. The Robertson and Donelson children were soon assembled with my own near the sand box, ready for a distraction. For once the sky stretched blue and cloudless above our heads, and the sun shone down, warming us in spite of the cold wind.

I began by asking how many had heard the story of Noah. All raised their hands, but when I asked for volunteers to retell it in their own words, no one spoke.

"Rachel," I said. "Why don't you tell us the story."

Rachel declined, saying she could never tell it as well as I, so I took one of the pointed sticks and wrote two words in the sand, NOAH and ARK.

"For you beginning spellers, these are your words for the day. And when I've finished with the story, I want you to write each of them ten times."

Betsy and Delilah nodded. Then Betsy added, "Yes, Mrs. Johnson."

"*Mrs. Johnson*? What's wrong with calling me Mama?" I asked.

"I'd feel better if I can call you Mrs. Johnson like all the others."

The children laughed and Betsy managed to look proud and embarrassed at once.

"The most important thing I want you to remember about this story is that God was with Noah and his family on their trip just as sure as He's with us today. And they knew even less about where they were going than we do."

"A long time ago, God looked down from heaven and saw that everyone in the world was evil except Noah and his family."

I explained that God became very angry at the situation and told Noah He was going to send the biggest flood the world had ever known. He instructed Noah to build an ark with room for his family, as well as a male and female of every kind of animal on earth. As soon as Noah was finished, God sent forty days and forty nights of rain which covered the whole world with water. The people and animals on the ark were the only living things that remained.

"But finally the rain stopped," I went on. "And when Noah's family complained about being shut up with all those animals, Noah scolded them and said they should be grateful for what God had already given them."

"The animals?" asked Polly.

"The animals, yes, but most important, they had each other, a community who could help one another, just like we have here on *The Adventure*."

I examined the young faces before me and thought how these children would people the Cumberland Valley just as Noah and his family had peopled the world. And for the first time that day I felt a stirring of hope. I took my long stick and drew a wide arch over the words ARK and NOAH.

"Who can tell me what that is?" I asked.

No one answered.

"If I had some paint, I would make it many colors."

"A rainbow," squealed Polly and Peyton at once.

"A rainbow indeed. God promised Noah and his family that He would never again destroy the world with a flood, and He put the rainbow in the sky as a sign of His promise."

"I like that story," said Betsy, her upturned face caught in a spot of sun.

"And so do I," I said.

I divided the children into two groups, with Polly, Randolph and Severn sitting against the cabin's wall, memorizing the story of Noah from a Bible that lay open in Polly's lap. Betsy, Peyton and Delilah practiced writing "Noah" and "Ark" in the coarse sand. They seemed happy to be busy, and I was grateful that my black mood had lifted, if even for a little while.

Colonel Donelson kept the boats moving all day and into the night before he finally felt assured he had put enough distance between us and the Indians. It was midnight when he blew his horn, and our company wearily landed on the northern shore of the river. A full moon lit the sky allowing us to see a shallow inlet with ample trees for tying up. The water made lapping sounds against the side of our boat, while our oars squeaked and groaned as Somerset and John Junior paddled toward land. *The Adventure* thumped against the shore and Jeremy was quickly over the side of the bow, locating a good sized tree for mooring.

Although my girls had slumbered for hours in the cabin beside the fire, I was unable to sleep. After *The Adventure* landed, I left the children sleeping beside Hagar, took my buffalo robe in my arms, and made my way across the dark deck and over the side with Bruno close at my heels. A large valley spread before me in the moonlight, revealing tall mountains thirty miles away, and the call of an owl lifted plaintively in the night like a warning. Bruno barked in return while smaller boats landed, one after another, slamming into the riverbank with crunches and thuds. Putting the robe around my shoulders, I thought how wonderful it would be if we were arriving at the French Lick, with Jamie and the others waiting for us, fires lighted, cabins built, our worries behind us.

The men called to each other as they worked to secure the boats, shouts that had a singing quality to them. I could make out Hugh Rogan's bold lilt and Major Cockrill's low reply as they pulled up not twenty yards from where I stood. I didn't want conversation so I crossed to a hulking pile of driftwood, and letting the robe fall to the ground, began to sort out small pieces to use for kindling. Fortunately I found logs that were dry to the touch.

"Let me help you." The Major's voice came from behind me.

I hadn't heard him approach and jumped, dropping my wood.

"I'm sorry," he said, putting his hand on my arm to steady me. "I didn't aim to frighten."

"I'm skittish," I answered. "So many terrible things have happened."

"I'm sorry for that too," he added. "Your friends . . . "

The pale light of the moon revealed the pain in his dark eyes. His eyelids seemed even heavier than usual, pulled down at the outer corners.

"I miss them," I said. And to my surprise a sob escaped. Major Cockrill put his arm around me and his warmth unleashed a torrent of emotion. My first sob was followed by a series so deep I sounded as if I were choking. I allowed myself to lean into him, pressing close, and he patted my back, as if I were a child. His gentleness made me cry even more, all my sorrows gathering in my throat and demanding release. When my chest finally stilled, with great effort I stepped backwards, wiping the tears from my face with the back of my hand.

"I'm so sorry," I said. "I've gotten your cloak wet."

"Don't apologize."

"I never cry. I can't imagine . . . "

"It's all right, Mrs. Johnson."

I looked around nervously, wondering if anyone had seen us together. "We need to start a fire, and here I am . . . " I gestured at the driftwood. "Wasting time."

"It wasn't wasted," he answered.

I longed to be rid of my embarrassment and turned to reach some branches for the fire.

"Let me help you," he said.

I nodded gratefully and took one long stick from the pile, dragging it to a flat space that was adequate for a fire. I used the stick to sweep the earth and then stamped my feet to flatten it. I worked in silence with the Major to build a pyramid of wood that he lighted with a flintlock box. The sparks ignited first the dry leaves, then the small sticks. Finally the logs caught until a great fire roared and crackled.

I could see his face clearly now from the bright firelight. I hesitated to look at him directly but couldn't resist sidelong glances. Other fires, at least ten in number, were started along the banks, and people arranged their robes and blankets around them for warmth. Bruno returned from a hunting expedition and whined at my side, then wrinkled up his brow as if to ask what he could do to help.

"May I sleep here by your fire tonight?" asked the Major. "In case you need anything."

I pulled Bruno to my side.

"It would not be proper, Major. I'm sure you know that." I couldn't look at him.

"Proper has lost its meaning here I would imagine."

Finally I lifted my face to study the weary smile that played across his thin lips.

"I'll ask Hugh to join us," he added before I could say anything more. "Then no one can say a word against it."

"Major Cockrill," I called, but he had already withdrawn. "Oh, Bruno, how did you let me get into this pickle?" I asked rubbing his soft ears. He only shook his head.

I returned to *The Adventure* and climbed onto the deck, hoping not to run into Charlotte who definitely would not approve of my sleeping arrangements. I checked my girls to make sure they were all right, removed one of the canvas ground cloths, and returned to the fire. If I hurried, I could pretend to be asleep when the Major and Hugh returned. I spread the ground cloth and wrapped myself in the buffalo robe, a caterpillar nestled in a cocoon. I lay still, eyes closed, and played possum when I heard them return.

"Bonny fire," Hugh said. "Looks like you two work well together."

The Major didn't reply, but slung his gun to the ground and followed it with his own weight, a thump, then a scratching sound. I felt his presence, saw him even through my closed eyelids, sensed the heat of him as if we lay side by side.

"Full moon makes me want to howl," said Hugh, slamming down his supplies.

"Doesn't take much for you to want to howl," added Cockrill. Hugh chuckled.

Bruno shifted beside me, pushing his back even closer to my side, and I realized I felt a sense of peace for the first time that day. It wasn't long before I dropped into a deep sleep.

I didn't know how long I was in the grip of dreams when loud shouts shattered my sleep. The first cries were indistinct, but then I heard, "Help us." The sound came from some distance down river, but was moving closer and closer. Soon I could recognize Mr. Jennings' voice! I wrestled my way from under the buffalo hide and sprang to my feet, Bruno joining me, barking loudly. In seconds Major Cockrill was at my side.

"It's Mr. Jennings. I'm sure of it," I told him.

"I hope to God you're right," he answered. We hurried to the water's edge where I could barely make out a dark shape moving toward us and hear the shout of Jennings' voice. Bruno continued barking and ran in circles beside me.

The whole company was awake now, even the children. My daughters spilled over the side of *The Adventure* and quickly found me. They jumped at my side yelling, "Mama! Is it really them?" I could see more clearly now as the boat came out of the trees and into the broad moonlight. Two shapes stood poling the small vessel and a larger shape was on top of the cabin controlling the tiller. But I still couldn't see how many other people were on board.

Our land party cheered as if George Washington himself were approaching. I could make out Mr. Jennings standing at the bow with a rope, ready to throw it ashore. Major Cockrill waded into the river to receive it. The rope fell into the water, but he retrieved it quickly and Hugh joined his hands on the sodden hemp as they pulled the boat to a safe docking spot. It was still too dark to count the whole Jennings party, but I could see Mr. Jennings clearly: his brow deeply furrowed, his neck stiff as he shouted loudly to be heard over the crowd.

"I need help," he called. "We've got an injury on board." Major Cockrill and Hugh broke through the crowd and followed him into the cabin. They returned with Nancy Gower, working deftly to get her off the boat without further injury.

"Watch her leg," called Mrs. Jennings. "She took a ball in her thigh."

Nancy's face was gathered in a grimace of pain, but she made no sound as they lifted her over the side and to the shore. Finally I saw Elizabeth with Mrs. Jennings' arm around her waist, both of them wearing stunned expressions and moving across the deck with a staggering gait. Because of the darkness, it was impossible to see whether they had any wounds.

"Let me help," I called, reaching my hand to steady Elizabeth as she climbed clumsily over the side of the boat. Once on land, she leaned heavily against me as I gripped her around the shoulders in a strong embrace.

"Oh, Elizabeth, Praise God!"

"My milk is near to bursting," Elizabeth said. "It wouldn't come when he was first born."

A chill went through me as I pulled away from her. Elizabeth's face was expressionless, as if all life had been pressed out by a hot iron.

"I want my baby," she said woodenly.

"I'll ask your Mama, Honey," I said as I led her to my fire where Nancy had been laid out as well. Mrs. Donelson knelt beside Nancy, binding her leg wound with torn pieces of cloth. "You sit right here on my robe," I said to Elizabeth. "I'll be back before you know it. And you, girls," I added to my daughters, "Go find us some blankets and be quick about it."

The children scampered off as I hurried to find Mrs. Jennings but came instead upon their slave, Hannah, the only person remaining at the boat. Hagar was at Hannah's side, rubbing the servant's arms and back.

"Where's Baby Ephraim?" I asked. "Miss Elizabeth's calling for him."

"Oh Miss Ann," Hannah said. "He's not here."

"What are you talking about?"

"Ephraim. Baby Ephraim," said Hannah, crying.

"Talk some sense," I said, shaking Hannah's arm until Hagar stopped me with a frown.

"You ask Miss Jennings. She'll tell you what happened to that baby. She was the bravest lady I ever saw," said Hannah.

I left Hannah and hurried back to the fire where I found both Mr. and Mrs. Jennings, the whole flotilla surrounding them. Many were standing and hurling questions into the night air. I lowered myself beside Elizabeth and held her hand in my own. My children returned with a stack of blankets and settled beside me.

Mr. Jennings appeared very small standing in the firelight with so many people crowded around him. His eyes were dark beneath the heavy overhang of his brow. Mrs. Jennings sat beside him with her head lowered, her bonnet entirely covering her face.

"I guess you saw how our boat got stuck on the rocks back yonder," he said. "We had us a terrible time trying to fight all alone, but I know the river was moving too fast for any of you to help. When those Indians saw our situation, they fell upon us like ducks on a June bug. They know how to take advantage of a man's misfortune, make no mistake about that. We were in a desperate situation. It was pretty clear to me that we were never going to get off those rocks with all our gear aboard. So Mrs. Jennings, Elizabeth and Nancy Gower started unloading the boat right away. For awhile Johnny and his friend Robert pitched in, along with our girl Hannah and our man Lucius. I provided the cover with my rifle, although it wasn't clear I was hitting anything at that distance. Some of the Indians were still on the top of the mountain, but others were moving down toward us, and I aimed at them."

Mr. Jennings paused, ducked his head at this point and stood silently for a few moments. The assembled crowd grew absolutely still. The only sound came from the crack of the fires.

"Go on," his wife prompted. "They've got to know about Johnny."

He lifted his head, and bit his bottom lip as he squinted into the fire. He continued to speak but looked no one straight in the eyes.

"I've been a soldier," he said. "And I know that most men are afraid when they go into battle. No shame in that. It's what you do with that fear that makes you a man or a coward. And I'm sorry to say my son is a flat out coward.

"We were making some progress in lightening our load when Johnny caught sight of a canoe pitching toward us in the river. I guess it had come loose from one of your boats, and it must have looked like salvation to him. He yelled at Robert and Lucius to join him and the three of them took to the river, swimming as hard as they could to get away from us. Johnny left his own mother, his sister and her little newborn baby without a second thought."

He shuffled his feet and drew a deep breath.

"When the Indians saw what was going on, they turned their guns on those deserters and plugged Lucius right in the head before he'd gotten even thirty yards. He went down leaving nothing but a bloody spot in the water. Johnny and Robert made it into the canoe, but I think Robert took a shot too. If Johnny hadn't been my own son, I think I would've gunned him down myself, abandoning his family that way.

"It like to broke Mrs. Jennings' heart, but she and Nancy and Elizabeth got to working even harder. They were throwing things off the boat this way and that, even with bullets ripping their clothes. It was clear that we were going to be slaughtered just like the Stuarts unless we could get our boat off the shoals."

He stopped after his voice caught, almost strangling him. He cleared his throat and continued with difficulty.

"And this brings me to our second tragedy. In all the confusion of throwing things into the river, baby Ephraim got tossed in too. Elizabeth had made a bed for him in one of the boxes while she helped the others and somehow, in all the ruckus, with the bullets whizzing and the cargo sailing into the river, his box got pitched in too. We never even saw it go over the side."

I felt Elizabeth shudder beside me and heard Hugh Rogan exclaim, "God Almighty."

"When Elizabeth went to check on Ephraim and realized he was gone," Mr. Jennings continued, "she started screaming, and I thought she'd received a mortal wound. She fell on the deck crying, and when I didn't see any blood on her I couldn't figure out what had gone wrong. Finally Mrs. Jennings discovered the baby was gone, and laid down right beside Elizabeth. The bullets were still coming as thick as bees, and Mrs. Jennings told

Elizabeth that getting herself killed wasn't going to bring back that baby. She had to pull herself together to help save the rest of her family."

Mr. Jennings stood taller at this point, jerking back his shoulders.

"Well, I have to say my daughter showed her mettle. She raised up and jumped back into the water with her Mama, Nancy, and Hannah, and they pushed that boat until it tore off the rocks with such a force it almost drowned them all. On top of those exertions, they had to swim some distance to catch up with the boat. Nancy couldn't swim a lick with her bad leg, so she put one hand on Elizabeth's back and the other on Mrs. Jennings', and by the Grace of God they made it safely to the boat."

Here he paused with a sigh. "I don't know what became of Johnny or Robert. I expect we'll never know for sure."

Heartsick for Elizabeth's loss, I didn't know how I could relieve her pain.

"I want my baby," Elizabeth said. "I want to touch him."

"Of course you do," I said. My children stared, their eyes wide, their mouths screwed up tight.

"It's going to be all right," I said to them. "You girls spread your blankets beside us. We'll sleep here for the rest of the night."

They did as they were told without a word of protest.

"What am I going to tell Ephraim? He's waiting for me, expecting to see his first born son."

"He's lucky you're alive, Elizabeth. You were as brave as anyone could be. Sometimes God has a way of doing things we can't possibly understand."

"I ache for that baby. I had him bundled up so carefully. I lined his box with a fine feather pillow that Mama brought from Virginia, and he was sleeping so soundly, in spite of all that racket. I thought he was safe. God knows I thought he was." Elizabeth spoke in a tone that was frightening in its flatness.

"Of course you did," I said. "You did everything you could."

I thought how different the outcome might have been if Johnny had jumped into the river to save Ephraim instead of jumping in to save his own cowardly skin. In all the stories I had heard tell about adventures on the frontier, I had never heard one that included such a family betrayal. Johnny Jennings was a despicable wretch, and I couldn't keep myself from wishing him the very worst.

"Mrs. Peyton," came a low voice. "I just wanted to stop and pay my respects."

It was Major Cockrill who removed his hat and knelt beside Elizabeth.

"Major Cockrill," replied Elizabeth with a slight nod. It was clear from the way she turned her head from him that she wanted no further conversation, so he rose, putting on his hat with a slight tip.

"I wish I had died," said Elizabeth. "I left my heart in that river."

"Your poor body's so tired your mind can't think straight. Let's get you settled."

Elizabeth let me coax her into lying down, and I nestled close. Now that my friend had returned from the dead, I didn't want to leave her for a minute. How horrible to lose the baby. And how lucky I felt to have my daughters gathered around me by the fire.

# Eight

MARCH 11, 1780 — *If there is anything more devastating than losing a child, I don't know what it is, and yet God continues to take our little ones. It is bad enough when they die of disease, but to have a baby thrown overboard, swallowed up into eternity. It is unbearable even to imagine! If only we could stop time and return to that moment when Ephraim's box flew through the air. Then Elizabeth, alert to his peril, could stretch her hands and grab him just in time. Oh, if only!*

*As I look at her lying beside me in the early morning light, she appears peaceful, but her long blond hair is stripped of its usual light and matted with water weeds. Just before she went to sleep, I heard her repeat the word "Ephraim" in a whisper only a little louder than the sound of breath. Can her pain ever go away?*

*And how much was Johnny Jennings a part of this awful outcome? I know it's my Christian duty to forgive him, and I'm trying to do so because he was young. And foolish. But I am making no progress. We are taught from birth that our survival here depends on loyalty to our family and friends. And yet, Johnny left his family without ever looking back. His deed strengthens my conviction of the importance of community, that those of us on this trip who are not relatives must become like blood kin. For aren't we all the children of Noah?*

*And finally, though it shames me to admit after all the tragedy that has befallen us, I am thinking selfishly of Major Cockrill and his warm support. How comforting it was to lean against his side to unleash my tears. And how long it has been since I was held in that way. If Charlotte had seen us, she would have preached about propriety, but our lives are so uncertain here on the river. If an Indian's bullet could easily kill me tomorrow, how does that affect what I do today? And what is wrong with warmth of feeling between an unmarried man and woman? Oh, I wonder if the devil is behind even these questions.*

*My first duty is to my children, and I will not compromise that responsibility.*

*Here is what I think. Adam and Eve brought a great deal of confusion when they ate the apple that gave us the knowledge of good and evil, for it is sometimes so hard to distinguish the difference.*

It was later than usual when our group awakened. Gray clouds were marked with occasional dark striations, and a hint of snow flavored the air, rare for March. Hagar poked the fire and Patsy returned to the boat to stir corn mush into the kettle. The thought of eating mush yet again caused my stomach to clench. Only the empty feeling in my belly and the desire to set a good example for my children made me swallow it in spite of my reluctance.

Nancy Gower groaned quietly as she touched her wounded leg, so I crawled to her side. Sweat beaded her upper lip even in the cold air.

"Can I get you some whiskey?" I asked.

She shook her head, her eyes dreamy with pain.

"They'll take the ball this morning," she said. "Dr. Henry couldn't see well enough to do it last night." She kicked at the blankets with her good left leg. "I'm so hot," she complained.

I put my hand to her forehead and found it feverish.

"Can you take off my blankets?"

"But it's freezing. I'm afraid you'll get a chill."

"Just for a minute," she begged.

I reluctantly pulled back the red and blue blankets and was shocked at the condition of her brown homespun skirt. It was soaked with a crimson tear-shaped stain that ran from her thigh to her ankles. The tattered fabric revealed a bloody bandage that made me gasp.

"That's not my worst suffering," said Nancy as she gripped my hand. Pulling me close she whispered, "I can't forget about Ephraim. I think I threw that baby overboard myself." She began to cry softly.

"Shhh," I said, hoping Elizabeth and my daughters would remain asleep.

"I never saw him," continued Nancy. "I promise I never saw a thing, but it must have been me," she anguished, rolling her head from side to side.

Elizabeth began to wake as well, and I was at a loss as to who might need comfort the most. Nancy thrashed her leg again, as if the effort would help to run away from memories, while Elizabeth slowly rose to a sitting position. Her gray eyes puffed with misery.

"It's all true then, isn't it?" Elizabeth asked. "Last night I dreamed he was alive at my breast," she said, mechanically raising her hand to her bodice and cupping it under her right breast. "I could feel his little mouth tugging at me. We were still joined together."

Nancy cried louder now and tried to rise. I pinned her down with the blankets, securing my hands at either side of her shoulders.

"Doctor Henry will be here soon," I said. "You must lie still."

"He can't bring that baby back," said Nancy. "What else matters?"

"Stop it," said Elizabeth, scrambling to her knees and crawling to Nancy's side.

"No one knows who threw him over," said Elizabeth, pushing me aside and startling Nancy to stillness. "If I'd kept better watch, it never would have happened," she continued. "It was my fault. All mine."

Elizabeth dropped her head slowly until it rested on Nancy's chest.

They were both sobbing now, and I was greatly relieved when Mrs. Jennings arrived with Dr. Henry bustling behind her. She gently pulled her daughter to stand facing her, while Dr. Henry prepared Nancy's wound for surgery.

"This blaming doesn't help that baby one iota," said Mrs. Jennings, wiping the tears from Elizabeth's cheeks with her hand. "It's no one's fault. It just happened." She took Elizabeth's face between her rough palms. "I lost a son and grandson in one day. I don't aim to lose you too."

Elizabeth absorbed her mother's firm gaze, and I could almost see the strength spring from mother to daughter. Elizabeth's crying stopped, and she stood erect.

"We'll leave Dr. Henry to care for Nancy," said Mrs. Jennings, "while we see to breakfast." They trudged side by side toward the cook fire, like the brave soldiers they were.

I returned to my children who huddled near *The Adventure*, their blankets tented around their shoulders, and sank to the hard earth beside them.

"They're going to be all right," I sighed, trying to relieve the gloom I read on their faces. "It's time for breakfast."

"You told me baby Ephraim would be fine too," said Polly. "That he wouldn't die."

"I know, Honey. And I'm sorry I was wrong."

"This is a terrible journey," said Polly. "I wish we'd never come."

"Hush. We couldn't stay at Fort Caswell when all our family was going west."

"Yes, we could. Uncle Charles stayed. Ephraim would be alive if we had."

"We don't know that," I said, narrowing my eyes for emphasis. "There are plenty of Indians at Fort Caswell too."

"Mama," interrupted Betsy. "I'm thinking of something. We're going through bad times, aren't we?"

"Yes, Honey," I answered, unable to deny that fact.

"Well, there's something in our box you said we could have one day to lighten our troubles." I could think of nothing I owned to ease their heavy hearts. "The maple sugar, Mama. Remember?" said Betsy. "You said we could have it with our corn mush one day."

And I did remember, but sugar seemed a paltry treat in the midst of so much heartache.

"Why of course I do," I answered with all the enthusiasm I could muster. "And I'm going to get it right now, for you to share with your friends."

I climbed aboard the boat followed closely by my daughters who were excited in spite of their sorrow. The girls circled tightly around me as I took down our trunk and dragged it to an opening on the deck. I removed my iron key and put it in the lock.

"What if the sugar's gone?" asked Polly.

"It'll be there. Don't you worry."

I opened the squeaky lid, releasing a musky odor of mildew, decay and neglected fabric, a sharp contrast to the crisp morning air. On top of my quilts, beside the corn husk doll, was the small pouch holding the precious sugar. When I took it out, the little bag felt firm as a rock, and I wondered how I could share a stone among all the children.

"Polly, can you get my rifle?" I asked. "It's in the cabin on the wall."

"Are there more Indians?" whispered Betsy tearfully, reaching out for my arm.

"No, Honey. I need some help to break up this sugar. That's all."

Polly returned with the rifle across her arms and I took it, pointing the barrel to the sky. I placed the pouch on deck and crushed the sugar with the firm butt of the gun.

"Now hold out your hands," I said as I opened the pouch's draw string top. I shook the amber lumps of sparkling sugar into each of their hands and their plump fingers curled around it in protection. They stared at the nuggets as if they were gold, letting them roll in their palms to catch the sky's light.

"But Charity has more than me," said Betsy.

"Everybody's going to have enough," I said. "Don't you worry. For this one morning, everybody's going to have enough."

———

Later that morning, Colonel Donelson, Major Cockrill and Mr. Jennings carefully inspected the Jennings boat from front to back and top to bottom. Major Cockrill used a flat iron tool to test the damaged sideboards, while Mr. Jennings inspected the boat's deck, and Colonel Donelson worked the tiller to see if it moved properly. Finally the Colonel pronounced it unfit for further travel.

"I'm afraid we'll have to abandon it," he said to Mr. Jennings. "It's a wonder you made it this far."

"All the same to me," said Mr. Jennings. "That boat's meant nothing but sorrow."

So the Colonel assigned the members of the Jennings family to the Harrison boat, and Nancy returned to the one where her parents traveled. I wished I could petition for Elizabeth to travel aboard *The Adventure* so I could keep a close watch over her, but I knew the idea was impossible. Our boat could not accommodate the entire Jennings party, and more than ever, Elizabeth needed her mother's protection.

With a sad heart I returned to *The Adventure* and watched as all the vessels prepared to leave. After what we had experienced, it seemed monstrous for life to go on exactly as it did every other day. And it was odd to set off under nothing more dramatic that a canopy of mouse-colored clouds when a brilliant display of lightning would be more appropriate. I spent the rest of the day in reflection and said little until evening when we tied up, and I found Elizabeth at the Harrisons' fire.

"How are you feeling?" I asked.

She shrugged, her face dull in the firelight.

"I bet Mrs. Harrison was glad to have you and your mother aboard," I said. "After nothing but male company."

Elizabeth didn't speak. She had changed from her ragged dress, but still wore a garment enlarged for her pregnancy, one that folded over itself like a half-spent feedsack.

"You need some different clothes. I've got two dresses in my box I haven't worn since David died. I saw them only this morning."

"I couldn't take your dresses," Elizabeth said with a wave of her hand.

"But I've no use for them, Elizabeth. You can't keep wearing that smock. It's too much a reminder of the baby."

"Everything reminds me of the baby."

"At least take my blue one. It will be so pretty on you."

Elizabeth ignored me. "When I was growing up in Virginia, I was never afraid, or sad," she said. "I wonder if I'll ever be that way again."

"Of course you will." I stroked her blond hair that was straight as a horse's tail. "You can't lose your faith."

"Can't I?" responded Elizabeth, looking at me as if I were a child.

I was relieved when the Major interrupted us and began speaking rapidly. He was so engrossed in his message that he didn't notice my cheeks flushing at the sight of him. I remembered our embrace, even though he had apparently forgotten it.

"I've talked with Colonel Donelson," he said. "According to his map, tomorrow may be an important day. He thinks we should reach the Muscle Shoals before night fall."

Since I had heard the water at the Shoals boiled even more dangerously than at The Suck, I grew uneasy. Indians might lie in wait to take advantage of our possible foundering.

"We may find Captain Robertson waiting for us. Or signs that he's been there," the Major continued.

"What do you mean?" asked Elizabeth. "That we're almost home?"

Major Cockrill explained that before Jamie set out in October, he had agreed to journey from the French Lick to the upper part of the Muscle Shoals to meet us if the miles were few in number between the Lick and the Shoals. Then he would lead us to the new settlement.

"I might see my husband soon?" asked Elizabeth.

"It's possible," said Cockrill.

Elizabeth smiled for the first time since her ordeal. Although glad to see the light return to her face, I feared her hopes would come to nothing.

"But we have no way of knowing how great the distance is," I added.

"All I'm saying," said Cockrill, "is that Captain Robertson vowed to be at the Shoals if he could. Or leave a sign."

I wondered if Elizabeth really heard the qualification of his statement.

"Have you seen the Shoals?" I asked.

He shook his head. "I've only heard they go on for maybe forty miles."

Forty miles! Pray God that Jamie might spare us going through that. But the distance between the Shoals and the French Lick would have to be a short one to make a land journey practical. Otherwise, we would have to abandon many of our household goods.

"Well, I'm off to tell the others. The Colonel wanted me to spread the word," Cockrill said. "Good to see you ladies." He certainly had a way of leaving abruptly, I thought, but perhaps it was just as well. As long as we spoke only of the trip's details, I would be safe from my emotions.

I left Elizabeth by the fire and as I returned to my children, I studied the night sky where stars dotted the inky blackness, far away jewels, unapproachable, unreachable. I knew as much about where we were going as I knew about the moon and stars. Our travels were a plunge into darkness and I felt terribly alone, even in the midst of company.

———

Around ten the next morning, we reached the Muscle Shoals at last, and I was stunned at the sight. Before me was a vision of God's wrath, as if He had upended the sky to pour an avalanche of rocks into the river, and followed this furious dumping by uprooting trees and flinging them in the water to churn and pitch upon the riverbanks. Until now the rocks in the river had been rounded limestone or soft sandstone, but these were made of flint and protruded sharply from the water like jagged teeth. The flint extended to ledges lining the river, knifelike threats to be avoided at all costs. And finally islands of various sizes stretched before us, additional obstacles to our progress.

My desire to find signs of Jamie increased greatly at the daunting sight since I wanted to avoid crossing the rapids if at all possible. With the river galloping faster and faster around us,

Colonel Donelson signaled for the boats to tie up. Somerset was the first to jump overboard when *The Adventure* luckily hit upon a shallow part of the riverbank free from treacherous ledges. He waded through the water and tied the boat to the trunk of a straggling tree bending over the river as if looking at its own reflection. Charlotte followed, dragging her moss-colored skirt through the swirling water in her haste to find signs of Jamie. She struck off down the riverbanks, and I scrambled after her, instructing Hagar to get the children off the boat as soon as possible. I searched the trees for a sign that Jamie had been there: a gash in the bark, a tree obviously felled by a man instead of nature, but I saw nothing. The bare oaks, maples, and sycamores stared back mutely. I quickened my pace to reach Charlotte's side where she frantically scanned the shore.

"Sometimes James will leave a rock tower as a sign," Charlotte said nervously, pulling up the sleeves of her dress until the cuffs slid over her elbows. "He lays down the big rocks first and then puts the small ones on top, interlocking them until they're strong enough to withstand a flood if necessary."

I joined Charlotte's search but was fairly sure further looking was in vain. Jamie would have put any signs close to the head of the Shoals. Charlotte continued to march along the river, and I followed for some minutes until the rocky shore ended at the dense forest, blocking our path. We stood silently listening to the river roar.

"He promised to come," Charlotte said, a tear sliding down her cheek like melted tallow on a candle.

I bent closer to hear more, but Charlotte only repeated, "He promised."

"Maybe the distance was too far. Or his responsibilities kept him. It could be anything."

"Why does he always think of others besides his family? We need him here," Charlotte added, balling her slim fingers into fists. "Sometimes even I get tired."

"Of course you do," I said. "But he's all right. I know it in here." I pointed to my heart. "Let's go back now. We can't do anymore."

Charlotte nodded and allowed me to lead her to the area where the boats were uneasily moored, bobbing dramatically on the river's stormy surface. But this time her tread was heavy, as if she carried large stones in her pockets. The Colonel was talking earnestly with Captain Blackmore, while a number of people knelt along a rocky promontory examining something in the water. Betsy saw me and came running with an open mussel shell in her hand.

"Look, Mama," she called. "They're everywhere. We can eat them right out of the shell," she said, tipping the shell to her lips and swallowing the mussel in one gulp.

"Ooooh. They're slimy," she said, making a face. "We found piles and piles of empty shells too," she added. "Major Cockrill says the Indians have been eating them here for hundreds of years. I guess that's why they call this Mussel Shoals."

"Maybe," I agreed.

"Whatever the reason, I'm going to get some more," Betsy announced and joined the other children who picked among the rocks where the mussels were attached.

Major Cockrill came toward us, a mussel shell in his hand. Charlotte passed him on her way to *The Adventure* without speaking a word.

"Is Mrs. Robertson all right?" he asked, frowning as he looked after her.

"Severely disappointed I'd say," I answered. "And I am as well. Either our map is wrong or something terrible has happened to Jamie."

"Maybe this will cheer you," said the Major, extending a dark gray mussel shell.

I took it reluctantly, holding the rough surface in my palm.

"I'm not hungry," I hesitated, handing it back to him.

"Open it," he urged.

I lifted the top of the shell slowly and saw to my surprise nestled in the opaque interior was a single pearl, gleaming and perfect like a child's small tooth. It caught the light, its creamy surface showing a faint pink tinge.

"I found it in the first shell I opened. It's a good omen," he said smiling. "We're going to make it through those Shoals, Mrs. Johnson. You'll see."

I studied the pearl and wanted to believe him, but it was just one pearl among so many mussels. What kind of a chance did we really have against the tumultuous Shoals?

At the sound of Colonel Donelson's horn, I put the pearl in a pocket at my waist and joined the others to listen to his decision. We formed a large semicircle three hundred strong and made little conversation as we waited. I noted how shabby we had grown from two months of wearing the same clothes with little opportunity for a good laundering.

"We have a dangerous stretch ahead of us," the Colonel began. "I'm told the Shoals extend for many miles. But without a sign from Captain Robertson, I am convinced we must proceed." He paused. "I know many of you are sorely disappointed."

A grumble drifted through the crowd.

"The best advice I can give you," he continued, "Is to keep a good distance apart. We have enough obstacles ahead without bumping into each other. And those of you in canoes and dugouts must be particularly vigilant. You may tip over without a moment's notice. *The Adventure* will go first. Captain Blackmore will bring up the rear."

"And one more thing," added the Colonel, raising his hand. "Take time for a prayer."

We returned to our respective boats, and Charlotte stood by the cabin door, her face ashen but resolute, her dark eyes glittering like jet.

"Almighty God," she began as she closed her eyes and we bowed our heads in turn. "Since you have sent no one to guide us overland to the French Lick, we know it is Thy will that we journey through the Shoals before us. Be present as we travel these rough waters, even as you parted the Red Sea for the Israelites. We pray in the name of your Son, our Savior, Jesus Christ. Amen."

"Amen," I repeated quietly. And God helps those who help themselves, I added to myself.

Without further discussion, Donelson instructed Somerset and Jeremy to lash the barrels to the deck while John Junior and Severn secured the farm implements. I took my walnut box into the cabin where I wedged it under one of the benches for safe keeping. As we prepared to cast off, I found a long rope which I tied around the waist of each of my daughters and then affixed to my own middle. Colonel Donelson advised me against it, saying we might all drown in an accident, but I maintained I could save them better if they were bound to me. I would not risk losing a child.

As planned, *The Adventure* broke into the tumbling waters first. When we encountered the Shoals, I felt a new horror. Muscle Shoals spread before us like a thousand boiling pots. The noise entered my mind, suffocating all other thoughts. If our boats had been empty, we might have passed more easily through the foaming caldron, but as it was, *The Adventure* immediately struck at the rocks and lurched first one way and then another. A large drifting branch raked across the port side of the boat, catching Jeremy on the head and slamming him to the deck. Piles of logs jutted into the river looking like the skeletons of nature, graveyards of wooden bones. Black and pointed branches threatened like a hundred crooked weapons. Even the smell was ominous — the rank odor of decay.

The children shrieked as the boat fell a four-foot drop, but their voices could barely be heard above the powerful bellowing of the river, mouse sounds in a conversation with a giant. Sometimes the boat seemed to fly, only to be dashed to the river's surface with a crash. Colonel Donelson shouted commands while Somerset and John Junior used their poles as best they could to ward off the protruding rocks.

The other boats behind us pitched into the air, and I heard screams above the river's roar. It seemed the shoals would never end . . . that the river would thrash us until every last boat was added to the piles of wooden skeletons. As we progressed, the river sped faster and faster. Waves dashed, foamed and whirled over the rocks. Often the foam tumbled over the side of *The Adventure* as well, and we struggled with buckets to return the water to the river. Minutes stretched agonizingly into hours and still the war went on.

Finally, after three of the longest hours I had ever known, the river relaxed as if it had come to the end of a temper fit. The water stretched before us once more as a silver lake under the gray sky. Not a single boat had been lost, undoubtedly because of the unusually high water, but not a single soul would ever want to repeat the experience. I decided the stretch of river was named Muscle Shoals because of the great strength necessary to endure the passage.

# Nine

MARCH 14, 1780 — *Our day on the Shoals was followed by twenty-four hours of smooth sailing. Because the river was high, we moved rapidly, making good time. Colonel Donelson guessed it would not be long before we reached the mouth of the Tennessee River where it flows into the Ohio. Even though this river has been a mighty foe, I still love its name, Tennessee. It rustles on my tongue as I say it and writing the word in sand is a joy. I encourage the children to join me, to line up the pairs of n's and s's and e's like little playmates in a row. Tennessee. Tennessee. The Indians may be our enemies, but they often create beautiful names.*

*Yesterday I was actually able to give Charlotte some advice. I suppose I was giving the advice to myself as well. The river was smooth enough to allow Colonel Donelson to sit with us at noon for our shortest meal of the day. The Colonel enjoyed a philosophical mood and brought up the subject of the Declaration of Independence, the document that helped to start this long war of ours. Colonel Donelson reminded us of the freedoms we are all fighting for — life, liberty and the pursuit of happiness.*

*Charlotte said that after what we have been through, she was ready for our happiness to begin soon. But I reminded her that happiness was not our guarantee, only the pursuit of it. She gave me the strangest look, but I know we have few guarantees of any kind.*

*Major Cockrill joined us around the fire last night. He said little but spent a long time looking at my hands until I put them under my cloak. I am ashamed that the skin of my fingers has grown as rough as that of a chicken's foot. Is that why he stared?*

*MARCH 15, 1780 — Shakespeare wrote we should "beware the Ides of March." Today may have its trouble ahead, but yesterday was a day we should have watched out for as well. Just when we thought we had seen the last of the Indians, we found to our sorrow it was untrue. The boats of Major Cockrill and Ben Belew strayed too near the shore at one point, and it was as if the trees turned into Indians, so mystically did they appear. First we saw nothing on shore, and then the spectacle of painted faces and smoking guns. I feared for Major Cockrill's life and yelled and flapped my arms in warning, but my actions were useless. Their boats were too far away to hear me. Thank God the Major was spared! Five others were injured, but none seriously.*

*As soon as we had landed for the evening, arranged our goods and lit our fires, the dogs started their barking. First my Bruno gave a few stray yips which I credited to the presence of deer in the forest, but his barks were followed by a crescendo of hoarse howls from the other dogs. At that point their meaning was as clear as if they had shouted the word "Indians" louder and louder.*

*We hastily gave up our camp and moved a mile down the river where we spent the night sleeping nervously on the opposite shore. This morning, at the urging of Mrs. Donelson, the Colonel sent John Junior and John Caffrey to our first site to recover some of her goods. They found one of our slaves had accidentally been left behind, and still slept undisturbed by a fire. I can't explain why the Indians didn't kill him because I'm sure they lurked nearby last night. John Junior brought back his mother's favorite kettle and other items we'd abandoned in our hurried flight. She is most fond of that pot.*

MARCH 20, 1780 — *The last few days have gone hard on us. The river is much easier to travel, but the frigid rains continue to cover us like an icy second skin, the cold making my old wounds ache. And our food supplies have dwindled to almost nothing. Someone spoke of killing the dogs for food. Impossible. Those brown-eyed creatures have become as close to us as first cousins-once-removed. Bruno is more dear to me than certain people I will not name who hoard food while children go hungry.*

*I must admit that Colonel Donelson sets a noble tone. He asks nothing for himself or his family that is not available to all. At night I see him walk the boundaries of our campsite like a worried shepherd tending his flock. And weary sheep we are too.*

*The children grow impatient with their lessons. The boys frequently break off study to pretend their writing sticks are guns and kill each other without mercy, falling into writhing heaps. My girls are distracted by their hunger and stay close to me. In fact, at every chance, Charity nestles under my arm like a baby bird pressing itself into the fork of a tree. I wish I could teach her to fly away to some safer spot, a place where berries are plentiful and birds are not apt to freeze upon the bough.*

This morning continued as gloomy as all the days preceding it, but the rain held to a light mist. The river expanded to a mile in width, and we saw the first subtle suggestions of spring in the bordering forest, a faint lemony green strung through the trees. At midmorning, I was teaching with mixed results when Colonel Donelson pointed to two islands and beyond them a body of water that loomed almost as big as the sky. We had come to the end of the Tennessee River at last, and before us swept the wide and gray Ohio . . . which led to the Cumberland River . . . which led to our new home.

The flat earth was fringed with white sycamores and cane brakes that stood twenty feet high. The cane foliage has an unnatural color, as if painted green to resemble make-believe trees. As soon as the boats landed, we tumbled out to examine the new Leviathan, the next beast to be conquered. I knelt by the Ohio, letting its icy tongue wash over my hand and listening to the language of its current. My solace was disturbed, however, by a squabbling from *The Adventure*. Mrs. Donelson was shaking her daughter by the shoulders while the Colonel walked briskly toward them. I hurried forward too, arriving just as the Colonel managed to persuade Mrs. Donelson to release Mary.

"Mrs. Donelson, please," he pleaded.

"I won't have it," said Mrs. Donelson, her face flushed, strands of gray hair escaping from the knot she wore at the nape of her neck. "We've come too far for them to abandon us now."

Mary struggled backwards and stationed her feet wide apart, thrusting out her chin in defiance.

"We must handle this in an orderly fashion," said the Colonel, stepping between them.

I understood from the ensuing conversation that Mary and her husband, John Caffrey, wanted to leave the flotilla. The endless difficulties of the trip had worn heavy on them, and Mary was prepared to exercise her rights as a married woman. She and Johnny C. had decided to strike out on their own, down the Ohio River to the Natchez country.

"The family must stay together. What can you be thinking of?" shouted Mrs. Donelson, her anger undiminished by the Colonel's presence.

"Our future," said Mary. "We don't know how much further it is to the French Lick. Or what we'll find when we get there."

Johnny C. joined them, undoubtedly drawn by the loud argument as were others. He was thinner and more wiry than any of the three Donelson men, and no taller than Mary. His chin was covered with a sparse blond beard which he may have thought made him look more manly, but didn't. When he spoke, however, his deep baritone voice belied his slight appearance.

"We hoped to talk with you privately," he said with authority. "We reckon there's a better future in the Natchez country. Plenty of folks have set up there already, and I hear tell the Indians are friendly."

"You hear tell! That's a fine recommendation," said Mrs. Donelson, looking as if she wanted to give him a good slap.

"Better than what we hear from the French Lick. Which is nothing," said Mary, looking pleased with herself.

"Now, Mary," Colonel Donelson began with a low calming voice. "You know Captain Robertson saw no Indians at the Lick last year."

"A year ago," said Mary almost snorting. "No telling what's there now. Especially if our party has started to build cabins. They draw Indians quicker than flowers draw bees."

Mrs. Donelson, making an obvious effort to contain her fury, cleared her throat, brushed back her hair and began again.

"We've held together this long, girl of mine," she said. "Let's stick it out to the end."

"We should be at the Cumberland River soon," added the Colonel, nodding. "According to all accounts."

"All accounts said we'd be there by now," said Mary, growing even more agitated. "All accounts said the river trip would be the safest route. If this journey was the safe one, we can assume Captain Robertson's party is half dead by comparison."

"Now, Mary," said Johnny C., trying to soothe his wife.

"I can't let you go," said Mrs. Donelson drawing up her formidable body as if she planned singlehandedly to block their escape.

"We must make our own way," said Mary, drawing up her own good-sized bulk as well.

"We respect you, and all," added Johnny C. "But married folks have got to make their own decisions."

"You'll fall prey to the Indians. They take advantage of lone travelers. You've seen horrible examples of that already," said Mrs. Donelson. "I can't have your souls go unmourned."

"I mourn already," said the Colonel and turned from his daughter and son-in-law.

He brushed by my side, his face etched with defeat, his shoulders slumped. For the first time I could see straight into the heart of the man.

Following the argument, a rumbling as ominous as thunder shimmied through the entire company: thoughts of abandoning the flotilla were as contagious as smallpox. The cold, fatigue and hunger had stripped bare our nerves. For three months we had been together in this loose alliance of people and boats. For three months no alternatives were available to splinter our group. But now the Ohio swept away before us like a silver road. Downstream lay the promise of a more established life. Upstream lay uncertainty.

For me there was no question but that I would remain with Charlotte and the others. However I could understand that Mary and Johnny C. might want a future on their own, untrammeled by the long shadow of John Donelson. Was separation inevitable? Did the founding of the West mean that grandparents would never know their grandchildren? I recalled how maple trees sent their seeds fluttering into the wind, looking for the most fertile ground, wherever that might be. It was Nature's way, but I fervently hoped that my daughters would remain close beside me until the day I died.

To settle the crowd, the Colonel hastily assembled the group.

"I don't have to tell you we've reached the Ohio," he said gesturing toward the river. "You can see that for yourselves. You can also see the force of its current and imagine the strength we'll need to fight our way upstream."

He walked among us with a heavy stride. "I don't have to tell you that you're hungry either. That the game we've killed lately has been poor and stringy. Even the fish hide from us.

"We need more food for the job ahead so I'm asking for volunteers to go hunting in the morning. Hugh Rogan and Ben Belew will take the rest of the day to scout out the best areas, so those who're willing to set out tomorrow, come stand by me."

Reuben Harrison stepped forward to be the first to volunteer. His father also started toward the Colonel but his wife put her weathered hand on his arm to stop him. I knew I could shoot better than Reuben and most of the others who ambled forward to stand with Donelson. And what good could I do remaining with the boat? The children would be in no mood for a school lesson, especially since this was one of their few opportunities to explore a new shore in the daylight. I advanced toward Donelson, shoulders back and said in a voice loud enough for the whole company to hear, "I'm ready."

"Mrs. Johnson," the Colonel answered, his face pinched into a frown. "Your place is here, with your children."

"My place," I replied, "is where I can do best by my hungry children. I know how to hunt." Captain Blackmore threw back his head and laughed. Several of the other men followed. "I've used a rifle since I was ten years old. I challenge any man to out-shoot me. Pick a distance, short or long."

"We'll not be wasting good powder on a contest," said the Colonel sharply. "If you went, you'd be no help to us, Mrs. Johnson. Just another worry."

"She can go with me," said Major Cockrill, his hat tipped back, framing his dark face. "And I can vouch for her gun. It shoots straight and true."

I harbored conflicting emotions at his offer; frustrated that anyone needed to stand up for me, but grateful that he had done so. The Colonel nodded in response to Cockrill's gesture, not wanting to waste any more time on the subject. The crowd broke up, and Charlotte approached the Major where he stood beside me, leaning so that her mouth was near his ear. "I trust I can count on you to be a gentleman, Sir. Even if Ann refuses to act like a lady."

"I have only her best interests at heart, Mrs. Robertson. I can assure you," the Major answered gravely.

Now that I had won my point, I wasn't so keen on going into the woods with the Major after all. As I walked toward *The Adventure* to check out my rifle, questions flew through my mind. Would the fact that I once welcomed his embrace make him think I would welcome it again? Would I blush like a fool the moment we were alone? I had worked myself into a state of agitation by that evening when the Colonel called the volunteers before his campfire to hear Hugh Rogan's report. The twinkle in Hugh's eyes was evident even in the darkness as he joked that he'd passed up a bear and a buffalo because he knew he was only supposed to scout, not shoot. But he turned serious as he described how he and Ben were encouraged to find fresh animal droppings in a number of places: deer, elk and even the small round pellets of turkey scat. They discovered three springs within several miles of our camp where it might be possible to find game the following morning. They had cut through the canebrake that fringed the river and established the beginnings of three paths to set us in the right direction. The Major and I would take the nearest spring, while the other eight hunters would split up and proceed to the two more distant hunting spots.

"All right then," the Major said in a matter-of-fact manner. "See you beside *The Adventure* at first light."

"First light," I responded, doing my best to match his seriousness.

———

Back on *The Adventure*, I feared I could not sleep for thinking about the upcoming expedition. But fortunately, after covering myself with the buffalo robe, and warming my face at the fire, I forgot all my concerns and slept until I felt someone shake me.

"If you're going hunting, it's time," Hagar said, holding my rifle, powder horn and bullet pouch. I sleepily took the powder horn, looping its strap over my shoulder. "I'm going all right," I said, as much for my own benefit as Hagar's. "If I'm lucky, I'll bring back a deer," I added, fastening the pouch around my waist and taking the gun. I checked to see it was loaded with a single bullet, the gun powder in the flash pan ready to go. "And let's pray I'm lucky."

————

I followed the Major who carried a ten-inch scythe to hack at the dense undergrowth. The cane was a friend when it provided a food source for our animals, or when hunters could hide from Indians within its depths, but it also served as a barrier as dense as any fort palisade. Soon, however, we emerged from the cane-brakes, and walked silently through the forest, watching for game as we wove through the trees.

"You shoot something besides Indians, Mrs. Johnson?" the Major asked.

"Rabbits, turkeys. Jamie taught all of us to hunt."

"Ever come across a bear?"

"Not yet," I said. "Can't say as I'd like to. But a big bear would feed a lot of us."

"I'm partial to bear," he said. "Bear oil is God's gift to the hunter. You can cook with it, drink it, cover yourself with it to keep the bugs away. A bear's hard to kill though."

"I'd settle for something smaller," I said, pushing aside a supple tree, but letting it swing back too soon, scratching my hand. I felt a bit weak from hunger and pressed on, making sure my boots dodged the rocks. When I tripped on a root, however, the Major suggested we sit for awhile, and I nodded in agreement. We used a fallen log for a makeshift bench, and I sat down heavily, keeping a respectful distance between us. In the stillness, his familiar smell mingled with the scent of pine needles and wet leaves that lay beneath our feet. He took off his slouchy hat and rubbed the sweat from his forehead with the back of his hand.

"May I ask you a question?" he said, looking into the trees.

"Certainly." I felt an odd, prickly sensation in my skin for fear of what he might ask.

"Why is it you wear men's clothes?" He turned to look at me.

At his inquiry, the memory of David became palpable, as if his ghost sat between us.

"Have you ever been married, Major?" I asked.

He shook his head but didn't turn away.

"It's a terrible thing to lose someone you love. I wear these clothes to feel near my husband."

"I'm sure he'd be proud," said Cockrill, returning his interest to the trees. "A wife like that is hard to come by."

He straightened himself, tucked his head, and rolled his eyes sideways toward me.

"I expect he'd want you to keep on living though. Even if he's gone."

I felt a confusion of emotions rise inside me, an unexpected urge to cry.

"I aim to live, Major. That's why I'm searching for food. I don't want my family to be six feet under in a God forsaken place like this."

I turned my eyes to the forest, scanning the upright trees for the slightest movement, any horizontal shape that signaled an animal. I saw no trace of action and heard nothing but the thud of my own heartbeat.

"You can depend on other people you know," the Major said. "We all need help."

Suddenly I saw a shuddering of trees. "Shhh," I said, and without thinking touched his thigh to be silent. My hand lay there for only an instant but the touch bloomed. With some effort I drew my attention back to the woods.

"I thought I saw something," I whispered. "Over there."

"If you did, our talking sent it a mile away," he said, standing. "We'd better find that spring so we can do some serious hunting."

He began to walk again, without even turning to see if I followed, and I trailed quietly behind him for several minutes until we came to a space where the trees opened to a small meadow with a spring. The Major pointed to a large tree that had fallen and motioned for me to follow him. We took positions behind the log which was large enough to shield us from animals that might come to the water. As quietly as possible, we placed our rifle barrels on its surface to brace our guns.

I directed my eyes to the line where the trees stopped and the meadow began. Back and forth I followed the line until my eyes blurred for a moment, and I thought they might be failing me. But in the woods, just to the left of a cedar, I saw a tip of white, a flicker. And sure enough a deer slowly materialized from the forest.

I followed the animal with my rifle, tracking it, aiming for the neck, letting it move closer and closer in a diagonal path toward the spring. Then I fired. I heard Cockrill's gun crack as well, providing a double staccato effect. The doe lurched forward in a final leap that was too late to save her life. Her body slammed into the grass and flipped to the side, the graceful head thrown back in surrender. The Major and I scrambled to her body to make sure she was dead, ready to help her avoid unnecessary suffering. And dead she was.

I knelt beside her warm body and stroked the soft brown coat.

"Thanks be to God," I said.

"Not as large as I'd have liked," said Cockrill. "But not as skinny as some."

He pulled a knife from his belt and drew the blade hard across her underside from neck to tail, letting the blood spill on the long soft grass. Because the doe was hit in the neck rather than the gut, he could remove the entrails fairly easily, but even so his arms were covered with blood when he hoisted the deer to his shoulder to trek back to the river. I fell in behind him without a word, grateful for success and the end of our hunt. When we returned to the camp, other hunters had returned victorious as well, but no one with an animal as large as our deer. I found Hagar and Charlotte waiting anxiously with my daughters.

"Before you say . . . " I began, but Charlotte shook her head.

"I am reconciled," she said. "James always told me to avoid fights I cannot win."

"It was my shot that brought down the deer," I said, still feeling the need to defend myself.

"We thank you," was all Charlotte answered before she left me to join Mrs. Donelson who stood admiring the deer's carcass. Hagar remained with me, holding Charity's hand.

"I understand why you went," Hagar said, her brown eyes lit from a fire deep within. "If I had a baby, I'd do anything to get food too."

————

That evening our stomachs were a little fuller. Numerous squirrels and rabbits helped to sweeten the cooking pots, and our deer was strung up for preparation later. When all had finished their suppers and the youngest children were put to bed, Colonel Donelson called still another meeting.

He stood atop a trunk so the assembled group could see him plainly, the fire casting wavy shadows on his face. He had heard many grumbles during the day from people who were losing faith in our journey, and he wanted to bring their concerns to the forefront.

"We are at a crossroads," he said. "Our hungers are many. We hunger for the food that is so abundant east of the mountains, and for our friends and families who have gone overland. We hunger for rest and peace and a land of plenty. I share these hungers."

He paused to let his gaze settle on each one of us individually, finishing with a long look at his daughter, Mary, who avoided his glance.

"Downstream the Ohio leads to the great and terrible Mississippi River and the country known as 'the Natchez.' It's a land where Spaniards reign who have made alliances with the Creeks and Cherokees. There's not a one of them I would trust. And between this place and the Natchez you can be sure to encounter pirates whose very livelihood depends on plundering any vessel that might drift by unprotected."

He turned and stretched his arm into the darkness, pointing at the river.

"Upstream leads to Captain Robertson, your friend and defender for more years than you can count. I cannot promise you a protected journey to the French Lick. We have been fired upon before, and we may be fired upon again. But I can promise my solemn oath that I will pursue the course, no matter what happens. You have my word."

I glanced at Mary and John Cafferty, the two for whom this speech was fashioned. It was impossible to read their expressions, but they huddled together, creating their own island. Mrs. Donelson rose to stand by her husband, much more composed than she had been earlier.

"Colonel Donelson and I are older than most of you," she began. "And by all rights we should be inclined to take the easy route at our time in life. But my husband and I have pledged ourselves to the future of this country. We look forward to living in the new land, and we'll do whatever it takes to get there."

She faced Mary directly. "Come with us to build a new community and leave the Natchez country to the Spaniards," she finished.

No one lifted a voice in argument. The meeting, such as it was, concluded and only the next day would reveal the decisions made separately this night.

# Ten

MARCH 21, 1780 — *Last night, time and again I woke from dreams of Major Cockrill that make me redden at the remembrance. What a storm of emotion I started with that touch. If shaking my head could rid me of these thoughts, I would shake until people thought I suffered from St. Vitus' Dance! Charlotte is right as always. I am too impulsive.*

*I must concentrate on other things. For instance, the happy signs of spring. The willow has begun to leaf, as if hundreds of tiny green moths were attached to its graceful boughs. More birds greet the early light with a busy chatter, encouraging us to get on with the day. I have always envied the birds. The smallest robin sees the world from a perspective we can never know. I wish I were the silvery mockingbird perched on the bough above, and I could fly to the French Lick. I would inform Jamie we are alive, that he should not give up hope. But since I cannot fly, I pray this will be the last trip of my life. May God let me settle at the French Lick and sink my roots deep into that promised soil!*

*If I slept badly, I suspect that Mary and Johnny C. had an even more fitful night. At least I have chosen my path, however arduous, while they still waver. I hope their prayers lead to the right decision.*

When Colonel Donelson called us to cast our lots, it reminded me of the Bible story when the sheep were separated from the goats, one group to be saved and the other damned. But which will be which? Right away I saw Mary Caffrey walk with a strong stride toward her father where he stood in front of *The Adventure*. She planted her feet solidly on the brown earth and looked her father squarely in the eyes. Her mind was made up, no question about it. Johnny C. trailed behind like an afterthought and stood at her shoulder. Mrs. Donelson waited amidst the crowd, her back straight, her gaze resting resolutely on her husband's face.

"We'll start with Mary and Johnny C.," the Colonel said, his face a rigid mask. "Have you arrived at a decision?"

The crowd was still, the only sound coming from the river's rushing current.

"Johnny and I talked and prayed," said Mary, never letting her eyes stray from her father's face.

"We thought it was high time we made our own decisions," added Johnny C.

His words hung in the air and Mary waited for just a second before she spoke. "And we're sticking with you," she added, smiling at last. "I guess we can get up the Ohio as good as anyone."

The Colonel's face melted, a smile replacing the rigid set of his mouth. Mrs. Donelson let out a grand hallelujah and hurried to her daughter, lifting Mary slightly off the ground with her embrace. Rachel, Severn, John Junior and the other Mary encircled the couple that had decided to stay with the family. Amid all the rejoicing, it was hard to hear the few families who announced they were leaving us: two to head for Natchez and one to go to the Illinois country.

After bidding farewell to the three departing vessels, we set on our way. It didn't take long before each of us was aware of the abrupt change that had taken place. The Tennessee River with all its bends, curves, rocks and islands, at least had been a river that carried us with its natural flow, whether going south or turning north. The Ohio, however, insisted we fight for every inch of progress. Because of the tremendous strength necessary to move the boats forward, some of us women took our turns at the tillers, giving the men time for rest. At the end of the first day when we landed some five miles upstream, pain surged through my arms as I helped set up our campsite. At dinner the effort to lift a fork made my hand tremble. So much effort for so little reward. I could have walked more miles than our boats had advanced that day.

After dinner I fell asleep by the fire while sitting bolt upright, trying to listen to Polly spin a tale. I was dreaming of the Major holding the reins of two black horses, seventeen hands high at least, when I heard his deep voice. I opened my eyes to see him kneeling beside my children, his hat on the ground, his large right hand concealing something. Never had dream and reality fused so seamlessly.

"Can your mother sleep standing up as well?" he asked, smiling. He wore his wide shoulders like heavy wings.

"Sleep?" I asked, trying to adjust my eyes to the firelight.

"Sure looked like it," he said, sitting beside me without an invitation.

"Maybe I am a bit tired." I rubbed my eyes in an effort to see more clearly. Then I added, "The truth is, I'm as tired as I've ever been in my life."

"It was bad today, but I've seen worse," said the Major, holding out his hand to Betsy, opening his fingers to reveal a doll made of horseshoes welded together. One horseshoe formed the arms, another the legs, and part of a third served as the body and head. Betsy squealed with pleasure.

"Where did you find this?" Betsy asked.

"Just pulled it out of the flames," he answered.

"He made it," said Polly. "Anyone can see that."

"After a day like today, I don't see how you had the strength to bend a twig, much less a horseshoe," I said.

"When I was in the army, we once went three days without a mouthful to eat. Not a bite. And six days without the food to make one good meal. Marching in knee-deep snow too."

"Horrible," I said, but finding it difficult to concentrate on his words.

"We were looking for General McIntosh."

"Did you find him?" asked Betsy.

"Reckon I did," said the Major laughing. "Although he wasn't too glad to see any of us. Sent me straight home with only a packet of flour to eat and nothing else. If I could live through that, I can live through anything."

Hearing of other people's miseries had never made me feel one whit better, and I struggled for a reply to his story.

"I wouldn't want to be any hungrier or more tired than I am right now," I said.

"You can play with my doll if you want," suggested Betsy. "Playing always makes me feel better."

I reached for the iron doll, fingering it, using a large helping of imagination to recognize it was a doll. The arms and legs were easily discernible, but the head was fashioned out of scraps and tilted at an odd angle, as if it were perplexed. The simple gift merely complicated my emotions further. Why was the Major paying this attention to me and my children? Was he courting me? Is this how a man did it? When I married David, I had been so young. I wouldn't have recognized courting even if David was doing it. I had made my decision to wed him with no more thought than I would have used in deciding to swim on a summer afternoon. I was used to being surrounded by my brothers, and spending time with David was almost like being with them. It was only after I married that I realized the magnitude of my decision.

But now that I was fully grown, the idea of marrying again frightened me more than any of the physical challenges of our journey. Besides, why would Major Cockrill be interested in a widow woman with three children? Any number of women on the trip were younger than I, and prettier too, without the added responsibility of daughters.

"You were kind to make this doll Major. But I'm afraid we can't accept any more gifts," I said.

"Mama!" cried Betsy, snatching the doll away and burying it in her skirt.

"You've been too generous already," I added.

"Do I have to give it back?" questioned Betsy, taking the doll gingerly from her lap and holding it up.

"I've no use for it. I assure you," said Cockrill. "Let the child keep it."

Considering that my children had few enough pleasures, I relented and told Betsy, "It's all right. Just thank the Major."

Betsy shyly looked at Cockrill and smiled her most ingratiating smile.

"Thank you, Sir," she said. "I'll tuck it under my covers every night and tell it the best stories I know."

"Good girl," he said. "And then you can tell them to me."

"Off with you now. All of you. I want to speak with the Major alone."

Betsy eyed me suspiciously but scampered off to show Delilah her new treasure. Polly followed reluctantly, holding Charity's hand but frequently looking over her shoulder.

"I need to speak plain," I said when I was sure the children were out of earshot.

"I can't imagine you talking any other way," he said with some amusement.

"I'm afraid," I started. "I don't want you to think . . . ," I added. "Oh, Major Cockrill. Just because I wear men's trousers doesn't mean I'm not a lady. Well, maybe not exactly a lady. But I'm a decent woman, and I won't be . . . "

The right words wouldn't come. I felt like a blithering fool. What if he were merely being friendly to a woman in need? Maybe I was creating a problem where none existed.

"I consider you more than a lady," he said gravely. The fire light hit squarely on his wide forehead, and highlighted the broad bridge of his nose. "And my respect knows no bounds."

I studied him carefully for the slightest hint of mocking but none was present. Respect was the last word I expected to hear him utter. Respect even though I dressed like a man and allowed myself to touch his leg when we were alone? He seemed completely serious and still I found his words hard to believe.

"May I ask how old you are, Mrs. Johnson?"

My aching bones said I was a hundred and three. My experiences placed me even older. I didn't like the question.

"Twenty-three," I answered. "Why?"

"I'm twenty-three myself," he said. "But I've been a man since I was seven years old, when my Daddy died. I know what it's like for a woman to be left alone with no protector. Like my mother."

He let his eyes stray to the fire and continued talking without looking at me.

"My father was a fine man, Mrs. Johnson, what I can remember of him. He was tall, thin, with a nose shaped like the beak of a hawk. He came to this country from England, a Captain under the command of General Braddock. Fought with Captain Henry Harrison in the war with the French and Indians. A brave man who did his part and then settled down to being a planter."

The Major stopped, sighed, picked up a stray twig and threw it into the fire.

"When he died, he was a man of property and how he loved the red clay of Virginia. The crops that rose up from it too. He would walk with me at his side to inspect his long rows of corn. Every growing season he'd measure the corn's height against my own. 'John minus twelve,' he'd say when the corn was just getting started. 'John plus six,' he'd say as it climbed six inches higher than my head.

"He knew all the great men of his time in Virginia. Served in the House of Burgesses. Life was good when I was a boy, but everything changed when he died. My mother was bereft for over a year, roaming through the house like a woman possessed, sobbing, pulling at her clothes. Then she met and married David Collinsworth."

The name tumbled from his tongue with distaste.

"Mr. Collinsworth gave my mother only one thing, another son. Everything else he took and wasted until we had nothing at his death. My only education after that was from the blacksmith my mother bound me to when I was twelve. She had no other recourse and wanted to make sure that I could hold my own in the world. I served five years with him until I was drafted into the army."

Finally Major Cockrill turned his eyes to me. He had no tears in them, but his brows were drawn together in an expression of intense sorrow.

"I tell you this so you will know who I am, a man who will always respect a woman left alone in this world with children who lack a father's love."

All suitable responses flew from my mind. I watched dumbly while he stood as if to dismiss himself.

"I give you my good opinion, Mrs. Johnson, and I offer my protection."

I had been completely wrong about him. He had no thoughts of me as a wife. He thought of me in the way he thought of his mother! I had imagined a romance between us when it was only filial respect. He towered above me as he waited for a reply.

"I thank you, Major," I said woodenly.

Respect. Never had the word held such disappointment. Well, Charlotte could be both pleased and relieved. Respect. The very thing I had just asked of him, and yet his offering left me feeling as chilled as an icy rain. It had come to that. I was one hundred and three years old after all. I might as well take to wearing black dresses and heavy kerchiefs covering my head. Thank heavens he was unable to read my mind and the foolish thoughts I had entertained.

"We're much obliged," I added since he appeared to expect more.

"I hope I haven't offended you," he said without a trace of humor.

"It's high praise to be compared to a man's mother," I said, trying to avoid an ironic tone. "But I'm rather tired this evening, and it's time I gathered my daughters and prepared for sleep."

Major Cockrill nodded, picked up his hat and returned it to his head.

"And one more thing, Mrs. Johnson," he said, leaning close to my ear so that the brim of his hat brushed my hair. "Your hands are as graceful as white doves." With that startling remark, he straightened and walked away.

I shot a glance at my hands and saw only red skin and raw knuckles. But my heart flew.

# Eleven

MARCH 24, 1780 — *Day follows upon day, each more exhausting than the last. The rains continue to fall, swelling and strengthening the beast we call the Ohio. We have seen no Indians in this territory, and I thank the Lord for that, but neither have we seen many animals. Our food supply dwindles as our physical tasks increase.*

*Elizabeth spent the evening at our campsite last night. Although she is still pale, life is returning to her eyes. She has begun to talk of her husband which I take as a sign she looks forward rather than back. I'm sure she and Ephraim will have more babies, though none can ever replace the one they lost. They will always be haunted by thoughts of that tiny infant sunk deep in the river, lying on the cold rocks.*

*Yesterday Hugh Rogan shot a buffalo, but it was a traitor to its kind: lean and sinewy, with a tough hide that fought his hunter's knife. We might as well have eaten shoe leather for all the nourishment it provided.*

*I am willing to consider almost any possibility for food, even the bag of tulip bulbs that Charlotte keeps in her trunk. Their size and shape suggest onions which could be boiled for a soup, but the broth would only prove another bitter disappointment. Besides, those bulbs are the beginning of Charlotte's dream to bring forth flowers at our new home.*

*And she has brought precious seeds of another kind, seeds for a better and more civilized way of life: a matching lace cap and collar carefully packed away that she hopes will take root in the life to come and breed a world of fine houses and damask cloth upon the furniture. Oh, how she dreams. On the other hand, I consider items the color of brown dirt: wooden bowls, beds of oaken planks and hemp, tables the hue of an earthen floor. Only my quilts capture the brilliance of flowers.*

*I try hard to picture how my own dreams might come true the way Charlotte's will. The sole image that comes to mind is of my children growing healthy and strong. I certainly do not fill my head with thoughts of becoming a mother to Major C!*

On the fourth day of travel up the Ohio, I caught sight of a convergence of rivers ahead. At three o'clock we passed a large island on our left, and the new river swirled and kicked its way impudently into the wide waters of the Ohio. A storm further up the smaller river had stirred up sediment, and its waters entered with a murky rush and were quickly assimilated, a minnow eaten by a whale.

"Sound the horn, Colonel," I called. "I see a river ahead."

The new river was not what we had expected, so small in comparison to both the Ohio and the Tennessee. Somerset took my post, and I went to Donelson's side where his wife and Charlotte had joined him in observing the damaged shoreline ahead. Repeated floods must have been responsible for the fallen logs that lined the banks, some with enormous roots extending like writhing snakes.

"What do you think, Colonel?" I asked.

"Looks sort of puny to me," answered Mrs. Donelson, pinching together her dark eyebrows. "I thought Captain Robertson called this a good-sized river."

"It must be the Cumberland," said the Colonel. "I never heard of another one between the Tennessee and the Cumberland. Look at my map." He pointed to the much used piece of paper.

"I dare say we've seen a great deal on this trip we've never heard tell of," said Mrs. Donelson, pushing it aside. "The Tennessee River turned out to be twice as long as it shows on that."

"We'll try it anyway, won't we?" I asked. "We can't take much more of the Ohio."

"It's a friendlier river, I think," said Charlotte, "even with its muddy color."

"Friendly or not," I said. "I hope to heaven it's our river."

The Colonel marched about the deck making harrumping sounds, trying to decide what to do. We had been gone so long, that any wrong turn would demoralize the whole flotilla even further. I approached him with some trepidation, knowing he didn't want to be interrupted.

"Colonel," I began, clasping my hands behind me in an effort of restraint.

"Mrs. Johnson," he said before I could proceed. His face flushed darkly and instead of looking at me directly, his gaze focused on my neck, just below the chin. "I am fully aware of your desire to choose this river, but I am in charge, and I will make my decision in due course."

A hot retort rose in my throat, but I knew he wanted none of it, so I kept any further counsel to myself. At last the Colonel instructed Somerset to turn *The Adventure* up the new river but only until he could tie up at a clearing. The boat thrashed its way across the Ohio's current and plunged into the far milder waters of what I hoped was the Cumberland.

When the entire fleet had landed, the Colonel invited a few to join him as he sat on the trunk of a fallen tree to study the map. Captain Blackmore, John Junior, Hugh Rogan, Major Cockrill and Johnny C. sat with him while I walked the deck, waiting for his decision. Charlotte teased me, saying I might wear out the planks, but I couldn't stop. I knew the Colonel had decided when he stood and headed to *The Adventure*. To my surprise, Major Cockrill followed him.

"We've agreed to try it," Donelson said, removing his wide brimmed hat and slicking back his thin gray hair. "At least for a few miles."

He'd decided to raise *The Adventure's* sail for the first time of our voyage to take advantage of the prevailing winds, and since an unattended sail could bring trouble when the winds shifted, he asked the Major to help secure the lower corners of the sheet.

As we set off, John Junior and the Major raised the sail which slapped against the mast until it was tamed. Because it had been stored for months, its color was brighter than anything else aboard *The Adventure* and provided a symbol of hope as it billowed in the wind. Although we were still traveling upstream, the current was ever so much more gentle than the Ohio, and the boat relaxed into a slow and steady pace. I avoided the Major, concentrating instead on the banks which began to widen. The sun scattered on the sparkling surface and broke into a thousand pieces, as if God were lighting our way at last. After the dangerous shoals of the Tennessee and the fierce power of the Ohio, it seemed as if we had indeed found our way home, albeit a home we had never seen.

That night when we settled our camp beneath a stand of willows, Major Cockrill spread his bedding with the rest of us. I sat beside Charlotte at the fire and watched as Rachel Donelson brought him a bowl of watery soup. Her black hair was freshly braided, circling her head like a crown, and her cheeks dimpled charmingly. There was no chance the Major would think of Rachel as his mother. At thirteen, she was at the peak of prettiness, and even though the hardships of our trip had stripped the ripeness of her former beauty, nothing could change those dark eyes that promised fun and mystery.

My stomach ached from something even more unpleasant than hunger, a longing for my own lost girlhood. I must have been handsome myself when I was Rachel's age. David was not a man for compliments, but even he had described my red hair as brighter than the hearth's fire. And my waist was tiny before the children came. In fairness, it was still small but I was too thin from the rigors of the journey, not the bright flower I was as a girl. It was foolish to grieve for lost youth when so many people younger than I had actually lost their lives during the last few years. And I didn't like the uneasy thoughts brought on by Rachel's attention to the Major. She was doing nothing wrong. Why shouldn't a pretty young girl move gracefully before a young man, swaying her skirt, smiling prettily? Of course she should. And old matrons like me should watch from the shadows and make sure nothing came of it unless the man's intentions were honorable. That was the way it was, and I might as well get used to it.

I hastily slung the contents of my bowl into the fire and listened to its hiss as sparks exploded upwards. The thin gruel had made me feel worse than ever, and I couldn't bear the assault to my stomach.

"Ann," Charlotte said, grabbing my wrist. "What are you doing?"

"We wouldn't feed our pigs that slop," I said, shaking her off. "If we had any pigs."

"Someone else could have eaten that food. You should be ashamed," Charlotte added with exasperation.

I was ashamed of myself, but not because I hadn't eaten the miserable food.

"Tomorrow I'll catch a fish. Or shoot a deer," I vowed.

"Maybe you will or maybe you won't," said Charlotte. "But right now you are setting a poor example for your children. When will you grow up?"

When would I grow up? How could I be both old and young at the same time? And why was I in such a temper? Because

Rachel Donelson was younger and prettier than I? It was ridiculous. I was jealous, and I didn't like the feeling one bit. Maybe this was exactly how the devil worked, wormed his way into one's mind and seized the soul. I resolved to cast out the demon, and I found the feeling of righteous indignation improved my disposition immediately.

———

MARCH 30, 1780 — *We are almost sure that we sail the Cumberland since the river has widened. What we do not know is how long we must travel before we reach the French Lick. But as I say to the children, it won't be as long as it has been.*

*I have resolved to conduct myself in Major Cockrill's presence as if I am an elder member of our party. For the past few days I have practiced nodding gravely when he speaks. I do it quite well, but he seems a bit amused. Nevertheless, he will get used to my new ways and will be calling me "Granny" before the voyage is over. Charlotte has not commented on my new demeanor, but I'm sure it pleases her. She can relax her guard for awhile.*

*The children progress nicely with their reading. Polly is much taken with* Genesis *and the word "begat." Betsy has learned her letters and can count to ten. At night she lines up sticks before the fire and counts them as seriously as she would gold coins. Severn Donelson is intrigued with bloody battles and loves to read the story of David and Goliath. He has made a crude slingshot which he calls his flipper and hurls stones into the river at unseen Philistines. I try to keep the children as busy as possible to take their minds off the hunger.*

*Luck has been with us lately, and we have killed two buffalo. Their humps and tongues were particularly nourishing, but still our hunger is a constant presence. Three days ago John Junior killed a swan and was as proud of himself as if he had brought down a buffalo. We roasted the bird and the Colonel gave orders that it would be cut into pieces small enough that all aboard would have a taste. This made for very small portions, but it was the most delicious taste we have had for months.*

*Then only yesterday, Patsy the cook, spied vegetation growing in the river bottom which she thought to be edible greens. We dispatched a canoe to investigate, and they brought back fresh plants which some called "Shawnee Salad," and Patsy called "Ingun Patch." She cooked up a mess of those greens and never have I enjoyed anything so much. More important, we all had enough to eat until our bellies were full.*

*Colonel Donelson has been quite agitated lately since he bears the burdens and uncertainties for each of us. His concern deepens the furrows between his brows more and more. His face has lost a great deal of flesh since we began and his cheeks droop, giving him the aspect of a hound dog.*

*Yesterday the Colonel heard tell of a family whose name I will not reveal here. The rumor was that they were hiding a supply of corn on their boat and making bread for themselves alone. When we tied up for the night, the Colonel approached Mr. M. with the accusation. He protested in a loud voice that the Colonel could search every inch of his boat for corn and he would find nothing. Mrs. M. fairly cowered in a corner, and it was difficult to see whether guilt or fear was written on her dish-shaped face. The Colonel did not lower himself to search their boat, but reared up like a wounded bear and announced, "Woe to anyone who harbors food when children go hungry." Either the Colonel is changing or I am. My respect for him grows daily. Through our adversity he becomes stronger and as angry as the Old Testament God when he sees selfish behavior.*

**MARCH 31, 1780** — *We are living almost entirely on buffalo now, with only a little salt to make it palatable. I have taken to dreaming of food every night, but I guess that is better than having no food at all. Or dreaming of the Major. Last night we sang hymns to lift our spirits, and the music made our souls soar. The Major has a powerful baritone that rises over the others and seems to hang in the air. I joined*

*in the singing and felt I was participating in the music of the spheres,*
*of heavenly angels singing. It was a healing experience.*

*Maybe today I will see my brothers, not only Jamie but also Mark*
*and John. How long it has been since I've seen those dear faces.*

———

All morning we sailed without incident, but early in the afternoon Major Cockrill surprised us with a loud shout. He dropped his end of the sail and rushed to the Colonel's side, waving in excitement. What caught his attention was a sight we had not witnessed since leaving Fort Patrick Henry. White men. Lined up on the riverbank were five holding survey equipment, their horses tied behind them. A thrill spread through our party as we shouted and hugged one another in happiness. This was the sign we had waited for, the proof we were indeed on the Cumberland River. All the boats in the flotilla followed *The Adventure* toward the shore, darting as swiftly as a school of fish toward food.

I recognized the tall gray-haired man in the center as Colonel Richard Henderson who had bought the Cumberland territory from the Indians and started our long endeavor. Two of the others were Henderson's brothers Pleasant and Nathaniel, and a fourth was Nathaniel Hart. The fifth man I recognized as my childhood friend, Sam Butler, who had left for the Cumberland long before we had.

*The Adventure* hit the shore, joined swiftly by the other boats and Colonel Donelson was the first person to go over the side, followed by Charlotte and me. Colonel Henderson abandoned all the severe trappings of his former life as a judge, and impulsively grabbed Donelson by the shoulders as soon as he was within reaching distance.

"We feared you were lost forever, sir," said Henderson, his long, thin face as creased as a leather pouch. His mix of sandy and gray hair stood up like porcupine quills.

"By George," answered Donelson, "I wondered about that myself."

I threw my arms around Sam's neck and hugged him for all I was worth. It was almost as if I were seeing my own brothers. As much as I wanted to talk with him, however, I wanted even more to hear what Colonel Henderson had to say about Jamie and the others. So we joined the crowd pressing around Henderson. Charlotte was quick to question him, her face filled with apprehension.

"My husband, Captain Robertson?" she asked breathlessly. "Have you heard tell of him?"

Henderson rewarded Charlotte with a wide smile. "I'm please to tell you 'Mam, that he and his party arrived at the French Lick on Christmas Day," he said, gently taking her hand in his. "All present and accounted for."

Charlotte was unable to speak at first, but then cried out with a vivacity she hadn't shown in months.

"James is safe! Oh praise God. And Jonathan and all the others too!"

"One thing's changed however," he added. "Your husband's a Captain no longer. The people have promoted him to Colonel and elected him leader of the new settlement."

Charlotte's face filled with animation. "Tell me everything," she said.

Henderson firmly shook his head in the affirmative, but Sam stepped forward to continue the story.

"I was there just two weeks ago," he said. "Colonel Robertson is well except for worry over you and this party. As soon as he sees you, his heart will be eased."

Sam was a fur trapper who had ventured to the Cumberland country because of the great quantity of beaver, but had lately joined Henderson in his surveying activities as a chain carrier. All the girls found him very handsome, his dark curly hair caught with a deer hide strap, his eyes the color of bluest sky. But I still saw him as the boy I had grown up with, my younger brother Mark's best friend.

"Is there corn at the Lick?" I asked him. "The corn Jamie planted last year?"

"I'm afraid not. What corn the buffalo didn't trample, the Indians got."

"There's no bread then?" Charlotte asked, her joy tempered somewhat.

"Not yet," he replied. "But they've planted more corn. A new crop's coming."

"I do have some good news about corn," said Colonel Henderson, taking charge of the conversation. "Earlier this very month I asked my friend William Bailey Smith to bring hundreds of bushels of corn to the French Lick."

"Hundreds?" asked Charlotte, as if she couldn't imagine such abundance.

"I raised most of it myself,' added Nathaniel Hart. "It's rich country out here, Mrs. Robertson. It won't be long before hunger's just a bad dream of the past."

So our dreams might come true after all. The overland party had actually arrived at the Lick and was preparing for us. And they had been there for three months, time to build cabins if the Indians had given them a chance.

"And cabins?" I asked. "Can we expect those?"

Henderson explained that because of the extreme cold and rain, there were few cabins, but progress was improving with the advent of spring. Most were being built within the perimeter of a stockade, but some were scattered within several miles of the new fort. He answered other questions as well: how long the rains had lasted in the Cumberland country, how much game we could expect to find between our present location and the French Lick. He assured us that our party would reach our destination before the month of April was up, no more than thirty days. The distance was longer than we had hoped, but its length was certain for the first time, and we were grateful.

When Colonel Henderson had finished answering questions, I pulled Sam aside to tell me more of all he had seen. He described the location of the new camp they were calling "The Bluffs," which the men were building atop a hill that rose sharply above the Cumberland River, sixty feet of chalky stone. It was an excellent spot for protection against the Indians, he explained, since the river formed a natural barrier against attack.

"And they're all alive," I repeated. "You're positive?"

"Alive as that red hair of yours," he said. "You've got the garden spot of all the Cumberland for your home. And I've seen it from one end to the other."

Sam himself had decided to remain in the Cumberland Country and had already built a cabin at Eaton's Station.

"Is that near the Bluffs?" I asked. But before he could answer, Major Cockrill interrupted us, obviously wishing an introduction.

" This is Major Cockrill, Sam. A . . . family friend."

"Always glad to meet a friend of Annie's," Sam said enthusiastically, using the name he had called me since we were children. Cockrill shook his proffered hand stiffly.

"I expect Eaton's Station is a far piece from the French Lick," said Major Cockrill. "Hard to get to."

"Less than two miles," said Sam. "And it's downstream if you're coming from the Bluffs. Takes no time at all."

"Neighbors indeed," I said with pleasure. Sam Butler might think of me as his sister, but at least he didn't regard me as his mother.

"You'll like this country, Annie. We've had a hard winter, but you're here in time to see the forests come alive. The buffalo at the Bluffs are so plentiful they've made wide roads on their way to the salt lick. In some places they've carved out paths two feet deep and four feet across. And in the trees are flocks of red-billed parrakeets."

"Oh Sam, you make it sound like Eden," I said.

"Just waiting for an Eve," he added.

At that remark Major Cockrill jerked his head back, as if he'd been struck.

"Guess we shouldn't tarry here then," he said with deliberation. "Not with Eden in the offing. I'll speak to the Colonel and we'll be off as soon as possible," said Cockrill.

"Before you go maybe you'd like some good peach brandy?" Sam suggested, returning his eyes to me. "Made it myself."

"I'm not one for spirits, Sam. But maybe one day a drop or two won't hurt me," I answered.

"Till then," he said, gesturing as if he were drinking a toast.

"Well, I must be going," the Major said, turning abruptly on his heel and striding off.

"A man in a hurry," said Sam smiling.

"And it came on him rather suddenly too," I answered, trying to look very serious.

We returned to our boats in short order, no less hungry, but cheered to know that our loved ones waited safely in the new land. As I walked toward *The Adventure*, I was joined by Elizabeth who seemed in a state of ecstasy.

"Ephraim is alive," she said, "Did you hear it?"

I took her outstretched hand to warm it between my own two palms.

"Oh, Honey. They're all alive. Waiting for us. Our faith has been rewarded."

Elizabeth shook her head with enthusiasm as we stood in a puddle of sun at the water's edge. Anyone watching us might think we were poised for fiddle music to kick off a dance. And maybe we were.

# Twelve

APRIL 1, 1780 — *If all proceeds as we expect, we shall arrive at our new home this very month. I know we will survive until that time since we have come so far already. Last night we camped near the mouth of a small river with rich bottom land in every direction, land anyone would be proud to own. In fact, Hugh Rogan discovered a pair of hand millstones that had been set up for grinding corn and later abandoned. But why?*

*I ran my hand over the rough stones, asking for their owners' stories. Had Indians killed the settlers at this deserted site, or did they manage to escape with their lives? How many had lived here? How long ago? The stones remained mute as stones always do, but my mind spun out a tale of families slaughtered in this isolated spot. I don't know why I had such terrible thoughts, except that an eerie sadness seemed to permeate the place. I must not dwell on sadness when so much good will soon come our way.*

*In fact, there is positive news already. Elizabeth is more herself, and her mother has lost the pallor that matched her gray eyes for so long. She is charged with new energy as she anticipates reuniting with her son, Edmund. And Nancy's leg has healed to the point where she limps only slightly. These improvements occur in spite of hunger that still gnaws at us daily, its effects making it difficult for me to write. Perhaps because of her need for food, little Charlotte cried throughout last night, although Charlotte always feeds her first. Whatever the cause of her misery, her loud wails spoke for each of us.*

*I must rein in my thoughts from the bad and concentrate on the good. It was such a relief to come upon Colonel Henderson yesterday and to hear that all our men arrived safely. Although Henderson has aged since last I saw him, he is still a fine figure of a man at the age of forty-five. Charlotte says he is the most ambitious gentleman she has ever known. Jamie is ambitious too, but while Henderson pursues building wealth, Jamie pursues building community. A vast difference.*

*I must say, if I didn't know differently, I would think that Major Cockrill showed signs of jealousy over my old friend Sam's attention. But why do I even mention such a trivial idea? What fools we mortals be! This mortal, at least.*

**APRIL 14, 1780** — *It has been a fortnight since I last wrote. Two days ago we lost more of our party as Moses Renfroe and his group left us at the Red River. I hope it is not called red because of blood from previous settlers. Again I am drawn to a negative conclusion, but we have seen so much trouble, and the length of our trip wears us all down. Somehow the nearness of our goal unravels the nerves.*

*Charlotte's concern over little Charlotte has added to her general agitation. Her relief in discovering that Jamie and Jonathan are alive has been followed rapidly by an increase of other worries. It is an odd thought for me to have, but removing one big problem to discover other small ones reminds me of removing ticks from a dog. Sometimes when one removes a big tick, a swarm of baby ticks lies underneath, just the way a big problem sometimes hides a horde of little ones. And those problems, like the ticks, burrow in and suck the spirit.*

*Now that I know my brothers are safe, I begin to wonder about my own life in this new country. We have many lone women in our party, but most of them have husbands waiting. Even now their men are splitting logs and building cabins in preparation for their wives' arrival. They have planted seeds for corn to feed their families, and they tend cows that will give milk to their babes.*

*Of course I know Jamie will always provide for me. He shares his pocket on my behalf as surely as he shares his love. He has been like a father to me for as long as I can remember, and I am truly grateful. But as dear as a brother's love is, it cannot take the place of a husband. Although I still wear David's clothes, they comfort me less and less. In fact, I sometimes feel they have become a sham. Yes, I wear these clothes in remembrance, but the deerskin is no longer supple the way it was when he was alive. The color fades even as his memory does. Does God takes these precious memories from me as a gift to avoid further suffering, or as a punishment to teach me I should not be so attached to the things of this world? A mystery I ponder in my heart.*

*Only the children bring me out of myself. They seem to have forgotten life before their existence on this boat, and go about their work and play as if being confined to these four corners is as natural as breathing air. Thank God for that. They have made such progress in reading and writing during the voyage, that I suppose their confinement has been a Godsend to their education. They wouldn't have held still for so much learning otherwise.*

*This same confinement has no effect on my relationship with Major Cockrill. Although we have the opportunity to observe each other in all things, we speak little. Some days when he trades his duty at the sail for the poles, I take note how his long years spent at the blacksmith's trade have readied him for the task. I admire his abilities, but my lips fall silent in his presence.*

**APRIL 23, 1780** — *A new development has taken place in the last week. Although the Major avoids looking directly at me, he has taken to spending time each evening entertaining my children with stories. After our paltry meal, he invites Charity onto his lap while*

*Polly and Betsy arrange themselves on either side of him. They study the fire for animal shapes and call out what creatures they see in the flames. The Major weaves these animals into a tale that delights the girls until bedtime.*

*This ritual began last week. Night had fallen and a full moon illumined our camp site. Even as the moonlight brightened the clearing where we camped, it made the shadows in the woods seem even darker. Wolves in the far distance howled in mournful tones, their calls setting our dogs to barking in a fierce answer. The children feared the dogs were barking at Indians who lurked in the dark beyond our fires. Nothing I could do would lessen their terror. That was when the Major approached and devised his game with pictures in the fire. Every night since that time they have delighted as he repeats his performance. Then he sings a full bodied rendition of Mr. Watts' song for children which he croons softly until they curl into sleep.*

> Hush my dear, lie still and slumber
> Holy angels guard thy bed.
> Heavenly blessings without number
> Gently falling on thy head.

*The tenderness of these moments affects me greatly. I find tears stirring deep inside, fountains hidden in underground caves.*

It was late in the afternoon when we came upon Eaton's Station, the first fort we had seen in almost four months. It was a structure similar to the ones we left behind, with a stockade fence fifteen feet high, each picket pointed at the top to discourage Indian assaults. The familiar blockhouses sat at each corner: tall square buildings looming above the stockade, providing lookout stations and excellent vantage points from which to defend the fort. Colonel Donelson rang the ship's bell himself and had Somerset fire the four pounder to celebrate the occasion. Men and women dashed through the fort's gate at the sound, scattered along the river bank, and shouted to us.

"Is it the French Lick?" asked Polly, leaning over the side of the boat.

"Not yet," I replied as Major Cockrill came to stand beside me. "But Mr. Butler told us it's only two miles away."

"Major Cockrill," said Betsy joining us. "I bet there are real cabins inside the fort, with real beds!"

"Bet so," he replied, patting her blond curls.

"When we have our own beds, will you still sing us to sleep?" Betsy asked, looking at him with pleading eyes, putting her small hand in his big one.

"The Major will have his own home," I said. "We can't be bothering him like that. Now come over here."

Betsy reluctantly removed her hand from the Major's and shuffled to my side.

"But we could still play the animal game," said Polly, "Couldn't we?"

"We'll talk about this later," I said. "Now you girls find Peyton and Delilah so we can be ready to go ashore. Scoot now!"

Polly and Betsy scampered to the cabin where the Robertson children played a game of make believe.

"I'm sorry," I said to the Major. "They've come to think of you as a playmate. I'm afraid you've spoiled them mightily."

"That was my aim," he answered.

"Once my girls get a thought in their heads, they're like dogs worrying a bone."

"Wonder where they get those hard-headed ways?" he replied, surveying the river bank.

"I wouldn't know," I answered, wondering if he had insulted or complimented me. He turned to stare most intently into my eyes, as if he had asked me a question and waited for an answer. All around us people scurried, preparing to land at the fort, Somerset unwinding the rope to toss overboard, the children shoving one another to be in the best position to exit. All the while, the Major and I stood still, as if we had created our own island in the midst of havoc.

"Mrs. Johnson," he started but added nothing more.

"What is it Major?" I asked.

"I'd like to speak with you this evening, after the children are asleep."

"What's wrong?" I asked nervously in response to his gravity. "Please tell me now."

"It's nothing of concern," he said. "I hope," he added, increasing my alarm.

"Then tell me, Major, for heaven sakes," I said, breaking my eyes away from his and studying the deck.

"I'd be much obliged if we could speak later," he said. "I don't want to talk in the midst of all this."

He gestured to the activity that surrounded us. I didn't want to wait, but there was nothing I could do about it. Of course I didn't want him to reveal some deeply private thought in front of all the others. But why hadn't he waited until that evening to say something rather than giving me apprehension for hours to come? Hadn't I been plagued with enough waiting?

The Major left me to join Somerset and the others as they prepared to land the boat. Now that we were closer, I could see the smiling faces waiting to greet us, many of whom were our former neighbors from the Holston. I recognized an old friend in the crowd, Sarah Lattimer, who had joined me many a morning to milk the cows. She was short and round, with blond curls springing from her head. I jumped to shore and grabbed my old friend.

"Ann, Ann," Sarah squealed, returning my hug and then holding me at arm's length. "Let me look at you. Mercy, you poor thing. You are skinnier than ever!"

"And you've stayed as plump as a Christmas goose," I said laughing at Sarah's enthusiasm. "How did you ever manage it?"

"Bear oil," said Sarah proudly. "Better than mother's milk." With that she danced in a little circle, showing off every pound.

"I guess we wasted our time feeling sorry for you people who went by land," I said with my hands on my hips. "Your journey was no trouble at all."

"What a thing to say," replied Sarah with a little pout. "I deserve every bit of sympathy you can give me. Don't forget I walked almost every step of the way from Fort Patrick Henry, while you came cruising down the river on a pleasure boat."

"Pleasure? Oh Sarah. If you only knew," I said, the fun hissing out of me at once.

"We had to huddle under our tents at night," continued Sarah, not noticing the change in my demeanor. "And sleep next to our cows for warmth!" said Sarah. "Fancy that. It took me weeks to quit smelling like old Bossy."

"And Indians? What about them?" I asked.

"Didn't see a one. We traveled through their hunting grounds, but who would hunt in a winter like this one? I'm sure they stayed close to their warm fires."

"The Indians we saw were pleased to hunt," I said. "They hunted us."

"You don't mean it!" said Sarah, noticing my tone at last. "Tell me everything."

And so I recounted the terrible stories, the slaughter of the Stuarts, the tragedy of the Jennings party, and all the other trials we had endured.

"Merciful God in heaven," cried Sarah. "What a terrible voyage! You get those daughters of yours into our cabin and let me pour them a pitcher full of milk. It's been too long since they had a proper meal. Come on now."

Nothing could have pleased me more as we followed her for

an abundant meal: milk, eggs, bacon, chicken and warm, succulent corn pone topped with mounds of butter. I had never known a better feast.

Colonel Donelson decided we should stay at Eaton's Station for the night to ensure a fresh start for our final two miles. We joined our former neighbors for fine dinners and protected sleeping quarters, some in tents, some in cabins, but all within the safe confines of a newly constructed stockade.

That night around a large campfire in the center of the fort's acre enclosure, the talk swiftly turned to the future threat of Indians in the Cumberland Valley. The Eaton party was greatly disturbed to hear our stories of atrocities. They had been lulled by their own experience to think Indian battles were a thing of the past. I sat with Sarah, but could barely concentrate on the conversation for thinking of Major Cockrill's request for a talk that evening. I wasn't sure what I wanted him to say; I just wanted it over and done. It was only when Frederick Stump rose to address the group that I turned my attention to something other than the Major. I knew that Stump considered himself an expert on Indians, so I was interested in what he might say.

Stump was in his mid-fifties, and as he strutted before the fire, he looked like an old tree stump himself, gnarled and twisted, but with a dynamism that drew my full attention.

"I know Indians," he said, slamming his fist against his palm. "And my advice to you," he continued, "is to always see them before they see you."

I considered this observation less than brilliant, but he went on to tell about his first encounter with Shawnees twelve years before when he lived in Pennsylvania. He was at home on a bright moonlit night, settled in for the evening, his servants returned to their cabins, his wife sleeping quietly by his side.

"And then I heard the yelps and screams of savages as they slammed at my door with their tomahawks. Drunk as skunks they were, but still strong enough to hack their infernal way into my house. I ran to the hearth where we kept the meat axe and turned to face those monsters, prepared to defend my home to the last breath."

With this remark he threw his body into a crouch, as if he could see the Indians coming through the door at that very moment, fire in their eyes and blood in their hearts.

"My wife had rolled under the bed. Thank the good Lord she couldn't see what happened next, for it was a bloody scene. Let me tell you Brothers, at the end of that fight, nine Indians lay dead at my feet, and this old hide of mine bore twenty-seven wounds. Two of those devils got away, but the next morning I tracked them down, cut their throats, and sent their souls straight to hell."

He stood as straight as his twisted body would allow.

"And do you know what I got for my pains? How my Quaker neighbors rewarded me for ridding those parts of murderous savages?" He swaggered in front of us. "They threw me in jail! How do you like that? Thank the heavens there were enough sane men in those parts to help me. A mob of 2,000 fellows broke me out, and I've not been back to those parts since. Those Quakers take brotherly love too serious.

"But I give you my word this night. I don't plan to move again. This is where I take my stand and no golldarn Indians are going to run me from this place. Like I say, if I can see them first, I can out shoot 'em, outrun 'em and out climb 'em. Keep your eyes peeled, Fellows, is all I got to say."

"Old blowhard," Sarah whispered, shaking her curly head. "I've heard enough from that old man to last me until I'm grayheaded without a tooth in my mouth."

Happily, one of the Eaton party began to fiddle, his bow speeding faster and faster, and the group joined in singing, as if to blow away Stump's bloody words. Polly and Delilah kicked their legs high in the firelight, locking arm to arm. What a relief it was to see my most solemn daughter so joyful.

Then Sarah poked my side.

"Who is that man staring at you?' she asked.

I assumed it was Major Cockrill although I couldn't see him in the darkness.

"Over there," Sarah poked again. "On the other side."

I squinted into the fire's brightness and saw Cockrill singing.

"Well?" said Sarah. "He's not one of ours."

"Major Cockrill," I answered, feeling a blush spread over my face.

"Looks like you put a spell on him," said Sarah mischievously.

"Don't be silly," I replied.

"I mean it. That man couldn't be worse off if a snake dug fangs into his leg."

"That's a pretty way to put it," I said defensively. "The Major and I are friends."

Sarah whooped. "And I'm a three-eyed pony," she said. "Do you think he's gonna sit there mooney-eyed all night or come over here and talk?"

"Looks to me like he's enjoying himself just where he is," I said.

"Looks to me like he's slack-jawed and mouthing his words. Motion for him to come," said Sarah.

"No," I said. "I'm not going to intrude on his privacy."

"Then I will," said Sarah, standing.

"No, Sarah. No!"

But I had no effect on Sarah who waved her hands, gesturing for the Major to join us, and to my distress he got up.

"Now look what you've done," I said.

"You said he was your friend. I'm being neighborly, is all," added Sarah.

The muscles tensed in my neck. What was he going to do now? Surely to God he wouldn't say anything personal in front of Sarah. It would be like informing every man, woman and child in the fort.

"Evening, Mrs. Johnson," he said, his voice low and melodic. Sarah stared at me impatiently, waiting to be introduced.

"My friend, Sarah Lattimer," I said reluctantly. "Major Cockrill."

"How do you do, Major," said Sarah. "You sit down right here, make yourself comfortable and tell me all about yourself. Will your wife be following you here to the Cumberland?" I wanted to throttle her.

"I have no wife Miss Lattimer," he said smiling. "I can tell Mrs. Johnson's told you nothing about me."

"She only told me about the terrible things that happened, not about any nice gentlemen," said Sarah, looking at the Major as if he were a dish of bear stew.

"It was a river trip, Sarah. Not a social," I said.

"Goodness gracious. I can't think of anything more social than being together, day in and day out, for four months."

"And you, Miss Lattimer. Where might you be from?" asked the Major, giving me some hope that he might shift the topic of conversation.

"Oh, Virginia, like almost everyone. My parents decided to come here to make their fortune, and what else could I do? Mother needs me to help with the little ones, so here I am."

She looked at the Major, waiting for more pleasant repartee, but he said nothing.

"Of course I'm hoping to have children myself someday," Sarah continued, keeping the conversation going. After an uncomfortable pause the Major spoke.

"Excuse me, Miss Lattimer. But I'm going to steal away Mrs. Johnson. I've grown attached to her girls, and I want to discuss them for a moment."

"Why certainly Major," said Sarah. "I'm sure talking about the children is the perfect thing to do on a beautiful night when the stars are scattered in the sky like a fist full of jewels. Don't let me stop you."

She shooed us off as if we were a pair of errant chickens. "Go on. Go on. Get!"

As we walked across the fort yard, people spilled in and out of the few cabins that had been built. Most of the assembled company still sang by the camp fire, but others paraded in the open space, chasing children, playing with dogs, drinking whisky, and laughing at private jokes.

The Major led me to a corner of the fort nearest one of the blockhouses where he came to an abrupt stop and turned to face me. Although the air had finally lost its deep winter chill, the wind was still cool against my face, and my body quickly lost the fire's warmth. The Major's wide brow was crimped and his eyes wore a distressed expression.

"Is something wrong with the girls?" I asked.

"So far as I know they're fine," he said. "It's not the girls I want to talk about. Or maybe it is, but not exactly."

His agitation easily transmitted to me, and I also grew edgy and concerned. He was usually so calm that to see him like this was distressing.

"When I was a boy in Virginia," he began, "before my Daddy died, I can remember fine houses brightened at night by a hundred candles. The women wore dresses of silk, and the men powdered wigs."

I thought I would scream. What was he talking about? Surely he had not made such a commotion to tell me of his boyhood life.

"I wish we were in such a room tonight," he said.

"Major, we're lucky to be alive and safe within this fort."

He nodded gravely. "But in a room with all the civilities of life my words might come more easily. I could pass you a cup of tea and ask you how much sugar you required."

I searched his face in disbelief. Here was a man of action unable to say the simplest thing.

"Peach brandy is a more suitable drink here, one that helps to loosen the tongue," I said.

"You're thinking of Mr. Butler?" asked the Major.

"No, I'm thinking of peach brandy."

"But Mr. Butler seems to have adapted quite well to the frontier life, don't you think?" said Cockrill.

"You brought me here to talk of Sam?" I asked impatiently.

"He's the last person I want to discuss," said Cockrill, turning away.

"Major Cockrill, all evening I have anticipated our conversation. You led me to believe you had something important to say."

"And I apologize, Mrs. Johnson. I'm afraid I was mistaken."

Mistaken? I had waited nervously all day for this! My apprehension turned to anger.

"And that's all you have to tell me?"

"I'm afraid so," he said, staring at the distant fires.

I wanted to shake him until the words tumbled out.

"Then I'll be getting back to Sarah and the others," I said instead.

"Of course," he replied, stepping back to clear a path.

"In the future Sir, I hope you will spare me this needless worry," I said, acid tinging my voice as I marched past him. He only nodded as I went by.

Well, didn't that just beat all! Here I had endured all that agitation for no reason whatsoever. What was he thinking? That just because he had been good to my children he had earned the privilege of tormenting me? He had been ready to speak his mind until Sam's name had dropped into the conversation with as much welcome as a spider dropping into a cup of milk.

Oh, it was too frustrating to bear. Major Cockrill had been on the threshold of saying something important, and had let the mere mention of peach brandy dissuade him. If he was put off so easily from declaring his love, then it wasn't a love worth having. But maybe he had been ready to declare no such thing. Maybe he had planned to discuss new stories he wanted to tell the children. How was I to know? By the time I had reached my place beside Sarah, I was in a terrible temper and threw myself to the ground. She eyed me warily.

"You look as mad as a bee-stung bull," said Sarah. "He must have talked about the children after all."

"He didn't talk about anything," I said. "So there's nothing to report."

" Oh, Honey," said Sarah. "That's the worst kind of conversation."

"I told you Major Cockrill was a friend. No more than that."

"I don't know what happened, but the way he was looking at you this evening was not the way a man looks at a friend," said Sarah.

"You are apparently wrong. Now I don't want to discuss it further," I said, picking up a large stone and throwing it into the fire. The stone shattered a hollow log and released a spray of sparks.

"Don't worry, Honey," said Sarah, patting me on the back. "You've got a couple of hundred men waiting for you at The Bluffs. The Major will have to get in line."

The image of men lining up to court me, a widow with three children, made me laugh out loud. Why in the world was I letting myself stew about the Major when tomorrow we would arrive at the French Lick? Our journey was about to end, and I would see my dear brothers at last. I turned to Sarah who studied me closely for a response to her prediction.

"Oh, Sarah. How can I be unhappy? We're coming to the promised land. Home at last!"

# Thirteen

APRIL 24, 1780 — *As I lie on the bed with Sarah, the scent of freshly hewn wood from the cabin's wall mingles with the smell of dying embers. The dim light of morning reveals the corner of Sarah's mouth turning upwards in a smile. I smile back at her because she is as full of goodness as she is of mischief. Last night after cheering me, she gave each of my girls a spoonful of honey with the promise it would bring them sweet dreams. I hope she had her own sweet dreams.*

*Outside somewhere Major Cockrill, is sleeping or maybe already awake. How can I look at his face today without embarrassment? I must conduct myself with dignity. I will consider how Charlotte might act under these circumstances and let her behavior be my guide. Of course, Charlotte would never have gotten into such a predicament in the first place.*

*Maybe Sarah is right about the unmarried men at the French Lick. I suppose a great many anxiously await our arrival, and maybe it's my destiny to remarry. At least my future lies within the short space of two miles, and I shall know soon enough.*

❦

Sarah's mother rose to poke the fire and add more logs, the noise setting the household in movement. The baby cried, the children turned under their covers, stretching, emitting yawns. Mr. Lattimer rolled from his bed fully clothed, took his gun from its place above the hearth, and left without a word. I slipped from the bed and followed him to get my first glimpse of the long awaited day.

Recently my hunger had dulled my senses to the beauty of the April woods, but now with a full stomach I could appreciate the spring in all its loveliness: the vibrant pink of the red bud trees still lingering in the forest, the rising sun igniting cloud banks with a peachy glow. Robins danced on the branches of a tall cedar just outside the stockade, and I had my first sighting of a parakeet, yellow with a touch of red. Never had the world looked so bright, and I was joyous in spite of the previous night's conversation with the Major.

People milled about the fort yard, and I spotted him kicking dirt into his fire to extinguish it, looking perfectly miserable: a fact which pleased me no end. The sound of a horn drew my eyes from the Major to the center of the enclosure where Colonel Donelson motioned for us to assemble. Charlotte appeared at the door of Amos Eaton's cabin where she and her children had spent the night and crossed the fort yard holding the hand of young Charlotte who was extremely pale, a slight bluish tinge to her lips. Thank heavens we were almost home so she could get proper nourishment every day.

"Mr. Eaton sent a man to the Bluffs last night with news of our arrival," said Charlotte, smiling. "I wish I could have seen James' face when he heard."

"And today you will see it, Charlotte," I said. "Think of it."

Elizabeth and her mother joined us. She had finally discarded her smocks of pregnancy and wore a blue skirt of woven flax covered with a short gown of blue and white striped linen. The garments were simple but served to highlight her recaptured beauty. Mrs. Jennings smiled at her daughter, obviously grateful that Elizabeth bloomed like the spring.

"Can you believe it?" said Elizabeth. "I'm going to be with Ephraim this very day."

"And I'll see my son Edmund," added her mother.

"And dear Edmund, of course," Elizabeth said.

Given the terrible news Elizabeth had to impart, I knew the meeting with Ephraim would be bittersweet, but they would be reunited, and what pleasure that would bring.

"Edmund has our livestock with him," said Mrs. Jennings. "Even the rooster and laying hens. I'm hoping he'll have a bushel full of eggs to feed us when we get there."

Our group clustered in the fort yard before Donelson, and we hastened to join them.

"Friends, I know you're as ready to be on your way as I am. And I'm sure I speak for all when I say a word of thanks to the good people of Eaton's Station for taking us in. They can count on receiving the same hospitality whenever they come to visit."

Applause and shouting broke out and the Colonel raised his hand for silence.

"Just give us a little while to build up our liquor supply."

Whistles and shouts greeted his last remark and someone in the crowd played a run on his fiddle which brought more laughter.

"We will reach the end of our voyage in a matter of hours, and I am more sure than ever that God intended us to embark on this effort," the Colonel continued. "He has sent us on a special mission: to bring civilization to this rich and blessed land."

Donelson slowly lifted his arm and pointed to the forest beyond the fort's walls.

"As all of you know, the cane grows only on the richest soil, and we can see canebrakes thriving all around us, God's message of fertile fields and the promise of abundant crops."

He glanced at the solid blue sky that held not the smallest cloud, and continued, as if he had just received a message from the heavens. He brought his hands together, palms touching in the posture of prayer, and bowed his head.

"For God has led us to this land of milk and honey, even as he led the Israelites to their promised land. And we will take His blessings and use them in His name."

"Amen," Donelson finished. A resounding "amen" followed from the assembled crowd.

"And now," he said raising his head. "Let's go home."

A loud communal shout greeted his words, as we broke up to prepare for our exodus. I hurried to the Lattimer cabin to gather my children and to secure a promise from Sarah to come visit soon. The Major was already on *The Adventure* helping to raise the sail for departure when we came aboard, and Betsy raced to his side.

"Major Cockrill!" she shouted, tugging on his trouser leg. "God sent us to the right place. Last night we had milk and honey!"

"Good for you!" he shouted over his shoulder.

"Stand back, Betsy," I called. "The Major has work to do."

Polly skipped toward her sister.

"Remember who we get to see today," said Polly.

"Uncle James. And Uncle Mark and John," said Betsy, counting to three on her fingers.

"And somebody else," said Polly.

"Daddy?" asked Betsy, her eyes searching Polly's face with great expectation.

"No," said Polly, unhappily. "We get to see our cow, Miss Priss."

"You don't get to see Daddy till we get to heaven," I added, kneeling beside Betsy.

"Oh," she said sadly. But then she brightened. "You know Mama, I think I can smell Miss Priss already."

"Well, maybe you can," I said. "If you sniff really hard."

The boats shoved off in rapid succession and in less than two hours we saw a steep bluff on the southwest side of the river, covered with a dense forest of cedar trees and privet bushes and crowned by the new fort standing on the precipice. A mineral spring flowed from within the fort and tumbled down the bluff's side. Since our friends were alerted to our arrival, I counted five scouts outside the palisades keeping watch for us. They were soon joined by others who made their way down to the river's edge. As we neared the shore, I could make out Jamie's shape, his servant, Henry, standing behind him. Also unmistakable were the Peyton twins, Ephraim and John, whose copper hair glinted in the sunlight. More and more men appeared on the shore until a hundred crowded the banks to greet us.

At the bow Charlotte had lined up her children according to size: Randolph, Peyton, Delilah and little Charlotte in her arms. They waved to their father as well as their twelve-year-old brother, Jonathan, who stood beside Jamie. Colonel Donelson was also at the bow, surrounded by his family. He looked as proud as if his wife had just given him another child, and it was a birth of sorts. He had seen us through our most difficult days and brought us safely home. I had been harsh in my judgment of him but had gradually gained respect for his unfailing commitment and fortitude. He had made mistakes, but so did every living person.

I crossed the deck to thank him, and he returned my thanks with a smile that transformed his weary expression.

"He's a natural born leader," said Mrs. Donelson. "I've said it before and I'll say it 'til the day I die." She beamed at her husband as if he were Moses himself.

"And thank you for teaching the children," the Colonel returned graciously. "Every time Severn shoots his slingshot, I'll be reminded of you . . . in addition to David and Goliath."

"Prepare for landing," ordered Major Cockrill who was now at the tiller guiding the boat to its most important docking yet. Somerset moved in front of the Donelsons, ready to throw the rope. No sooner had we struck the earth than Severn Donelson scrambled over the side to be the first to set foot on the new land. Randolph Robertson followed and was immediately grabbed by both his father and brother. Within minutes we were swallowed into the community of men who welcomed us with embraces, shouts, and even a few tears. Someone struck up a tune on a Jew's harp, and a young boy ran down the bluff banging a drum of buffalo hide. In short, it was a reunion that lived up to our grandest expectations.

My children joined their cousins and uncles, and I watched Mark pick up Betsy and swing her twice in a wide circle. I had a special fondness for Mark, mainly because he was the family member closest to my age and temperament. He was only a little taller than I, with light brown hair and a face that still held a sprinkling of freckles like my own. After spinning Betsy, he picked up Charity, tucked her under his arm as if she were a sack of potatoes, and then pulled Polly to his side in a bear hug.

Jamie grasped Charlotte in a tight embrace that was touching to see. He was dressed in his finest clothes to mark the occasion, the three piece suit Charlotte had made of linsey-woolsey, dyed blue with Indigo. The coat, accented with covered buttons, hung to the bottom of his knee breeches and white wool socks covered his calves. The whole outfit was set off with shiny oval brass buckles on his black shoes. Jamie was not as tall as the Major, but tall enough at five feet ten inches to command respect in the community. I admired his long straight nose and clear blue eyes, and was fond of the way his dark hair tumbled across his forehead. Watching the tenderness between Jamie and Charlotte, I turned instinctively toward the stern where I had last seen Major Cockrill. When I saw him walking toward me, however, I climbed over the gunwale to join my family.

My brother John, the tallest of the boys, blond haired and thin as a post rail, broke through the crowd to give me my first welcoming embrace.

"Look at you, girl! Still in pants. I knew those Indians wouldn't bother killing someone they couldn't tell was a boy or a girl," said John. "Lord Almighty."

Mark grabbed me next and twirled me just as he had spun Betsy.

"Put me down, you silly goose," I said, hammering his back lightly with my fists.

"Gander," Mark corrected, setting me down and surveying me just as John had done.

"Girl, you are skin and bones," said Mark. "I don't think you've eaten since you left Fort Patrick Henry."

"We had iced cakes and tea every afternoon," I said, pantomiming a lady drinking tea.

"Just the same for us," answered Mark, reaching forward to toast my imaginary tea cup.

Jamie and Charlotte joined us. He held baby Charlotte with one arm, but stretched out his other to embrace me.

"Little sister, you're just what we need to add spirit to this place," he said. "God Bless."

And at that moment, with my head nestled against his shoulder, my arm encircling his familiar waist, I knew that I was really home. We had only a moment to embrace, however, before Betsy and Polly were at our sides. "We want to see our cabin, Uncle Jamie," said Betsy. "Uncle Mark says there's beds and a table and everything."

"Then I guess we'd better go see it," said Jamie. "I welcome you to Fort Nashborough," he added, gesturing toward a path that led uphill to the fort.

"Nashborough?" I said. "I thought you'd named it 'The Bluffs.'"

"That's not a proper name for the Advance Guard of Civilization," said Jamie. "Colonel Henderson and I decided to name it for our old Carolina comrade in arms, Francis Nash. He died at the battle of Germantown where we both fought, and we wanted him to be remembered."

Jamie led us up the steep incline. At the crest of the hill stood the new fort with block houses at each of the four corners and eight cabins already erected. The horses were tethered outside the walls, the cows fed on the new spring grass, and nearby the chickens pranced as if showing off for us. In all the business of greeting my own family, I had failed to see that Hagar was reunited with Henry, and the two of them had followed us up the bluff.

"We're safe, Hagar. It was worth everything just for this moment."

"I hope you're right, Miss Ann," Hagar replied. "Seeing Henry is a balm. But I've been getting my uneasy feeling."

It wasn't a time for dark speculation, but a time for rejoicing. I glanced back at the river where our boats were nestled like birds come home to roost, and I thanked God for creating a perfect day.

———

That night the children and I were among the luckiest new arrivals at Fort Nashborough, ones who slept in a cabin. My brothers had worked hard to construct and furnish it before we arrived: a one room structure with a wooden floor and a fireplace at one end. It contained two large beds with two underbeds that slipped beneath them, a newly made chest, a table, and four chairs. We had no cupboard, but Jamie had made two shelves out of boards that rested on wooden pegs set into the logs. On the top shelf was his homecoming gift, a nosegay of spring flowers in a gourd, their stems bent over the side as if giving us a welcoming bow.

We gathered around the fireplace to exchange stories of our difficult journeys, Jamie in a chair by the fire, puffing his pipe, sending the sweet smell of tobacco throughout the room. Charlotte had arranged her chair by his side so that their arms could touch, while their favorite hound, Caesar, lay at her feet. We had pulled the low beds to the center of the room and the children wiggled and giggled on top of them, while I sat with my brothers on a buffalo robe, Bruno curled close by.

Jamie was amazed to hear of our numerous Indian attacks, for his group had not experienced a single act of Indian violence. The weather, however, had been enemy enough. Many a morning they woke to find a cow had frozen and died during the night. In addition to worrying about the weather's effect on the animals, they had the constant challenge of finding food for them. The cane was the animals' principal source of nourishment, but it was lean pickings. Their entourage made a cold and miserable sight as they moved along, first the men on horses, followed by the extra brood mares, the hogs, the cattle, and finally the sheep.

"Not finally," spoke up Jonathan from his perch on the bed, shaking his mop of dark hair the color of his mother's. "I was always bringing up the rear, Mama. Chasing old Sampson."

It was Jonathan's special duty to herd the sheep, and Sampson was a ram of unusual vigor and stubbornness who often took it into his head to break away from the group and scamper into hills where no horse could follow. Jonathan was then obliged to dismount and chase the ram until he caught him, however long it took.

"I'm afraid Jonathan had the hardest duty of all," said Jamie. "We camped every night at sundown, but many an evening it was dark for three or four hours before we'd set our eyes on Jonathan."

"James, how could you let him roam like that!" said Charlotte, motioning for Jonathan to come to her side. Jonathan refrained from moving.

"I'm not a little boy any more," he said, his bottom lip sticking out in the slightest pout. "And I always captured old Sampson. Got him by the horns and dragged him back to the camp, even after he'd knocked me down a dozen times."

"Every night," said Jamie, taking a puff on his pipe with satisfaction.

"Papa says I'll get my reward when it's shearing time. He's going to let me clip Sampson, to see if he loses his strength when he loses his hair."

Mark laughed loudest and grabbed Jonathan's leg where he stood by the bed.

"He was the bravest of us all," said Mark. "The only one who traveled alone in the dark."

"Thank the good Lord you didn't run into any Indians," said Charlotte. "I can't bear thinking of my son in the wilderness all alone."

"I trusted Jonathan same as any man," said James. "He's grown up, Charlotte."

Charlotte did not look convinced, but since Jonathan remained out of reaching distance, she put her hand on Jamie's arm instead.

Jamie continued tales of their rugged journey: how they crossed creeks filled with large blocks of ice that slammed into their horses, how they continued to ride with wet clothes that slowly froze on their bodies. The only positive outcome from the biting cold occurred when they arrived at the Cumberland River on Christmas Eve. The water was frozen so solidly that the men and animals could easily cross its width.

"When we were half way across, we heard a sound that chilled our blood in a way the weather hadn't accomplished," said Jamie, leaning forward with an expectant air.

"Indians?" asked Charlotte. "I knew there had to be Indians."

"A crack and a bang, but it wasn't gunfire. The weight of our party put cracks in the ice that extended for miles. They heard the noise all the way down at Eaton's Station," said Jamie. "I have to say, that noise sped us quite a bit."

"I should hope so!" I exclaimed, imagining the lost lives of men and animals if they had fallen through a crack into the icy waters.

"We thought you'd never get here," said Mark. "I searched the river looking until I thought my eyes would fall right out of my head."

"You." I ruffled his hair with my hand. "You were just looking for girls to flirt with. I don't know how you got along for almost seven months without female companionship."

"It was a hardship for all of us," said Jamie in a serious tone, taking Charlotte's hand.

"I guess you can't be too sympathetic," said Mark. "I saw you didn't have to suffer without an admirer. There was a fellow on the boat looking as smitten as anyone I've ever seen."

"Major Cockrill," said Charlotte, with a stern tone. "He's been quite attentive. Even gave Ann a gun."

"Ah, I knew it. And I bet our Ann slipped the ship's anchor round his ankle, to make sure he didn't get away," added Mark.

"You hush up, Mark," I said. "There is nothing between the Major and me. He cares for the children, that's all."

I looked to the bed and sure enough Polly and Betsy were studying me intently, trying to understand what was being said about Cockrill. Only Charity was already asleep.

"The point is," said Jamie, "we're happy to have our family with us at last. This cabin was no home without you."

"We're expecting more newcomers tomorrow, too," said Mark. "Colonel Henderson and his party are on the way. He sent Sam Butler to alert us that Henderson wants to draw up a constitution, now that everyone's here."

"Then it's high time we got to sleep," Jamie said. "I've got to get my rest if I'm going to write a constitution!"

"We want to sleep with Delilah," said Betsy.

"I'm sleeping with Uncle Mark and Uncle John outside," said Jonathan proudly.

"Me too," shouted Peyton.

"You're too young," said Randolph, "but I want to go. Can I Mother?" he asked Charlotte.

"You'll have to ask your father," said Charlotte, greatly pleased to say those words.

"For this first night, I say you can sleep anywhere in the fort you choose," said Jamie. "But in the morning, I want all of my family by my side. We've been separated too long."

And so it was that I spent my first night in Fort Nashborough sharing my bed with Charity, while Polly, Betsy and Delilah cuddled under quilts in one of the trundle beds. Jamie and Charlotte were together in their feather bed, and Hagar slept on the floor next to little Charlotte's small bed. All safe.

# Fourteen

APRIL 25, 1780 — *My first morning at Fort Nashborough. A memorable occasion. I sit on the ground outside our cabin because the closed door and lack of windows made it too dark to write inside. Jamie built the cabin in this manner for warmth and as a protection against the Indians, but I wish he had included a small window looking to the fort's interior. We could leave such a window uncovered in fair weather and seal it with oiled paper when winter comes. The back of the cabin is built right into the palisade wall itself to avoid wasting lumber and to add additional fortification against our foes.*

*I am struck by how similar this fort is to the ones I have observed so many times before. The stockade of pickets surrounds a two-acre area, a bare expanse of dirt dotted with the odd clump of hearty weeds. Families gather around their fires, sleeping on the ground. It is an unsettled scene, but in the future more cabins will be built into the palisade walls, as well as cabins stretching down the center of the enclosure.*

*Some of the families I watch this morning will be in those cabins, but most will move on to make their homes in other locations. They wait at Colonel Henderson's request, since it is imperative for as many men as possible to sign the governing document he and Jamie will prepare. In signing, the men bear witness to obey the laws and uphold the community in this new land.*

*Only a few people move about the enclosure under the stunning lavender sunrise, but in another week or so, those of us who remain will rise early each morning to get on with our new lives, using various tools to conquer this rich land. Some will set up spinning wheels to turn the spring crop of wool into yarn. Others will operate looms to weave fabrics to replace our shabby clothes. We will dig and prod and plant this earth to fulfill the covenant we made with God, to populate the land with Godfearing citizens.*

*I look forward to the sound of the hoe as it thuds and scrapes the soil, making way for my precious seeds: cotton, flax, gourd, peas, potatoes, beans. I love the pungent smell of newly turned earth and the moist feel of it against my palm. The fort yard is quiet, but soon the dogs will trumpet their barks into the air. That sound will mix with the noise of spoons clanking against the sides of kettles. Fathers will tease children they have not seen in months. Wives will smile shyly following a night of lying with their husbands after so long a time. Our real lives have finally begun.*

*I search the crowd of more than a hundred people to see if I can find Elizabeth. Upon waking I thought immediately of her, wondering how she managed to tell Ephraim her sad news. I hope he was strong when he heard of the baby's death. That he held his wife close to his heart, knowing he could easily have lost her as well as the child. Thank goodness she had her mother and father to help her tell the story. Grief is always easier to bear with the sharing.*

*I can't locate Elizabeth, but I can identify Major Cockrill, reunited with Hugh Rogan at a fire near the fort's gate. The outline of his shoulders has grown so familiar I could recognize him anywhere. Of course I know only the exterior of the man; what goes on within his mind is still a mystery. His words and actions can set my blood to stirring at one moment and make me feel like a fool the next. If he is interested in me romantically, he certainly has an odd way of showing it. Will he build a cabin inside Fort Nashborough or will he strike out into the wilderness to make his place elsewhere? And if he leaves, will I miss him?*

*Jamie recounted that a number of the men had already found and laid claim to springs in the area and bitter rivalries have grown up as to ownership. When I think of the whole wilderness that spreads around us, it's hard to understand such pettiness. I don't know why I am surprised though, for isn't that the nature of man? After all, God gave Adam and Eve everything except the apple and still they were dissatisfied. The fall from grace was blamed on Eve, but it's my experience that men are always more discontented than women. Haven't all our long hunters been men, from Daniel Boone to Jamie himself, men always searching for some better place? Some new Eden? I believe that Adam was just as restless and guilty as Eve, only not as quick witted. No one can make me think any differently.*

*I must quit writing, for a man is coming toward me and unless I'm very much mistaken, it's Sam Butler himself. It's been a little more than three weeks since I last saw him, but how my life has changed since that time. Then I was rootless; now I am home.*

Sam Butler marched across the barren ground, his dark hair loose across his shoulders, wearing leggings and a fringed deerskin hunting shirt similar to mine.

"We meet again so soon," I said.

"I've come to see your brother, James," he said.

"I think I heard him stirring," I answered, and sure enough Jamie emerged from the door behind me. He had dressed in haste, his shirt blousing at the waist.

Sam's message was a short one. Colonel Henderson had arrived from Eaton's Station late the night before and wanted to meet with Jamie as soon as possible.

"Where the two of you won't be disturbed," Sam added. "Outside Fort Nashborough."

Jamie agreed to meet within the hour at Henderson's camp, a mile down the path toward Mansker's Station. Sam nodded at both Jamie and me, and hurried off to relay the message, his rifle slung against his back.

"Henderson thinks we should structure a government right away," said Jamie, absently patting my shoulder. "He had good luck putting together resolutions in Kentucky, and wants to do the same here."

"You don't need Henderson for that," I said, disturbed by his words. "You helped write the first Constitution this side of the mountains," I said, referring to the *Articles of Association* that Jamie had drawn at Watauga. "Don't let the Judge take credit for everything."

"It's not important who gets the credit, Ann. It's what's in the document," he said. We had engaged in this conversation many times. I would point out how other men claimed credit for things he had done: drawing up documents, calming the Indians during times of unrest. He would answer that he'd let his actions speak for themselves.

"Look over there at Edmund Jennings," he said. "He doesn't brag, but he's a man you can count on. That's why I picked him to bring up the rear on our overland trip. When Edmund's walking behind me, I never fear for my tail side."

I looked where he pointed and saw Edmund and Elizabeth with her parents.

"I didn't know Elizabeth was awake," I said. "I must see how she fared the evening. Tell Charlotte I'll be back in a moment to help her with breakfast."

"Give her my regards and sympathy," Jamie called after me.

Everyone was waking, and I found it somewhat disorienting to see so many men after being so long in the company of predominantly women and children. The Jennings party was gathered around their fire, a few trunks stacked on the ground haphazardly since they planned to move to another location soon. I studied the one member of their family who was new to me, twenty-seven-year-old Edmund who had his mother's gray eyes and heavy brows. He wore the traditional deerskin shirt and leggings, but with a significant addition. At his waist was the usual leather belt, but a hideous collection of Indian scalps hung from it. The very sight of them filled me with disgust, and the thought that white men could be as ruthless as Indians was horrifying.

Elizabeth had warned me of Edmund's habit of wearing scalps and defended the practice by explaining it was his response to a terrible incident he had witnessed on a trip with Boone to Kentucky. Edmund had found the bodies of several men who were brutally murdered, including Boone's son James. Before killing James, the Indians had tortured him by tearing out the nails from both his hands and feet. Ever since that time, Edmund wore the scalps in memory of and retribution for the deaths he had seen that day. The explanation was a reason, but not a suitable excuse for Edmund's barbaric behavior.

When I joined the group, I was disturbed at seeing Elizabeth's troubled face. I could guess at her new calamity.

"Oh, Ann, I'm so glad to see you," she said, grabbing my hand.

"What is it?"

"Ephraim," said Elizabeth. "After I told him about the baby, he was so upset. He made me repeat the story of how it happened over and over until I was crying so hard I couldn't speak."

"I told him it was no one's fault," said Mr. Jennings, squinting into the morning sun. "But he was looking for someone to blame."

"He didn't have to look far," said Elizabeth. "I'm the one he blames."

"That's nonsense," said Mrs. Jennings. "Redheads are excitable, that's all. He'll cool."

"I don't even know how long Ephraim's been gone. When I woke this morning, he wasn't beside me."

"You need to sit down and rest yourself," said Mrs. Jennings. "There's not a thing you can do anyway. I'll send Hannah to milk one of the cows, and the fresh milk will soothe you, you'll see."

Elizabeth answered her mother with a bitter laugh.

"His brother John is out looking for him," said Edmund. "He'll find him. If I didn't believe it, I'd be out searching myself. John and Eph are like two sides of the same coin. They may have different natures, but one always knows what the other will do."

"The only ones to blame," said Mr. Jennings, "were the Indians who were shooting at us."

Edmund drew his knife, lifting it so that the blade glinted in the slanting sun rays.

"I can't kill all the Indians, Lizzy, but I promise you I'll kill as many of them as I can," Edmund said.

"Killing!" shouted Mrs. Jennings as she seized Edmund by the wrist. "Has all your killing brought one person back to life?" she asked, looking fiercely at him.

"No," Edmund answered, lowering his knife, and staring at his mother until she released his arm. "But it's saved my own skin more than once. And a score of others too."

"Do we have to talk about killing all the time?" asked Elizabeth. "It brings us nothing but pain. We came here to live."

"Of course we did," I said, pulling her to the ground beside me. "And we will, too. Jamie and the others have been here for four months and the only Indians they've seen have been peaceful ones who came to trade. We left the Chickamaugas far behind."

"I say it's high time we had some breakfast," said Mrs. Jennings, trying to calm herself as well as Elizabeth. "Edmund's got some squirrels we can roast on a hickory stick, and Hannah can cook up some of those eggs we've been dreaming about. Would you join us?" she asked.

I explained that I needed to help Charlotte. Before I stood to leave, however, I squeezed Elizabeth's knee through her linen skirt.

"You've had almost two months to get used to the baby's death. Ephraim's had less than a day. Give him some time. He'll come to accept it just as you have. You'll see."

Elizabeth gave me a faint smile. "I guess that's the problem," she said. "I don't think I'll ever accept it. How can I expect him to?"

"Maybe acceptance is the wrong word. But you've got to find peace with it," I added, rising, my body throwing a shadow across her bowed head.

"Please let me know the minute he comes back," I said to Mrs. Jennings.

She nodded and nervously pulled up her sleeves, exposing wrinkled elbows. "It's time to see to breakfast," she said.

Thinking about Elizabeth's sadness drained some of the joy from the morning, but I refused to let my spirits be dampened. The very business of living could keep one from dwelling too much on unhappiness. Fires had to be lit, food cooked, and tools made. Life went on in spite of our tragedies. All around me people were engaged in a myriad of activities. The Major was awake, facing my way, but it was impossible to determine if he was actually looking at me. I was so busy assessing him that I almost bumped into Rachel who was helping Mrs. Donelson set up an ash hopper.

"Goodness gracious," said Mrs. Donelson as she prepared to make soap. "I never thought I'd be so happy to make soap, but every last piece of clothing we have needs to be scoured. So many things to do! Rachel!" she called with some volume, even though Rachel was only six feet away. "You go through that storage box of mine and get my wooden paddles, the ones I use to beat the dirt out of the clothes. And find Severn to set up my wash pot."

"He went down to the boat with Papa and Somerset," said Rachel. "I wish I could have gone too."

"Lord help us," said Mrs. Donelson putting down her bag of straw and placing her fists on her generous hips in a gesture of exasperation. "I'd think you would have had enough of that boat by this time. Go down there and bring him back."

"They're getting the cannon, Mama. Papa said he needed two people to bring it up the hill."

"Then find Patsy to help with that pot. I am way past my heavy lifting days, I can tell you that. Old age and child bearing have taken their toll. I told Severn just this morning. Severn, I said, I brought you into this world, the least you can do is bring me a pot of water. But off he scampers like a rabbit, just as soon as he gets the chance. I have a big family and I still can't find any-one to help when I need it. But excuse my manners for running on, Ann. Tell me, how did you find your brothers?"

"Fine, Mrs. Donelson. I'm on my way to feed them breakfast."

"People eat breakfast entirely too late in the morning to suit me," said Mrs. Donelson, poking the fire. "I had to chew on some parched corn this morning just to get myself going. It tasted about as good as eating rocks, but it gave me some energy."

"Well, I must be getting on, Mrs. Donelson." I backed away slowly.

"You give my best to your family. Rachel, what are you doing standing there gawking. Say goodbye to Ann and go get Patsy."

When I turned, I saw that Mark was almost upon us and then I understood Rachel's reluctance to move. She was waiting to speak to Mark since she had often made eyes at him back at Fort Caswell.

"Morning Mrs. Donelson," Mark said. "Rachel," he added, tipping his hat. "I've been sent to retrieve my sister. Her poor lit-tle children are crying for her."

"Poor indeed," I said. "I bet they've already milked the cow and set the table."

"Morning, Mark," said Rachel with a pretty dimpled smile. "I heard from your brother that you killed a buffalo last week."

"With my bare hands," said Mark, smiling back. "Grabbed him by the horns and wrestled him to the ground."

"The same way he wrestles with the truth," I said, linking my arm in Mark's. "We'd best be getting back to the cabin. Since my brother was so kind to come searching for me."

"Next buffalo I catch," said Mark over his shoulder, "I'll save the tongue for you, Rachel."

"I don't know how you had a chance to become such an outlandish flirt, without a single female out here to practice on," I said pulling him along.

"Didn't have to learn," said Mark. "Born that way. The way you were born to break men's hearts. Look at the Major, reduced to hammering out his sorrows on the anvil."

Cockrill was setting up his blacksmith tools near the gate in preparation for the heavy work of bending and twisting iron.

"Why don't you speak to him? Light up his morning," asked Mark, nudging me with his elbow.

"Like you did for Rachel? No thank you. I've better things to do and so has the Major." With my free hand I took the key from around my neck. "At last I can open my trunk and store my goods."

We entered the cabin to find Hagar stirring a pot which hung from an iron support in the fireplace while Charlotte arranged pails, trays and the butter churn by the hearth. They had already smoothed the quilts on the beds. John whittled by the fire while Peyton and Randolph guessed what he was making from the hickory wood. Jamie leaned over the table with his wooden document box, the top slid back revealing a pile of papers within. Charlotte and Betsy played on the puncheon floor with Delilah, their corn husk dolls talking with one another in a busy game of pretend. Polly and Charity examined a shiny object by the fireside.

"Look, Mama," said Charity. "Uncle Jamie let us look at his compass."

She proudly extended the foot long brass compass. "No matter which way I turn, the arrow always points in the same direction," Charity said, turning in a circle.

"Uncle Jamie says that's north," added Charity pointing to the end of the arrow. "Only I don't know what north means."

"You remember how Colonel Donelson had a map that he studied every day while we were traveling?" I asked. Charity looked doubtful.

"Let me try to explain directions this way," I said, sitting on a chair. I positioned Charity in front of me. "If you were to stand outside the cabin all day long, with your right arm stretched in the direction where the sun rises, and your left arm pointing to where the sun sets . . . " I lifted Charity's right arm to point east and her left arm to point west. "Then you'd be facing north all day. Can you understand?"

"I can understand that if I stood this way all day," said Charity, "I'd be very tired."

The whole family laughed, and Charity didn't know whether to be pleased or hurt.

"Right you are," I said, lowering her arms. "But then you'd never forget which way was north."

"All right," said Charlotte. "Put those things away, James. We're going to have our first breakfast together."

Henry helped Hagar bring the pot to the table and held it while she spooned out the usual corn meal mush, only this time it was flavored with dried apples that Jamie had saved from his rations. Charlotte filled our cups with the miracle of fresh milk from our very own cow. After Jamie said the blessing, we ate from our pewter bowls with enthusiasm, the children laughing and planning a game of hide and seek after breakfast.

"Play?" I said. "You haven't forgotten about your lessons, have you?"

"Oh, Mama," said Polly and Betsy in unison.

"Charlotte told me how you taught the children, Ann. I'm very proud of you," said Jamie.

"It's the least I could do," I said. "After all, Charlotte has taught me so much, I was happy to pass it along."

"You won't have to bother with that any longer, though," he said, taking a big swallow of milk. "We have a real school teacher here. Zachariah White. He'll relieve you of that burden."

"Burden?" I repeated.

" He had his own school back in Wake County, and he's agreed to teach here too."

The mush turned to a leaden ball in my stomach.

"Maybe Ann could help him," said Charlotte, observing my distress.

"I thought you'd be pleased, Ann," Jamie said. "Teaching was a way to pass your time on the boat, but you don't want it to keep you from your duties here."

"It was more than passing time." My hands dropped heavily into my lap. "The children advanced in their reading. They learned to do their sums."

"You'd understand if you'd been with us, James," said Charlotte. "Ann was as good as any teacher I've seen."

"I have no doubt that she was excellent," said Jamie, "But Zach White is our teacher now. It's been agreed to. You know teaching is a man's job."

I pushed away from the table, my chair making a scraping sound as it moved across the floor. I could feel my face redden in spite of myself, and I had a fierce desire to slam my fist on the table so hard it would split the walnut plank.

Mark spoke up quickly, trying to avoid a confrontation between Jamie and me.

"Good. You've finished breakfast, Ann. It's time for me to show you around," he said. "Get the lay of the land."

"I want to go too," said Polly, putting her spoon on the table.

"Please, Uncle Mark."

"Me too," said Betsy, jumping up.

"And me," chirped Charity from her low stool on the floor.

"I guess you can't play hide and seek until you've seen where there is to hide," said Mark.

"Me. Me," said little Charlotte, looking up at her mother's face.

"You can go with me after I wash these dishes," said Charlotte, concerned that rough play would worsen the child's lungs. "I don't want to go all alone."

"All right then," said Mark. "Clean your bowls and let's get started. Randolph, Peyton, Delilah."

"Yippee!" exclaimed Peyton, kicking back his chair. "We can find sticks to make flippers like Severn. So we'll be ready to fight the Indians."

"Slow down," said Mark. "One thing at a time. Line up. If you're going to be soldiers, you must learn to march. Oldest first."

Avoiding a look at Jamie, I took Charity's hand, and stood at the door waiting.

"Now soldiers," said Mark. "Forward. March."

The children made a happy if ragtag army, as they marched stiffly through the open door and into the fort yard. Mark and I followed into the morning's sunshine.

"You'll like Zach," said Mark. "I imagine he'll welcome your help."

"I won't like him at all, and I've done very well without his help," I said, kicking a loose stone in front of me.

"Now that you're home, you'll want to spend your time making new clothes for the children, and tending your crops and . . ."

"You never could get me out of my moods, Mark. You might as well quit trying," I said, frowning. "I was good at teaching. I really was."

"There's still Sunday School. I don't think Zach's much good at Bible verses," said Mark as we neared the gate.

Our conversation was interrupted when Betsy broke ranks with the others and ran to the Major where he studied the cannon with Colonel Donelson and Somerset.

"Major," Betsy shouted. "We're going for an adventure."

"Don't be bothering the Major," I called.

"No bother at all," Cockrill said, leaning over to greet Betsy. "But my hand's too dirty for shaking," he said as he showed a palm blackened by his morning's work.

Betsy pulled her horseshoe doll from her pocket and held it toward him. "I did just like I said I would. I let her sleep with me last night, and she liked her new bed."

"And you kept her covered?" the Major asked with a look of concern.

"I let her head peek out, of course, just in case she wanted to see things in the fire."

"Or to breathe," added Cockrill with a smile.

"Come on, Betsy, the Major's busy," I said, tugging at the back of her dress.

"What are you doing, Major?" asked Betsy, ignoring me.

"Colonel Donelson thinks we should mount the cannon above the gate, and it's up to me to figure out how to do it. First I've got to build a platform, high at the top of the fence; and make some brackets to anchor it."

The other children gathered around the cannon and Randolph ran his hand along the barrel.

"When I get big," he said. "I'm going to have a cannon even bigger than this one. Big enough to blow up a whole forest."

"That's silly," said Polly. "Why would you want that?"

"The best thing about this weapon," said Colonel Donelson. "is that the Indians are afraid of it even if you never shoot a ball. I'm hoping you can use it to scare them away from the fort."

"What do you mean by 'you?' Won't you be with us?" I asked.

"I'm afraid not. I plan to look for some good land up on Stone's River and put in a corn crop as soon as possible."

"You're leaving?"

"Not until James and Colonel Henderson finish drawing their guidelines. Then I'll head off."

I was surprised to find myself sad at the thought of his leaving. I had grown fond of the whole family.

"And John Junior and Johnny C.?"

"We're all going. I'm sure we can find enough land to suit us," said the Colonel.

"Then I shall miss you," I said, looking Donelson straight in the eyes. "All of you."

"But you're not going to leave us, are you Major?" Betsy asked Cockrill. "Please say no."

"Not today," said the Major. "But I'll soon be looking for my own place too."

"But you'll be back to visit," continued Betsy, much to my embarrassment.

"I will," said Cockrill. "When I can."

"The land's filled with good springs bubbling out of the ground," said Mark. "Fresh water enough for all of us."

"Then show it to us, Uncle Mark," said Peyton, growing impatient. "I want to see."

"Back in formation," said Mark, and the children quickly lined up. "All right. Stand up straight, Delilah. You too, Randolph. That's good. Now, forward, march!" The little soldiers paraded past the cannon and through the gate until they reached the area outside the palisades.

As I followed them, I was filled with a mixture of joy and sadness. Why was it that nothing ever worked out quite the way one expected? I thought I would continue to be the children's teacher, but Jamie was denying me that pleasure. I'd thought the Major might become my husband, but he was going away. I tried to cheer myself by surveying the grand new land that stretched before me. The horses were tied close to the fort wall, but the cows grazed near the cedar forests to the left. On the right lay a wide expanse of open fields which had been cleared by trampling buffalo who had come to the salt lick for perhaps centuries, creating land ready for cultivation.

The children broke ranks and ran rapidly through the brown grass that stood tall from the previous year's growth, a new layer of green hugging the earth's surface beneath their feet. They ran like animals who had been penned up for a long time and were at last put out to pasture. The girls veered off to visit the cows, Betsy heading straight for Miss Priss while the boys galloped to the field's edge and then circled back.

"It's as beautiful as Jamie told us it would be," I said, watching my children's delight.

"Within the month the wild grape will be growing," said Mark. "Cherries will be ripe for the picking. It's all ours to make of it what we will."

The wind ruffled the grasses, and I listened to the happy shouts of the children while I willed myself to be happy too. Everything seemed so peaceful. But across the clearing in the far distance, set off against the forest behind them, two figures appeared like dots in the meadow. My first thought was of Indians, but as they slowly advanced I could see they wore the hats of white men. I called to the children to come, and they reluctantly started in my direction.

"What's wrong?" Mark asked.

"Two men," I answered. "There."

Mark shielded his eyes from the sunlight and looked where I indicated.

"What's wrong, Mama?" asked Polly, the first child to reach me. "We were having fun."

"Strangers," I said.

Polly scanned the meadow, alert as a hawk. The other children soon arrived, panting from their race. I gathered Charity into my arms.

"It's the Peyton twins," said Mark.

"Are you sure?" I asked.

"Won't take us long to find out. They're headed our way."

The dots became larger and soon one of the men took off his hat and waved it in the air. His red hair confirmed that he was no Indian and strongly suggested it was one of the Peytons. Reassured, I sent the children playing, and off they ran with a whoop. I lowered Charity to the ground and told her she could join the others. Off she toddled into grass taller than her head.

"The children look like young colts, don't they?" said Mark. "Doesn't it make you want to run too?"

"Another time," I said.

"You've changed," said Mark. "I guess you're not a girl any more."

"I've known that for some time," I said, striding toward the distant figures. "But I'm a fast walking woman, and you'll have to go some to catch up with me."

I marched through the grass, enjoying the way it slapped against the side of my trousers, Mark following me. The earth beneath the grass, however, was not as flat and level as it looked. Signs of buffalo were nestled in the grass: their droppings and the holes their feet made as they'd sunk into the soft dirt.

We walked for ten minutes before we met the two men who were, indeed, the Peyton twins. Their red wavy hair scalloped across their foreheads, and they made quite a striking sight, slim, with long slender faces. Although their features were identical, I thought Ephraim's eyes had a wildness not present in John's, just as Hagar had said. It was more than his current distress that made me feel he was a troublesome man. He laughed too loudly, and drank too much, and was quick to see the makings of a fight in many situations. But I had to admit that he could be quick with a funny remark, followed by a booming laugh. While John was also clever, his wit was apt to be more subtle and dry than Ephraim's. Even the way they wore their hats set them apart. John's sat level on his head while Ephraim's was often tipped back or to the side.

But today neither of them looked in the least cheerful. John seemed apprehensive and Ephraim wore a scowl.

"Ephraim, thank heavens," I said. "We were all worried about you."

Ephraim, at a loss for words, stared past me to the fort.

"Found him under a sycamore tree," said John. "I knew he would be all right."

"That's not how I'd describe myself," said Ephraim. "All right."

"Safe, then," added John.

"Elizabeth is waiting for you," I said. "She needs you very much."

Ephraim nodded but didn't speak.

"She was so brave, Ephraim. It was just a terrible accident."

I stopped, realizing my words were useless. The baby was gone. Nothing could relieve that sorrow but time.

"Thank you," said John, taking his brother's elbow. "We'd best get on."

The Peytons continued up the hill, moving through the fields to the place where my children played. How painful it must have been to pass those happy, laughing faces while suffering the loss of one's own child. I felt ashamed for feeling sorry for myself. Why did I keep forgetting that I had everything I really needed: my children safe at our new home.

# Fifteen

MAY 1, 1780 — *A week has passed since I had the time or concentration to write, and more has happened in that past week than in a month on the river. Then our activities were narrowly confined to the boats, but now events explode in a hundred locations. Down at the dock, many of our vessels have been torn asunder, the lumber to be used for building more cabins. The Jennings and Peytons have taken leave of us and moved a mile upstream to start a new home. And Major Cockrill has struck out for parts unknown to stake his claim. We exchanged only the most formal goodbyes, so I am left with no idea of his plans for the future.*

*Although he is gone, many other men have poured through our gate like water rushing over the Muscle Shoals. We have almost two hundred here now, for the word has gone out that today is the day to sign our new constitution which Jamie and Colonel Henderson are calling "The Cumberland Compact." They have come from seven other stations: Eaton's, Gasper Mansker's, Bledsoe's, Asher's, Freelands, Stone's River and Fork Union, as well as from all over the Cumberland country. That grizzly old Frederick Stump who bragged about killing Indians was the first one here from Eaton's. I might have known he wouldn't miss the action.*

*Yesterday I had the opportunity to meet the legendary Gasper Mansker who has been in this country longer than almost any other white man. He credits his longevity to the fact that his eyes are set so widely apart in his head that he can see not only on both sides, but also entirely around himself. No Indian has been able to take him unawares. I am hoping to see Thomas Sharp Spencer as well, an enormous man whose feet are said to be so large that the sight of their prints frightened off a party of French traders who thought a giant roamed the region. This past winter he lived in the trunk of a sycamore tree which he vowed was one of the best homes he had ever enjoyed, the tree purporting to measure twelve feet across. This cast of characters is worthy of Mr. Shakespeare himself.*

*The only negative aspect to the large number of men milling about is that I am a constant target for sidelong glances or open stares. Heaven knows I am not dressed to entice, and yet one would think I was a fairy princess set down on this mortal earth. At first I was alarmed by this practice. Then amused. And finally, offended. These men do not look at me because of my wit or charm. They regard me only because so few single females reside here, and they need a woman to share their burdens. I can't help but think of hungry dogs fighting over yesterday's soup bone. If this treatment continues, I will never put on a dress. I don't want to encourage their advances.*

*In this competition for eligible ladies, I know that Mark can hold his own. It's John I worry about. John is every bit as fine a young man as Mark, and when he is at home with us, he is as sunny as his blonde hair. But when he encounters the young ladies, he stares at his feet as if measuring them for moccasins. For instance, Nancy Gower came over to visit one evening this week, and I feared John would jump into the fire rather than speak with her. I know he likes her, and yet his tongue was stilled. If only he could put himself out more, he would display the tender qualities that a woman appreciates. This week he carved toy guns for Charlotte's boys and dolls for the girls. He will make a good father if he can ever bring himself to speak to their future mother.*

*Last night was the most important time of the whole week. Colonel Henderson, along with Sam Butler, came to finish the document that the men will sign today. The Compact sets up a "Tribunal of Notables" who will act as judges for our new settlement. Based on population, Fort Nashborough will have the most representatives with three, followed by two from Eaton's and Gasper's Station, and one from each of the other five. These men will be elected to settle all disputes over land, provide equipment and food for those who may arrive without provisions, provide for widows and orphans whose husbands or parents are killed by the Indians, promote peace, happiness and well-being, and of course suppress vice and punish crime. Very high minded intentions. The document contains a great deal more words as well, but they add little in the way of sense. It's just that Colonel Henderson is a lawyer and can't help himself when it comes to spilling words. I still think Jamie should have written it, for clarity's sake if for no other.*

*As Sam and the Colonel left, Sam made quite a point of saying he looked forward to seeing me today. I wonder what he meant.*

The time set for signing the Compact was early afternoon. No more exact hour could be fixed because no one knew precisely when the maximum number of people would assemble. To meet the challenge of feeding so many new arrivals, we busily prepared as much food as possible. Hugh Rogan organized a hunting party which brought in six buffalo and ten deer, one a large buck with a fine rack of antlers. A family recently from Kentucky brought several sacks of corn, enough to make cornbread for everyone.

Charlotte instructed Henry to build a fire outside for her largest pot and a venison stew simmered over the flames. I stirred the pot when Mark approached, followed by a short, thin man whose most distinguishing characteristics were a prominent Adam's apple and round brown eyes that appeared almost lidless.

"I wanted to introduce my friend Zach White," said Mark. I wanted to meet the school teacher as much as I wanted to greet a case of smallpox. Mark's smile was designed to charm me into accepting the man, an impossible mission. Instead I considered how much he looked like a startled bird, and how the children would laugh at him. The words, "pleased to meet you" stuck in my throat like a turkey bone, and all I could do was nod in return.

"I've heard about your work on *The Adventure*," said Zach. "I gather you had some trying times."

"Indeed," I said. I added nothing more, but turned to the pot and continued stirring.

"Ann, Zach has some questions. Could you let the pot tend itself for a few minutes?" Mark said, giving me a pleading look.

I removed the long-handled iron spoon from the pot and held it impatiently as I appraised the unfortunate looking White. His appearance did not improve upon scrutiny. He seemed strong, though wiry, but his short black hair had been tamed by a goodly quantity of bear oil, causing strands to stick out stiffly like dark feathers, adding to his bird-like quality.

"I thought we might have a few words about the children's progress," Zach said mildly. "So I'll know where to pick up with their studies."

It was clear the man would not leave until I spoke with him, so I relented.

"The best way to proceed, Sir, is to give them reading and numbers tests on your own."

"Would you be willing to help me, Mrs. Johnson?" he asked so politely it irritated me further. I knew he was trying to placate me, offering the olive branch of peace, but I was simply in no mood to accept it. I had no taste for the fruit of that particular tree. At least not when presented by the lamentable Zachariah White.

"Mr. White. It is my experience that children want one teacher and one only. Division of authority only slows their learning. So it would not be in the interest of the children or you for me to offer my help, however modest."

"Is that the best you can do, Ann?" asked Mark, visibly exasperated.

"I believe so," I replied, lifting my spoon and depositing it into the stew once more, effectively communicating my dismissal. Both men took a step back.

"I see that maintaining discipline over your students was never a problem, Mrs. Johnson," said White.

I looked up, surprised that the little man possessed the backbone to give me such a retort.

"No, Sir," I answered, and returned to my stirring.

"Careful, Ann," said Mark. He paused, measuring his words. "The way you're thrashing that stew, we won't even recognize there's meat in it," he added.

With that remark both men withdrew and left me to my vigorous stirring. I was joined shortly by Charlotte who wore a dress I had not seen since Fort Patrick Henry, dark red cotton, pulled tight at the waist, with long, full sleeves. Charlotte had drawn her black hair into a knot, leaving a few loose tendrils to curl about her face.

"Isn't it marvelous?" she said, gesturing broadly to the crowd of men. "They're coming from all over the country in the interest of good government. It's a sight to make us proud."

"I'd say your fine disposition has more to do with being beside Jamie than your love of democratic principles," I said.

"Ann! Please," Charlotte exclaimed, coloring.

The blush on her cheek added to her beauty, and I remembered that Charlotte was only thirty, after all, and had every reason to appear pretty and youthful.

"You know how proud I am of James," said Charlotte indignantly. She moved close to whisper in my ear. "And it is wonderful to be with him once more, to feel his rough whiskers against my face."

Charlotte pulled back to reveal an impish expression, instinctively bringing her hand to cover her mouth, as if to keep her tongue from unleashing more secrets. I smiled and resisted the impulse to tease further. I remembered that feeling of closeness Charlotte described and felt a passing tremor in my own heart. We were interrupted by Hagar who returned from outside the fort where she had been milking the cows. The dogs, Caesar and Bruno, accompanied her, displaying an acute interest in the contents of the pails she carried.

"These dogs wouldn't leave off barking," said Hagar. "Indians are hiding in the cane."

"That's foolishness," I said. "If Indians were about, we'd surely hear from them. The dogs only want some of that milk."

"I know what I know," said Hagar. "Henry said he'd seen their tracks in the woods. The way the toes were pointed inward, he knew the prints belonged to savages."

"We're not going to think about Indians today," said Charlotte. "I forbid it. Today is set aside for ourselves and our future. So hurry and get that milk into little Charlotte. She coughed for hours last night and needs something for her strength."

"Soon the red horsemint will be growing, and I'll make her a tea to soothe that cough," I added.

"I can see nobody but me is going to worry about those Indians," Hagar grumbled as she started toward the cabin door. "I don't want to be right, but I know."

"Do you see James?" asked Charlotte, surveying the crowd, anxious to put Hagar's remarks behind her.

I didn't. Nor did I see Major Cockrill, but I caught sight of Colonel Henderson. I had heard a number of the men calling him "Carolina Dick," a nickname that summoned up less than the distinguished gentleman before us. Yet some people accused him of being a ruthless speculator, and they were questioning his legitimate right to sell land in the Cumberland country. He was a speculator and an opportunist, but so were all the men here. To avoid the appearance of being dishonest, Henderson had written into the Compact that he expected no money from anyone until the dispute as to the ownership of the land was decided in his favor. At that time, and only at that time, would he expect the twenty-six pounds, thirteen shillings and four pence per hundred acres to be paid. I imagined that clause should muffle the more mischievous tongues.

Jamie and Johnny C. brought a rough-hewn table into the center of the clearing and placed it on top of a patch of spring grass. They were surrounded by a number of the new arrivals who had begun their celebration by drinking rum and whiskey, even though the morning was still young. But still no sign of the Major. I abandoned my pot at last and worked my way through the company of men to stand at the gate where the mounted cannon almost made me feel his presence. He had bought one of Jamie's Spanish mares before venturing into the wilderness, so I walked outside and along the palisades, looking for his large bay horse. Although some of the men had arrived by foot, many had come by horse, and at least a hundred animals stamped and worked their bridle bits as I walked behind them. It wasn't Cockrill I found, however, but rather Sam Butler rubbing down his brown and white spotted horse.

The morning light poured through the trees, turning his hair spotted as well, inky dark in the shady places, with glints of red and even a touch of blue in the sun.

"Morning, Annie," he said, rubbing his horse with what appeared to be part of an old blanket. "How are you this fine day?" He pitched the cloth to the ground, and eyed me as if he had something important to say. I replied that I was fine. How could I be otherwise on such an auspicious day?

"The perfect day for a walk by the river, don't you think," he said.

"And take a chance on missing the ceremony? Why would I want to do that?"

"'Cause I'm a man who wants to spend some time with you, Annie. Alone."

If those words had come from the Major I would have welcomed them, but the idea of a romantic stroll with Sam made me want to explode with laughter. He was a handsome, strapping young man to be sure, but I would never consider him other than a boy.

"What is wrong with you, Sam Butler?" I exclaimed. "You're forgetting I've known you since you were a pup!"

"I'm no pup now," he answered, standing straight and squaring his shoulders. "Haven't you noticed?" He advanced toward me until he was so close I could feel his breath on my face.

"You stop that," I said backing away. "Or I'll forget you're my friend and give you a wallop."

"Oh, Annie," he said sorrowfully. "Can't you give me a chance?"

"No," I replied. "One day you'll find someone your own age, Sam, who isn't saddled with three children. And she'll be lucky to have you."

"Oh, Annie, I've favored you for as long as I can remember," he continued.

"Shhhh," I replied. "Save those words for your future wife." I gave him a pat on the shoulder. "I'm going to forget this ever happened so we can still be friends." He looked so sad at hearing my words that I thought no one had ever deemed friendship so worthless.

———

About two o'clock Colonel Donelson assembled the company of men for the signing ceremony. At the table in the center of the enclosure sat Jamie and Colonel Henderson: Jamie square and muscular, Henderson sitting taller and thinner in his chair. Colonel Henderson stood first, stretching his long, slender arms over his head to quiet the crowd. We grew silent except for a few children, who scuffled among themselves until they were subdued by their parents. Henderson summarized the major points of the document and urged all who could read to study The Compact before they signed it. He went on to add that the record would remain open for signatures for a full two weeks to accommodate those men who were unable to sign that day.

"It's important that we all participate in the origins of our government," said Henderson. "The power to govern ourselves is why we're fighting this war. It's why our comrades in arms like Francis Nash died, and why we have come to this new land. Colonel Robertson and I have served our time in battle and we think the best way to fight the British is to colonize the land."

Here he paused and dipped his pen into the pewter inkstand on the table.

"I take the liberty of signing first as a symbol of my commitment, but I don't consider myself first among you by any means. For that honor, I nominate my good friend and longtime associate, James Robertson."

Spontaneous applause spread through the crowd like wind cutting through long grass. Henderson called for quiet.

"You have already elected him your Colonel, and I can think of no more judicious man to be Chairman of the Committee of Notables than James Robertson."

Again applause broke out, punctuated by whistles and shouts. I felt buoyed up, as if I floated on the crowd's approbation. My Jamie was acknowledged by all the others to be the man of courage and principle I knew him to be. I was fortunate to have such a brother, even if he did not endorse me as a school teacher. And we were all fortunate to have such a leader. Jamie stood to accept the new post he had been awarded by acclamation. As

Chairman, he would assemble the eleven other notables to bring order to our community, and if possible, order to our lives. Jamie seemed embarrassed as he cleared his throat and shifted his weight from foot to foot.

"My friends, I will do my best to live up to the trust you've shown me today," he began somewhat stiffly. "We have come to this place at great cost, and more sacrifices remain in our future. But here we can live as free men and women, and I truly believe God has led us to these hills and valleys."

He picked up the pen and offered it to the crowd.

"So I encourage you to step up to this document and add your name firm and true alongside your neighbor's, that we may register as a community of faith our intentions to do right by our friends."

Jamie turned to Nathaniel Hart, who stood at his right side, and with a gesture invited him to sign under Colonel Henderson's name. Reverently the other men formed a line behind Hart, rough men, with the dirt of their labors clinging to their clothes, but all capable of signing their own names, committed to building a community, and woebetide the selfish or the conniving.

———

That night the fires crackled throughout the encampment and created twenty bright earthbound rivals to the stars. Sam Buchanan played his fiddle and dancers flashed in the firelight. The children had been put to bed, and I sat on the ground with my family in front of the cabin. John went about his familiar whittling, Jamie smoked his pipe, and Jonathan used a stick to play catch with Caesar. Only Mark inspected the crowd for the dancing partner of his choice.

"You were pretty hard on Zach today," Mark said as he squinted into the crowd before us.

"What's this?" asked Jamie, immediately interested.

"I brought Zach White to meet Ann. Thought they might work out a way to teach together, but it was all we could do to escape from Ann without mortal wounds."

"Ann!" said Jamie with alarm. "Zach is one of my most trusted friends."

"I'm sure there's room in this country for the both of us," I said tartly. "As long as he stays out of my way."

"You'd better reread The Compact, Ann," said Jamie. "We're pledged to help each other. Not to squabble."

"I did not squabble," I answered so loudly that Bruno turned his yellow eyes to study my face. "I spoke my mind. I can't help it if I'm not a saint like you."

"I'm no saint," said Jamie softly. "But I try to do what's right."

The conversation agitated me as it always did when Jamie scolded me . . . and I suspected he was right.

"John," I said, determined to put the subject of Zach White behind me. "Lay down that whittling and come with me. "We both need to dance."

"Oh, Ann," said John hesitantly. " Can't you see I'm busy."

"If you're too shy to ask a girl for a dance, the least you can do is respond when a girl asks you."

"I'll dance, Aunt Ann," said Jonathan eagerly leaving his game with Caesar, who still dangled a stick expectantly from his mouth. "I want to learn."

"Our nephew puts you to shame, John," I said as I took Jonathan's hand. He was as tall as my shoulder, every inch of him reaching to be a man. We ambled toward the music where other couples danced arm in arm around the fire. A crowd of mostly men stood clapping and singing, *"Nappycot and petticoat and the linsey gown, if you want to keep your credit up, pay your money down."*

"Start with your left foot," I instructed and off we went like a couple of mismatched carriage horses. I shortened my stride to complement Jonathan's and soon we arrived at a comfortable rhythm that matched the beat of the music. Little by little the music increased in speed until Jonathan and I flew in the circle. It was then I noticed Sam Butler at the edge of the crowd, gazing at me, and I wished for all the world it was the Major instead. But since it wasn't, I let myself give in to a larger dance, one with some vast purpose beneath God's bright stars.

# *Sixteen*

**MAY 15, 1780** — *A fortnight since I last wrote. The day after Sam asked me to walk by the river, he departed with Donelson and Henderson to build cabins on Stone's River. I confess I was not sorry to see him go. His group was not the only one to leave of course. Since the signing of the Compact, most of the men have gone, the majority looking for land in this general vicinity, but some returning to Kentucky.*

*Word has come back that the Donelsons are calling their new settlement "Clover Bottom." I hope it is as delightful as it sounds, with fields of white blossoms tinged with pink. Colonel Henderson's group is building full-fledged cabins there, but Colonel Donelson is satisfying himself with half-faced camps. I suppose these makeshift homes will be like others I've seen: about eight feet by ten feet in size, with a bark roof, and the front wall supported by poles. The roof is always tilted backwards so that rain won't drip into the fire. Mary and John Junior's baby will be born in a primitive dwelling, but still a superior place to the Indian cabin where baby Ephraim was born.*

*Hugh Rogan and the other men with Donelson spend the majority of their time putting in a good crop of corn. Donelson has even ordered a patch of cotton to be planted. How fortunate we will be to spin new cloth once more. Although my buckskin clothes hold up well enough, the children's dresses have grown both shabby and too small.*

*We have heard no word of Major Cockrill. He disappeared into the wilderness, as if the canebrakes swallowed him whole. At first Betsy asked about him, but after three weeks she no longer mentions his name. She still places the horseshoe doll beside her when she sleeps.*

*Henry and five other slaves plow from sun up to sun down, preparing the earth for our crops, and I have planted my seeds in a plot of land outside the fort. I took Hagar with me into the forest to search for pawpaw and cherry that will soon give us summer fruit, and we found them in abundance. The cherry trees' branches have lost their flowers, and already fruit is forming. I can almost taste the sweet juice of the berry and delight at the thought of cherry picking parties this summer. Picking pawpaws is less rewarding because one's hands turn red and itchy when touching their skin, but Hagar says they don't bother her one whit, and she can provide us with an abundant harvest soon.*

*Even with warming days, little Charlotte's health continues to decline to the point where I fear for her survival. Although Charity is eager to play with her, Charlotte will often go to her mother's side instead, and beg to be held. She'll have nothing to do with her father, and cries when Jamie lifts her into his arms. The child finds comfort only from burrowing into her mother's lap, and the sight of her frail body must break Jamie's heart.*

*How can I worry about selfish things like the whereabouts of Major Cockrill, when real troubles sleep at my own hearth?*

It was early morning when the Major bolted through the fort's gate as if he were pursued by the devil. His face was flushed and sweating, and he waved his hat excitedly in the air. People in the fort yard stopped their activities to watch him head straight toward me where I sat making a broom of corn husks. He stopped abruptly, not noticing that his boots scattered dust over my trousers and onto my pile of husks. His tall frame cast a shadow on my face, and the sun radiated behind his head like a halo.

"Is your brother home?" he asked. His left trouser leg, which was only a foot away, was smeared with blood. "Something terrible has happened," he added.

Alarmed, I struggled to my feet, letting the broom fall to the earth.

"What is it? Have you been hurt?" I asked, reaching out to him.

"I must find your brother," said Cockrill, scanning the fort's enclosure. "Joseph Hay's dead body is just outside the walls."

"Jamie's gone to Eaton's Station," I said. "What can I do?"

Without answering, the Major pivoted and ran toward the Buchanan cabin yelling, "John. John Buchanan. Come out. I need your help."

John Buchanan emerged followed by his father, John Senior. They looked like two versions of the same man, twenty years apart. Both were of medium height, built as thick as water barrels, with noses as dense and lumpy as potatoes. Only John Senior's thatch of gray hair set him apart. From the fort yard Zach White joined them, as well as James Leeper, a tall, skeletal, black-eyed man whose very presence radiated nervous energy.

The Major explained he was coming to record his land claim with Jamie, but just as he approached the fort, he discovered Hay's bloody body. He asked the four men to grab their guns and follow him. While they went for their weapons, I returned home to gather a linen sheet from my trunk as a burial wrap. It was a sheet David and I had once slept on, and I pressed the folds to my face before I tucked it under my arm and returned to the men.

"No women," said old Mr. Buchanan when he saw me walking toward them, but the Major guided me along as he led the group outside. I assumed he expected no ambush since he surged ahead of us, and it wasn't long before a terrible odor advised me we were near. With a few more steps, I saw Hay's mangled body for myself, still fully clothed in a suit of rust-colored homespun, the garment darkly stained with blood. He had been scalped, a four-inch strip of hair and skin removed down the center of his head. I would have expected scalping, but his torso had also been hacked repeatedly, the head almost severed from his body. Blood, bone and gristle were laid bare. His gun, shot pouch, powder horn and hunting knife had been stripped away.

"They've left him here as a message," the Major said. "To warn we'll have no peace in this place."

The other men shouted amongst themselves, yelling threats into the bright day which seemed to mock our horror with its cheerful sunshine.

"We'll make them pay," threatened James Leeper. "This is our land. Henderson paid a fair price for it. Let's go get them!"

"No," said Cockrill, silencing Leeper. "Our first job is to tend to Joseph, and our second is to spread the word of his death. From now on we must defend ourselves at all times."

He explained that the thirty families who were scattered nearby would need to build forts of their own, or return to stations like ours. Anyone who lived alone was asking for slaughter.

"As soon as we can find Colonel Robertson, we must organize a fighting group," Cockrill said. "And starting today, we'll need guards posted at the gate day and night."

It was war all over again. The very thing we had traveled so far to avoid. I knelt beside Hay's body and wept, not because I knew the man, but because of what his death meant for all of us. I had been living in a dream world to think that there would be no Indian attacks, but I couldn't possibly misinterpret this sign. Hay had been shot a number of times, enough bullets to have killed him easily, and yet the gun shots were followed by the needless hacking of his body, the axe plunged into his chest and neck. How they must hate us, to violate his body in this way. The only time that I could remember violently killing one of God's creatures was long before when I was working in the garden at Fort Caswell.

Polly had been just a toddler the day I carried her to the field to play in the dirt with a stick while I dug for potatoes. During one of the many times I looked up to check on her, I discovered a long brown snake advancing through the grass in her direction. I grabbed the hoe, cautioning Polly to sit still, while I moved toward the glistening snake until I was close enough to strike. I clubbed it thoroughly with the first blow, but continued to hit it again and again, chopping its body into twenty parts. Later I explained that my frenzy was due to fear the vile reptile would kill my child. But now I believed it was more than fear. It was hate that made me bash the snake long after it posed a threat. Joseph Hay's murder was also a product of hate and fear, and we would surely be subject to the Indians' wrath in the future. With sadness in my heart, I silently handed the sheet to Major Cockrill and made my slow return to the fort.

That evening Charlotte invited the Major for dinner, and after Jamie returned, we gathered around the fire, a comfort against the cool evening air. Mark and John arranged themselves on the floor beside Cockrill's chair and eagerly questioned him about his adventures in the weeks he had been absent. John was particularly interested in the quality of the land, while Mark enquired about the availability of game. As soon as our meal was finished, Hagar and Henry cleared the dishes, and Betsy jumped into the Major's lap to ask for a story, proud that she had restrained herself for so long a time. I admonished her to leave him alone, so Cockrill carefully slid her to the floor, promising a good yarn the next day.

"I'm sorry," I said, pulling a chair beside the Major. "She thinks she has a claim on you."

"She does," he answered, leaning forward so that his elbows rested on his broad thighs. As he inspected the fire that had grown low, he appeared more weathered, his skin darkened. Silence fell between us, and I struggled for what to say.

"We looked for you at the Compact signing," I said lightly, as if his absence was immaterial to me. After what must have been a full minute he explained that he had been detained because of the land he had claimed. It was part meadow and part forest, with a strong spring of fresh, sweet water. He had even started a cabin, cutting logs and gathering stones for the chimney.

"Got to put that behind me," he added. "It's not safe to be so far from the fort."

We were interrupted by the unexpected arrival of the Buchanan men, John and his father, as well as James Leeper. Leeper marched quickly to the hearth and turned to face us, as if he had been commissioned as the commanding officer for the evening.

"Don't hang back, Leeper," said Mark, smiling. "Just make yourself at home."

The others laughed while Leeper scowled back at them.

"I see nothing funny about murderous Indians," he said. "I didn't hear you laughing about our headless friend out there," he added, gesturing toward the darkened meadow. "Colonel Robertson, we've come to discuss what must be done."

Charlotte moved quickly across the room to Jamie's chair. "Can't we have this discussion after the children are asleep?" she asked Jamie, her forehead wrinkled with concern.

"The more they know, the safer they'll be," he answered.

"But James," Charlotte continued, putting her hand on his arm in protest.

He took her hand and pressed it tenderly. "I'm right about this," he said sternly, and she pulled back with a defeated air.

"Sit down, gentlemen," said James. "I'm afraid the floor will have to do."

"Zach White would be here, but he volunteered as sentry for the evening," said Leeper, too agitated to sit. The Buchanans settled on the floor beside Mark and John, old Mr. Buchanan moving more stiffly than his son.

"Oh Jamie," I said, turning toward him. "Could Dragging Canoe have followed us here? Would he come so far just to torture us?"

"It's not the Chickamaugas," said Jamie, drawing on his pipe. "I heard talk at Eaton's that Spanish agents have paid the Chickasaws and Choctaws to wage war on us."

"But Spain is supposed to be our ally against England," said Leeper, pacing before the fire.

"That's their official position," continued Jamie, pulling himself into a more upright position. "I'm afraid their unofficial position is something far different. We heard from a friendly Chickasaw that the Spanish learned North Carolina has promised land grants to soldiers in the Continental army. They want to scare off any of those veterans . . . to keep this land available for Spaniards who may come in the future."

"But that's disgraceful," said Leeper, stopping abruptly and then raising slightly forward on his toes. "What kind of country is Spain?"

"Like any other, I'm afraid," said Jamie.

"Well, no dirty Spaniard or Indian is going to drive me away," growled Leeper. "I'm planning to marry Susan Drake and start my family here."

"Susan Drake?" I asked. It was an unfamiliar name.

"She'll be moving here from Eaton's Station," he added. "She said she'll have me, and I guess this is as good a time as any to ask Colonel Robertson if he'll do the honors."

Jamie put his pipe on the table and stood to shake Leeper's hand. "It would be my privilege," he said. "Charlotte! This calls for a celebration. In the midst of our sorrow, we've been given a cause for happiness. Bring out the rum!"

Hagar distributed our odd assortment of pewter cups and wooden bowls so there were enough vessels to go around. Charlotte followed her, pouring a small ration into each container.

"To your happiness," said Jamie, addressing us all. "And to God's blessing for a long and happy life for the newlyweds-to-be!"

All the men drank, but it was clear the alcohol had no enlivening effect on Major Cockrill.

"We're got real problems," said Cockrill, effectively halting the celebratory mood. He rubbed his forehead thoughtfully. "I've seen signs of Indians throughout the area. I believe they've been watching us for some time, developing a war strategy. Joseph's death is just the first sign of their intentions."

"I say we get a party together and kill every last one of them," suggested Leeper, his black eyes lustrous in the fire's light.

"They've been hunting these woods all their lives, know all the hiding places," said Cockrill. "Trying to kill them all would be next to impossible."

"So we have to sit here like fish in a barrel, waiting to be shot?" asked John Buchanan. "That's not the way I do things."

"Major," Jamie began, "Would you be willing to alert our friends in the wilderness, and scout out the Indians' whereabouts on the way."

"I'll do my best, Sir," he answered with a solemn nod.

"And we'll continue to have sentries watching for Indians," added Jamie. "But I don't think it's likely they'll attack the fort. They'll go for easier targets. Men out hunting. Cabins alone in the wilderness."

"Cowards," said Leeper. "Let them engage us man to man."

"The Indians are no cowards, Leeper," Jamie said, stopping Leeper's diatribe. "Their ways are different from ours. And often a lot more effective."

"But they kill innocent women and children," exclaimed Leeper.

"Our savagery has matched theirs, I'm afraid," said Jamie. "One of our own has sunk so low as to kill a pregnant Indian woman and pierce the heart of her unborn child."

"James!" said Charlotte.

"Savagery begets savagery," he went on. "I believe we are beginning a long war with the natives. Our hope that this was unclaimed land was apparently wrong. We must fight the Indians here, even as our brothers fight the British across the mountains."

"Maybe you're wrong," said Charlotte. "Maybe Joseph Hay's death was an accident."

"You didn't see him, Ma'am," the Major said sadly. "It was no accident."

"We're lucky in one respect," Jamie added. "We could have lost many more victims because we have not been vigilant. I'll give the word that from now on, no one will leave the fort unaccompanied. And every man who works outside these gates will have another guarding him. We'll be like the crows. No one ever comes on a crow unannounced; they always have a scout to sound the alarm."

I didn't want to be like a crow: dark and foreboding. I had come here so that my children could run and play freely, and yet Jamie had pronounced a prison sentence.

"Oh, Jamie," I sighed. "We have come so far, and for what?"

"We don't know the full extent of the danger," Jamie continued, knowing my question had no answer. "Cockrill will bring back the latest information about our enemies, and tomorrow I'll organize a militia. I can promise every onslaught will be met with a full retaliation."

Jamie's words and enthusiasm gave me no comfort. All I could think of was the need to protect my daughters. In our three weeks at Fort Nashborough, the girls had grown used to playing outside the palisade walls, even foraging in the woods for acorns. Last week, one of the mares had given birth and all the children watched as the new colt took his first shaky steps and within minutes was kicking up his tender hooves in the grassy meadow. What a sign of promise that event had been. But now hope was gone. Joseph had been the sacrificial lamb, offered on the altar of our trusting innocence.

While the men drank their rum, I took the opportunity to study James Leeper with some diligence, wondering what Susan Drake saw in his lean face and fevered eyes. He certainly seemed to have the fire necessary to protect his family, but was it a fire that would burn too brightly and too hot? At least he was a man of passion. One unafraid to declare himself and take the responsibility of a wife, unlike Major Cockrill who sat contemplating the interior of his cup.

"Drink up, gentlemen," said Jamie. "Let's enjoy every ounce of happiness this evening. To Captain Leeper and his bride," he said as he lifted his cup high. "To the future," he called with a smile that seemed to challenge any threat. "Man proposes. God disposes. He is surely on our side!"

The rest of us showed less cheer than Jamie. Leeper, of course, joined in the drinking with enthusiasm, holding out his cup for another round, enjoying the special privilege of a prospective bridegroom. I left to organize bedtime for my children where Hagar was already preparing the bed. I took Charity's nightgown from the trunk.

"You were right about the Indians," I said as I watched her turn back the freshly laundered sheet, folding it with a snap. Only that morning she had taken the laundry outside the fort and spread it across the privet hedge where it dried in the sun. Her ability to carry out that ritual was over unless someone stood watch.

"Wasn't nothing but listening. First to the dogs and then to Henry," she said. "Nobody else wanted to hear the truth, but just 'cause you don't want to hear bad news, doesn't mean it goes away."

I threaded Charity's small arms through the sleeves of her white gown and settled the garment over her head.

"Do I have to go to bed?" asked Charity. "Charlotte gets to stay up."

"Charlotte can't sleep because of her coughing, you know that. You wouldn't want to trade places," I said.

"But I wish I was held all the time like Charlotte is."

"Hush up," said Hagar. "You don't know what you're asking for. That child didn't draw a decent breath this whole day. You thank the Good Lord for being who you are."

"Into bed," I said, not wanting to dwell on little Charlotte's problems. "That's a good girl," I continued as I deposited Charity into the center of the bed. She pulled the covers under her chin and looked at me, her bright blue eyes fringed with dark lashes.

"I thank God for lots of things, Mama. But I didn't know I had to thank him for each breath."

"It's something we all forget, Honey," I said. "Even me."

Not long after we had put the children to bed, Cockrill, Leeper and the Buchanans departed, and we turned in shortly thereafter. I lay beside Charity and considered both the fort's situation and my own. Particularly my own.

I was sorry I had not been able to speak to the Major alone. What had he been thinking when he laid out his parcel of land, notching the trees that marked the boundaries, maybe even carving his initials on them? Did he envision his own children playing on that grassy land some day? Did he see a wife sitting before some future fire, patching the holes in his trousers? While imagining the Major building his new cabin, I inched my way deeper and deeper into sleep.

Some time later I was awakened by a petrifying scream, my neck instantly covered with sweat. In a few moments my eyes adjusted to the dark, and I saw Charlotte kneeling before the fire, little Charlotte in her arms. She was rocking back and forth, emitting low terrible wails in front of the flaming logs. It looked as if she were tumbling toward some dangerous precipice, only to be pulled back, and then lurching forward once more. Jamie hovered over her, mumbling words I couldn't hear because of the cries.

"Mama," came a voice beside me. "Mama, what's wrong?"

"Shhh," I said, positioning myself so that Charity couldn't see the scene before the hearth. "Go back to sleep."

"But I'm scared," said Charity. "Is it the Indians?"

"No baby. Not the Indians. Go back to sleep. You'll be all right."

"Promise?" she asked.

"I promise," I said, kissing her forehead.

I knew my words weren't enough to put Charity back to sleep, but I slipped from the bed and moved toward the fire where Charlotte wept. Hagar was there already, putting on more logs for what promised to be a long night of grief.

"Charlotte," I began, stooping so that I saw what I had feared, the lifeless form of little Charlotte. The child was swaddled in blankets, but her face was visible; the skin an ashy hue, the lips a dull gray in the firelight. Such a beautiful child, barely two years old, and never once was she graced with a full day of abundant health. Why had God given her such a life of suffering?

"Charlotte," I said, reaching forward to embrace her, but she shook off my arms and continued crying and rocking. I glanced at Jamie, but he only shook his head as if to say he had no idea what to do. Looking to see if Betsy and Polly were still sleeping, I saw instead a cluster of children assembled with their backs against the bed's footboard, staring in silence at the dreadful scene.

I joined the children, and as soon as I had settled on the floor between Polly and Betsy, Charity scrambled into my lap. The older children asked no questions. What had happened was all too apparent. They had lost a sister and a friend.

"An angel took her," I whispered. "God surely sent an angel for someone as sweet and innocent as that child."

"With wings?" asked Betsy.

"I imagine so," I said. "Maybe even wings of shimmering gold."

"I didn't see anything," said Polly.

"The angel could have taken any of us," said Delilah with fear in her voice. "Maybe it's still here."

Charity began to cry softly. "I don't want to go to heaven," she said, grabbing my shirt.

"But Daddy's there," said Betsy.

"It's not your time," I said. "Baby Charlotte was sick and couldn't breathe. This was God's way of helping her."

"I'm never getting sick again," said Polly.

The children were justified in their alarm: death hovered over us like an unseen presence. This very day had affirmed that the weak or the unprepared could easily lose their lives. I clenched my jaw until it seemed my teeth would crumble. I would be vigilant for us all. Or die trying.

# Seventeen

MAY 22, 1780 — *Another week raced by as we tried to recover from little Charlotte's death. Jamie officiated at her burial ceremony, and the pain of it tore our hearts asunder. The first time in my life that I have seen him cry. The morning of the funeral was gray, unseasonably warm with a threat of rain. An oppressive atmosphere hung thick upon us, as if steam from a thousand pots filled the air. I believe God sent such humid weather to remind us of the difficulty little Charlotte experienced with every breath. We made a grim procession as we filed across the meadow to the spot where Joseph Hay had been buried the day before. It is a terrible omen that in only three weeks, we have already begun a cemetery.*

*The funeral crowd was a large one; maybe fifty people marched in line to that pretty spot where wild flowers grow near the sulfur spring. John and Mark carried the little wooden coffin as Major Cockrill and three others brought up the rear, armed in case of Indian attack. As I walked in the procession I was reminded of David's death three years ago, and I realized I have almost forgotten what it is like to have a husband. Now that we are far away from Fort Caswell, so little reminds me of him. Of course when I look into the children's eyes, I always see hints of his expression, but every year they become less a part of us and more individuals of their own.*

*At the grave site the sound of Charlotte's weeping was overtaken by the raucous and unseemly call of crows circling in the air above us. We should have enjoyed a choir of songbirds instead to lift our hearts to heaven. Jamie began the service by reading from Ecclesiastes, "To every thing there is a season, and a time to every purpose under the heaven." He continued with the whole verse which always brings comfort to the grieving heart. Afterwards in private, he added his own sad note to the occasion, a confession that he was the one to blame for Charlotte's death. If he had not brought his family into this wilderness, the child might be alive today; since the cold and deprivation of the journey surely led to her death. At the sight of his tears, Charlotte renewed her crying and the rest of us joined in. For what can we do but weep?*

*Maybe he is right, that our journey was the determining factor in Charlotte's death, that her daily exposure to the river's dampness made things worse. But who can know? The winter was surely as cold at Fort Caswell as on the river. It is useless to speculate. We must see to it that Jamie and Charlotte do not harbor blame in their hearts, but instead focus on the new challenges ahead. We know there will be challenges because Major Cockrill returned from his scouting expedition to report numerous signs of Indian campsites. Although he saw no savages nearby, as surely as the sun rises in the morning, they will return, whether or not we are ready. We must put away our old sorrows to bear the ones that are to come.*

After lunch I sat on a stool outside, mending Polly's skirt to make it presentable. My hair fell across my face so I had to stop repeatedly to push it back, a nuisance. I refused, however, to wear a foolish ruffled cap.

"You need some combs, Mrs. Johnson," said Major Cockrill. I had not expected a visit from him, and he shifted from foot to foot, as awkwardly as an unsure rooster.

"A hat like yours would do," I answered.

He removed his hat and set it on my head where it quickly slipped to my ears, managing to cover even my eyes.

"Now that's a big help," I laughed, pulling it off and handing it back to him. "Have you come to say goodbye?" I asked. "Last time you took off without so much as a word."

"I'm not going anywhere," he answered wistfully, looking toward the forest.

"But what about your land?"

"It'll wait," said Cockrill. "Too dangerous to work alone now."

"But you were ready to build your cabin."

"Guess I'll have to build one here first," he answered, brushing the side of his trousers with his hat. "Get in some practice while I wait for things to settle down. Looks like there's enough cedar trees for everybody to build a cabin or two."

So, he was going to stay!

"Well, there are plenty of folks here to help you," I said. "I'm sure John and Mark will lend a hand."

"I'd be much obliged," said Cockrill. After a short pause when he seemed to study intensely a dandelion growing at his feet, he continued. "I came to say something else. Something that's been on my mind for some time."

He cleared his throat and the next words tumbled out louder than the first.

"I'd like to come calling," he said, his brow wrinkled as if in pain.

"Come calling?" I repeated, as if I didn't know what he meant. "Looks like you're calling right now."

"Mrs. Johnson," he said with a sigh of exasperation. "Can't you make this easier for me? If you don't want my company, just say so. I don't want to waste your time."

I was ashamed at the pleasure I had gotten from teasing him. He was making a serious proposal and deserved a serious reply.

"I like your company very much, Sir," I said, a little more enthusiastically than I'd planned. "And the children are always happy to see you," I added carefully.

"I see," said Cockrill. "Do you give me hope with one hand and take it away with the other? It's only the children who want to see me?"

"Oh Major, please." I put down my mending. "You are welcome at our home. Always."

A shout drew my attention to the gate where three horsemen entered and pulled up short in the middle of the yard: the first, none other than Johnny Jennings, come back from the dead! He was accompanied by Sam Butler and a trapper whose horse was loaded with brown and gray fur pelts. Johnny Jennings bore signs of torture, his head scalped and covered with a mixture of scars and scabs, his right arm hanging loosely at his side.

The sound of arrivals brought Jamie and others to cluster around the newcomers who had dismounted. The third man introduced himself as Ralph Rogers, who explained he was hunting beaver when he came upon the Chickamauga village where Johnny was held captive. He soon learned from the Indians that Johnny's companion, Robert Wood, had already been killed, and that some wanted to make sure Johnny received the same treatment. When Rogers learned that Johnny was the brother of Edmund Jennings, a man he had often hunted with, he paid his ransom of two hundred fur pelts, and was on his way to Fort Nashborough when they reached Clover Bottom. It was there that Sam had volunteered to show him the quickest route to the fort. Jamie approached Johnny and carefully placed his hands on the return captive's shoulders. The boy was terrible to look at, with raw skin running in a brutal path across the top of his scalp.

"Your family's prayers have been answered," Jamie said with some emotion. "They have settled just up river, and once you've rested sufficiently, we'll send you home. I hope you won't mind telling us your story in the meantime."

Johnny didn't speak, but nodded somewhat reluctantly, and Jamie led the way back to his cabin. As we followed them, Sam made a point of passing close and giving a pleading look.

"Why don't you come too, Major?" I said, ignoring Sam. "It's not exactly what you had in mind by calling on me, but I wish you'd join us just the same."

"I wouldn't think of missing it," he said, possessively putting his hand at my elbow.

The cabin was packed thoroughly with our neighbors, all eager to hear Johnny's adventures. Hagar brewed some peppermint tea for Johnny, but it was obvious from her stony eyes that she had forgiven him nothing. Charlotte hustled the children outside while the adults settled in chairs around the table, on the beds, and on every square inch of the floor as well. There was little conversation in the room as everyone anxiously waited to hear Johnny's story. He lowered his terribly injured head and seemed struck dumb.

"Go ahead, boy," Jamie coaxed. "We need to know what happened."

"He's hardly said a word since we've been traveling," said Sam, crouching on his knee beside Johnny. He put his hand under Johnny's chin and lifted it.

"It's all over, son. It's safe to talk now."

"If you tell us what happened," said Jamie evenly, "it may help to save other lives."

"I can't help anyone," said Johnny bitterly. "The only reason I'm alive is because the chief protected me."

He stared down, as if he could make everyone in the room disappear if he didn't look at us. But he knew he was obliged to tell his story before we would let him leave, so after a few minutes he began. The room was still except for the occasional crack of the fire. I strained to hear the words he spoke in a whisper.

"I was half crazy when I jumped into that river with Robert," said Johnny, massaging his bad arm in a distracted manner. "I just wanted to escape, but by the time I reached the canoe, I knew we didn't have a chance. The bullets were hitting the boat, and my buddy, Robert, took a ball in his shoulder as he climbed into the canoe.

"Instead of trying to paddle away from the Indians, I steered right toward them while Robert stood in the bow, waving his arms in surrender. But when our boat hit the shore, a group of twenty wrestled us to the ground."

"Did they speak to you in English?" asked Jamie.

"Not a word," answered Johnny, forcing himself to look at Jamie. "But we could tell by the way they hollered and swung their tomahawks that most of them were ready to kill us right away. They were a terrible sight. One side of their heads was painted black and the other side red as the devil."

Johnny seemed so rattled by his memories that Charlotte put a hand on his good arm.

"You can tell us the rest later if you want," she said.

"No," he answered. "I want to get this over with."

Johnny went on to explain that after maybe ten minutes of arguing, the Indians tied them behind pack horses and set off on a long march. He pointed to his feet which were covered by a pair of roughly made moccasins.

"These feet of mine still hurt from that journey. Our shoes rubbed blisters on our feet until the leather completely fell apart. We must have walked twelve miles until we came to their village filled with cabins as good as any white man ever built. They took us to the center of town where we found more Indians covered with war paint and looking as if they'd dearly love to separate our heads from our bodies. In the middle of them was a surprising sight: a little old white man, stooped over with hair as thick and white as a pile of cotton bolls. He acted as the Chief's translator."

Johnny warmed to his story somewhat as he continued with a more energetic tone.

"We stood there kind of hang-dogged in the middle of maybe fifty Indian men while our captors told our story to Chief White Horse. He was a fine looking man, six feet tall with well-muscled shoulders and arms as thick as the trunk of a small oak. After a lot of shouting the chief motioned to the old man to tell us what was going on: that the Indians were arguing about whether Robert and I were old enough to be men or if we were still boys. If we were men, they would kill us straight away. If we were boys, they would keep us as servants. I never thought I'd be so pleased to be called a boy."

Here the assembled crowd laughed, relieved to have an occasion to break the tension.

"Who was the old man?" asked Sam. "A half-breed?"

"No," Johnny replied. "He was a trapper who fell in love with an Indian woman and gave up everything to stay with her. He felt plenty sorry for us, but the only advice he could give was to prepare to meet our Lord. When I fell to my knees to ask God's mercy on my soul, I remembered a Bible story Mama used to tell about Stephen being stoned. In the middle of his ordeal, he lifted his eyes to the skies where he saw a vision: the heavens parting and Jesus sitting on the right hand of the Father. Course I knew what a sinner I was, but I hoped maybe God's mercy would let me see a vision too. So I lifted my eyes for a glimpse of the Lord, but all I saw was Robert running for the woods as fast as he could. It was the dumbest thing he could have done because it made the Indians madder than if they'd been stung by a hundred bees. About thirty of them set off after Robert, whooping and firing their rifles. One of the first bullets caught him in the leg, and threw him to the ground. The Indians fell on him pretty rough and dragged him back to the chief."

Johnny was sweating with eyes wide like a frightened animal.

"I was still on my knees, and looked to the old man to translate what they were saying, but he didn't need to tell me that Robert was a goner. It wasn't any time before they took him to a mound of earth where an upright pole was stuck in the center and tied him with leather thongs. They piled wood and brush around him, yelling and chanting all the while, Robert begging for mercy, the Indians keeping to their task. There was nothing I could do but watch them light their cane torches and set fire to the timber."

Johnny had tears in his eyes and stopped to ask for more tea. Hagar silently poured it, while we waited for the obvious end of the story.

"That wood was so dry it blazed in a second. Even though the Indians were whooping and shouting, I could still hear Robert's screams as his skin turned to black and his hair burst into flames like a candle's wick. I closed my eyes and fell to praying, trying not to think of what was in store for me."

He was listening to the fire finish its work when an angry argument broke out among the warriors. After a prolonged squabble about his fate, Chief White Horse called for a vote as to whether or not he should live. The chief wanted to adopt him, as many Indians did with their captives, but others were in favor of killing him right away. They reminded White Horse of Dragging Canoe's warning that prisoners would merely learn their ways, escape, and bring others to destroy them. Johnny was saved by a single vote. Many of the men were extremely disappointed and glared at him hostilely as the chief gestured for Johnny to stand. He told Johnny in broken English that he was going to be received into the tribe, and that in the future, he should address the chief as "uncle" and all the other warriors as "brother."

"Most of them didn't look like brothers to me," said Johnny, "Unless it was Cain and Abel, but two of the friendly ones took me to their cabin where they did their best to make me into an Indian."

They cut his hair, shaving both sides of his head, leaving only a small scalp lock on top where they tied a collection of bird feathers. They replaced his old clothes with a coarse piece of dun-colored cloth four feet long and fifteen inches wide that substituted for his breeches, and finished his costume with a pair of leggings and a shirt which hung to his waist.

"The boys I lived with were kind to me, but the ones who held allegiance to Dragging Canoe swore to kill me, in spite of the chief's protection. I had to watch my back all the time, but finally they got me at dusk one night. My friend and I were returning to our cabin when a dozen braves set upon us. Two grabbed my friend while the others beat me, took my scalp and left me for dead. I guess when Chief White Horse heard about my attack, he realized I would never be safe, so he traded me to Mr. Rogers, and here I am."

Johnny leaned back into his chair, closed his eyes and sighed deeply.

"Did you learn anything about their plans to attack us?" asked Jamie.

"Sir," Johnny said, without even opening his eyes. "I never understood much of what they said unless the old man translated for me."

"I've known White Horse for many years," added Rogers. "And he's changed. When I was one of the few trappers through here, he was happy to trade with me. But now he's been listening to Dragging Canoe and sees us as a plague of insects destroying their crops."

Jamie thought for a moment and then addressed Johnny. "Thank you for telling your story, Son," he said warmly. "You've come through a rough patch, and I expect you could do with a bit of rest now."

Johnny nodded and John Buchanan spoke up.

"He can come to our place," he said. "We've got some spare beds. We can take you too, Sam, and you, Mr. Rogers."

There was a hum of talk as the crowd disbursed and Sam Butler helped Johnny from his chair. As they filed toward the door, Sam paused briefly in front of me.

"Can I have a word with you later, Annie?" he asked politely.

I could feel the Major stiffen beside me.

"I suppose so," I answered, stepping aside to let them pass.

The Major and I followed into the afternoon sunshine, and I returned to my mending. The Major paced in short, quick steps in front of me.

"Oh do sit down, Major," I said, surprised to see him fidget uncharacteristically. "I have a question to ask you about the Indians," I continued. "How could Chief White Horse have considered adopting Johnny for even a moment, if he knows how Dragging Canoe feels?"

"The Indians believe in transmutation," said the Major, finally sitting down, crossing his legs but still managing to look as if he were at attention. "They believe if certain rites are performed, like ceremonial washings and hair plucking, then the captive can take on the soul of a dead relative."

"Mercy," I said. "How can they believe such a thing? That the soul of a dead father, for instance, could somehow slip into the body of their sworn enemy!"

"I guess it's no more strange than thinking Jesus ascended into heaven."

"Major, that's blasphemy," I said, really shocked.

"My point is that we all believe things we can't prove, that seem beyond logic."

"Oh, Major," I said, suddenly forlorn. "I don't see how we're ever going to get along with the Indians. We're too different."

"We want this land, and they want this land. That doesn't sound too different to me."

"Oh, for goodness sake. You know we're nothing like the Indians."

"I disagree," he shook his head, "but I can see you're not about to change your mind." He slowly rose. "I've got to go. Promised Leeper I'd help him with a wagon wheel."

"Good day then, Major," I said, peeved that he was ready to go before we had finished a proper conversation. Our exchange had been anything but courting.

"And one more thing, Mrs. Johnson," he said, looking down at me with a cautionary air. "I'd use every care around that Butler man."

"Thank you for your concern," I said, but knew his warning was unnecessary. Sam was just an annoyance I would deal with as soon as I had the opportunity.

I waited all morning and most of the afternoon for Sam Butler's return, irritated that he hadn't come more quickly so I could put his attentions behind me once and for all.

"Looks like our Annie's got a burr in her breeches," Mark said, playfully shoving my foot. "Anything to do with Major Cockrill?"

"I'm upset," I said, pulling away my foot. "As mad as I was when Johnny abandoned Elizabeth and the baby, I wouldn't have wished him such dreadful treatment."

"It was terrible to hear about Robert Wood too," said Jamie. "You don't hear much of Indians burning folks. I'm afraid it's a measure of how their anger has grown of late."

"Chief White Horse told Mr. Rogers that many of his braves had died of the small pox," added Mark. "When the fever seized them, they lost their minds and jumped in the river to drown."

"They wouldn't have gotten the pox if they hadn't slaughtered the Stuart party," I said. "They deserved it."

"God has a way of bringing justice to the world," said a voice from the door behind us. I turned to see Sam at last, hat in hand, leaning against the door frame with his gun by his side.

"Evening, Sam," said Jamie, standing. "Won't you join us?"

"I wonder if I might have a word with Annie," Butler said.

"I guess you might," said Jamie, when he saw me advance toward Sam. He chuckled and sat down.

I didn't bother looking at my children or anyone else as I darted through the door. I knew my brothers would be smiling and making much of this development, but I didn't care. As soon as we were through the door, I abruptly faced Sam, and he stumbled back to avoid bumping into me.

"I have told you to leave me alone," I said abruptly.

"But I've spent the day preparing a surprise for you."

"A surprise?" I responded. "I would think Johnny Jennings was surprise enough."

"Have you ever been fire hunting?" he asked.

I had not, and I couldn't imagine what such activity had to do with the two of us. On summer evenings, men would venture to the creeks where the deer gathered to avoid the mosquitos and eat mosses that grew along the banks. The hunters took torches with them, and the deer, startled by the unexpected light, would stare at the flames, transfixed. Their glowing eyes provided perfect targets.

"No, I've never been, and I don't intend to go hunting now. Certainly not after hearing Johnny Jennings' story."

"Come on Annie. The Indians who captured him were more than a hundred miles away. I spent the day looking around here, and I saw no sign of savages. I found the perfect spot to hunt deer though, and it's not too far away."

"And what has that got to do with me?" I asked, irritably.

"I've heard the fort is almost out of meat," he said, stepping closer, raising his hand as if to touch me, but lowering it when he saw my frown.

I couldn't disagree with that. The need for fresh game was an ever present one, and the visitors passing through constantly drained our supply.

"At least let me show you how I've rigged my boat for hunting. It's just down at the river," he added.

I supposed it would do no harm to see the provisions he'd prepared. And I'd feel more comfortable confronting him away from the earshot of others. I followed him down the bluff until we reached the water's edge. It was a clear evening, with the setting sun reflecting red and orange on the river's surface. Little waves kicked at the sun's reflections and multiplied them. He pointed to a birch wood canoe that contained a bowl made out of rocks filled with pine knots, ready to be lit. I wasn't sure how to begin my onslaught against him, so I started with a question about Colonel Donelson's progress at Stone's River.

"Well," Sam answered, "the Colonel's had us burn a forest full of cane, and we've gathered brush, cut down trees, and made rough fences. We've planted cotton and enough corn to feed every animal and person in the settlement. I've never seen such a pretty sight, Annie, rich bottom land filled with cane and trees. And on the hills sloping down to the valley are fields of clover, shimmering white, like clouds fallen from the sky."

"Clover Bottom," I said, remembering. "It's as beautiful as it sounds."

"Prettiest place I've ever seen," said Butler.

He gestured for me to sit down. "Your freckles are fading," he said. "Like those little flowers that close when the sun goes down."

Suddenly a terrible yell filled the air, and before we could move, an Indian fell hard upon Sam, brandishing a long blade. I watched in horror as they wrestled, the Indian whooping ever louder. Sam had unsheathed his knife somehow, and he and the Indian rolled on the ground in a deadly embrace, each straining to kill, first one on top, then the other. Sam's gun had been thrown to the ground, and I dashed toward it, praying it was loaded, but even when I hoisted it to my shoulder, it was impossible to get a clear shot at the Indian.

He was fearless and finally succeeded in wrenching away Sam's knife by grabbing the blade and twisting it from Sam's hand. Although it cut the Indian horribly, the blood bursting from his fingers, he now had both weapons and Sam was defenseless. The Indian stabbed Butler once, rendering him senseless and then jumped up to attack me.

I was already running for the fort, my heart thudding in my chest, my breath coming fast. Briefly glancing back, I could see his face drawing closer, painted entirely black, hideously contorted. He was naked except for a breechcloth, and the outline of his knife was raised against the darkening sky. I prepared to die and cursed myself for abandoning my children in such a senseless way.

Even before I heard the rifle's shot, I felt blood spring from the Indian's body and hit my neck. I screamed as he slammed me to the rocky ground. His hand fell two inches from my face, so close I could smell his blood. With difficulty I wriggled from beneath his body, sobbing at the horror. Sobbing, sobbing, aware that someone was coming toward me, feet thudding through the underbrush.

"No . . . No, no, no," I screamed through my tears.

I drew myself tightly into a ball, shivering, screaming, almost blind from the ordeal. I lashed out at the man who knelt beside me until I recognized the reassuring sound of his voice. Then I let Major Cockrill gather me into his arms and hold me tightly until the terror began to subside.

# *Eighteen*

MAY 24, 1780 — *Two days have passed since the Major rescued me. Although everyone gossips about my foolish behavior, I care only for his good opinion. He learned of my whereabouts when he came to call shortly after Sam and I left. Charlotte told him we had just set off, and he was alarmed for my safety. I don't know if his actions were driven by the wish to see what would transpire between Sam and me, but I hope he witnessed enough to know it was nothing.*

*When he escorted me back to our cabin, he explained to Charlotte that I had suffered a fearful shock from an Indian's assault, but that I was unharmed. He then withdrew to take Sam to the Buchanans for assistance. I must have been a fearful sight, my face and clothes splattered with blood, my hair in disarray. Charlotte offered no reproaches, instead summoning Henry to go at once to the spring to bring water for my bath.*

*Never before has Charlotte been a dearer sister to me than on that evening. She put away her own grief to tend my every need, bathing me, all the while assuring me that I would be all right. The warm water soothed as it coated my skin, but it could not calm my distressed mind. I kept reliving the sight of the Indian coming toward me with his knife raised, as if I were flipping through a book and every page contained the same dreaded picture. On top of this terror, I became possessed by the idea that Charlotte should burn the shirt and trousers that I had worn for so long. I believed that in destroying those clothes I could erase the memory of what had happened. Charlotte tried to comfort me, saying that she was sure they could be washed properly, eradicating the stains. But I would not stop my wailing until the hunting clothes were placed on the fire and began their transformation into ash. They had long since served to remind me of David, and I had no regrets about their destruction. I wear a simple gray dress now, with a white apron, and even a ruffled cap. Although these clothes seem burdensome, they are the symbols of my new life as a thoughtful woman.*

*I know that when I agreed to go to the river with Sam, I had no dishonorable intentions. My error was in being foolhardy as to my safety. I will not make that mistake again. They tell me his wound was not a serious one, and he has returned to Eaton's Station to recover. Friendship between us is no longer possible.*

**JULY 4, 1780** — *Almost six weeks have passed since I last had the inclination to write. It has been a lonely time, for I have kept very much to myself. I am trying to reform in every way. Without the smallest grumble, I send Betsy and Polly to Zach White each morning for their lessons. Even when I'm very angry about some foolish remark, I hold my tongue. Jamie teases me and says one Indian has accomplished what a whole family could never achieve: the taming of sister Ann. He says this with humor, but I know he frets because I sometimes catch him stealing worried looks in my direction. It is true that I have slipped into the skin of some more timid character, but I'm sure this is all to the good.*

*Most afternoons a guard watches over me as I chop bull nettles that threaten our young corn. As I work amid the crops, I marvel at what a wonderful gift God gave us when he supplied the corn plant. We can roast and eat it plain or grind it for our bread. We feed it to the hogs, and they in turn provide us with lard and meat. Its fodder we use to feed the horses and the cattle, and its surplus we turn into whiskey. When it reaches its full height, we no longer need to tend its stalks because they hold themselves above the plundering of turkeys and racoons. And each plant beautifully wraps its ears as gifts for us; plump columns covered with golden coins. I can only wish to be as useful as one of these plants I tend. With God's grace, I will become so.*

*Major Cockrill has finished building his cabin within the fort, and I often see him working on its furnishings. Betsy visits him on the way home from her classes, and she sometimes brings stories of his progress, but he never comes calling. I'm afraid Major Cockrill is a door that has shut behind me.*

*Today is Independence Day and we are expecting arrivals from all over the Cumberland to join in a celebration. I have heard that the Jennings and Elizabeth are coming. I look forward to the sight of my old friend.*

The full strength of summer descended on us that morning. The air was thick and muggy, but the warmth was a positive sign as well, of crops maturing and the earth bringing forth its bounty. It had been four years since I experienced such heat while wearing a long skirt, and I couldn't help but think it foolish that women wore such things. But I had made up my mind never to complain about a skirt, so I whistled as Hagar and I took our stools a little after dawn to milk the cows. As we passed the fort's guard on duty, I thanked him for watching over us and stood a moment to note the fat little puffs of cloud stuck on the orange and azure sky. We rounded up Miss Priss and another cow who seemed unimpressed to see us but submitted blandly to our daily ritual. I leaned my cheek against Miss Priss, feeling her soft hide and enjoying the smell.

"I wish I were a cow," I said to Hagar who milked only a few feet away. "She does her job and never gets into trouble."

"A cow can find trouble same as you," said Hagar, wearing a blue head scarf and a dress of brown homespun. "Get into an onion patch. Or go nosing into the forest."

The milk clanged as it hit the pail.

"And she can set her eye on an old bull too," added Hagar, slyly.

"Enough," I warned. After a moment I added, "All right. I wish I were an angel instead."

"If you were an angel, you'd be dead and no use to those sweet girls of yours. You'd better be glad you're you."

I continued to pull on the cow's teats in a rhythmic way.

"I suppose I don't have any choice," I added. "But I'm getting better aren't I? I do my chores. I keep my opinions to myself."

Hagar didn't answer.

"Surely you can compliment my good behavior," I said, turning abruptly to look at her.

"If you think it's good to scuttle around like a pale-eyed possum, then you're doing good, Miss Ann. You're doing a good job, all right."

"I'm behaving myself," I said defensively. "No one can say any different."

"And your children think they've lost their Mama on top of losing their Papa."

"They'll never lose me. I'll see to that . . . even if I have to tie my leg to the bed frame."

Hagar just laughed. "I got to be a slave. Nobody says you got to."

We finished milking in silence and returned to join Charlotte in preparation for the party. Jamie was admiring the wrinkled copy of the Declaration of Independence which he had carried for three years. He announced that in light of the occasion, he would read it to the assembled group later in the day and then instruct the men to fire their rifles thirteen times in honor of the thirteen states.

"You might as well fire the cannon too," I suggested as I put my pail on the hearth beside Charlotte. "Make a mighty blast to tell the Indians we're here to stay."

"Think of the waste of gun powder," said Charlotte, looking into the pail, pleased at the large amount of milk for the children.

"I believe it will cheer the spirits," said Jamie. "And tonight we'll have a dance as well!"

Others might dance, but I made up my mind to join the old women and bow my head.

———

It was ten o'clock when I sat in front of the cabin rinsing fresh greens. Just as I was holding a large batch of the leafy vegetables in both hands, I looked up to see the Jennings enter the gate. Elizabeth and Mrs. Jennings appeared first, followed by the Peyton twins who supported Johnny Jennings between them.

"Ann Robertson Johnson!" she cried. "Look at you in a skirt! What is the meaning of this?" she asked, embracing me.

It was not a subject I wanted to discuss, so I tried to change the topic by asking about Johnny's health instead.

"I won't say a thing until you explain yourself," Elizabeth answered and collapsed on the grass, clamping her lips together. She seemed so determined that I reluctantly told my story.

"Whatever possessed you to give up your trousers?" asked Elizabeth. Her blond hair was almost white in the glare of the July sun.

I was so hot and sticky I could only think of one answer. "The very devil himself," I replied.

Elizabeth laughed so hard she almost tumbled over, and I was gladdened to see my dear friend so happy, even at my expense.

"And what makes you so cheerful, Miss?" I asked, shaking the water from another handful of greens.

"Well, of course we thank the Lord for Johnny's return. Even though it looks as if he'll never be quite right."

I glanced at the Peyton twins who held Johnny as Mrs. Jennings spread a blanket for him. She no longer had to worry about his trouble-making; he would be hobbled for the rest of his years.

"That's not what's giving your cheeks a bloom," I said. "Come on. Tell me."

Elizabeth dropped her head in shyness and then shot a look at me.

"I think I'm pregnant," she said softly. "You mustn't say anything, though. Promise, Ann. I only told Ephraim last night."

"Oh, Honey," I said. "That's the best news I could imagine."

"God's answered my prayers," Elizabeth went on. "I'm ashamed to be so happy, though, when others are not so fortunate. Have you heard about the Donelsons?"

I had heard nothing on that score so Elizabeth explained that two weeks earlier Mary Donelson had given birth prematurely to a son whom she and John Junior named Chesed. No one understood why they chose such an odd name, for in Hebrew it meant *destroyer*. Maybe they picked it because they knew such a tiny baby would never survive, and that his loss would destroy their happiness. And lose him they did.

Elizabeth shook her head, as if to clear the memory of her own loss and went on. Following this tragedy, it rained without interruption for days, flooding the Donelsons' entire cotton and corn crops until they could no longer see the tops of the stalks above the water. All the work they had accomplished in months of effort was destroyed in a few days. In addition, the Indians managed to kill three men in Colonel Henderson's party by catching them unattended. After so much misery, the Donelsons decided to give up working the land at Clover Bottom and move to the safety of Mansker's Station.

The air was abruptly split by a piercing scream, and I caught my breath as I looked for its source. A woman entered the fort who clearly had not come for the day's celebration. She fell on her knees and howled, her clothes shredded, her face darkened with dirt and sweat.

Jamie rushed out of the cabin to aid her.

"Who is it?" Elizabeth asked.

Because of the woman's altered state, it was impossible to tell. Jamie reached her side at the same time as Major Cockrill, and they lifted up her crumpled body. Those of us who had gathered in the fort yard followed them, trying to guess what had happened. When it became clear the Major was taking her to his own cabin, I stopped about twenty feet from the door. I didn't want to see a single item in that cabin where I would never live.

"Come on," said Elizabeth. "Don't you want to hear what happened?"

"I'll know soon enough," I said, planting my feet firmly, balking like a stubborn horse.

"It's Nellie Jones," said Mrs. Jennings, coming up behind us.

Nellie Jones had been a part of our flotilla, but I did not know her well. She and Mr. Jones had left the rest of the group at Red River with the Renfroe party. I remembered worrying about the river's name, and how it might mean danger, but things had gone well at first, the station doubling in size. Now it appeared my fears had been realized.

"You're coming with us," said Elizabeth, pulling me into the cabin.

The interior was dark with only a smoldering fire on the hearth. The desperately hot air pushed in on all of us as we crowded around the bed where Nellie lay. Although the light was dim, I could still see her anguished face. She was about thirty years old, with dark chestnut hair that lay in matted ropes on the pillow. Her face was all sharp angles: jutting chin, pointed nose and bony cheekbones.

"Please stand back," said Jamie, holding Nellie's hand. Major Cockrill knelt on the floor beside her, as anxious as all of us to hear every word.

"We need to hear what's happened, Mrs. Jones," Jamie said, "but take your time."

"We made a terrible mistake," she began with more vigor than I would have imagined possible. "We never should have gone back."

Their settlement's problems had begun after two men were savagely tomahawked and scalped one morning as they fished near the mouth of the Red River. The brutality of the event, coupled with stories of other Indian attacks in the area, convinced them it was time to move, so they quickly gathered a few small items and started their escape. It was only later that evening around the campfire that some of them had misgivings about their quick departure.

"I kept thinking how nice it would be to have my pewter dishes," said Nellie, lying still as death. "And Mrs. Renfroe was hankering after her quilts. We decided we'd been too hasty in leaving. That it wouldn't be too much trouble to go back for our favorite things."

About half of the group, twenty men, women and children, returned that evening to gather the goods they had left behind. They spent all night in their cabins packing their things and set out early the next morning, pleased to have their belongings. They traveled from sun up to sun down without coming on a single sign of Indians. When they camped that night at the edge of a small stream about two miles north of Sycamore Creek, they felt pleased with their decision to return.

"We'd unloaded our pack horses and tied them to trees so they wouldn't stray, and cooked ourselves a fine dinner of fish the men had caught. When we got ready to sleep, my husband, Howard, wanted to spread our blanket away from the others since the mosquitos at the creek were bothering him something terrible."

The Joneses didn't stray too far, however, for they wanted to remain close to the others for safety. They had been asleep for several hours when they were awakened by the chilling sound of Indian war cries.

"Howard grabbed his gun and jumped up, ready to help the others. I begged him not to leave. I knew there was nothing he could do to save anybody, but he took off running and that was the last I saw of him."

At first she waited for his return, but when the shooting and screaming were over and all she could hear were the triumphant whoops of the Indians, she set off and walked a full twenty miles to Fort Nashborough.

She began to cry, the tears trickling down her newly washed cheeks.

"All that killing," she said with a sob. "Even the little children."

She turned her face into the pillow and let the heartache spill.

Jamie motioned for us to leave, and I bolted for the door, as if in leaving I could separate myself from the terrible story. Stepping outside, I shaded my eyes from the sun's bright rays as Elizabeth and her mother followed me.

"It's like the Stuarts all over again," said Mrs. Jennings. "I don't know how much more of this we can stand."

Mrs. Jennings' gaze was settled on Johnny where he sat beside his father and brother. At least Johnny had survived his terrible experience, and although his scalp had little hair, the wounds would heal . . . not like the forty travelers from the Renfroe Station who were gone forever.

"I don't see how we can celebrate after what we heard in there," I said as we trudged back to my cabin.

"It won't be easy," said Elizabeth with a frown on her face. "But we've got to look to the future and hope for the best."

"It'll take more than a speech about freedom to give me hope," said Mrs. Jennings gloomily. "It'll take real freedom. Major Cockrill warned us we'd best move back to a fort, but I can't bear living like chickens in a coop."

Elizabeth saw Ephraim by the blockhouse and left us to tell him the news.

"Sometimes I can't understand God," said Mrs. Jennings. "So much suffering."

"We'll have good times ahead, Mrs. Jennings," I said. "Once this war with Britain is over, and the Indians quit fighting, we'll flourish."

Mrs. Jennings looked doubtful.

"Flourish?" she asked wearily, her thick black brows drawn together. "I'd like to believe that, but when I look at Johnny, all I see is a road of pain rolling out before me."

She turned her back and started for the cabin door.

"I want to pay my respects to Mrs. Robertson," she added, tossing the words over her shoulder. "I heard about her little girl dying." She looked at me with an expression that said, "You see what I mean?" And of course I did.

———

Despite the morning's sorrow, the dance started after dark. And it wasn't just one dance either, for there were two fiddlers in attendance that evening. The big celebration took place around a large fire, with a smaller dance in the Leeper cabin — in part to mark their wedding which occurred the week before. In keeping with my vow to stay out of trouble, I made a point of sitting with Elizabeth and her family.

I marveled that so many of us could act as if we had never heard Nellie Jones' account of the massacre . . . how we could sit with Johnny Jennings in our midst and ignore the scalping knives that awaited us in the forest. It was the only approach that made our lives bearable. Even I had begun to pass most of a day without thinking of my near brush with death. Nevertheless, I felt quite gloomy watching the others dance as if worries belonged to another world. Elizabeth was joyful as she clapped to the music, but she had good reason with a new baby on the way.

"Don't you want to dance, Ann?" she asked, clapping and swaying to the music. "Edmund." She nudged her brother playfully. "You dance with her."

"I don't want to dance," I said, hunching over in protest.

"She might as well dance with a buffalo as dance with me," said Edmund, taking a puff on his pipe. "I'd step on her toe and do about as much damage as one of those beasts."

"I'll dance with you, Mrs. Johnson," said Ephraim, leaning in front of Elizabeth to give me an intense, unwanted stare. "You're looking awfully pretty this evening in your new skirt."

His smell of alcohol blasted my face.

"No, thank you," I replied, leaning away from him.

"You do look prettier than ever," said Elizabeth, smiling. "That new cap favors you."

"I look like a ruffled toad," I said, "And I have no intention of dancing."

"We'll see about that, Mrs. Toad," said Ephraim who stood somewhat clumsily, and to my surprise, reached for my hand. Before I could resist, he pulled me toward him with such force I almost flew to his side. The reel sent us round and round in dizzying fashion, Ephraim's face becoming as red as his hair. I pretended to trip on my skirt, a movement that tripped Ephraim as well, but allowed me to break away and head for the safety of my own cabin.

Although I hoped Ephraim would return to Elizabeth, I heard the thud of his boots following. Panic seized me as I ran across the empty yard, only to hear him running too. At last I reached the cabin and entered, slamming the door behind me. The heat of the day still clung to the interior which was lit by one lone candle. I dragged a chair in front of the door but feared it would provide a poor barrier if Ephraim was determined to enter. I collapsed on the red quilt, breathing heavily and staring at the door.

I heard him knock first and then begin to pound. The force of his beating made the chair dance against the door and finally fall aside. When Ephraim's dark figure entered the room, I shot up from the bed and ran toward the hearth where the fire tools leaned against the stone chimney.

"I heard tell you went to the river with Sam Butler," he said, closing the door behind him and shoving the chair from his path with his foot. He walked unsteadily toward me.

"Go back to your wife, Ephraim," I said. "You don't have any business here."

I held the poker in front of me where he could see it easily.

"You'd better go," I warned. "I won't hesitate to use this."

"Don't be unfriendly," said Ephraim, stopping to assess the situation. "You and my wife are such good friends, I thought we'd get to know each other too," he added, advancing.

The candle illuminated the whites of his eyes, giving him a fiendish appearance.

"Get out of here," I said, raising the poker, preparing to swing.

"Your high tempered ways don't scare me," he laughed.

At that moment the door opened and to my relief, Major Cockrill walked in as calmly as if he were taking a stroll, his rifle by his side.

"Evening, Mrs. Johnson," he said evenly. "You trying to get rid of a varmint?"

"Indeed, Major," I replied, light-headed with relief. "We seem to have a rat on the premises, and I was trying to kill it. Mr. Peyton here was kind enough to offer his help."

"I can take over now," said Cockrill, advancing to Ephraim, his composed demeanor a stark contrast to Peyton's drunkenness. "I believe your wife's looking for you, Ephraim."

Ephraim didn't respond, but anger boiled on his face.

"Elizabeth . . . ," I began, but couldn't choose the right words to follow. What a shame this man was her husband.

Ephraim glared at us both as he moved backwards toward the door. When he reached it, he adjusted his posture with an unconvincing attempt at dignity, lifted the latch, and was gone.

I breathed out a sigh, letting the poker slide to the floor and sagged into the nearest chair.

"You have saved me again," I said, too embarrassed to look at his face.

"Seems like you were amply prepared to save yourself," he answered, picking up the poker to examine it. "Don't think Ephraim would have cared for a piece of iron lodged in his skull," he added, leaning both the poker and his gun against the chimney.

"I did nothing to encourage that man," I said, gripping the chair's seat until my knuckles turned white.

"Mrs. Johnson," said the Major, standing a good ten feet away.

I still couldn't bear to raise my eyes to meet his. Instead, I studied the weave of my gray homespun skirt.

"Ann," he added, softly, coming close until his legs almost touched my knees.

I turned up my head. He had never before called me by my given name.

"If I'm going to spend the rest of my life defending you, we might as well make it legal," he said, putting his hands under my arms and drawing me up. "I'm asking you, plain and simple. Will you marry me?"

I couldn't believe I had heard the words correctly. I couldn't speak.

"You don't make this easy, do you?" he said, putting his hands tenderly on either side of my face. "I love you, Ann Johnson."

His warm brown eyes reflected the candle's light, and I thought I had never loved another man the way I loved him. I tentatively moved my arms until they rested first on his shoulders and then around his neck.

"And I love you, John," I said, his name fire upon my lips.

We kissed, and I melted into his body with a warmth that would blaze for a long time. He released me from the kiss and pressed my head against his chest, whispering low as he continued.

"If these were ordinary times," he said softly, kissing the top of my head, "I would take the time to court you. Pick you flowers. Sit on one of these chairs to talk with your brothers until my legs turned to wood."

He gently leaned me back so that he could look into my eyes.

"But these are terrible days, Ann," he said. "And listening to Mrs. Jones tell her story today made me realize I don't want to wait any longer. I don't intend to die before I've slept with you by my side. Or had a chance to be a Daddy to your girls."

These were words I had been so sure I would never hear. Hot tears filled my eyes.

"Every log I put into my cabin," he continued, "I laid for you. Every piece of furniture I built, I made with you in mind. You're the only woman I have ever loved."

He gently removed my cap.

"Yours is the only hair I ever wanted to watch shine in candlelight."

He brought me close to his chest.

"Even if you can be as stubborn and unbending as that iron poker," he added, chuckling, "I still can't help loving you."

I hugged him back as hard as I could and thanked God for bringing me a man as good and loving as John Cockrill.

# Nineteen

SEPTEMBER 1, 1780 — *I have just read my last journal entry and am amazed at my despair. Who would have thought that a little less than two months later, I would be the happiest woman in the world? For this very day I am going to marry John Cockrill. Oh, thank you God for leading me on this blessed path, and may I always remember that when life seems at its darkest, the possibility for joy remains.*

*Since he proposed to me in July, John has spent all of his time readying our cabin. He has built three chairs for the children that fit them perfectly, each according to her own size. I protested that it was a waste of his energy to create those two small chairs for Charity and Betsy, as they are growing so quickly, but he wanted to demonstrate how dear they are to him. And he crafted a special bed for Polly as well, a gesture that made her feel quite grown up.*

*My Polly. She is the only daughter I feared telling about our marriage. She is the one who remembers her Daddy well, making it difficult to open her heart to another man. But I told her that even though John isn't her real father, he loves her and will take care of her as though he were. She cried a bit, but has visited her new bed many times and asked to cover it with the red quilt David and I shared.*

*Betsy, of course, loves John extravagantly and always has; I believe she thinks he is marrying her instead of me. Charity is young enough to love him for his good stories alone.*

*I have more good news. Charlotte is three months' pregnant. The tiny baby must have been growing in her body, even as little Charlotte was dying. If the new baby is a girl, they plan to name her Charlotte after the sister who went before her. Hagar thinks it is a bad idea, and although she doesn't tell Charlotte, she is casting spells to ensure it will be a boy instead. But I'm sure the baby will be healthy in any case.*

*I do have one terrible incident to relate. In late July, the Indians set upon Mr. Jennings and murdered him in a most horrible fashion. On that particular day, Edmund and Ephraim were hunting, and Mr. Jennings tended his garden without protection. The Indians apparently crept upon him from behind without a single war cry and took him down silently. They followed the murder by hacking his body into pieces and hanging the dismembered parts on nearby bushes for Mrs. Jennings and Elizabeth to discover. How is it possible to exact justice for such an act?*

*The pain of Mr. Jennings' death tempers the happiness I feel, but it also reminds me that I must never let a day pass that I don't savor the good things that arrive unbidden. And today I will become Mrs. John Cockrill. The jubilation surrounding that event will fill the landscape and soar to the heavens.*

Our wedding was scheduled to take place at 5:00 in the afternoon, to give enough time for preparing dinner and allowing the late summer's heat to dissipate. By 4:30 most of the one hundred wedding guests lounged on the soft green grass, listening to Sam Buchanan's fiddle music. Four large fires blazed, and women worked over their pots, each tending portions of the wedding feast: bear meat, buffalo tongue, stewed venison and green corn roasted and made into succotash.

I observed the scene from the cabin door: children playing tag, chasing dogs, and occasionally throwing pine knots into the fires to see the flames dance. By late afternoon, the air had become perfect for the occasion, cool with the crispness of a newly cut apple. The tips of maple leaves glistened scarlet in the dying sun, a sure sign that fall was approaching.

Inside our cabin, Charlotte put last touches to our makeshift wedding cake of corn meal sweetened with honey. Mark and John, proving the best of uncles, had taken all the nieces and nephews to the meadow and took turns entertaining them with horseback rides. Meanwhile I was dismayed to find myself filled with nervous apprehension. I, who had never given my appearance the least consideration, studied my face and hair in the four-inch square of tin that served as a mirror. First I piled my hair on top and secured it with combs, only to despair at the result and let it tumble down. Displeased with that result as well, I tried again, torturing it into a new design.

"For heaven sakes, Ann," Charlotte said. "You'd think John Cockrill had never laid eyes on you."

"I hate this thing," I said, tossing the shiny piece of tin onto the table "No matter what I do, it reflects the fact that I'm ugly as a mule."

"Ann Robertson Johnson," said Charlotte, rolling up her sleeves in disgust. "You ungrateful girl. God made you beautiful, and you tempt fate with this kind of nonsense."

She picked up a brush and drew it through my hair with steady purpose.

"I'm going to make you a fancy braid, anchor it with these combs, and I don't want another word of complaint."

At the table Hagar arranged dried hydrangeas in a bowl and couldn't resist a comment.

"There are those who have hair and those who've lost it," she said, taking one of the blossoms and placing it squarely in the center of the wedding cake. "You'd better be glad for every strand you've got."

"I'm a terrible person. I know it," I said mournfully. "What will John do when he finds out how ungrateful I am?"

"Will you stop this foolishness!" said Charlotte, giving my braid a good tug. "The Major has had ample time to get acquainted with your shortcomings. He loves you for your virtues."

"But he hasn't seen my scars, Charlotte. I told him about them, of course, but knowing's not the same as seeing."

"We'll not speak of that," said Charlotte, winding the braid in a circle around my head. "Some things are only between husband and wife."

"Oh, Charlotte. Whatever made me think I could go through with this?" I asked, pressing my palms to my cheeks. "I can't bear to disappoint John."

"An hour ago you were dancing with the broom you were so happy," said Charlotte, fastening the braid on one side. "Now get hold of yourself, girl."

"Miss Ann needs some tea made out of boneset leaves," said Hagar, placing the kettle on the hearth. "I'll brew a cup to settle her nerves."

"A cup?" asked Charlotte, finishing her job. "She needs a whole pot."

"I couldn't drink a drop." I reached for the tin mirror. "It would hang in my throat."

Charlotte removed the tin from my hand before I could get another look.

"You look lovely, my dear," she said gently. "Trust me."

At that moment Jamie entered and flashed a wide smile.

"Oh little sister," he said with appreciation. "Stand up and let me look at you. What a beautiful bride."

I got up self-consciously and turned in a circle. I had borrowed Charlotte's dark green homespun dress with the lovely white lace collar.

"I must say, you make a prettier bride in a skirt than you might have in trousers."

"Oh, Jamie," I responded, lacing my fingers together, still unable to rid myself of the jitters. "Tell me I'll make John a good wife. Please."

"I wouldn't perform the ceremony if I didn't think so," he said, hugging me. "You'll be a wonderful wife: as loyal as the day is long and as fearless as a bobcat."

"Huh," I said into his shoulder. "You might have said something about my being tender and loving."

"Anyone who's seen you with your girls knows that," said Jamie, stroking my back. "Now the crowds have gathered. John and Mark just brought back the children, and the groom's outside, looking as if he can't wait another minute without fainting and falling in the fire. I'd say it's time for a wedding."

"Just one more thing," said Charlotte, rolling down her sleeves, and retrieving a Bible from beside her bed. She placed it in my hands.

"I carried this on the day James and I married. I pray you two will be as happy as we have been . . . that's the most I could wish."

"Oh, Charlotte," I said, tearing up. "Now I will cry on top of everything else!"

They couldn't help but laugh, and Hagar handed me a much needed handkerchief. I gratefully blew my nose in a most unbride-like fashion, causing them to laugh all over again.

"Shall we go?" Jamie asked, taking my arm. I nodded resolutely, and we proceeded through the door to face the assembled guests. As soon as I was across the threshold, my daughters gathered around me, Polly instinctively reaching up to touch my face.

"Mama," she said, her brown eyes wide with surprise. "Is it really you?"

Betsy and Charity chanted in a singsong fashion a phrase they had obviously rehearsed.

"Mama is a bride. Mama is a bride," they sang.

I released Jamie's arm and embraced the three of them at once.

"I'm a bride, all right, and I want all of you to stand beside me when I say my vows. The Major's marrying a little bit of each of us."

I felt the familiar touch of John's arm as he pulled me to his side. He appeared different too, dressed in a jacket and vest of faded blue homespun rather than his usual hunting shirt. His brown eyes were filled with a mixture of passion and apprehension, expressing the feelings that so perfectly matched my own. I motioned to the girls to follow us until we stood before Jamie.

"I seem to have a new job these days," he said as he faced the crowd. "Earlier this summer I had the great pleasure of marrying Susan Drake and James Leeper . . ."

A loud whoop rose from the Leeper contingent. "Making them the first couple to wed on the Cumberland. Now I have the added honor of marrying my own sister to one of the finest men I've had the pleasure to meet."

I discerned a flush steal across John's tanned cheeks.

"Your future husband has asked me to read this passage, Ann. To express the feelings he has, not only for you, but also for the rest of our family."

I was surprised. I had no idea that John had made a special request.

"I read from the Book of Ruth, Chapter One, Verse Sixteen. As you all remember, Naomi has just spoken to her daughter-in-law, Ruth, instructing her to return to her own people after the death of her husband, who was also Naomi's son. And Ruth replies to her mother-in-law. *Intreat me not to leave thee, or to return from following after thee: for whither thou goest, I will go: and where thou lodgest, I will lodge: thy people shall be my people, and thy God, my God.*"

Jamie closed the Bible and looked at us seriously.

"I don't need to tell you that marriage is for the good times and the bad," he said. "We have already seen plenty of the bad. But now you will have your love to provide a fortress against the vicissitudes of life. And may God bless this precious union."

Jamie reached into a vest pocket and brought out a gold ring I had never before seen.

"This ring," he said, "belonged to Major Cockrill's mother, God rest her soul. And he wants you to wear it now and for always."

He handed the ring to John who nervously placed it on my finger. The gold gleamed on my hand, encircling me with love.

"Mr. and Mrs. Cockrill, you may exchange a kiss now. With God's permission."

I was unprepared for the force of John's embrace which almost shook the Bible from my hand. But I returned his kiss with all the enthusiasm my love brought. It was an awkward moment, displayed in front of so many people, but no one in the assembled crowd could have doubted the love that lay behind our embrace.

"And now, we've some celebrating to do," Jamie addressed them all.

The first wedding guests to greet us were Elizabeth and Ephraim Peyton.

"Oh, Ann!" She cried as she threw her arms around me. "You deserve the very best." "And," she added surveying John, "You've got him."

She stepped back, taking Ephraim's hand. "We're so happy for you both."

I expected Ephraim to exhibit some shame, but he showed no hint of embarrassment. In fact, he had the nerve to wink at me, as if we shared a delicious secret.

"Thank you," was all I responded, even though I wanted to shout a warning to Elizabeth. Fortunately it was a fleeting desire, and they quickly moved on to allow others to express their congratulations. All evening as John and I enjoyed the good wishes and hospitality of our neighbors, I felt as if I played a part in some lovely dream. When the sky darkened, even the stars and moon paid tribute to us. The fires for cooking were joined by three other fires set to light the dancing. This was one dance I didn't dread, for now I had my true life partner, the man I would walk with until death parted us. From time to time as we danced, fire reflected on my new wedding band, making me feel as if I were a bride for the very first time. It was an odd assessment, given I was a widow with three children.

After many hours of dancing, eating, and much drinking of whiskey, our guests were ready for us to fulfill our marital vows. James Leeper, acting as if he were a longtime veteran of marriage, hit one of the cooking pots with an iron spoon, shouting the names of Mr. and Mrs. Cockrill, and calling for us to take to the wedding bed. At the sound of the commotion, Polly ran to my side, asking if it was time for us all to sleep in our new home. I took her face in my hands and explained that the first night John and I would be alone, but Polly could sleep in her new bed the very next evening.

"But Mama," she pleaded. "How can you ever sleep without us?"

I pulled her tightly to me. "It will be hard," I said. "But it's only for one night."

After much shouting and calling, John and I retreated to our new home. As I passed through the cabin door, it was a curious feeling to know that the two of us would be alone for an entire night, maybe the only time for years to come. John slid a bolt across the door behind us, guaranteeing our privacy. The cabin was more spare than what I was used to, but he had made every effort to create a welcoming place. On the table stood a lamp flickering with bear's oil, as well as a pewter cup filled with yellow, pink and blue wild flowers. He had bought a featherbed from the Harrisons, and it lay plumped on top of the newly hewn bed. Around the hearth were cedar branches whose earthy smell permeated the cabin.

My submerged fears returned to plague me now that the two of us were alone. In a matter of minutes he would see me naked for the first time. I wanted to hurry the process the way I learned to conquer icy water, with a swift plunge, but John was in no rush. Instead, he walked to the hearth and knelt to light the fire he had previously laid. After the flames started up, he turned to me.

"You have always reminded me of fire," he said. "The color of your hair. The heat of your temper," he added, smiling. "The light you shed everywhere you go," he added, drawing me from the chair and into his arms. I breathed deeply to take in his pungent animal scent, and leaned into him, hoping that his warmth would still my nerves. But no matter how hard I tried to relax, I could only imagine his pained expression when he saw my scars for the first time.

"John, you must see them," I said, pulling from him abruptly to stand three feet away.

"What?" he asked, knitting his brows in a worried expression. "See what?"

"My scars," I said, anguished, pulling nervously at my circle of braid. "I know it isn't fair to you. When a man buys a mare, he gets to examine her thoroughly. Even ride her, but with a wife . . . "

"Oh, Ann, I love you," he said, stretching out his hand. "I didn't marry you on account of your skin."

He pulled me close and kissed me softly, barely touching my lips. "And besides, I did get to see your teeth first."

"I'm serious John," I said, putting my hands on either side of his lapels. "I've got to show you now. Before another minute passes."

I withdrew to the table where I removed Charlotte's lace collar, placing it carefully on the surface. Then I kicked off my shoes, pulled off my white cotton stockings and untied my green skirt, letting the fabric pool around my ankles. Slipping out of my bodice, I stood before him dressed only in my shift. Taking a deep breath, I stepped over my skirt and toward the fire where I examined the flames as if trying to get a last bit of courage from the dancing tongues.

"You don't have to do this, Ann," came John's voice from behind me. "Come here."

I ignored him and pulled the shift over my head, flung it to the floor, and stood with my back to him, entirely naked. The scars were scattered across my body: seven large ones — on my left shoulder near my breast and on my thigh. John's rough hands caressed my skin as he turned me toward him and kissed me firmly on the mouth. Then he knelt, adjusting my body slightly so the fire illuminated my skin.

"Why, they're nothing at all," he said in the most reassuring way, kissing one of the scars on my thigh that ran two inches in a diagonal slant.

"They're like minnows swimming in a pond. Magic fish. See?" he said as he swayed me back and forth slightly, the light dancing on my scars.

"You are the most beautiful woman in the world," he added, still kneeling, taking my right hand and kissing it on the top. Then turning it over to kiss the palm and stare into its shadows as if reading an ancient map.

"Do you know how long I have loved these hands? How I've wanted to hold them and call them my own?"

I shuddered deeply, finding myself hot and cold at the same time.

"You're cold," he said, getting up. "Here I'm fully dressed and I've let you stand there with nothing on."

He lifted me easily, carried me to our bed, and laid me gently on the quilt that Charlotte had given us. Since the fabric was rough against my back, I worked my way between the linen sheets, watching my new husband take off his clothes.

He undressed slowly, ritually, in the firelight, first removing his boots and placing them to stand like sentinels beside the hearth.

He hung his jacket around the back of a chair, folded the vest methodically and laid it across the jacket. Finally, he unlaced his trousers and pulled them off, standing with only a loose shirt billowing around his body to the tops of his knees. I studied his legs, how thick and muscular they were.

John performed the last act of undressing, pulling his shirt over his head, the cream colored fabric sliding up like a curtain to reveal the full wide strength of his chest. He walked toward me, his feet making the floorboards creak as he stepped. Although I was no virgin, I somehow felt virginal with the knowledge that after this evening I would be a new person. Lifting the covers, he gathered me into his warm encircling arms. But before I let him kiss me, I slid my hands to his chest, curling the hair around my fingers, as if I were looking for rare flowers in the darkest forest.

"Let me take down your hair, he said, running his thumb across my nose. I nodded, and he pulled out first one comb and then the other. I turned my head aside as he unraveled the braid and combed through the ropy strands with his fingers.

"Mrs. Cockrill," he whispered in my ear. "Mine," I thought I heard him say as he buried his face in my hair. As I lay beneath him, I felt as if he had somehow fastened me to the center of the earth. The muscles of my arms ached from holding him so tightly.

"Oh, John," I said, turning my face aside. "This is our one night to be alone."

He laughed and curled his muscular body around mine until we lay as close as a potato and its skin.

"Then I guess we'll have to make the most of it," he said into my ear.

And we did.

# *Twenty*

OCTOBER 3, 1780 — *Oh, the joy of a life well shared. I don't know how it is possible, but my love for John grows daily. When I see him at the supper table, I want to weep from bliss. Even my children seem more precious. The adorable way Charity brings the spoon to her mouth is a miracle to me. Betsy's blond curls shine more brightly than ever, and Polly speaks with the wisdom of a mature adult. Charlotte and my brothers laugh at my new happiness and warn it cannot last, but I laugh in return. We shall see.*

*How was I so unaware of what my life lacked? Certainly I have been surrounded by men all my life, with brothers to spare. But a husband is another thing altogether. Did I feel this way with David? I don't remember his touch igniting my spirit the way John's does, like flint striking metal. I find that my whole day is lived in anticipation of lying beside him at night. Oh such pleasure! Like falling into a barrel of warm honey.*

*John accompanies the girls and me for leisurely walks in the woods, both to look for autumn nuts and berries and to appreciate the beauty of the leaves. Sassafras saplings display an array of colors from green, to bronze, to bright red. The oaks have turned a* darker crimson, and the Witch Hobble bush shakes with a bounty of red coin leaves.

Yesterday as we strolled, the leaves drifted in the stillness of the afternoon like the slow notes of some exquisite song. John considers autumn a melancholy season, with the leaves withering and dropping from the trees, but I reminded him of its bounty by sharing the secret I have been holding in my heart. For two weeks now, I have known that I am pregnant. No. The truth of it is, I have known a child was planted ever since our wedding night. Never before had my heart, mind, and body seemed so complete. I knew God was sending us a child.

At first he was so taken with the news that he said nothing, did not even look me in the eyes. Instead he stopped short, took off his hat, and circled the floppy old thing in his hands for a full ten seconds. Then he threw it into the air with such a whoop you would have thought him an Indian, and he hoisted me into the air as well. The girls were startled and ran back to see what was the matter. Although I hadn't planned on telling them so early about a new baby, it seemed the thing to do, given John's excitement. The five of us fairly danced back to the fort in our exuberance.

Mark came back from a trip last week to report on seeing an enormous buffalo herd, a sight well worth telling about. During the early summer the cows, calves and yearlings travel together, eating the plentiful grasses and growing fat and strong. At the same time, the bulls keep to themselves, scratching their backs, feeding, and wallowing in deep, muddy holes. But now is the rutting season when the two groups come together to mate and the herds are more spectacular than usual.

Mark was traveling to visit Thomas Spencer at his home near Bledsoe's Lick when he came across a herd that filled the trail, leaving his horse little room to wind its way through the mass of thick animals. The males are huge of course, standing up to six feet tall at the shoulder, the females almost as large. When he finally was able to make his way to the Lick, he discovered about one hundred acres filled with thousands of these beasts, turning the landscape black with their bulk.

*A great concentration had gathered at the sulphur spring itself, a circular area with a diameter of about two hundred yards, and they had used their huge tongues to lick the dirt away, making a hole several feet deep. Mark killed not a one, fearing the sound of his gun would start a stampede, but he watched the majestic animals for several hours and vowed he has quite a story to tell his grandchildren. We believe the presence of such an enormous herd bodes well for the winter, providing us with a good source of meat. And the Indians have been quiet lately. Once more we thank God for His bountiful mercy.*

**OCTOBER 17, 1780** — *Well, I never would have believed it. Brother John has surprised us all by getting married. The bride is Sarah Maclin, a sweet girl every bit as shy as John. I can't say she's a beauty. Her nose spreads rather wide across her face and her small brown eyes peer out like a little bird's, but her dark hair is thick and lustrous. The most important fact, of course, is that she makes my brother happy so nothing else matters. Here we thought he'd grow into a gnarled old bachelor uncle, and he has made us feel very foolish indeed. My mother always said that "still waters run deep" when she talked about John, and it seems she spoke the truth.*

*Tonight John and I are hosting a celebration for the newlyweds, and my girls will prepare their favorite recipe, corn pones in the shape of their little hands. First I make a stiff batter, and the children press their hands onto its surface. I cut around the imprints and bake the little cornbread hands on a slanted board in front of the fire. They make a delightful dish. We will have a fine time, for the groom is bringing his Jew's harp and after dinner we will strike up a dance.*

*We won't have many more sumptuous meals, however, before the long winter sets in, and we are back to dried fare and whatever fresh game we can kill. Our crops have not been as plentiful as we had hoped because of the heavy rains and occasional animal and Indian mischief. Fortunately the flax crop fared well, and Charlotte, Hagar and I have managed to lay aside a good amount of fibers which we will weave into cloth during the winter months. Already we have soaked the plants until the chaff rotted away, leaving the fiber to be pulled through a hackle, bleached and spun into linen thread. John is at work constructing a loom so that I can make cloth for the family, including the new baby.*

*And another surprise. Hagar is pregnant too. She speculates her time will be in June just like mine. This child will be the first for Hagar and Henry, and you would think no baby had ever before been conceived. She is casting spells and studying omens everywhere. Charlotte will give birth first in January. We shall be like three plump setting hens come winter.*

**NOVEMBER 3, 1780** — *Just when concern was rising about our short supply of corn, we received news from Mansker's Station. Colonel Donelson has discovered the corn crop he thought was ruined by the summer's floods has thrived instead. And the cotton too. He and John Junior returned to survey the damage last week, and to their astonishment, the corn was growing splendidly, and the cotton flourishing. And because the Colonel realizes we are equally in need of corn, he has volunteered to share it with us. What a generous man. How I regret all the dreadful things I thought about him less than a year ago.*

*My uncle, Abel Gower, has agreed to lead the harvesting expedition, and both my husband and my brother John have volunteered to accompany him. Jamie has volunteered Henry's services as well. It is terribly selfish of me, but I don't want my John to go. Since our marriage, he has slept every night by my side, and I find myself missing him even before he has gone. Maybe my apprehension comes from knowing what it is to lose a husband.*

The only clouds I saw on that cold November morning were the ones that spouted like puffs of smoke from our mouths as we gathered to see the flatboat set off for Clover Bottom. The sky was clear, though not so brightly blue as it had been, and a smell of dead fish scented the air. I hated to be left behind, but accompanying John was out of the question, given my condition. Uncle Abel stood at the stern, giving orders to his crew, his voice carrying across the water. My husband and Abel Junior were already aboard, as was my brother John. The three black men who would accompany them were still on the bank, sorting the goods they were to take: axes, hoes, empty baskets and sacks. They included Henry, of course, as well as the Gowers' slave, Joshua, and Jack Civil, a free black man of dubious reputation. The ten dogs they took for protection were already on board too.

Uncle Abel had asked each family to contribute baskets and hemp sacks to hold the corn they would bring back. Rather than think of how I would miss John, I tried to concentrate on the pleasure of seeing them return in a few days, those sacks filled with much needed corn. For safety's sake, the Gower boat planned to meet the Donelson party, led by John Junior, at Mansker's Station, a half-day away. Then they would travel together up Stone's River to harvest the fields at Clover Bottom, an undertaking that should take no more than four days. I looked longingly at John in his long brown coat as he helped the others finish loading the boat. I never fail to get a feeling of pleasure when I watch him work, his strong body bent so ably to whatever task he performs. When he had finished stacking the last of the tools, he lightly jumped over the side of the boat and approached me to say goodbye. I smiled at the feel of his chin gently rubbing the top of my head.

"I'll be back before you've had a chance to miss me," he said in a low voice.

"I wish you'd take Bruno with you," I answered. "I'd feel better knowing he protected you."

"And I feel better knowing he's here safe with you," said John. "Old Bruno's gotten so comfortable he thinks he's one of the family. We'll fare better with the dogs who are trained to attack Indians." The chosen dogs nervously paced the deck, and I had to admit they looked more keen to hunt than Bruno.

"You will be careful," I admonished. "Promise me you'll be sure someone is on guard at all times."

"You know we'll take care," John said, pulling back to look at me directly. "Your uncle is a good navigator."

"John," I said, reaching up to hold his face between my palms. "You won't forget you've got a baby to live for now."

"I've a whole family to live for," he answered solemnly. "I never forget that."

We were able to embrace for only a short while longer before it was time to cast off. All the men assembled on the boat and took their stations. Henry manned the sweep on top of the cabin, while John and my brother took their positions at the oars. Both Gowers stood at the stern as Jack Civil and Joshua pushed off.

I watched the boat depart with Hagar and my new sister-in-law, Sarah. We listened to the dogs' eager barking as the boat swirled into the river's current to begin its bumpy, lumbering journey upstream. The remaining leaves on the trees nodded a farewell as a breeze shook its way through them.

Sarah was crying openly, tears running in gullies down her cheeks.

"I'm no good as a wife," she sobbed. "Now everyone knows it. The whole fort."

"What foolishness," I said, embracing her. "The dew's not even off your wedding. Why would you suggest such a thing?"

"John never would have volunteered to go with the Gowers if he loved me," said Sarah.

"You're not thinking straight, Sarah," I said, taking her by the shoulders. "My John chose to go, and I know he loves me better than anything in this world. And my brother feels the same about you. I'm sure of it."

I was peeved rather than sympathetic as I looked at Sarah's tear-drenched face, perhaps because I would have liked nothing better than to cry myself.

"Let's get back to the cabin," I said, pointing up the hill. "We have enough work to take your mind off those silly thoughts."

As I followed Sarah up the bluff, I made a point to walk beside Hagar.

"What kind of feelings are you getting about the trip?" I asked softly so that Sarah wouldn't hear. "Are they going to be all right?"

Hagar shook her head. "I can't say," she said. "I've been studying it, but I just don't know."

"Oh, Hagar. They have to return safely," I said, keeping my voice low in spite of my concern.

"I can tell you one thing," answered Hagar. "We won't have to wait long to find out."

———

No matter how many times I concentrated on the security of having a full crib of corn, I couldn't stop worrying about John. I knew I was being foolish . . . intemperate . . . useless, even. The fretting was like sitting in a rocking chair, going back and forth and getting nowhere. But worry I did. At every meal the children and I ate, I studied John's chair, as if he might magically reappear. I couldn't go through my entire married life agonizing in this manner. It was the nature of the frontier for husbands to be separated from their wives, often for months at a time. I had to improve my behavior and remembered how Charlotte bore the burden with grace. I would have to do the same.

Early on the morning of the fifth day after John's departure, when only a faint light sifted through the cracks outlining the cabin door, Bruno began to growl, low at first, and then accelerating to a full, vigorous bark. He paced the floor from fireside to door, back and forth, waking everyone. I cautioned the girls to stay in their beds while I seized my rifle from its place above the hearth. I had just turned to face the door when it opened abruptly to reveal John, his face a terrible sight, blackened with dirt and sweat. His coat hung from his shoulders in shreds, like a long rag fringe. I ran to his side and supported him as we struggled to the bed.

"Are you injured?" I asked, searching his clothes for signs of blood. He shook his head to indicate no, but I could see his face was hatched with a maze of scratches, some superficial but others deep and oozing. I asked no more questions but stretched him out on the covers.

"Polly," I called. "Heat some water." I pulled up his shirt, looking for wounds that needed tending. He gestured that a search wasn't necessary, but then let his arms collapse by his sides. Although grateful to God he was home, I hated to imagine what calamity had returned him in such a wretched state. Indians. It had to be Indians. When Polly brought the warm water, I dabbed gently with a cloth at the injuries until the dried blood softened, wiped away, and I saw his face more clearly. The wounds, indeed, were superficial. He seemed to suffer more from exhaustion than anything else, but I desperately wanted to know what had happened.

"The other men, John," I said softly. "What happened to them?"

His face contorted as he squeezed his eyes tightly shut. "Henry survives," he said and then opened his eyes to look at me intently. His face was a study in grief, his eyebrows straining together above the bridge of his nose. "I don't know about the others."

Did this mean that perhaps my brother was dead? And my uncle and cousin too? Or were they captured? I desperately wanted to know, but he seemed unable to say more. A knock on the door was followed quickly by Jamie's entrance. Without a word he headed for the bed, picking up a chair which he placed beside John. Jamie took his hand and said without looking at me, "Get his boots off. Henry says they've walked for twenty hours straight."

I moved to the foot of the bed where I tugged at his right boot.

"Did Henry say how they were able to get back into the fort?" I asked, struggling to remove the boot from his swollen foot. "I thought the gate was still locked at this hour."

"Found some loose pickets and pushed them aside," Jamie said. "We're lucky the Indians didn't find that spot first."

"I'm afraid I may have to cut off this boot," I said as John's face grimaced with my every effort.

"No," said John huskily. "I'll not lose my boots."

"Better to lose a boot than a leg," said Jamie, gesturing for me to stop for awhile. "Can you talk to me John?" he asked, leaning close to John's face. "I asked Henry what happened to our brother John, but he says he doesn't know."

My husband called upon some hidden strength and roughly rubbed his mouth with his free hand before speaking.

"I think he took one of the first shots," he said, staring at the dark ceiling. "I can't say if he's alive or dead."

"What can you tell me?" Jamie asked. "Do you know what tribe it was who attacked?"

"Chicamaugas," said John. "I saw Dragging Canoe myself."

Fear stabbed my heart. I had thought the chief was content to attack settlers who passed by his town on the Tennessee River, but now it appeared he was willing to take his revenge all the way to the Cumberland. John shifted on the bed and continued his terrible story.

The expedition had begun with great promise. The Gower boat met the Donelson craft with no difficulty, a party including John Junior, Somerset, and four others. Donelson had brought along his pack of dogs as well, and a horse to help tow the boats upstream and pull a rudely constructed slide to transport the corn from field to boat.

"It all went well," John said, rolling his head slowly from side to side, as if he couldn't believe what happened next. "The corn was plentiful, and we camped easily on the bottom land. But we should have paid more attention to the dogs."

The animals had barked almost incessantly every night, but the last night was particularly bad. The dogs had rushed furiously in every direction as if they had gone mad, the woods echoing all night with their barking. Of course John and the others feared their agitation meant Indians lurked nearby in the canebrakes. But the first thing in the morning, my husband himself had gone to look for signs of the savages.

"I saw nothing of Indians," he said, "But at the place where we'd killed some buffalo, I found that wolves had already picked their bones clean. I figured the dogs were just barking at the wolves."

After he returned to make his report, the Donelson party left to harvest cotton on the other side of Stone's River, Gower's men remaining behind to eat breakfast before starting out. Some members of the Gower party were uneasy and wanted to return home right away, but John and my brother thought it best to remain with Donelson to provide a united front as they traveled home. Gower was in charge, however, and he made the final decision: they would depart immediately.

"John Junior was surprised when he saw our boat wasn't coming to land on the shore beside his," John said. "He thought we needed the cotton as much as they did. But Abel called out that he wanted to reach the Bluff before nightfall."

As they shouted to each other, the Gower boat drifted downstream toward an island in the river where suddenly a force of more than a hundred screeching Indians rushed out of the canebrakes to fire on them. The smoke of guns plumed in the air and a hail of arrows shot toward them.

"At the first sound of gunfire, I took to the river," John said. "The water was only about three feet deep at that point, but trying to move my legs was like trying to cut through molasses. I heard someone thrashing behind me, but didn't stop to see whether it was friend or foe. All my efforts were given to reaching the woods without getting killed."

As he spoke, I could imagine the scene . . . my uncle calling to Donelson as he held an oar in his hand, unafraid, anxious to get home. The morning sunlight dusting his shoulders, the other men busy at their tasks, anxious to get home. Then the fearful Indian howls shattering the air, and the sight of arrows arcing through the air. The smell of gun powder.

"When I reached the woods I turned to see what was happening behind me, to see if there was anything I could do to help, and I discovered it was Henry who followed. I managed to shoot at the Indian chasing him who fell face down into the water, but there were too many of them to stop and fight. Our only hope was to run."

And run they did, all day, weaving through the cane, cutting through the underbrush, pounding their way home. As I listened to John's story, I was barely able to breathe. My fears had been justified, and it seemed impossible that my brother John could have survived.

"I'm sorry," said John, retrieving his hand from Jamie. "That I couldn't save the others."

"You've nothing to apologize for," said Jamie, standing abruptly, as if the story had made him want to run from the cabin. Bruno barked at the sudden movement.

"What will you tell Sarah?" I asked Jamie as I took his place in the chair beside John.

"We've nothing to tell yet," he said, shifting nervously on his feet. "I've seen many a man survive an Indian fight. Including your husband, here. We'll just have to wait and see."

Jamie gave John a pat on the shoulder in a distracted manner and leaned to kiss the top of my head before he left the cabin. As soon as Jamie had gone, Betsy jumped from her bed and ran to John's side, crying in relief. Polly moved to my side while Charity crawled into my lap. Each seemed to know how close we had come to having a hole carved from the center of our happiness.

————

All morning I attended to John, feeding him broth from a venison stew. When John tried to lift himself from the bed, I scolded him, but he ignored my protestations. Because his feet had been elevated for several hours, the swelling had receded. When he stood, he swayed slightly.

"You belong in this bed," I said severely, motioning to its rumpled surface.

"I'm not a man who can stay in bed while the sun's up," he answered, shaking his head and starting for the door. "I've got work to do . . . repair my gun barrel . . .

He stopped when the door opened of its own accord and Sarah Robertson slid inside. Her chestnut hair was pulled back tightly from her face, her brown dress a dark cloud around her. The fire revealed her small eyes were swollen from crying. She stood with her back against the door's rough wood, as if to bar anyone from escaping.

"Tell me about my husband." She spoke with uncharacteristic calm, her arms folded tightly in front of her.

"I'm afraid we don't know anything," I said, starting toward Sarah, wanting to save John the pain of repeating his story.

"Henry won't tell me a thing," she said coldly. "You must tell me, John." Her small eyes burrowed into him.

"I wish I knew something to tell," he said, raking his fingers through his still tangled hair.

It was the first time I had ever seen him so reticent. I wondered if he really knew more than he was willing to share, but it was more likely that he wanted to offer hope.

"I'll be as honest as I can, Sarah," he addressed her with level eyes. "We were set on by an army of Indians. But John was as strong and agile as any of us . . . "

His voice trailed off.

"I can't stand not knowing," said Sarah, clasping her hands together tightly, her calm dropping away like a discarded veil. "What if he's dead already?"

Her voice echoed in the small room, and I was aware that my children had come near enough to touch my skirt, their faces uniformly frozen in fear.

"You girls need some fresh air," I said. "Sarah, if you'll step aside." I took Charity by the arm. "Polly, gather the coats," I added. "And John, I know you have work to do, but please keep an eye on them while you're at the forge?" In a matter of moments I was able to accomplish the exit of my entire family. After they departed, I faced Sarah alone, but she had lost all resolve, her face collapsing. I took her by the hand and led her to the hearth where two chairs sat before the fire.

"I can't bear it," she said, digging her fingernails into her palms as she settled into the chair. "It isn't fair, Ann. We've been married less than three weeks."

"Let's not borrow trouble," I said. "We don't know yet that John is dead."

"But an army of Indians against so few of us! Who could survive that?"

Who indeed? My husband and Henry, but was it likely that anyone else did so? In my heart I suspected that Sarah was right. I thought of my kind, gentle brother, John. Even though he was older than I, he had always seemed younger because of his sweet, shy demeanor. My mind traveled to thoughts of the boy he had been, who whittled by the fire, making things for others, a bright, loving presence. How could he possibly vanish from the earth?

"We have to pray," I said, taking a deep breath and gathering Sarah's hand into mine. We bowed our heads but I couldn't close my eyes. I focused on the flames eating the logs in front of us.

"Almighty Father," I began. "We most humbly pray for Thy loyal servant, John Robertson."

"For his survival," added Sarah quickly. "We pray that he may live to serve you for many years to come."

I looked with pity at her earnest face and continued. "He is a good man, Lord, with much to accomplish in this life."

Tears stuck in my throat, and I didn't think I could continue. Although Sarah wanted the prayer to be for John's deliverance, I also had to acknowledge the fact that he might already be dead. And if so, he needed God's protection in the afterlife.

"But if it is Thy will to call John to Heaven," I went on, still studying Sarah's face, "we commend his soul to you. He has been a good Christian all his life, and we pray he will dwell in Thy house forever."

As I spoke, Sarah's eyes flew open and she sprang up, her arms flailing, as if she might strike me. It was clear she thought the prayer for John had been sabotaged, that I had willfully offered him up to God. Instinctively I drew back, pressing my back into the hard spindles of the chair, and under Sarah's withering gaze, I felt a mixture of fear and guilt.

———

At four in the afternoon, the sky was pressed low with ashy smudges for clouds. The children were laughing as they practiced tossing a pen knife into a lazy circle drawn in the dirt, while Bruno watched them with liquid brown eyes that peered dutifully from under his wrinkled brow. Suddenly, a shouting from the riverfront shattered the air. All activity stopped, capturing us like statues.

"What is it, Mama?" asked Polly, alert as a fox, her voice breaking the spell.

"You children stay here," I called over my shoulder as I hurried to John at the forge. His face glowed orange and gold as he held long tongs over the fire, dangling a horseshoe that pulsated like a misplaced orange smile.

"John?" I called, giving him a questioning look.

"I don't know," he answered, wrenching the horseshoe from the fire and dousing it in a kettle of water. He pulled the leather apron over his head with a swift jerk and the two of us started toward the fort's gate. As we passed the children, I barely grazed Polly's hair with my hand.

"We'll be back before you know it," I said. "You stay here. And hold Bruno so he can't follow us."

I shoved on quickly before Polly could protest. At the gate we met Sarah and Charlotte who had joined the rest. Charlotte's dark hair sprung from her white ruffled cap and her cheeks were flushed enough to suggest a fever.

"They say the boat's come back," said Charlotte, grabbing my hand and pulling me down the path, threading through the roots and rocks.

"John's come home," said Sarah, following us. "He's alive in spite of your prayer," she called defiantly toward my back.

As we scrambled down the bluff, the cold air seared the inside of my nose and burned my lungs. The descent had never seemed so steep, so long to traverse. "God, let my fears have been unfounded. Let them be all right," I repeated to myself.

When we reached the river's edge, thirty people huddled together under the solemn sky, straining to see as the boat drifted nearer, growing larger as it approached. And what we saw, or rather didn't see, was a most chilling sight: no man stood at the oars, no man held the sweep or guided the boat to shore. Instead of men for guards, the flatboat was accompanied by four vultures circling in the sky and barking dogs dashing about the boat amid the sacks of harvested corn.

John and Mark launched the nearest canoe and paddled toward the boat, their paddles sending up plumes of white water. As soon as they reached the errant vessel, Mark jumped aboard, followed by John who tied the canoe to the flatboat's tug. Mark fell backwards against the cabin as he tried to defend himself against the dogs, and John used a paddle to flog at the frenzied animals. It was not until Mark shot his pistol into the air that they retreated, and he was able to grab the sweep and guide the boat to shore.

When I heard the first words Mark shouted, I no longer had any doubt about my brother's fate. "Take Sarah home," he called, and Sarah fell down, screaming all the while. Charlotte dropped to the ground to comfort her, but I couldn't take my eyes off the boat as it continued toward us. Mark wore the grimmest possible expression on his face, his features drawn tight like a closed fist. John had herded the barking dogs into one corner of the bow where the five beasts snarled and climbed each other's backs.

James Leeper and Zach White waded into the water to receive the boat. As they pulled it to shore, I was amazed to see so many sacks of corn piled high around the deck. It appeared that the Indians had taken none of it. And when the boat was finally close enough for me to see its contents, I was stunned almost to unconsciousness. There, lying prostrate in a lake of blood, were the bodies of what must have been my brother, uncle, and cousin, their faces gnawed to bloody pulp by the dogs, portions of their white skulls visible even in the gray afternoon light. I fell to my knees and vomited, retching until my stomach was a knot that couldn't be untied.

The dead were buried before nightfall and a runner sent to Mansker's Station to tell of the calamity that had befallen the Gower party. The man returned the following morning to report that none of the Donelson party had yet returned. As we assembled in the fort yard to hear his message, despair settled over us like a coarse, suffocating blanket.

# Twenty-one

NOVEMBER 8, 1780 — *I have spent the last week submerged in grief over the loss of my brother, as well as my uncle and cousin. When the image of their ravaged faces comes to mind, I try to drive away the anguish with memories of good times together: how John taught me to ride a horse without a saddle, to squeeze the animal's velvet sides with my knees and lock my fingers into its mane. I remember too, Uncle Abel's birthday gift as we waited for our journey to begin: my mother's bowl. And how my cousins, Abel and Nancy Gower, would join my family each year to celebrate our birthdays. Our mothers shook out quilts, letting them float to the springy grass where we children arranged ourselves for the special treat of honey-drizzled wheat cakes.*

*But in the middle of these happy thoughts, a picture of those demolished faces flashes inside my head. I was wrestling with those memories yesterday when about two o'clock a great commotion in the fort yard interrupted me. I ran out to discover that John Donelson Junior had arrived from Mansker's Station and was surrounded by a crowd of men near the gate. I rejoiced that he was alive and quick as a flea jumps to a dog, I hurried to hear him tell what had happened.*

*Jamie invited Donelson to his cabin, and my husband joined me as we squeezed inside with all the others to stand as tightly as straws wrapped for a broom. James Leeper, of course, needed to be in the center of things, and pushed forward to the chair where John Junior sat. Those nearest the crackling fire stripped off their coats, but others, like John and me, pulled our garments tightly about us for warmth. I found it impossible to see John Junior's face from my place wedged behind the two Buchanan men, so I climbed on the children's bed for a better vantage spot. John Junior's face flushed deeply from his ride in the cold, dry air, his brown eyes glowing as he sat beside a bear's oil lamp. We could see his every expression as he shook his blond head, seeming unable to believe his own story. I don't want to forget a single detail, so I have tried to put down the events as precisely as he told them.*

*He was able to see the Indians attack the Gower boat from his spot on the river bank, and confirmed what my husband had told us: that several hundred Indians had rushed from the bushes, both on the island itself and on the shore. When he realized what was happening, he left off gathering the cotton to return to the boat for his gun, cursing that he had not kept it by his side. He returned to the riverbank with his rifle and shot bag, and bore witness to the terrible destruction of the Gower party. When he saw John and Henry elude the Indians and vanish into the woods, he guessed their escape would have been impossible if the Indians had possessed better guns. I suppose I'll never know why God chose to let my husband live while allowing my brother to die.*

*He went on to tell how his gun was insufficient to reach the Indians attacking the Gowers' boat, so he began to fire at another group of Indians on the riverbank just opposite him. Fortunately the river was too deep for the savages to cross at that point, and they had to satisfy themselves with shrieking and shooting a flurry of arrows, doing little damage. He decided to rejoin his group of five men and after ten minutes of searching, found them crouching in the canebrakes. It was clear they would have to abandon their boat because the Indians expected their return for the corn and cotton. It was also clear that one of their party, old Mr. Cartwright, was too infirm to return to Mansker's on foot, so they insisted that he take their only horse. Donelson split them into two groups, John Junior taking three men for one party, and Somerset traveling with Mr. Cartwright.*

*At nightfall Donelson's group found shelter in a large hickory tree that had fallen to the ground, and hid amidst the ample boughs. Although it was dreadfully cold, they resisted building a fire since the flames would be a sure sign to the Indians of their whereabouts. Early the next morning, after very little sleep, they continued to the Cumberland without incident and happily found Somerset waiting for them on the banks with Mr. Cartwright. Their troubles were far from over, however, for the wide expanse of the river stood between them and the safety of their home fort.*

*For the remaining part of the morning, they tried to construct a small raft for crossing the river. Since their axes were left behind on the boat, they gathered small sticks which they fastened together roughly with vines. The failure of their efforts became apparent, however, when each time they launched a flimsy craft, the river's swift current returned them to the same side of the river from which they started.*

*They finally abandoned hope of ever succeeding with their raft, so Somerset volunteered to swim the river using the horse to cross the rapid current. The four men who remained behind watched the black man bob and struggle his way through the turbulent water. At times they feared he had gone under permanently, only to have their hearts lift when they saw his head reappear. At last he and the horse scrambled triumphantly up the muddy banks of the opposite shore. As John Junior described Somerset's bravery, I remember how many times the slave had helped us while we traveled on The Adventure and tears came to my eyes in appreciation of this fine man.*

*The rest of them were quite hungry by this time, having eaten nothing for twenty-four hours. Old Mr. Cartwright suffered might-*

*ily from the chill as well, a misery that intensified for all of them when an icy rain began to fall, soaking their clothes. Yet still they were afraid to light a fire in case of Indians nearby. Late the follow- ing morning, they were delivered at last. What they thought at first might be Indians, was actually Somerset emerging from the mist with four other men armed with rifles and axes. The newcomers immediately set to cutting down trees large enough to assemble a sturdy raft to ferry across the river. It was a weary group that made the final journey to Mansker's Station, but they had accomplished a miracle: they had all survived. When Donelson finished his story, something like a sigh went through those of us in his audience, as if we had been with him, fighting our way to safety, and could now give thanks for being delivered.*

*John Junior followed his story with a sad note, however. Because of this turn of events, his father plans to move the whole family to Kentucky. He has had enough of Indian attacks and heard that the people at Boonesborough have suffered very few onslaughts during the past year. The meeting broke up with a grumbling and cursing of Indians, and I understood how people could wish for relief. Who doesn't? But how can we think of abandoning the homes we have come so far to establish? Oh, I wish I could see into the future the way Hagar does, but only if it is a pleasant sight.*

**NOVEMBER 22, 1780** — *I must never again think I have seen the worst of times. Whenever I harbor that illusion, our situation plum- mets to new depths. No one else in the fort has been killed, but the Indians have devised a new manner to bedevil us: driving away the game animals, deer, bear and buffalo alike. This is a clever maneuver, for it is much easier to starve us than to go to the trouble of combat. We were forced to bring our livestock into the fort, since the Indians had stolen a good number of horses and cattle. The pigs we drove into the forest where they fend for themselves, but they are both difficult to cap- ture and growing thinner in the bargain.*

*John is safe by my side, and the children maintain their good health. Our cow, Miss Priss, remains, but her milk is only as good as her food supply, and that is growing sparse. We have rapidly consumed the ill-gotten corn that arrived two weeks ago on the boat from Clover Bottom, and it will soon be gone. Clover Bottom! How could those words have ever sounded sweet to my ears?*

*Ever since the Clover Bottom attack, I have seen a growing unrest in our community. Three families abandoned their homes and started for Kentucky, and it was a sad sight to watch them load their horses with everything the animals could bear. The only good outcome of their leaving is that empty cabins have become available for those who still live outside the fort's protection. Elizabeth and her family have just occupied one of those homes. Just yesterday she and Ephraim arrived, along with Mrs. Jennings, Johnny and their slave, Hannah. Edmund is away on a long hunt for animal pelts, but the rest of them will be within the protection of these palisade walls at last. Although the animal smells have made this fort a less desirable place to live than a few weeks ago, we are protected from the sort of surprise attack that took Mr. Jennings' life.*

*Elizabeth was ecstatic to hear that I am also expecting a baby. She is almost eight months along now, and has developed quite a plump belly. In fact, she and Charlotte have twin profiles. One happiness in the midst of trouble.*

**NOVEMBER 30, 1780** — *Our gun powder supply dwindles and our hunger grows. The corn is almost gone and the Indians shoot at our men every time they leave the fort. My neighbors no longer complain quietly, but raise their grievances to the skies. I am worried. Even John, who always views the future in the most favorable light, has expressed his fears for our survival as a settlement if we cannot contain the current unrest. A week ago, Jamie sent word to all the settlements nearby to convene this very evening. He hopes to rally those of us who remain, and I must say, his task is formidable.*

❧

Jamie's cabin had become a regular town hall, so many of our meetings had occurred there. We were all in attendance that night, accustomed to seeing the familiar arrangement of chairs and table, the beds pushed against the wall. When it appeared that all the company was accounted for, Jamie took his empty pewter cup and banged it solidly on the table to call for order.

"We've got problems to discuss this evening," Jamie said, surveying the room. "I know you have concerns."

"Anyone with half a mind has concerns," said the older John Buchanan. "The question is, what are we going to do about them?"

A loud grumbling caused Jamie to rap the table again.

"All our problems come from the damned Indians," said Leeper, his face darkly flushed. "I say we kill them all."

"All the Indians aren't our enemies," said Jamie, rubbing his forehead as if he had a headache. "You remember this was their hunting ground first and foremost, and some still come here to hunt."

"If any innocent Indians remain, I say they're too far from home," said George Freeland, a man with blond hair, thin and fine as corn silk, that hung straight on either side of his face. "A good rifle shot will help them find a way home in a hurry."

"We won't be launching an attack on the Indians," said Jamie. "They far outnumber us, for one thing. We'd have to take on the Chicamaugans and the Chickasaws first, and then try to deal with the Creeks and the Delawares." He cleared his throat, as if the thought of their multitudes suddenly blocked his voice.

"But we have to defend ourselves against them," said Isaac Bledsoe, his ears turning as red as if someone had twisted them. He had the crinkled face of a bull dog. "And we need more people to help us."

"First of all, we need gun powder," Jamie said emphatically. "This past summer I'm afraid some of us killed game needlessly."

"I killed to feed the rest of you at my wedding feast," said James Leeper, starting up from his chair as if he had thistles in his breeches.

"I'm not accusing any one person," said Jamie, his eyes leveled at Leeper. "We've all been guilty."

"We need salt too," said Ephraim, his red hair shining almost as brightly as the candle next to him. "We can get what we need for cooking here at the Lick, but my animals need salt too, and if we're going to preserve any of the game we kill, we must have salt for that."

"I know, I know," Jamie said, walking toward the hearth and picking up the poker.

"If we're not going to fight the Indians, then I think we should pack up and leave," said Jack Kneeland, a string bean of a man. "I'll not let my wife be a target for the Indians' tomahawk."

This bold statement set off the loudest protest of all, and I worried that the outburst might spell the end of Fort Nashborough. The group silenced, however, when Thomas Spencer pushed his way to the center of the cabin. Of course he was known for the giant size of his feet, but he had an enormous body to match and his presence filled the room. Everyone waited expectantly to see what one of our most seasoned pioneers had to say. Jamie remained immobile, the poker dangling in his hand.

Spencer knew how to get attention, for he waited until the voices stilled and the only sound was the snap and ping of the fire. He combed his waist-length beard with his knobby fingers and spoke at last.

"I take no steps backward," he declared while letting his dark eyes take in each man, one at a time. And he said no more but continued to glower at them.

Jamie smiled at his old friend. "Nor I, Thomas," he answered. "Leaving at this time is a poor idea, indeed," he added, and bent to stir the fire.

Spencer nodded, confident that he had been heard and returned to the corner of the room. Jamie poked at the fire a few more times, and at the sight of a flurry of sparks lifting upwards, he seemed satisfied and returned to the table. Putting his hands on its surface, he leaned forward to lay out the logical reasons why a retreat would be disastrous. Any sizable group of people traveling to either Kentucky or the Holston Valley would be an easy mark for the Indians. And their heavily loaded horses would make them desirable prey. If they thought of building boats to sail away, that method too was unlikely to be a success, for they couldn't leave the fort to cut down the trees necessary for building their boats without being shot.

"You're saying we're no better than a covey of partridges," said Ephraim. "Ready to be pounced on by the first predator."

"What we need to do," said Zach White, "is to move like the centipede instead of the partridge, with as many hands as legs . . . and as many eyes as legs and hands combined."

"Well said," answered Jamie, looking at White as though he were a prize student who had just given the right answer.

"What the hell is he talking about?" asked Gaspar Mansker, scratching his grizzled head in confusion. "I'm no centipede."

"But we've heard Colonel Donelson's family made it safely to Kentucky," said Ephraim, ignoring Mansker's question.

"Colonel Donelson's a rule unto himself," said Jamie. "With his big family and his retinue of slaves, he makes an army all his own."

"Something has to be done," said John Buchanan severely. "We can't sit here and watch our friends continue to be shot, one by one."

"I agree," said Jamie, straightening his posture and folding his arms emphatically before him. "I have a plan. I'll take a few men with me to Kentucky. And I'm asking each of you to contribute what animal pelts you've accumulated, to trade for gun powder and salt."

He would go to the Falls of the Ohio River where numerous boats passed with goods from the East, including gun powder. He also had heard a rumor of settlers who arrived at the Falls on their way to our fort, only to be told that it was abandoned. He determined to find these travelers and assure them we remained and would welcome them.

"Well," said Jack Kneeland, squinting his eyes, "That's all well and good for you, but you can't stop me and my family from going back to the Holston."

"Do what you must," said Jamie, "But I shall be the last to leave." He let the significance of that statement linger before he continued. "This is a rich country," he added. "We'll find no better. I've said it many times but it bears repeating . . . we are the Advance Guard of Civilization, and we must persevere only a little longer before we get reinforcements. We have just gotten word of our significant victory at King's Mountain, and it won't be long before the war will be over. North Carolina and Virginia have both passed resolutions to give liberal land grants to officers and soldiers, so we'll soon be joined by an army of new settlers."

"Who'll take our land from us," added Leeper sarcastically.

"That remains to be seen," said Jamie, returning to the table.

"You can count on me to stick with you," said Isaac Bledsoe, his entire bull dog face now as red as his ears. "If you go to Kentucky for powder, I'll go back to the Holston and see who I can find to join us here."

I was surprised to see this tough man so emotional. "And as God is my witness, I believe that if we perish here, others will come to avenge our deaths and finish what we've begun." His eyes had gone beyond the room and seemed to see a vision. "And if they find only our graves or scattered bones, they will revere our memories forever." He ducked his head and said somewhat more quietly, "It is sweet to die for one's country."

"But it is sweeter still," said Jamie, "To live for it. And live we will."

———

Later that night I lay in bed with my back pressed close against John's chest. I pulled his arms around my shoulders, burrowing into him like some hibernating animal, seeking shelter from the hard winter.

"How can anyone talk of leaving?" I said softly. "We went through such hard times to get here."

When John said nothing, I continued, "And that Ephraim Peyton! He should be more worried about taking care of Elizabeth than rushing out to find salt."

John gave me a little squeeze. "All of us have more than one thing to worry about, I'm afraid," he said kissing the back of my neck.

"If he tries to move Elizabeth away before her baby's born, I'll block the gate myself."

"That would be a pretty sight," he said, nuzzling my hair. As the warmth from his body sank into mine, my muscles loosened and a warm, liquid sensation overtook me.

"What were you talking to Jamie about after the meeting," I asked absently as I played with his fingers, rubbing them over my lips.

"He asked me to go with him to Kentucky."

"No," I said in a voice that threatened to wake my daughters.

"Shhhhh," he said, drawing me even closer. "That's exactly what I told him. No. I'm needed here."

"Thank God," I said, rubbing his hand against my cheek. "I know it's selfish of me, but I can't let you go."

As the fire hissed and sputtered, I thought of Charlotte and how she must be feeling this night.

"Oh, John," I continued. "I don't want Jamie to go either. He's bound to be absent when their baby is born. And what if he doesn't come back? How can we survive without him? The people will surely give up without his leadership."

Tears dampened my eyes. "And maybe I'll give up too."

"How many times has James gone into the wilderness?" asked John, cradling my face in his hand.

I couldn't answer. Jamie had countlessly launched his way into the unknown, maybe more than a hundred occasions. But this time was different. Never before had the Indians been so viciously on the attack.

"And he's come back every time," added John. "I think God gives James a special protection, Ann. I've seen that in a few men. He knows the woods the way some men know their wives. Every sweet mountain," he said, running his hand over my newly swollen belly. I turned in his arms to kiss his shadowy face. His beard was rough against my face as I kissed hard, with a certain desperation, as if this were the last night of our lives.

# Twenty-two

DECEMBER 2, 1780 — *It was a sorrowful day when Jamie headed off for Kentucky, taking both Mark and Henry with him. The sky joined us in crying as the men strapped animal pelts to their horses in the ropes of slicing rain. I'm afraid those four loaded packhorses will be a tempting sight to the Indians. Charlotte and I wept quietly to see them leave, but Hagar cried inconsolably. She must have portents of an evil outcome, but I didn't dare to ask what visions made her so distraught. I don't want to know. When it was time for her to say goodbye to Henry, she beat her fists against one of the horses until it reared up, threatening to throw off its treasured load. Henry had to seize her hands before she would give off thrashing at the air. Her violent agitation frightened me more than my own dread thoughts. How can I bear losing any more brothers?*

*They have been gone for five days now, and every night I pray both for their safety and their success at procuring gun powder. Our supplies are perilously low, and we are torn between saving the powder to protect ourselves, and using it to hunt game. When Jamie left, he cautioned us to make every bullet count: to bring down either a buck or an Indian.*

*Meanwhile we are newly infested with lice.*

DECEMBER 15, 1780 — *My husband John is the strongest, bravest man in our fort. I write this truth without exaggeration because during the past week he has saved us all from starvation. The corn is gone and my stews have been little more than boiled water. It is one thing to be hungry oneself, but far worse to hear one's children sob because their stomachs cramp with emptiness. Their cries tormented John every bit as much as they did me. Two days ago he came in from the forge to announce that no Indian was going to be the cause of their continued hunger. As he assembled his hunting equipment, I must admit I lost my wits. Every man I know who has ventured outside the fort recently has reported seeing Indians everywhere. In an effort to keep him from leaving, I went so far as to fall on my knees and beg. I told him that if he went, we'd never see him again, and he answered that he had no choice but to go: the children were starving. He added he could spot Indians as well as they could spot him, and he would stay clear of any path where they might waylay him.*

*The hours I spent waiting for his return ticked away slowly. Charlotte waited with me for several hours, and when she returned home she sent Hagar in her stead. But Hagar was no help at all because these days she wraps herself in gloom like a shroud. Not even the baby planted in her stomach gives comfort.*

*Finally, about four o'clock in the afternoon, we heard shouts from Ephraim who was on duty at the gate. I threw open the cabin door and saw my precious John, staggering under the weight of an enormous burden, carrying bear meat on his back wrapped in the skin of the bear. As he made for our cabin, he called for James Leeper to bring scales and by the time John had reached the cabin and set down his load, Leeper was there with his massive scales. We weighed the meat and discovered that my John had walked a good four hours carrying one hundred pounds on his back. In a few minutes everyone at the fort had heard the news and made a line outside our door, begging for food to feed their children. Given our great need, I thought perhaps we should save some of the meat to eat later, but John said no. He gave instructions to give it to whoever was in need. When I protested that it would be gone in a night, he gave me a flinty look with those solemn eyes and replied, "Then I will go again tomorrow for more."*

**DECEMBER 20, 1780** — *Elizabeth gave birth to a fine baby boy last night, with her mother once more in attendance, and this time her husband as well. They have named the baby John, after Ephraim's twin, and of course it is a name that cannot be improved upon. But Ephraim certainly could be. He drank all night to celebrate his son's birth, and his drunken behavior reminded me of the night of the dance when he would have done me harm if John had not arrived. For Elizabeth's sake, I will never say a word of his behavior, so I focus my attention on their baby. I made the little child a linen wrap and washed the cloth until it became as soft as rabbit fur. I pray the road will be straight and the burden light for this child, and that he will be a comfort to his mother. I'm afraid she will need it.*

**DECEMBER 25, 1780** — *Christmas day. The men who came in Jamie's party have now been here for one full year. We didn't celebrate that event, but our family did have a small ceremony to thank God for the birth of His son, Jesus Christ. John read the Christmas story from the Bible, and I followed by leading the children in singing one of my favorite hymns, "Joy to the World." For gifts, John made two additional horseshoe dolls and a pair of toy andirons for the children. But it was quite an effort to make merry when we are cold and tired and hungry. Still, no word from Jamie. He has now been gone for four weeks. A poor Christmas, I'm afraid.*

**JANUARY 1, 1781** — *The first day of the new year, and Charlotte has gotten it into her head to move away from the fort. She plans to take herself, her children and Hagar to Freeland's Station a mile away. I protested this idea because in my opinion a woman near her time should stay put if at all possible. But Charlotte is determined to* *go. She still believes that little Charlotte's poor health began with a birth injury, so she will do anything to avoid a repetition of that tragedy. There is a midwife, Mrs. MacGregor, who lives at Freeland's and is known to deliver babies safely, even in the most difficult of circumstances. Charlotte will stay in a cabin recently emptied by a family gone to Kentucky. I hate to think of her giving birth in a strange place with Jamie so far away.*

**JANUARY 11, 1781** — *When this morning's sun still shone crimson behind the eastern hills, George Freeland arrived to tell us of the birth of baby Felix Robertson, perfect in every way. May his eyes see a peaceful land that we can only dream of.*

**JANUARY 15, 1781** — *God Bless! Jamie, Mark and Henry are safe! They were able to secure a good amount of gun powder and lead, as well as a supply of salt, but the rumor was untrue that a number of people at the Falls on the Ohio wanted to settle here. Our Hagar is overcome with happiness at the sight of Henry and thanks God that her premonitions were untrue. But we had a terrible incident to balance our good news. Last night David Hood was set upon by Indians outside the fort. After several Indians fired at him, he fell to the ground, thinking he could "play possum," or pretend he was dead so they would pass him by. His trick was partially successful because the savages did believe he was dead, but that fact didn't keep them from dealing a most horrible scalping. All the while they were tearing his scalp from his head, Hood managed to refrain from uttering a sound or blinking so much as an eyelid. I can't imagine having such strength of will. It seems almost inhuman.*

*After kicking his body for a final insult, they abandoned him, and he waited a good long time before he began his bloody trip home. Imagine his horror when once again he confronted the very same Indians. They were so surprised to see their recent victim alive that at first they broke into boisterous laughter. Their good humor, however, didn't keep them from shooting him in the chest and tossing him into a brush heap. He was finally rescued last night when our men tracked his blood in the snow and brought him home. They put him in one of the sheds where his body could remain cold enough until burial today.*

*Mrs. Jennings, however, visited poor Hood and heard him making faint sounds. She summoned Jamie who arranged for him to be moved into one of the cabins. Sure enough, when the injured man was able to enjoy the warmth of the cabin, he thawed out. His wounds began to bleed again, and he gave every indication that he would live. Jamie told Hood that everyone had taken him for dead, and Hood replied with characteristic humor that he thought he'd live if only his friends would give him half a chance.*

*We cleaned him up and Jamie put off going to see his new baby in order to peg Hood's head. It is a most gruesome process that Jamie learned from a French surgeon and a task he has performed many times to save the life of a scalped man. Jamie first makes up rolls of lint to use for stanching wounds, and then begins his surgery. He drills holes in the skull with a shoemaker's awl, taking care to make the perforations close together. This allows the brain to swell, in addition to letting the oozings from each little hole form a thick scab which protects the delicate brain matter. I saw Jamie perform this operation once, but never again. After the surgery, he and Henry left immediately for Freeland's.*

**JANUARY 16, 1781** — *A terrible battle occurred at Freeland's last night, and everyone who took part has returned here for shelter. It seems there was much rejoicing over Jamie's return, and maybe that is why they did not attend to the dogs' barking. Also a full moon shone, and everyone knows that Indians don't attack under that circumstance. At least that is what we had always believed, but attack they did, about midnight. There was ever so much shooting and our men were severely limited because Jamie had left most of his ammunition here at Fort Nashborough. The savages also tried to set fire to the pal-*

isades, but the wood was too green to burn, so they satisfied themselves with destroying the corn and fodder stored nearby. Although the fort was saved, I am terribly grieved to report that two men were killed: Major Lucas and poor, dear Henry. Hagar was right in her fears after all, and she has become disconsolate.

Charlotte related that she and baby Felix spent the entire battle under the bed, hovering because a large crack in the chinked walls just above her head emitted a hail of Indian bullets. Some said there were fifty savages . . . some said a hundred. Whatever the number, it was far too many.

**FEBRUARY 10, 1781** — *My birthday again. I have now kept this journal for a full year, and what a remarkable twelve months it has been. I trust the next twelve months will not bring the kind of horrors we have seen, but will be filled with pleasurable surprises. I'll work to keep that thought. Just a year ago I was worried about our survival on the river trip and whether or not Jamie and the other men would make it safely to this place. A year ago I thought John Cockrill was a remote creature at best, and here he is, the dearest husband in the world. Now that I am four months pregnant, he loves to put his hand on my belly to feel the baby's delicate flutterings. He swears the child is a boy, but I have learned not to trust my premonitions on that subject. I lack Hagar's second sight. Poor Hagar. When I see how she is unable to shake her grief over Henry's death, I find my joy evaporating as fast as summer rain. I try to talk to her about our expected babies, but she turns her head aside. I fear the Hagar we have cherished in the past is gone forever.*

*Just now I am interrupted by much whispering in the cabin as John and the girls prepare a birthday surprise. My Betsy cast me a glance as sly as that of an accomplished thief. What fun they are having.*

**FEBRUARY 11, 1781** — *A baby's rattle. That was the children's gift to me. John found a tiny gourd which he helped the girls to deco-*

*rate with drawings of daisies and daffodils. A precious offering I will keep always.*

**MARCH 17, 1781** — *The snow still huddles in the earth's low places. Cups of white lie at the base of trees and alongside fallen logs like white shadows. The hills too still have a dusting of white at the higher elevations, but the winter signs are accompanied by evidence of spring as well. We have lately enjoyed warmer days, followed by cold nights, which are the perfect conditions to send the sap rising. The men have nailed heavy iron spikes into the maple trees to tap them and laid up wooden chutes and pails to catch the sap. Today John and three others arrived home about three o'clock from a trip to the area they call the Sugar Camp, a large stand of sugar maple trees. Their horses were loaded with buckets full of sap that we will boil down to syrup. It is hard to believe that it takes at least thirty gallons of raw sap to make one gallon of syrup. But John has promised to keep returning to the trees until every one of us has had our fill of syrup. If so, he will have little time for anything else.*

**MARCH 30, 1781** — *More signs of spring. The cherry trees have burst open their blossoms and the woods are dotted with their airy sweetness. It's as if the boughs are covered with pink clouds that might take flight and carry the trees to the heavens. Other trees have put forth rust colored buds that promise to open soon into fresh green leaves.*

*I'm afraid the Indians too might burst forth. After weeks of inactivity, some of them shot at Sam Barton yesterday when he was out on horseback searching for his cattle. Although a bullet penetrated his wrist, he was able to return to the fort without further injury. John and Alexander Buchanan were out searching for their cattle as well and were alerted by the gunfire to the presence of Indians. They hurried back to the fort without incident, but complained of having to flee like frightened rabbits to their burrow. I say they are lucky to be alive and should abandon their complaints.*

APRIL 2, 1781 — *Last night when James Menifee was on guard duty, he awakened us around one o'clock with a shot from his lookout post on the block house platform. The fact that an Indian spy was out at night worried Jamie so much that he assigned four additional men to guard the gate throughout the night.*

*Ever since that ominous interruption, I have been awake, sitting by the fire with Bruno. My fears fly about me like dry leaves in an autumn wind. As I stroke the dog's warm fur and look at my sleeping loved ones, I tremble at what might happen if Indians attack the fort. I don't know how John can sleep with the knowledge that somewhere outside in the dark, our enemy plots against us, and we have only forty men in the fort. I try to console myself with the fact that we are armed with plenty of powder and lead, and the cattle are safe within the fort's walls to provide the necessary food in case of a siege. The cabin and palisade walls are newly chinked with mud to fill up the cracks. We are safe here. I repeat it to myself, over and over in rhythm with my patting of Bruno. The dog and I both watch with a morbid fixation as the glowing coals turn to ash on the hearth.*

When the first morning light crept across the sky, my fears were realized when two Indians sped from the forest and fired at the fort's walls. Ephraim shot back from one of the port holes, but his bullets had little effect as the enemy marched boldly out of his range of fire. Ephraim's shot, however, was our call to arms. Within minutes men and women hurried into the fort yard and paced back and forth nervously.

I left the children in the cabin and joined John in the yard to hear Jamie's plan of how we would proceed. As we watched Jamie and Ephraim confer, most of the dogs barked and ran wildly through the crowd, adding to the general uproar, but Bruno remained obediently by my side. We all had reasons to hate the Indians who strutted outside the walls, calling insults into the fresh April air, but I was sure that as long as we stayed within the safe confines of the fort, everyone would be all right.

———

"Did you hear what those two devils shouted at us?" asked Ephraim as he turned from Jamie to address the crowd. He was breathless, the dark gun powder on his face providing a sharp contrast to his bright red hair. Elizabeth held the baby and stared raptly at him. "They called us cowards. Cowards!"

James Leeper had come from his cabin so rapidly he was still adjusting his belt. His wife Susan, pale and pregnant, clung to his arm, impeding his progress.

"By heaven," Leeper cried, "they won't get away with this." He absently shook off his wife's anxious hands. "There's only two of them, but there's forty of us. And I say, let's go get 'em."

Several of the younger men also chimed in with shouts, and Jamie had to raise his hands to quiet the noise that broke out among them.

"Just a minute," said Jamie, waving his hand back and forth for order. "We need to give our reaction some thought."

"What's to think about?" yelled Alexander Buchanan and the grumbling continued until Jamie shouted a booming "Silence!"

Some of the older men looked sheepish at their behavior, but the young ones were fired with a taste for vengeance. In the midst of them James Leeper's face turned such a bright red hue I thought his skin might ignite.

"Why do you think those Indians would stand before us in broad day light?" asked Jamie. "When have you ever seen them do that before?"

"I don't care why they're doing it," said Leeper. "No one's going to call me a coward and get away with it."

"They called us squaws, too," added Ephraim, shaking his fist in the air. Elizabeth backed away from him and leaned against her mother, clutching the baby in her arms.

"They are doing this for a reason," continued Jamie, pointing toward the woods as though he could see the Indians through the palisade walls. "I believe those men are decoys, setting us up for an ambush."

"I don't care," said Alexander Buchanan hotly. "I'm no squaw. Let me at 'em."

My own anger grew, not at the Indians, but at the young men who displayed their pride like strutting cocks. I suspected Jamie was right about the ambush, and I thought they were all fools.

"No offense, Colonel," continued Leeper. "But maybe this is a fight for us younger men, men who're not afraid of the savages. If we don't teach them a lesson now, they'll think they can have their way with us. I say we go after them and be quick about it."

"This is not a matter of fear," said Jamie evenly, his expression hardened at the inference he might be too old and afraid for battle. "I know the Indians, and I firmly believe they are setting us up for an ambush."

Leeper ignored Jamie and turned to the crowd.

"I say we fight, and fight now," said Leeper. "Those who are willing to join me, come stand by my side."

I was shocked as six men crossed in front of Jamie to stand with Leeper.

"You've got to do something," I said to John, desperately, tugging at his sleeve.

"What about you, Cockrill?" asked Leeper in a tone that dared refusal, as if he had heard my plea.

"I'm as ready to fight as any man, but I'll do whatever James says is right," said John, balancing himself firmly on both feet. "If he thinks we shouldn't go, I say we listen to him."

More angry conversation broke out, and I watched in amazement. How could any one of these men feel he had to prove his valor by responding to Indian taunts when each showed courage on a daily basis? Jamie raised his hand and this time the crowd readily became silent. The only sounds came from the animals: the dogs' continued barking, the horses' stamping and snorting, the chickens' crowing. I studied my brother as he stood before us. I had never considered him old, only wise, but this morning his face communicated a new fatigue. In the pale light, the grooves that ran from the sides of his nose to the corners of his mouth cast dark shadowy lines that made a triangle around his lips. Wrinkles between his eyebrows pleated into a frown. He would turn thirty-nine the coming June, and on the frontier perhaps he was old, especially when compared to the hot-blooded men in their early twenties who stood before him. But he was wise and experienced, and I believed those qualities counted for more than anything.

"All right," Jamie began gravely. "If your minds are made up to do this thing, I will not let you go alone."

"Jamie!" I called out in spite of myself. "You can't go. Your duty is to protect us here."

"I'll speak with you in a moment, Ann," he scowled.

"No," I answered, folding my hands over my large stomach in defiance. "We need all our men here."

I had never seen his face so filled with exasperation.

"These young men are going to ride out of here no matter what I say, Ann. I can't have them charging after Indians by themselves."

Charlotte emitted a cry. How could Jamie do this to her? She had suffered so much already. My thoughts were interrupted when John pulled me to his side, to quiet me as much as anything else. And he was right to do so because I wanted to scream. Our lives provided enough deprivations without riding out to look for them.

"I'll take twenty men with me and leave another twenty to guard the fort," Jamie continued, his voice maddeningly calm. "You women will not be left alone," he added, turning in a full circle so that his eyes could sweep across every face. His last glance was for me, a stern expression, as if chiseled in stone. The matter was all settled. There was nothing I could do to stop Jamie, but I could still try to stop John. I pulled away from his embrace and lifted my jaw determinedly.

"Tell me you won't go," I said, putting my hands to his shoulders. "I want to hear you say it."

"You know I must go, Ann," he answered, his eyes drooping at the corners. Then he stood even taller, as if to pull himself to military attention. "I know how to fight. They need me."

"They need you?" I cried in despair. "What about your family? You know Jamie's right about the ambush," I said, dryness cracking my voice. "They're out there waiting to slaughter you," I added, wishing for the power to keep him against his will.

"Look at me, Ann," he said, attempting a new approach, putting one hand on my belly, the other at the back of my waist. His warm touch permeated the fibers of my dress.

"Didn't I make it back from Clover Bottom?" he asked, raising his eyebrows quizzically, expecting a reply. When I didn't answer, he stroked my back gently. "Didn't I?" he repeated.

"What difference does that make?" I answered pulling away. "Don't treat me like a child, John. I don't deserve that."

"And how many times have I gone to hunt and come back safely?" he went on in the same vein.

"That was different and you know it," I snapped "Then you didn't have Indians taunting you to leave the fort. Counting on your foolishness."

"I'll come back to you, Annie," he said gravely, abandoning the effort to humor me. "I promise," he said. How I wished to God I could stop him . . . and time.

"I know you'll come back to me, John, one way or another. Just make sure you're alive when you do," was all I answered.

Jamie chose his twenty best fighters, a group that included Mark, John, Ephraim, and of course, James Leeper. With a great hustle they prepared for battle. I reluctantly returned to the cabin with John as he collected his rifle and ammunition. When we entered, the girls started toward me, but I could find no words of encouragement to give them.

"Mama," Polly asked. "What's happening?"

An ache lodged between my breasts at the sight of her terrified face. She grabbed my swollen waist, and I found myself kissing her red hair but unable to soothe her.

"Polly says the Indians are coming to get us," added Betsy, tugging at my skirt. Little Charity said nothing, but squatted on the floor and stared at us with wild, round eyes.

"You'll have to ask your Daddy about it," I said as I lowered myself into a chair. "I don't know how to explain."

"Daddy John?" Betsy asked, turning to him.

"It's nothing to worry about, Honey," he said as he strapped on his powder horn and bullet pouch. " Just a few pesky Indians. Your Uncle Jamie says everything should go on as usual. Mr. White will still be teaching your classes this morning. You can go to school."

"No," I shouted, my voice loud enough to fill the room. "They stay here. Under their beds. Just because the rest of you have lost your senses, doesn't mean I have."

John frowned at me in disapproval, obviously fearful that my words would frighten the children.

"You mind your Mama then," John said with resignation. "I'll be back soon," he added, and then bent low to the floor, opening his arms to them. "Now come give me a good-bye I can remember when I'm out there chasing Indians."

One at a time they enthusiastically circled their arms around his neck, and I wondered how he could possibly leave such precious children. The older girls went first and then little Charity threw herself against his thick chest, her hair a small dark spot in the middle of his wide tan shirt. I bit the knuckles of my hand to keep from crying.

"You play with your dolls, now," he said standing again. "I'll be back before you've had time to miss me."

I saw by their widely smiling faces that he was successful in his reassurance. I fervently wished I were young enough to believe him too.

I returned with John to the fort yard and watched as half the men took their stations at the port holes while the others prepared to leave, saddling their horses for the foray. My heart beat so hard I could feel it in my ears as I helped John slide the bridle onto his horse. The smell of the animal, coupled with the acrid smell of the leather straps, flooded my senses, adding further to a feeling of dizziness. As John leaned to tighten the saddle's buckle, I put my anger aside at last, and threw myself against his broad back, my arms encircling his middle. I felt the baby kick, as if it too were protesting his departure. I tried to shake the haunting vision of my brother being ambushed at Clover Bottom. My husband had escaped that encounter, but how long could his luck hold?

John straightened in response to my grip, but still I clung to him, lacing my fingers over the top of his belt, pulling him to me as tightly as possible. He laid his hands over mine and gently loosened their grip. Then he faced me, but I couldn't summon the strength to look him in the eyes. I focused on the base of his neck and studied his beating pulse. Could it be that in a matter of minutes that blood would stop its flow?

"You've got to live, John," I said. "Don't think of anything else."

He didn't answer but nodded and kissed the center of my forehead. As I held the bridle, he placed his foot in the stirrup and threw his leg over the horse's back. He was ready to do his job.

The sun had inched higher in the sky, and the day seemed unnaturally hot for an early April morning. Some of the women held the dogs at bay while old John Buchanan unbarred the gate, and John lined up his horse behind Mark's, in preparation for the expedition. It was only a matter of minutes before all the men were ready, and they kicked their horses to canter forth with great enthusiasm. John Cotten was the lone man to carry a sword, and as he passed by the weapon rattled against the side of his horse like an off pitch battle hymn.

When the gates were safely closed again, mothers took their children to the cabin that served as Zach White's school house. I marveled that they acted as if there was really no danger. Even Elizabeth calmly took her baby and returned to her cabin with Mrs. Jennings. It drove me mad. When I saw Hagar leaning against the door of the Robertson's cabin, holding baby Felix in her arms, I approached her, hoping to speak to a kindred spirit.

"Oh, Hagar," I cried desperately. "Are you as afraid of what's going to happen as I am? Any premonitions?"

"Doesn't take second sight to know what's going to happen here," Hagar answered bitterly, pulling with her free hand at the coral colored head wrap subduing her hair. Her round stomach matched my own. "It's a sad thing when dogs have more sense than men," she added. "They know what's out there, all right."

As soon as these words had spooled from her mouth like a deadly banner, shots rang out in the distance . . . not the few shots necessary to fire at a party of two Indians, but a long battery of gunfire. I whipped my head to stare at the gate, as if a message might be etched across its surface, and saw instead Charlotte climbing the blockhouse ladder.

I left Hagar and with some difficulty climbed to the ledge where Charlotte was poised, her hands wrapped around the points of the palisade timbers.

"You women have no business being up here," said John Buchanan, who was on guard duty.

"What is it?" I asked Charlotte, scanning the landscape.

"They went that way," she yelled breathlessly, pointing down the hill toward Lick Branch.

I could see neither Indians nor white men, but only gun smoke rising in the distance, little puffs of poisonous clouds wafting into the air. Then, to my dismay, I did see Indians. Not the original two Indians, but what looked to be as many as seventy pouring out of the cedar trees to form a line between our men and the fort.

"You women get down now!" shouted Buchanan gruffly, raising his gun to his shoulder. "It's an ambush."

"Merciful God in Heaven," I shouted. "They're doomed."

Charlotte and I stood paralyzed, watching the Indians stretch across the meadow in a thick line. We could no longer hear each other's words as Buchanan fired his rifle and sounds of battle filled the air: the Indians with their chilling war whoops, the explosion of guns and the snarling and baying of nearly fifty hounds in the fort yard.

I felt a tug on my skirt from Susan Leeper who was at the head of a crowd of anxious women. She was asking for news, but I could only look at her in fury. If it had not been for her husband, none of this would be happening. I turned back to Charlotte who pointed to riderless horses breaking through the Indian line and heading home to the fort. They were our horses, which meant our men had dismounted and were fighting hand to hand down by the creek.

"Should we open the gate to let in the horses?" I asked Buchanan. "Or will the Indians follow them?"

"By heaven, I don't care what you do, as long as you get down from here!" he said. His tone suggested he'd be willing to shoot me himself.

"It may be too dangerous to let the horses in," Charlotte replied, her face a vivid scarlet. "But we can let the dogs out."

She rapidly descended the ladder into the yard, pushing her way through the women who reached out, wanting to know what she had seen. I followed as closely as the crowd would permit. The dogs, responding to the increased sound of Indian activity, threw themselves crazily at the gate, an army of their own: brown, black and spotted fur armed with flashing teeth. Bruno was as wild as the others, his hair bristling on the back of his old neck. Big dogs, small dogs, long and short haired dogs, all barked with fervor, desperate to set upon our enemies.

The remaining men were ready at the port holes, holding their fire until the Indians got within shooting range. I helped Charlotte slide the heavy wooden bolt that barred the gate, but to my dismay, Zach White starting running toward us, his hair standing out like the quills of a porcupine, a rifle at his side. As he approached, he yelled in a voice louder than I would have thought possible.

"Stand aside," he screamed. "I'll not shrink from this fight."

I thought he must be losing his senses and turned my back on him to continue with the gate, splinters catching in my fingers as I shoved the massive wooden rail aside. Charlotte pulled the heavy door open a full six feet, and the dogs surged through the opening, as if the very gates of hell had been unlocked. I could see little but the receding backs and tails of the departing dogs. But then Zach bounded past me to a distance of about forty yards from the palisades. Taking a stance, he leveled his rifle to shoot at the approaching enemy and got off a round before an Indian bullet pierced him, sending him to the ground. When a few of the Indians started toward his body, I quickly slammed the gate, yelling to Charlotte, "Bar the gate. Bar the gate." Tears streamed down my cheeks in horror that I could do nothing to save Zach with Indians charging so rapidly. Why in God's name had he done such a foolish thing?

Still sobbing, I hurried to one of the unoccupied port holes with a desperate fear of what I might see: the Indians attacking my John. The sight I witnessed, however, was not what I had anticipated. As I wiped the tears from my eyes, I saw Zach, lifeless on the ground, but I also witnessed more of the enemy coming closer. Many of those who were previously dashing toward the creek in pursuit of our men, had abandoned that effort completely. Instead, some chased after the abandoned horses while many more tried to escape the dogs who tore at their ankles and leapt for their faces. One large blue tick hound caught an Indian by the throat and ripped the man's neck until it became a river of blood. All across the meadow Indians grappled with dogs, rolling in the grass, the men screaming in torment, the dogs snarling and tearing into their flesh. The Indians tried to sink their knives and tomahawks into the animals but had little success because of the dogs' strong muscles and determined mission.

I couldn't see Bruno among the swirl of men and dogs, but I could see some of our own men breaking through spaces in the line of Indians and retreating to the fort. Isaac Lucas came first, reloading his rifle on the run and streaking fast as a rabbit with an Indian close behind him. Isaac's face grew larger and larger as he approached, until a bullet downed him and he crashed to the earth. After he fought his way to a sitting position, he raised his gun and shot the man who pursued him, the Indian wrenching sideways from the blow and telescoping to the ground. Lucas began a desperate crawl toward the fort, appearing to be wounded in the leg.

Behind him came Edward Swanson with an Indian close on his heels as well. The two ran past the injured Lucas and headed straight toward my port hole, the Indian's face painted blood red, his long tail of black hair bouncing behind as he ran. At about twenty yards from the fort, the Indian slammed the butt of his rifle against Edward's shoulder, causing Swanson to drop his gun. Edward swirled to face his attacker, and I had a full view of the Indian as he prepared to shoot Swanson squarely in the face. The Indian whooped loudly as he pulled the trigger, but his cry stopped abruptly when the gun made a futile snapping sound. Miraculously, the rifle had misfired. Swanson grabbed the barrel and began to struggle, the two men making terrible grunts and yells. Finally the Indian succeeded in wrestling the gun from Swanson, throwing him to the ground where he landed on his hands and knees. I feared I would soon see Edward brutally beaten, but still I couldn't take my eyes off him as he crouched on all fours, awaiting the first slam of the gun stock to his skull.

Just when Swanson's fate seemed assured, the fort's gate swung open and old John Buchanan rushed out, his gun primed for one sure shot that entered near the Indian's left ear and sent him splayed onto the new spring outcroppings of grass. The blood gushed from the man's head and quickly became a crimson pool. Buchanan grabbed both the Indian's rifle and Swanson's arm and hurried him back to the fort. Two more men dashed out to gather Isaac Lucas and help him through the gate, returning to drag in White's body as well.

My heart froze as I saw my John, rising over the crest of the hill and followed shortly by three Indians, their whoops piercing the air, their tomahawks held high. I braced both palms on either side of the port hole, feeling the rasp of the rough wooden timbers against my skin. The sound of murderous dogs growling was still loud in the air. I screamed, "Watch out, John. Oh, John, be careful." Of course he couldn't hear my words; I knew that. But still I screamed until sound left me, and my lower jaw dropped, the air pressing rapidly in and out of my mouth. The inside tissues of my cheeks dried. I gagged, thinking I might vomit, but I couldn't turn my eyes away. I had the irrational illusion that John was safe so long as my gaze was trained on his face: that my persistent stare could ward off bullets. I prayed to God that something would stop the Indians, some bolt out of the sky. But still they came running, like four migrating birds tied together by an invisible thread: four birds in flight, with John the scout.

When he was within range of protective fire from the fort, he turned and fired on the middle Indian, catching him in the legs, sending his brown body headfirst into the grass where he slid forward, a plow set to digging. The two others continued to chase John, unfazed until one of them was struck in the shoulder by a bullet fired from the fort and his loud scream stopped his cohort as well. John continued running to the fort's gate. Closer and closer he came. He was almost to the walls when Buchanan swung open the gate and John entered at a rapid pace, one he couldn't slow until he had reached the center of the fort yard.

I abandoned my place at the port hole and ran to embrace him. I had only a moment to hold him, to put my head to his heaving chest, to smell his sweat and the fear that poured from him before he pulled away. He was off immediately, reloading his gun and hurrying to a port hole to defend the other men who staggered toward the fort.

Jamie and Mark came as fast as they could, but their speed was limited since they dragged the wounded James Leeper between them. Others came more slowly because of their injuries: George Kennedy, Alexander Buchanan and Gaspar Mansker. As the survivors made their way through the gate, they reported that four would return no more, left on the field with their dead Indian foes. It seemed as if the enemy had actually given up its pursuit at last, due to a combination of desires: to chase the horses and to avoid the dogs. And so the battle was over, at least for the moment. A few Indians continued to follow horses, but most returned to the trees and canebrakes from which they had come. In the aftermath, the uncaptured horses returned to the fort as well as those dogs who had survived.

Charlotte stood at the gate, welcoming the dogs, calling many of them by name. I watched beside her, anxiously searching for Bruno, noting each animal who returned. Some dashed through unharmed, baying triumphant barks into the bright sunshine. Others returned with missing ears, gashes in their sides, tails severed. But Bruno did not return at all. Somewhere on the field of blood outside the fort walls, Bruno lay dead or dying. I prayed that he was already dead, far beyond a long end of suffering.

When I had given up all hope that he would return, and Charlotte had barred the gate, tears filled my eyes and began to trickle down my cheeks. Sobs followed the tears, shaking my body until I feared I would lose my balance and fall. To avoid hurting myself, I eased down to a weedy patch of grass near the palisade wall and lowered my face into my hands. I cried for more than the loss of a dog who had been with me since Polly was born. I also cried in relief that John had survived, and Mark, and Jamie. And I cried for the death of Zach White and the mad passion that had welled in him, sending him to his end in such a useless way.

Tears fell too for my daughters who would soon grieve Bruno's passing. Who would long for his warm, friendly presence, especially on winter nights when they would remember using his sturdy back as a pillow before the fire. They had known Bruno all their young lives. I cried that his death was only one knot in the rope of sorrow that measured our lives, and that I could not protect them from the losses to come.

Once the tears began to flow I could not stop them. They streamed down my face and splashed onto the smock covering my swelling stomach where the growing baby twisted and kicked. John and I had created that baby with such love. What joy I had felt at the prospect of sharing a child with him. The baby was safe within me now, but soon it would begin its long swim into life. The poor innocent was being brought into the world to endure a life of war, a life of loss, upon loss, upon loss.

I was almost blind from tears when I felt John's familiar presence by my side as he lowered himself and draped his arm over my shoulders.

"Bruno's gone," I blurted out and then wondered if he thought me a fool for crying over the death of a dog.

"Bruno's dead," I repeated more accurately. "Dead, dead, dead."

"I'm alive," John answered simply, trying to stop my crying with his calm sanity, acting in his steady fashion like a compass, pulling the needle back to its rightful direction. A compass, always pointing north, showing the way.

"We need to go to the girls," he said, giving my shoulder a squeeze. "Think about them, Ann. Put your thoughts there."

I leaned heavily against his shoulder and tried to take strength from him. After all, John had just stared death directly in the face, looked into eyes set on murdering him. Still he could sit beside me and think, not of his own near death, but of my children. Our children now.

I drew back from his shoulder to appreciate the warmth of his mahogany eyes and the strength of his wide brow shining with sweat and gun powder. I traced my fingers along his thin lips, feeling their surprising softness in a face with so much power. I knew that no matter how difficult and harrowing our circumstances, whether we stayed on the Cumberland or went elsewhere, I was blessed in the most important way possible. I had this good man by my side, my partner for life. That thought made my tears begin again as I kissed him tenderly on the mouth, in the midst of barking dogs and squealing horses, and in front of anyone who might want to see. But those were the last tears I shed that day.

———

In the space of an hour, the children had rejoiced at seeing John alive and unharmed, had wept at the loss of Bruno, and had gone to the Robertson cabin to play with Delilah and the other children. I joined the women to set up a makeshift care station, and busied myself with tearing linen into strips for bandages. Charlotte knelt beside me, carefully binding the dreadfully injured head of Alexander Buchanan. His wound still oozed a sticky crimson through the fabric and into his blond curls. The blood continued to spread across his face, making a streak like the slash of a sword. No one expected him to survive the day from such a serious wound.

Nearby Susan Leeper sat with her injured husband's head in her lap. He was suffering from a deadly wound in his back between the shoulder blades. Studying Susan, who repeatedly stroked her husband's forehead without the slightest tear in her eye, I felt guilty for the animosity I had felt for her only hours before. It was true that Leeper's hotheaded insistence on chasing the Indians had been the main factor to rally the men that morning, but he had been punished for his fervor in the most terrible way possible. Providence might have put me in Susan's place just as easily. We were both seven months' pregnant. We had both surely wanted to stop our husbands as they rode out. But now John was safely inside the fort, examining the horses that had returned from battle, while James lay with his life slowly leaking into his wife's homespun skirt.

Suddenly we were startled by the cries of one of the men whom Jamie had deemed too young to go on the escapade. Everyone feared that his yelling meant the Indians had returned, but it was only Charles Cameran, looking for all the world as if he were possessed by the devil, his hair standing wildly from his head as he threw open the gate and ran outside. Jamie followed him swiftly with rifle in hand, but it wasn't two minutes before they returned, Cameran holding an Indian scalp and whooping like a savage. He took the scalp he had torn from a dead Indian's head and tacked the bloody piece of skin to the gate as a measure of his desire for vengeance. I felt nothing but disgust for his heartless deed. I had never seen a more horrid example of how savagery begets savagery. What in God's name have we become?

After the wounded had been attended to, we eagerly joined in a circle to hear the story of what had happened when the twenty had ridden out that morning. I sat in the hot sun with John on one side of me and Polly squeezed close to my other side. Betsy curled tightly in John's lap and Charity sprawled across my legs.

At first, Jamie knelt bare-headed in the center of the circle, poking the dirt with a stick, a deep frown creasing his forehead. Then he stood, and the vivid sun once more belied the tragedy of the day, making his face glow with radiance.

"We have just suffered our worst tragedy since coming to this place," he said, throwing the stick to the earth. "Three men lie dead outside these walls. Four more are dead or fighting for their lives here in the fort. If we had stayed here, all of these men would have been protected."

Jamie paused, his face twisted with pain, as if he had sustained a mortal wound himself.

"I want to say here and now that I feel personally responsible for these dreadful misfortunes," he added, his hands twitching at his side.

A murmur spread through the crowd like a sudden rushing wind. I wanted to jump up and refute him, but Edward Swanson answered Jamie instead.

"Not true," he called somewhat weakly, exhausted from his ordeal. "Every last one of us was ready to go."

Jamie went on, undeterred. "I saw the signs of ambush, and yet I still led you into a trap."

At this point, John removed Betsy from his lap and stood slowly to address Jamie.

"No one could have known so many Indians had gathered," said John. "We've never seen their like before."

"I'm your leader," said Jamie, shaking his head adamantly. "I should have known what was going on. The Indians spent some time in assembling so large a force. I saw signs out there during the battle that at least three tribes were attacking us. It's my guess they would have finished off our settlement if it hadn't been for the animals. We can thank the Lord that He gave Indians a fear of dogs and a love of horses."

"I'd like to say a word," said old John Buchanan, slowly rising to his feet. The activity of the day had worked hard on him, and we all silenced in a show of respect for his valor.

"No one is more grieved than I am about what happened today," he said, rubbing his blackened hands together, still stained from gunpowder. He looked all of his sixty-five years. "My son lies dying right now," his voice cracked and he cocked his head to one side. "But James. I know as well as every other person in this fort, that our young men were dead set on following those Indians, and nothing you could have done would have stopped them. And that's the God's truth."

Buchanan thrust his jaw forward, as if he dared Jamie to disagree with him, shook his head and sat down.

"You can quit this kind of talking, Jamie," added Gasper Mansker, hunkering on the ground with his left arm tied to his side like a broken wing. "And tell 'em what they're waiting to hear. About how damn lucky we are that any of us got back alive."

So Jamie told how their little band had followed the two Indians across the meadow and down toward the point where Lick Branch met the river. When the group was about four hundred feet from the river they saw the two Indians they were following disappear into the cane. They thought their mission was over, since they had long ago learned that pursuing Indians through the cane was an impossible business. But before they had a chance to turn their horses around, gun fire poured from the thicket in front of them and about thirty Indians rose up and began to charge from the brush, screaming their war whoops.

Jamie ordered the men to dismount immediately since it was impossible to aim with any accuracy while on a moving horse. The horses became wild, the smell of blood and the sound of the Indians' cries and gunfire, sending them into a fury. As they took off on a race toward the fort, Jamie glanced after them for a moment and was shocked to see that maybe seventy additional Indians had poured out of the woods behind them. The new warriors were strung in a line across the same hill the settlers had just descended, effectively cutting them off from any retreat to the fort.

"I didn't have much time to think about those Indians at our back, though, because the ones closest to us had murder on their minds. After we got off the first round of fire, some of us were able to reload our rifles while others were forced into hand-to-hand combat. John Cotten over there was mighty lucky to have his sword. Just when two devils were bearing down on him with their tomahawks raised, he beheaded them both with one swipe of the blade.

Here he paused and looked first at the blue sky where clouds gathered like a host of snowy giants. He turned his gaze on Charlotte where she sat on the ground amongst their children, baby Felix in her lap.

"There's not a doubt in my mind," he said gravely, addressing Charlotte, "that every one of us who rode out this morning would be lying dead by the river right now if it weren't for my wife's presence of mind when she set loose the dogs."

I watched with pleasure as Charlotte bowed her head in recognition of his praise.

"We all owe you a deep debt of gratitude, Charlotte," he said with great solemnity.

With what spirit that remained, the survivors in the fort shouted their thanks in appreciation for Charlotte's quick thinking.

Jamie seemed gratified by their response and continued.

"I think we've seen the last of the Indians for now," he said, striding purposefully before us. "But just in case they return, I've asked John Cockrill to gather any pieces of iron you might have to use as ammunition for the four pounder. We don't have any proper cannon balls for it, but I think we can put together enough scrap to make a mighty charge. We might not hit a single Indian, but the cannon will put a fear into them. I'm sure of that."

As I studied my brother's face in the glittering afternoon sunlight, I realized with a deepening sadness that he no longer had the power to inspire me with hope and certainty. Ever since I could remember, I had looked to him for a father's guidance, but now his voice rang hollow in my ears, as if coming from a far distance. I tried to shake off my melancholy, to take solace from the fact that my family had been spared, but that day I had seen him ride out from the fort against his better judgment, actually risking the future of the entire settlement with his rash decision. I wondered if I could ever again trust his judgment since he had lacked the will to stand up to an impetuous young man like James Leeper.

I lifted my eyes to the sky where the soft towers of clouds continued to dance and thought how much more appropriate it would be to have a cold rain drenching our skins, coursing in snaky rivulets around the grass where we sat. Without looking at him, I took John's hand, placed it on my swelling womb and gave a silent, open-eyed prayer, asking God to show me what I must do.

———

The meeting was over a few minutes later, and John and I were returning hand in hand to our cabin when Jamie fell in beside us.

I refused to acknowledge his presence until he placed his firm hand on my shoulder, stopping me.

"I want to talk to you," he said, and I reluctantly faced him. I wanted to speak out about my disappointment, but instead I pressed my lips firmly together and gave my attention to the ground.

"I know you were dead set against us going out this morning," he said. When I didn't reply, he added, "Ann, look at me, please."

I lifted my head to observe sweat trickling from his short brown sideburns.

"You heard me admit I did the wrong thing," he said.

I nodded, feeling John's hand still bound to mine.

"The truth is, at some time or another, we're all faced with impossible choices, Ann." His eyes searched mine for understanding. "These young men were bound and determined to chase out of here, no matter what I said or did. I couldn't let them go alone."

He paused, as if expecting me to say something, but I couldn't speak.

"We're lucky the Indians made mistakes as big as ours," he finished. "I just wanted to apologize to you face to face. That's all."

My heart melted at the sight of Jamie's wretched expression. How could I sit in judgment of him? It was clear that he had not been motivated by a lack of will. He had made his decision the way he always did, by going beyond his personal concerns to consider what was best for the group. He knew these young men in the fort weren't soldiers. They were only farmers and hunters whereas he had taken part in battles for almost ten years. If these men were determined to fight, then he was equally determined to do whatever necessary to protect them.

"God never made a more unselfish man than you, Jamie," I said. "And if He ever decides to create a man who never makes mistakes, I'm sure you'll be His first candidate."

I smiled at him and felt deeply relieved when he returned it.

"You are the best brother anyone ever had," I added and knew I spoke the truth.

———

They fired the cannon that evening, and even though I had for-given Jamie, I was still painfully aware of our precarious position and received little comfort from the gun's boom or the crashing sound of splintering trees in the forest that followed it. For behind the cannon's reach, the Indians still lurked in the dark wilderness, and even more Indians from the far reaches of the Cumberland Valley stood ready to provide reinforcements for those who now encircled the fort. We could only wait to see what happened next.

# Twenty-three

APRIL 3, 1781 — *Last night I chased sleep as diligently as a hunter pursues the deer, only to have it vanish into a tangle of fears. I couldn't rid my mind of Indians closing in on John, hard at his heels. To reassure myself that he was alive, I pressed my ear against his chest to hear the dull thump of his heart, then stretched my palm above his face to feel the warmth of his breath. But these actions gave me no peace.*

*Three times during the night I rose to light the candle that stands in its pewter holder beside our bed. With the burning taper in my hand, I approached my girls to gather strength from the sight of their sleeping faces, a ritual that usually reinforces my belief in angels. But on this long night, I found no cure for my soul's anguish. The very flickering of the candle gave our cabin a sense of wavering impermanence, as if we could easily slip from this world.*

*First I studied my Polly, admiring her features which are taking the shape of the woman she will become. Dark red waves of hair fell beside her freckled face, framing the cheekbones and slipping under her chin. I moved to Betsy, examining the smudge of dirt on her cheek she refused to let me rinse away. It is mud from Bruno's paw that she can't bear to part with. The dusky spot looked chilling in contrast to her white skin and blond curls, as if a sign of dark things to come. Beside Betsy lay Charity, whose brunette hair is turning even darker and whose chin reveals a new pointed shape.*

*Each time I made my ritual bed check, letting my hand slide briefly across the children's soft hair, one question disturbed my mind: how can I possibly save them from the dangers that lie outside the fort's walls? We cannot escape from this place until the new baby is born, but even after that blessed event, where might the six of us go? Crossing the land by horse to either Kentucky or the Holston seems more of a risk than ever. We came to this place because we thought it was God's will, but perhaps we've been misguided all along. Can it be that God wants the Indians to possess this land rather than us? For if He wanted us to settle this territory, then why did He make the process so treacherous?*

*These questions buzzed like hornets in my mind all night, and now that daylight sifts around the door's frame, I have come to no conclusions. I fear my prayers do not lift to God's ears, but remain here in this dark box that is our home.*

*APRIL 4, 1781 — Yesterday we waited in the fort all morning for further attacks, but fortunately nothing happened. This morning's unseasonable heat has made the stench of dead bodies outside the palisade walls unbearable. It was clear that someone would have to ride forth to deal with their remains. When Jamie announced he would lead a small party to bury the dead, something like the hackles of a dog rose up along my neck in fear and apprehension. We may have heard nothing from the Indians for more than twenty-four hours, but they might still hide beyond our walls, and I worried that my John would volunteer to go with Jamie. Sure enough, he and Mark were the first to step forward. I can't write another word until I know he is back safely.*

*APRIL 5, 1781 — Oh, thank you God that John was not hurt yesterday, nor was anyone else. My husband reported seeing no signs of Indians anywhere near the fort. He said that even though we had our doubts about the usefulness of our cannon, its explosion must have scared off the Indians, for the cannon fodder cut the bushes in half and split trees asunder. Our party found several knives and tomahawks that the Indians would never have left behind unless they departed with great speed.*

*John explained in ghastly detail how his group found our dead on the field of battle, their bodies stripped and their heads scalped. Of course they also discovered the bodies of the dogs and the murdered Indians who had been slightly covered by their brothers before they retreated. Our men made a long trench to bury the Indians and the dogs, and dug separate graves for our own casualties.*

*My John, however, made a special grave for Bruno's body. The hound died a hero's death, and John celebrated it as such. He has marked the grave with stones so that the children and I may visit it at a later time. After all the burials were completed, Jamie returned to lead us in a prayer for the dead, but I think we should have prayed for the living. And maybe even for the families of the dead Indians. Did their wives grieve any less for their souls' departure? How war makes us do such cruel and brutal things to one another.*

*Today I hover between two worlds, neither fully alive nor completely dead. I am a stranger to myself. Sometimes when I lie awake, I wonder if any of our family will survive these years, and if we do, will we become savage ourselves? John doesn't like to hear me express these fears, and tells me I will mark our unborn baby with my mournful thoughts. It is a shocking idea that gives me pause. This baby is a part of me after all, and what if my thoughts circulate in his mind the way my blood moves through his body? Assuming that is true, how can I possibly stop these thoughts? Prayer isn't working. I wish I could go to sleep tonight and wake up two months in the future to a newborn child.*

**APRIL 24, 1781** — *Today is the anniversary of our arrival at the Bluffs. I barely remember what I anticipated when I first set foot on* *the riverbank, but certainly I didn't expect this year would bring marriage and a new baby kicking within me. Nor did I foresee the dreadful death of my dear brother, John. Although I often lament the veil that God dangles between us and our future, I must admit it is good that we do not know what is to come.*

**APRIL 25, 1781** — *It has been three weeks since we last saw Indians. Jamie has gotten word from a friendly Chickasaw that our recent attacking party was composed of a combination of Indian tribes, not only Cherokees, but also Shawnees, Delawares and even Pottawattamies from the far north. Their thought was to put an end to our settlement once and for all, and to send a message to future settlers to avoid this place on pain of death. But with their defeat, they have become despondent and returned to their homes. Could this possibly mean that our battles are over? We have also received news that the war against the British is going well for our side and may soon be ended. Maybe, oh do I dare to hope it, we will see peace within the coming year.*

*With so many things to occupy my mind, I hate to complain about something so insignificant as the weather, but lately the heat has been oppressive. I long to feel cool water lapping against my skin, so I have begged John to take me for a swim in the river. He says if we see no Indians yet again tomorrow, he will keep watch as I swim near the river's edge, but he warned I could stay no longer than fifteen minutes. I am grateful to anticipate such a delicious respite.*

Before dawn the baby's sharp kick jolted me awake, snapping my eyes open wide as an owl's. I groped for a candle, lit it, and with some difficulty picked up my milking stool. The added weight of pregnancy makes me move clumsily, as if I am an old woman. I hope to live long enough for this elderly stagger to occur in the natural course of time. Outside I sat on the wooden stool and blew out the candle to witness the full wonder of daybreak. At first I heard no sounds other than my own labored breathing, shallow because of the baby's pressure. When the first indistinct light appeared in the sky, it was so subtle, I thought it might be my imagination. But slowly the glow was joined by a gathering of pale light that spread across the sky the way a patch of water creeps across a linen sheet.

The birds started their conversations, first the roosters with harsh crowing so familiar it barely registered in my mind. Then the song birds pierced the silence with their cheeps and tweets, a delicate counterpoint to the roosters' noisy tune. Cool air tingled against my face as the sky continued to lighten revealing the silhouette of trees — and gradually the palisade wall — and finally the squat cabins lining the fort yard. It was as if these things were being created all over again, pulled from the dark night.

The sky proceeded from inky gray to slate, then pearl with increasing striations of pink and orange. Three women left their cabins to start up fires and soon wisps of smoke rose to mingle with the gray sky. Two more women slid from cabin doors to milk their cows as the red sun grew fat and prosperous. Another day asserted itself, and it seemed as if nature cared not a whit for men and women who walked beneath the overarching sky. The sun was unaware that God had made man only a little lower than the angels, for compared to the sun, man was a puny thing indeed. I was lost in contemplation when John's hand rested upon my shoulder, and I instinctively reached to cover it with my own.

"Did the baby let you sleep at all?" he asked.

"Some," I answered, feigning good humor.

"I know how you hate this confinement," he added, putting my thoughts into words. "It won't always be this way. And today we'll get you out of here for a swim. I promise."

I smiled back at him. He was doing all he could to ease me through these difficult times.

"That will be grand," I answered, a little sadly. The falsity of my response bothered me, so I added. "I love you, John. No matter what happens, you'll remember that, won't you?"

He didn't answer but took my hand and pulled my heavy body to him. I let myself enjoy his tender embrace.

————

By two o'clock when John and I set out for the short walk down the bluff to the river, the air was almost oily in its density. Sweat gathered in a slick below my swollen breasts, and when I slapped my hand to the back of my itching neck, I retrieved a dead mosquito as well as a pasty layer of grime. Never had I needed a swim so much.

As we picked our way down the path beneath the cedars, low branches swept our faces. John carried two loaded rifles and enough additional gun powder and balls to hold off a dozen Indians, so I felt safe enough. Along the trail I noticed how the green of the cottonwoods and willows had deepened during the last month, turning from lime to emerald. Everywhere were indications that spring was behind us, and we had plunged deep into an early summer. When we came to the water's edge, I was surprised to see only three canoes tied to saplings. Normally there were more boats, but I supposed that most people had hidden their vessels in the thick underbrush to save them from the Indians' grasp. I stood on the narrow rocky shore and slipped off my loose moccasins.

In ordinary times, John and I would have chosen a more private place, but for the sake of safety we wanted to remain close to the fort. I pulled off my smock and handed it to John who spread it carefully on the rocks beside one of the rifles. Wearing only my shift, I looked like a large white boulder that had guarded the river since time began.

John took my hand and guided me across the small rocks and into the deeper water where the cold hit my feet and shot instantly through my body. I shivered with delight and shook off his hand as soon as my feet found soft sand. To accustom my body to the cold, I immersed my face in the water, letting it cover my head completely, allowing the icy liquid to saturate my hair. When my head was fully soaked, I flung it back and stood straight again, creating my own waterfall as the water streamed down my hair. I submerged myself fully, my shift catching little pockets of air as it floated around me, and relaxed into the gentle current, letting it cradle me. The baby within me relaxed as well, the river caressing us both with its soft waves.

Floating on the water's surface, I gazed up at the fort clinging to the rocky bluff above. Spring water dashed down the precipice, and I had forgotten what a truly beautiful place we lived in. Suddenly the water flowing from the rocky limestone surface reminded me of a Bible story concerning the Israelites. They were lamenting their decision to flee from Egypt into the desert and complaining that God had led them to an evil place. To teach them a lesson, God instructed Moses to call the grumbling travelers together. When they were assembled before a boulder in the dusty desert, undoubtedly still complaining about their fate, Moses admonished them for their rebellious nature and lack of faith. He then used his rod as God had instructed and struck the rock, causing a stream of water to burst from the stone and pour abundantly onto the ground before them. How astonished the Israelites must have been to see the miracle of water flowing in the desert.

It was then I realized that the beautiful spring tumbling above me had existed all along, but I had been oblivious to its message. Now, I saw its generous flowing as a sign that God looked over us as well. And not just us, but also the Indians who had hunted here for centuries before we arrived. Surely He would show us a way out of this constant combat: a way to live in harmony. This hope lifted my spirits as the water had lifted my buoyant body. At last I began to have faith that as surely as the river held me in its embrace, God would find a way to end the violence.

In that moment the whole scene took on special clarity. Sun sparkled on the river's surface like a net of brilliant stars. Shadows beneath the trees in the forest darkened with a deeper intensity; the canopy of sky gleamed a dazzling blue. And most important, on the riverbank, sitting as patiently as a rock, I saw the dearest person in the world. My John. I wanted to share my revelation with him and thrashed in the water as I pushed back to the shore, shouting to him. He was startled at my cry and sprang to his feet, his rifle at the ready, searching the river banks.

"No, John," I called, swinging my arms above my head. "It's all right. Everything is going to be all right after all."

John lowered the rifle and his crooked smile of confusion made me hurry toward him even faster. We were going to be all right, I repeated as the water fell from my body, pressing my shift into swirls against my skin. I emerged from the water like the spirit of the river to share my revelation with John: we would find a way to peace.

- *The End* -

# AFTERWORD

Battles with the Indians continued in the Fort Nashborough region far beyond the end of the Revolutionary War in 1783. The last death at the hands of the Indians was June 5, 1795.

**Ann Cockrill** lived to be sixty-four and all of her eleven children survived to adulthood, both the three she had with David Johnson as well as the eight she had with John Cockrill. In 1784, she became the only woman to be awarded a land grant of 640 acres from the state of North Carolina in recognition of her contribution as a part of the "advance guard of civilization" on the Cumberland. John Cockrill also received a land grant at that time which included what is now Centennial Park in Nashville, Tennessee. Today a marker dedicated to Ann Robertson Johnson Cockrill, the first school teacher of Nashville, stands in Centennial Park. Both she and John are buried in the old Nashville City Cemetery.

**John Cockrill** lived to be eighty years old and proved to be most successful in land speculation. When he died he was able to endow all of his children with significant land bequests. As a measure of his devotion to his three stepdaughters, in his last will and testament he treated all of his eleven children equally.

**James Robertson** continued to be a leader across the state of Tennessee. Robertson devoted himself to public service through-out his life, and in his later years when his friends tried to get him to pursue an easier life, he replied, "I know I am getting old . . . but I claim no exemption from labor until I can do no more good." He died at the age of seventy-two while serving as the United States Agent to the Chickasaws near present day Memphis, Tennessee. In his last illness he wrote to his wife and asked her to come to him with "My feathers and my comfort." Charlotte was by his side when he died. He is often credited with the title of "Father of Tennessee."

**Charlotte Reeves Robertson** lived to be ninety-one years old and bore eleven children. She lost three of these, however. Besides the death of baby Charlotte shortly after the river party arrived at Fort Nashborough, the Indians killed her sons Peyton and Randolph. Peyton was killed at the age of twelve in 1787 when he and a friend were out tapping maple trees for syrup. In 1793, the Indians killed Randolph, beheading him while he was trapping beaver. They later exhibited his head at their camp. He was twenty-two at his death.

**Mark Robertson** was killed by the Indians in 1786 as he was returning to Ann's house after visiting his brother James. In his will he left five thousand acres to his nieces, Polly, Betsy and Charity. He was in his early thirties at his death.

**Ephraim Peyton** abandoned Elizabeth and his four children in 1796. He fled to Kentucky with another woman whom he subsequently married after a number of years. His twin brother, John, married and had eleven children, two of whom became members of Congress.

**Susan Leeper** died accidentally when a rifle lodged above her fireplace fell, discharging a shot that killed her.

**John Donelson** and his family returned to Tennessee in 1785. In 1786, at the age of sixty-eight, he was killed by the Indians while on route from Kentucky to Tennessee. Mrs. Donelson continued to live in the Cumberland area where she kept a boarding house. Her many children grew up to have extensive influence in political and military matters. Most prominent, perhaps, was Rachel Donelson who married Andrew Jackson.

**Dragging Canoe** survived the white man's bullet and died in 1792 at the age of sixty. He had consistently refused to make peace with the settlers, and on the day before his death, had spent his hours in war dancing and festive drinking that lasted all night. For over fifteen years he succeeded in making his prophecy of a "bloody ground" come true.

## COCKRILL DESCENDANTS

One son of Ann and John Cockrill who remained in Nashville was Mark Robertson Cockrill, born in 1788 and named for Ann's beloved brother. Mark R. had a distinguished career in agriculture and was said to have been worth two million dollars before the Civil War. His principal claim to fame was the quality of wool from his Merino and Saxony sheep. In 1851 at London's World Fair, Queen Victoria awarded him a bronze medal and the title of "Wool King of the World."

His son, Mark Sterling Cockrill, was also devoted to animal husbandry, acquiring the title, "King of Shorthorns." He served as a Captain in the Confederate Army and was heavily involved in religious and civic affairs. The Cockrill School in West Nashville was named in his honor.

*Below is a picture of the author (on the left) as a child helping to unveil the monument to Ann Robertson Johnson Cockrill.*

—Staff Photos by Bob Grannis

Two great-great-great-granddaughters of Ann Robertson Cockrill yesterday unveiled a granite marker in her honor as the first teacher of Nashville and Davidson County. Catherine Peyton Cockrill, 6, left, and Nell West Foster, 10, are both students at Parmer School and were among the many descendants of the pioneer teacher who gathered with school children and other spectators to witness dedicatory ceremonies in Centennial Park.

# BIBLIOGRAPHY

Aiken, Lena Taylor. *Adventure II:Flatboats 'Round the Bend*. Rogersville, Tenn: East Tennessee Printing Co., 1976.

Alderman, Pat. *The Overmountain Men*. Johnson City, Tennessee: The Overmountain Press, 1970.

Arnow, Harriette Simpson. *Flowering of the Cumberland*. New York: The Macmillan Company, 1963.

Arnow, Harriette Simpson. *Seedtime on the Cumberland*. New York: The Macmillan Company, 1960.

Bond, Octavia Zollicoffer. *Old Tales Retold*. Nashville, Tennessee: Smith & Lamar Publishing House of Methodist Episcopal Church, 1907.

Burt, Jesse C. *Nashville, Its Life and Times*. Nashville, Tennessee: Tennessee Book Company, 1959.

Calloway, Brenda C. *America's First Western Frontier: East Tennessee*. Johnson City, Tennessee: The Overmountain Press, 1989.

Carr, John. *Early Times in Middle Tennessee*. Nashville, Tennessee: Mini-Histories, Reprinted 1984.

Crabb, Alfred Leland. *Journey to Nashville*. Indianapolis and New York: The Bobbs-Merrill Company, Inc., 1957.

Crutchfield, James A. *Early Times in the Cumberland Valley*. Nashville, Tennessee: The First American National Bank, 1976.

Davidson, Donald. *The Tennessee, Volume One*. Nashville, Tennessee: J. S. Sanders & Company, 1991.

Davis, Louise Littleton. *Nashville Days*. Gretna, Louisiana: Pelican Publishing Company, Inc., 1981.

Durham, Walter T. *Daniel Smith, Frontier Statesman*. Gallatin, Tennessee: Sumner County Library Board, 1976.

Faragher, John Mack. *Daniel Boone*. New York: Henry Holt and Company, 1992.

Gambill, Nell McNish. *The Kith and Kin of Captain James Leeper and Susan Drake, his wife*. The National Historical Society, 1946.

*Indian Battles, Murders, Sieges and Forays in the South-West*. Cool Springs Press: Franklin, Tennessee, 1996.

Irwin, John Rice. *The Museum of Appalachia Story*. West Chester, Pennsylvania: Schiffer Publishing Ltd., 1987.

Kelley, Sarah Foster. *General James Robertson: the Founder of Nashville*. Self published, 1980.

Kelley, Sarah Foster. *West Nashville, its people and environs*. Self Published, 1987.

Matthews, Thomas Edwin. *General James Robertson, Father of Tennessee*. Nashville, Tennessee: The Parthenon Press, 1934.

Putnam, A. W. *The History of Middle Tennessee or Life and Times of Gen. James Robertson*. Knoxville: The University of Tennessee Press, 1971. Originally published in 1859.

Roosevelt, Theodore. *The Wining of the West, Volume 2*. Lincoln, Nebraska: University of Nebraska Press, 1995. Originally published: New York: G.P. Putnam's Sons, 1894.

Spoden, Muriel M.C. *Kingsport Heritage, The Early Years 1700-1900*. Johnson City, Tennessee: The Overmountain Press, 1991.

Thomas, Jane. *Old Days In Nashville*. Nashville, Tennessee: Publishing House Methodist Episcopal Church, South, 1897. Reprinted by Charles Elder.

Williams, Samuel Cole. *Tennessee During the Revolutionary War*. Knoxville, Tennessee: The University of Tennessee Press, 1974. Originally published in 1944.